Legacy

G·K
Hall
&Co.

 **This Large Print Book carries the**
Seal of Approval of N.A.V.H.

Legacy

Leigh Bristol

G.K. Hall & Co.
Thorndike, Maine

Published in Large Print by arrangement with
Warner Books Incorporated.

G.K. Hall Large Print Book Series.

Set in 16 pt. News Plantin by Heidi Saucier.

Printed on acid free paper in the United States of America.

Library of Congress Cataloging-in-Publication Data

Bristol, Leigh.
   Legacy / Leigh Bristol.
     p. cm.
   ISBN 0-8161-5828-2 (alk. paper : lg. print)
   1. Large type books. I. Title.
[PS3552.R4957L44 1993]
813'.54—dc20   93-22679
                                                    CIP

Legacy

CHAPTER
One

Laurel Sinclair Laughton looked at the money remaining in the cash box, her expression still and dull with disbelief. One dollar and two cents. Only last month there had been almost fifty dollars in the box. Fifty dollars would have seen them through the year, and into the next if they had been frugal. Fifty dollars was the difference between a meager, though respectable, existence and abject penury. Fifty dollars was all they had.

Laurel raised her eyes slowly to her aunt Sophie, who met her gaze with a defiant jerk of her sausage curls. "You needn't look at me that way, Miss," she told her, though the sternness of her words was somewhat offset by the quavering of her voice. Not even Sophie wanted to meet Laurel in a temper, much less be the cause of it. Nonetheless, it was to her credit that she stood her ground and went on determinedly, "You just remember where that money came from and who —"

"You spent fifty dollars on a portrait." Laurel

enunciated each word with a terrible clarity, and with each syllable her hand tightened another fraction on the coins.

"Forty-five," corrected Aunt Sophie. "It was a bargain, really. Of course," she added vaguely, and her eyes drifted away, "there were paints and canvas and such . . ."

Laurel let the coins drop with a clatter back into the box. Her lips tightened and her eyes narrowed; it was not so much anger that she struggled against, but despair. Anger was a futile emotion, particularly where Aunt Sophie was concerned; but despair was something with which Laurel learned to live day by day.

Caroline spoke up quickly from her chair by the window. Her gentle face was etched with concern but her tone was soothing. "Now Laurie, don't be cross with Mama. You know she only did what she thought was best."

For most of her life, Caroline's simple tranquility had been the oil that could smooth any troubled waters for Laurel, but today the other girl's attempts at peacemaking only filled her with frustration and impatience. Caroline, for all her soft-spoken manners and charitable defense of her mother, was no fool. She knew what this meant, and Laurel could see from the anxiety that darkened her eyes that Caroline was just as horrified as she was. Irrationally, she wanted to turn on her cousin, to snap at her and demand that she show some gumption for a change and to stop constantly forgiving what was unforgivable. With a determined effort at self-control, Laurel squelched the impulse and said instead, firmly, "You must return the portrait, that's all."

Sophie Sinclair's tiny, mouse-like eyes fluttered and widened with alarm. "I can't do that! It's already finished — I just this very morning presented it to the elders of St. Michael's Episcopal Church . . ." The indignation in her tone was interrupted by a small, self-satisfied smile. "Oh, and weren't they surprised? They gave it a lovely spot right in the vestibule, where it will hang as a monument to my dear departed husband's unselfish devotion to his church and his community." She blinked, returning to the subject with a frown. "What you suggest is simply out of the question, my dear," she finished with a snap of her head which caused her double chins to jiggle. "It simply cannot be done."

For a moment Laurel lacked the breath to even speak. Caroline saw the emotions building on her cousin's face and tried to intervene. "Laurie, dear —"

"Don't 'Laurie, dear' me!" Laurel snapped at her. She saw the shock and the hurt cross Caroline's face as she shrank back into her chair as though slapped, but Laurel was far too upset to care. She braced her hands against the desk and pushed herself slowly to her feet, her eyes blazing at Sophie.

"You spent our last fifty dollars," she said, "on a portrait of Uncle Jonas for the vestibule of the Episcopal Church?"

Aunt Sophie blinked twice, then drew her plump figure up to its full five feet two inches. "I thought it only fitting," she responded, with dignity.

A renewed wave of outrage and incredulity swept over Laurel and left her impotent. She pushed abruptly away from the desk and walked across the room, turning her back on the two women who gazed after her nervously.

Through the open window the rattle of carriage wheels drifted, and a mockingbird chattered impudently; somewhere up the street a washerwoman sang a haunting Negro spiritual to herself as she snapped clean sheets onto the line and a small dog barked gaily. But inside the shabby little parlor at the corner of Lamboll Street all was silent and suspended in tension.

The infamous artist who had been responsible for the immortalization of Uncle Jonas and for the present difficulties of the women he had left behind might have entitled a painting of them "Portrait of Three Birds." There was Sophie, the plump little partridge, a woman of forty who still thought of herself as the sixteen-year-old debutante, the belle of Charleston society whose every whim must be gladly indulged. She had endured war, poverty, widowhood and the upheaval of all she had ever known, yet she defiantly sailed through it all with a willful refusal to recognize change or acknowledge loss. There was Caroline, as plain and shy as a brown wren, her eyes anxiously flitting back and forth between her mother and her cousin. And there was Laurel, who, with her white, tightly drawn face and the fire of anger burning in her eyes, might best be described at that moment as a hungry bird of prey.

The black mourning garb suited Laurel less than it did the other women, perhaps because the trappings of grief seemed uncomfortably at odds with the willful, restless spirit which was evident in everything she did from the way she moved to the way she spoke to the unladylike, and oftentimes unnerving, directness of her gaze. There was nothing shy or deferential about Laurel Sinclair Laughton, and the quiet dignity of mourning clothes was translated on Laurel into an air of severity and authority which could not, by any stretch of the imagination, be considered becoming on a woman her age.

The crisp black broadcloth sharpened a figure which might otherwise have been soft, if not particularly round, emphasizing her natural slenderness and making her appear taller than she was. Her fair complexion was, in contrast with the material, startlingly white, and her eyes, which would have otherwise been a soft gray, were reduced by her wardrobe to the flat dull color of steel. Her most luxuriant feature was a headful of rich chestnut hair, but Laurel had neither the time nor the inclination to make the most of her assets and wore her hair severely parted in the middle and tightly drawn back into a bun, and covered it most of the time with a black bonnet or veil to keep out the dust. She was not a beautiful woman and she was perfectly aware of the limits of her appeal to the opposite sex, but none of that bothered her. She had more than enough to worry about without fending off suitors like some empty-headed socialite.

Laurel was twenty-three years old and had been wearing mourning for most of that time — first for her mother, who had died when she was six, then for Johnny Laughton, her husband of three weeks who had died three years ago, and now for Uncle Jonas, who had drowned in the cyclone that had struck Charleston the year before. She did not consider her circumstances unusual or in any way pitiable; life and death were a matter of course that she had never bothered to question. The only thing she did have difficulty adjusting to was the added responsibility that seemed to be heaped upon her head year after year.

She had lived with Aunt Sophie and Uncle Jonas since the end of the war — which was to say, almost as long as Laurel could remember. Their daughter, her cousin Caroline, was sweet-spirited but sickly; Aunt Sophie was for all practical purposes as helpless as her daughter, and Uncle Jonas, who until the war had never done an honest day's work in his life, had gone about the business of supporting the four women in his household with a cheerful savoir faire and general incompetence.

In this environment Laurel had grown up very quickly. When demanding creditors came to the door, only Laurel had the presence of mind to deal with them. When Uncle Jonas came home late after a night of carousing, it was left to Laurel to scold him gently and put him to bed without disturbing the fragile dispositions of the other women. No one but Laurel seemed to be able to manage the household accounts, and when Aunt Sophie became embroiled in one of her feather-brained escapades, inevitably Laurel was the one who was left to untangle it.

But, oh, she was so tired of managing things and fixing things and making everything all right! Why couldn't life, just for once, be easy?

"Perhaps," ventured Caroline hesitantly, "if we all put our heads together . . ."

"Well, I for one don't see what all the fuss is about," pouted Sophie. "A fine man like my Jonas deserves a memorial, and —"

"Oh, hush up, both of you!" Laurel said sharply. She pressed her fingertips to her temples. "I have to think."

But all she could think about was Uncle Jonas, immortalized in oil for St. Michael's Church with their last fifty dollars . . . Jonas, who more often than not had sat through Sunday services with the stiff-necked misery of an incurable hangover, and whose only happy moments had been spent inside the walls of Miss Elsie's Crimson Palace. And when she thought of it, Laurel didn't know whether to laugh or cry.

After a moment Caroline took her courage in hand and offered, "Perhaps if we went to the bank . . ."

Laurel didn't even look around. "The only way the bank can be a help to us is if we rob it."

"Oh, my word!" Aunt Sophie snapped open her fan and began to flutter it furiously. "The things you say!" She turned away with a deliberate toss of her head and seated herself on the narrow settee, crossing her ankles and keeping her back straight, working the fan with finishing school expertise. "I declare I don't know where you girls get your manners, after all my hard work . . . ."

Laurel let the words fade out as she leaned her head against the window frame, frowning slightly with concentration. If there was one thing she had learned it was that there was no such thing as a problem without a solution. All she had to do was find it.

Caroline got up and crossed the room, favoring the twisted left hip which had been her curse since birth. She laid a light hand on Laurel's shoulder and said softly, "Please don't be angry with Mother. You know she can't help it."

Laurel looked at her, wanting to hold on to her irritation but finding it impossible to do so in the face of the other girl's sincerity. Caroline's face was small and earnest and wreathed with a cloud of light brown hair, her doe-like eyes large with pleading. Few people, looking into that face, could deny Caroline anything, and Laurel was no exception. She released an impatient, reluctant sigh.

"I'm not angry," she said, and the small scowl line that appeared on her brow was merely self-defense. Caroline, without meaning to, always made Laurel feel ashamed of her less than perfect temperament; and when Laurel was ashamed, she frowned. "But honestly, Caroline, I do wish you wouldn't go around trying to be such a perfect *saint* all the time. You're almost as bad as she is."

Caroline smiled, and an impish light came into her eyes that transformed her pallid features into something that was almost radiant. "But I'm not, you know," she confessed, squeezing Laurel's arm. "Sometimes I get so angry at her I could strangle her. But we mustn't let her know that, must we?"

Once again Laurel felt a surge of frustration that Caroline, of all people, should feel the need to protect Sophie, who, in Laurel's opinion, could have held her own with Sherman's army if the need arose and it did not inconvenience her too much. But even that annoyance gave way to amusement before Caroline's simple good will, and after a moment a grudging smile tightened her lips at the corners. "No, I suppose not," she agreed.

Caroline pressed her cheek to Laurel's briefly in a confident embrace. "Don't worry, dear, we'll manage a way around this, I just know we will. If we put our heads together we're bound to think of something."

But that assurance, far from comforting Laurel, just depressed her. She turned glumly to stare out the window again.

A barefooted black boy was rolling a hoop down the narrow, tree-shaded avenue while a black-and-white spaniel scampered at his heels. The milk wagon lumbered at a sedate pace to the carriage block across the street and its aged driver prepared to get out, then drew back abruptly at the passage

15

of a shiny coach and four. Laurel caught a glimpse of brightly feathered bonnets inside the coach and heard the trill of feminine laughter, and her interest was momentarily piqued. Then her scowl deepened when she realized that the occupants of the coach were some of Miss Elsie's notorious working women. It seemed to her that the world had come to a fine state when fancy women could career about town in feathered bonnets and new coaches while decent folk gave their last pennies to the church and faced starvation for their pains.

Suddenly she froze. An idea kindled in the back of her mind and sparked in her eyes, slowly working itself to a flame. She broke away from Caroline with a soft exclamation.

Caroline looked at her with alarm. "Laurie, what is it?"

Laurel took no time to explain. "I've just thought of something!" she said as she flipped her bonnet from the coat rack and sped out the door, taking the steps two at a time and showing a shocking amount of petticoat.

If asked, Hugh Casom of the Charleston Hotel would have reported that the gentleman occupying Room 110 was the model guest. Hugh, whose duties as desk clerk enabled him to function as one of the most reliable sources of gossip in Charleston, took almost as much pleasure in observing as he did in reporting, and the only observation he had to make about the stranger in 110 was that his conduct was above reproach.

16

True, he wasn't a very sociable fellow, and true, it was like pulling teeth to get anything of a personal nature out of him, but he made a point of paying his bill every day in advance and gave absolutely no reason for complaint.

He spent most of his time alone in his room; the only excursions he had made had been to the barber shop and the mercantile; he took his meals in the hotel dining room quietly and alone, though he seemed to have plenty of money to throw around and ordered the best the menu had to offer. He never tried to sneak women or whiskey into his room and he didn't put his boots on the counterpane. Those were all highly admirable qualities in a hotel guest and if asked, Hugh could not have said exactly what it was about the fellow that made him so uneasy.

Perhaps it was simply that in his thirteen years at the Charleston Hotel, Hugh had never run across a man who looked so distinctly out of place. Charleston was a port town and something of a center of commerce, and it would be fair to say that its populace on any given day could represent a fair cross section of foreigners. But this man was not a foreigner. He was merely . . . unusual.

Oh, he was a nice enough looking young man; an outdoorsman, judging from the darkness of his skin and roughness of his hands, quietly mannered and neatly groomed. His drawl was soft and undistinguished, and there was nothing particularly striking about his face. But something in the way he moved, the way he held himself, made the almost-forgotten defensive instincts of a city-bred man like Hugh prickle in wariness. And there was the matter of his eyes. They were watchful eyes, waiting eyes, and cold — as flat and hard as a dueling pistol at dawn, and only slightly less inviting. One did not see eyes like those much in an easygoing, friendly city like Charleston; certainly not in a refined hotel like the Charleston. The more Hugh thought about it the more he decided that what roused his suspicion about the stranger were his eyes. And if anybody asked, that was what he would report.

Hugh was standing on the street-side steps of the hotel absently picking his teeth and enjoying the morning sunshine. He nodded to the young Widow Laughton as she strode by, and was somewhat miffed when she didn't return his greeting. He started to call after her, but she looked preoccupied and like as not he would only get a cool nod for his trouble. Besides, she was already at the corner and he wasn't about to go chasing after her. He shrugged and settled back, resuming his lazy contemplation of the mysteries of the man in 110 with the hard-looking eyes, when a shadow fell over him and he glanced up to meet those very eyes. Automatically Hugh straightened up, casting aside the toothpick and fiddling nervously with the bow tie around his neck. A wide, obsequious smile came to his face which was only another sign of his uneasiness. The mere presence of the stranger had a way of making him inordinately anxious to please.

18

"Morning, Mr. Tait. Out to take in a little of the town, are you?"

"Might be." Seth Tait's gaze moved over the street with the absent manner Hugh had seen him use whenever he entered or left a room or departed the hotel. At first Hugh had been curious as to what he was looking for, until it gradually occurred to him that Tait wasn't looking *for* anything. He was just looking, checking, scanning. That habit, too, made Hugh uncomfortable.

Hugh said, perhaps a little too boisterously, "Well, then. Fine day for it." He was anxious for the man to leave, for no good reason except that every time he met with Seth Tait he was eager to be away from him. But one thing he had learned was that Seth Tait never did anything in a hurry. He moved when he was ready, silently, stealthily, and deliberately. Like an Indian, it occurred to Hugh now, though, with the exception of Old Joe Williams, who claimed to be half-Cherokee when he was drunk and half-Creek when he was not, Hugh had never met an Indian in his life.

"Can I help you with anything?" he offered now, quickly. There was an itch behind his ear but he manfully refused to scratch it. That wouldn't be dignified. "A horse, or a buggy, or maybe a hired cab?"

Seth Tait turned his gaze slowly back to Hugh. Hugh couldn't help it; he scratched.

"Maybe you can," Tait said in his flat, expressionless drawl. "I'm looking for a woman."

Hugh blinked and swallowed hard — not with

19

surprise, for that was not an unusual request (though at this hour of the morning it did seem to Hugh a bit indecent) — but with relief. A man who openly expressed such a common need could not be that much of a threat, after all.

"Well now." Hugh cleared his throat and stood a bit more easily on his feet. "We have some very fine — er — establishments in town, and if the pocketbook's not too much of a consideration I'd recommend Miss Elsie's, just around the corner there. Of course it's a bit early yet, but . . ."

A flicker of amusement crossed the other man's face. "That's good to know, but right now it was a particular woman I had in mind."

Hugh looked at him cautiously. "Oh?"

"Her name's Laurie Sinclair. Do you know her?"

This time it was surprise, pure and simple, that caused Hugh to blink. "Do you mean the Widow Laughton?"

Tait said nothing.

Conflicting instincts pulled at Hugh. The first and most prominent was self-preservation, which dictated that he tell the stranger what he wanted to know and be done with it. The more noble instinct had been ingrained in him since childhood — perhaps even farther back than that, chivalry being commonly thought to be instilled in Southern gentlemen in the womb — and demanded that he first and foremost protect the lady. The second impulse eventually won out and caused a fine film of sweat to break out on his upper lip as Hugh gathered his courage in hand

and met Seth Tait's dispassionate gaze.

"I wonder, sir," he managed with difficulty, "if you could give me some idea of the — nature of your business with the lady?"

Not a flicker of expression disturbed Tait's features. "We have mutual friends. I've got a message for her."

Hugh wanted to believe that. It would explain so much — what Tait was doing in town, where he was from, what kind of man he was (for if he were in any way associated with the Sinclairs, his character must be above reproach), and above all, why he was inquiring about the young Mrs. Laughton in such a cool, disinterested way. Of course the things it did not explain were just as numerous — why he had waited so long to look up a "mutual friend," why he did not seem to know her married name or where she lived, why he was staying in a hotel when Charleston hospitality had often been known to lead families to open their homes to perfect strangers for visits in duration of a year or more on nothing more than the strength of a letter of introduction from a distant acquaintance. But Hugh did not want to dwell upon the unknowns. He wanted to believe the obvious and the easiest, and he wanted to believe it so badly that he let the relief inside him break out into a warm and welcoming smile.

"I declare, Mr. Tait, you should've said so in the first place. They're over on Lamboll, little yellow house in the middle of the street, you can't miss it. And they'll be tickled to see you, I just know. Been a long time since they had any out-of-town company. Matter of fact," he added generously, "I just saw Miz Laughton pass by a minute or two ago . . ." He searched the street until he saw the familiar black-clad figure, now hesitating before a dressmaker's window. "That's her now, across the street at Miss Mason's. You might be able to catch her if you hurry."

Tait's eyes followed his gaze. He said briefly, "Thanks," and started down the steps.

Hugh leaned back against the railing, resuming his usual comfortable contemplation now that Tait was moving away. Laurel Sinclair, he thought, and couldn't help observing that Tait hadn't mentioned Miss Sophia or Miss Caroline, which seemed odd. All and all, he had to admit the whole thing seemed a little strange and he hoped he had done the right thing.

Laurie Sinclair, he thought again, and turned to go back inside. Now *that* was something he could report, if anyone asked.

Seth had no trouble distinguishing the woman from the many others on the street. Dressed in black from head to foot, she was the only one in widow's weeds lingering outside Miss Mason's shop. He crossed the street, not at all sure how he was going to approach her, but it didn't matter for she had already moved away. He followed her at a casual pace.

His gait was lazy and his expression bored, but his mind was busy. Laurel Sinclair Laughton, a

22

widow — and from the way the clerk talked, a respectable woman as well. A flicker of interest stirred within him.

He couldn't tell much about the woman from this distance and from the back, and he quietly moved closer. He considered overtaking her, or even passing her to get a good look at her face, but then she did something odd. She paused, glancing covertly right and left, and then slipped down an alleyway. Seth decided it was worth following her, just for a little while longer.

Laurel Laughton moved quickly for a Charlestonian. Everything else was slow in Charleston: the drone of the insects, the occasional breeze wafting in from the river, the plodding of horses' hooves, even the low, lazy accents of the city's inhabitants.

Seth had never known anything like the heavy, steamy heat that rose up from the streets and crept down from the trees like a fog, soaking his shirt by mid-morning and dampening the bed-clothes at night. It was the kind of heat a man had to wade through with slow, deliberate effort; it dulled his senses and ate away at his energy and Seth could not for the life of him understand why anyone would want to live here.

Nothing was ever urgent, nothing was ever rushed. In the world Seth came from a man was slow at the risk of his life, and he could not get used to the pace at which things moved in this part of the country. He wasn't sure he wanted to.

Every time he went out of his room he reached to strap on his gun and had to deliberately remind himself to put it down again. He hadn't been without a gun on his hip since he was twelve years old and he felt worse than naked without it.

But this was a different place, a different time. And he was a different man.

Peach Brady had no memory of the first five years of his life. Colonel Ike told him that he had been found when he was no more than three years old, wandering the desert some distance from a settlers' camp that had apparently fallen victim to an Indian massacre. For the next two years he hadn't spoken a word. The Colonel had called him Peach because the bristle of towheaded fuzz that covered the boy's head reminded him of a Georgia peach, and Brady after a man back east he admired who took photographs of the war.

The first memory Peach had was of a cobalt blue day and a field red with poppies, and a roan gelding rolling in the grass. He had looked up at the Colonel and laughed, and his life had begun.

In the beginning there had been the Colonel and himself. Then the Bartow boys came along, and Red English. They had ridden together for five good years. Then Jim Bartow fell beneath a bullet in Cheyenne, and his brother Kale was lynched when he went after the sheriff who had shot Jim. Matt Bartow never was good for much after that, and he took a fever one winter in the Sierras and died during the night. Red rode off on his own, and they heard he had been killed in a shoot-out over a poker game in Miles City. Then it was just Peach and the Colonel again, and times that were changing too fast.

Pat Garret got Billy the Kid. The Youngers, the Jameses — all were gone or going. The country was crisscrossed with telegraph wires and railroad lines, and schools and churches were popping up where buffalo wallows once had been. In times like these, a man either changed, or he died. The Colonel was wise enough to see that, if Peach was not.

The decades of Peach's life had spun out in a series of campfire tales, tales of the old days, tales of dreams once dreamed . . . and one dream in particular, repeated over and over until, at last, it had lost its luster. Colonel Ike and Augustus Sinclair, the frantic days of war, and the gold. . . . Even now, Peach could hear the Colonel's voice, telling it, without variation, just as he always did.

"Gus was like a brother to me. War joins people that way, you know. We looked after each other. His wife, and baby girl, they were like my own. He was a rich man, owned a plantation outside of Charleston. Chinatree. Me, I was just a poor farm boy from Mount Pleasant, but ole Gus and me, we took care of each other.

"The Yankees broke through near Charleston and Gus and me got separated from our regiment. That's when we came on the railroad car

— sidetracked, it was, the line cut by the Rebs. It was like a miracle, son. A miracle."

Seth let the voice of the past melt into the humid summer heat, willing his attention to fasten on the present. A wry puzzled smile touched his lips as he watched the woman in widow's weeds slip through a distinctive garden gate and approach the back door of an establishment whose function would be recognizable in any city, town, or trading post in the country. She scurried inside without a backward glance.

Seth had no trouble identifying the house for what it was — first of all because it was in a better state of repair than any other building on the street, with fresh paint, clean bricks, and polished brass door knobs, all of which indicated a residence of prominence. Secondly, there was the high privet hedge to guarantee the privacy of customers, and the window shades drawn all around at an hour when respectable homes and businesses had their windows thrown open to the air, which suggested this was not a home that welcomed morning callers. The only question remaining was what a woman like Laurel Sinclair was doing inside.

He stood there for a moment, studying the situation thoughtfully, for if there was one thing the Colonel had taught him it was the foolishness of acting in haste. After a time, he surveyed the street until he saw what he wanted: a black man, sitting on the sidewalk, watching the quiet bustle of morning traffic with sullen, discontented eyes. Seth walked over to him.

"How'd you like to make five dollars?" he asked.

CHAPTER
Two

When the dames and patrons of Charleston society spoke of Laurel Sinclair Laughton it was generally with a puzzled shake of their heads and a long-suffering sigh, followed by the observation that one never did know what she would do next. These were the Old Guard, whose family names formed the very foundation of the South, whose impeccable breeding had brought them through the Civil War, reconstruction, and natural disaster, with their heads held high and their dignity intact. Fortunes had fallen, sons had been lost, daughters had been forced to marry beneath their station and Yankees were invading some of the finest parlors in Charleston, but the rules that governed the behavior of a lady or gentleman of quality had not changed, and the line that divided the fine families of Charleston from the rest of the world was as straight and unyielding as ever. Laurel Sinclair skated dangerously close to that line but she had, so far, never crossed it. And for the sake of her name she could be forgiven a great deal; she was, after all, one of their own, and the Old Guard protected its own.

Her mother had been a Beaulieu of New Orleans, whose family, it was said, could trace its connections to the Emperor Napoleon. Her father had been one of the fallen heroes of the glorious Confederacy, and *his* family, which included the late Jonas Sinclair and his widow and daughter, had been among Charleston's first builders.

Laurel had made a respectable match three years earlier with Johnny Laughton of Columbia, and a general sigh of relief had been heaved when she was safely married on Christmas Eve and dispatched up country. But she had returned three weeks later, after her young husband succumbed to a bout of pneumonia on New Year's day. It was whispered about that her precipitous return after the funeral had been at her mother-in-law's request, for the lady was of a delicate constitution, like all of the Laughtons, and her nerves could not endure the prolonged company of her new daughter-in-law — a situation with which most of the matrons in Charleston could sympathize.

The list of Laurel's transgressions was long and varied. She did the daily marketing herself, instead of sending her maid as a lady should, and then haggled loudly over prices. She danced the polka until she was flushed and the way she carried on with Peter Barton was shameful — not that there was anything specifically untoward in her conduct with the young man, but her continued association with him effectively removed him from the running as far as marriageable young ladies were concerned, and in these times of shortages of men, that was not a crime to be looked upon lightly.

Most disturbing of all, of course, were her activities at the Veterans' Hall, where she spent three afternoons a week and where, it was reported, she not only listened to the men's rough talk without blushing, but actually had been known to play cards. This was a matter of such serious consequence that it was brought up for review by the Ladies' Memorial Society. The discussion had quickly become heated and might easily have turned vicious had not Caroline, in a timid and quavering voice, pointed out she was certain her cousin meant only to bring comfort to those gallant heroes of the Confederacy and should in fact be thanked for her generosity rather than condemned for it, for did they not all have a fallen father or brother or husband whose memories these brave men served?

As for the cards, since they only played for matchsticks Caroline could hardly see what harm could come of it, and if there were any shame perhaps it should be upon themselves, who lacked Laurel Sinclair's courage to cast aside convention and modesty and give of themselves to those in need. The meeting at that point had deteriorated into tears and sentiment liberally laced with self-recriminations and impulsive resolves, with the result that the Veterans' Hall was now visited on two afternoons a week by staunch matrons bearing fresh flowers and fruit baskets, much to the regret of the veterans themselves, who enjoyed the spirited Miss Laurel's company but devoutly wished she had never stirred up the whole fray.

None of that, Laurel realized as she stood nervously in the parlor of Miss Elsie's establishment, would stand her in good stead if she were discovered now. Dancing a polka might be forgiven, an outspoken opinion or two overlooked, but she doubted if even Caroline would be able to find a defense for Laurel being inside a house of ill repute at ten o'clock in the morning. For that reason Laurel had been very careful to use the back entrance, and had checked twice to make certain no one saw her slip down the alley. And as she stood alone waiting for Miss Elsie herself to appear, she alternated between a superstitious fear that lightning might at any moment strike her down, and a very natural curiosity about her surroundings.

She had counted upon the fact that a place such as this did its business at night, and would be empty at this hour of the morning. On that score she was relieved to discover she was right. In fact, what surprised her almost to the point of disappointment was that the interior of the notorious brothel did not differ greatly from that of any other home in Charleston — except, perhaps, that it was a bit more luxurious.

There were no mirrors on the ceiling, nor on the walls, for that matter. There was no scarlet velvet nor were there gauze draperies or crystal chandeliers. The only thing that was in the least bit offensive was a very large portrait of three women, two of whom were undressed to the waist, but Laurel found the painting embarrassing rather than provocative and could not imagine what appeal it was supposed to have.

The walls were flocked with gold and the carpet was a very fine Persian, and there were many chaises and settees and small tables around, but try as she might, Laurel could not see what distinguished this as a gentlemen's house of pleasure . . . until her eyes fell on the long curving staircase and a silk stocking that dangled from the banister. Heat rushed to her face, and such a succession of vague and confused images swirled through her head that she almost lost her nerve — even as she stared with a sort of morbid fascination at the lone undergarment decorating the staircase.

Laurel could scarcely imagine the kinds of depravities that went on beneath this roof, nor the kind of woman who would willingly give herself to satisfy men's base needs. Needless to say, she found the entire concept mildly repugnant — yet perversely intriguing. Were all their undergarments silk? she wondered. And did they really put perfume between their breasts and on the backs of their knees and on other, similarly unmentionable places? And what about the men who came here? Were they husbands and businessmen as her Uncle Jonas had been, or did the women have to contend with rough and bearded sailors with dirty fingernails and cracked teeth?

Her eyes were fixed on the dangling stocking as she pondered the mysteries of the upper regions that lone banner heralded; she did not even realize that her steps had unconsciously taken her closer and closer to the staircase until her hand was actually resting on the newel post. She knew she should leave this place, before someone discovered her here. There might actually be *men* upstairs, and what would she do if she encountered one of them? Or one of those painted, half-dressed women . . . She shrank from the prospect, even as another part of her quickened with the curiosity that she had often been warned would be the death of her. She should get out of here, quickly, while better judgment still prevailed and luck held with her. This was one time impulse had taken her too far.

Then she heard a sound behind her, and it was too late to flee.

She jumped and whirled guiltily, and found herself facing a short, solidly built man whose bald pink head and flattened nose put Laurel in mind of a shoat. Red galluses supported a pair of wrinkled pinstriped trousers over a faded union suit, and a gray bristle covered the lower half of his face. As she watched, he scratched his ribs in a lazy, vulgar way and demanded, "What're you doing here?"

Laurel stammered, "I — the door was open and I —"

The little man narrowed his eyes and swept a

gaze over Laurel that made her skin prickle with alarm. There was contempt in his tone as he met her eyes again and said flatly, "We ain't hiring."

Laurel drew herself up, rigid with insult, as the man started to turn away. Shock gave her voice the authority it needed as she replied frostily, "I assure you, I am in no need of a position. I have business with Miss Elsie."

The man stopped, gave her a narrow, speculative look that seemed to last forever, and then shrugged. "In there." He jerked his thumb toward the hall and a half-open door on the other side of it. Then he walked away.

When he was gone, Laurel released a breath she had not even been aware she was holding, and she felt her heart beating so hard inside her chest that it threatened to break her stays. Every instinct shouted, *Go. Go while you still can.* And she wanted to, very badly. This was not glamorous or exciting or adventurous. It was degrading and unpleasant and more than a little frightening. She had no business here. The best thing she could do was forget about this insane scheme and go home with all possible haste.

But Laurel had two powerful character traits. The first was stubbornness. The second was an almost self-destructive refusal to listen to her better judgment when it mattered. She crossed the hall, hesitated for a moment outside the closed door, and knocked.

By the time Seth, following Laurel's course in-

34

side the building, reached the back corridors, she was gone. But he wasn't entirely unfamiliar with places such as this, and he found his way toward the front rooms.

The hallways were dark and cool, faintly redolent of musky perfume, which was common to such places. Seth met no one until he turned a corner toward the front of the house and a short, angry looking man in red suspenders blocked his path.

"What the hell is this?" he challenged, though his ill temper seemed to be due more to the early hour than any real rancor. "A goddamn hotel lobby? Am I going to have to start locking the goddamn back door at night to keep the trash out? Get on out of here!" He reached out as though to grab Seth's coat.

Seth's hand came up in a smooth gesture that would not ordinarily have been suggestive of violence — until one looked at his eyes. Miss Elsie's top man looked at his eyes, and what he saw there stopped him cold. He had seen enough of what was good, bad and in between in men to make a fair judge of character; he wouldn't have lasted long in this job if he hadn't. There was something about the eyes of a man who knew how to kill; it didn't mean that he would, or he had, but just that he could. Once a man got that look, there was nothing he could do to disguise it. Lon Porter, who had worked for Miss Elsie for twelve years and prided himself on being the best in the business, had seen that look before,

35

and nothing good had ever come of it. He let his hand drop.

"We don't open till three, Mister," he said, more cautiously. "You come back then."

Seth reached into his pocket and flipped the man a silver dollar. He hated to throw away money like that, but when a man was unarmed sometimes cooperation was more effective than intimidation. He said, "You got a girl named Laurie here?"

Lon looked at the silver piece in his hand, turned it over in the dim light, polished it against his trousers, and made no attempt to hide his suspicion as he looked back at Seth. But he was also a practical man, and he made an easy decision.

"We got a Dolly and a Lilly. Which one you want me to wake up?"

Already Seth was beginning to think this was a foolish endeavor and he wished he'd never started it. Here he was in one of the finest whorehouses in Charleston and he was wasting his time tracking down some woman in widow's weeds. It had been a long time since he had been in a place that smelled as expensive as this, he had money in his pocket and two girls named Dolly and Lilly sleeping upstairs, and if he had had any sense at all he would have told the little man in red suspenders to wake both of them up and set about having the time of his life. He was in fact on the verge of doing just that — he had never had a whorehouse all to himself before — and reaching into his pocket to pay the man, when a shaft of irritation went through him. He was in no mood to enjoy himself, and he wouldn't be until he got this business of Laurel Sinclair behind him.

He said abruptly, "They call her Sinclair. Or Laughton. A widow-woman. Somebody said she came this way."

Lon looked startled, and then he frowned. He jerked his head toward the front room. "Up there."

Seth nodded his thanks and moved past him, then paused and added over his shoulder, "Do you reckon if a man was to ask real nice he could get a cup of black coffee while he waits?"

Lon hesitated, a dozen questions that he dared not ask roiling inside him. Then he grumbled, "Coming right up," and shuffled down the hall.

Elsie Kettle was not as old as she looked, nor as young as she pretended. Her beauty marks were painted on, her eyelashes darkened with tar, her lips painted with carmine. The brash yellow color of her hair was achieved through biweekly rinses of peroxide and lye soap, and sometimes great clumps of it floated away with the bath water. But the fine wrinkles that caught the powder on her face and sagged in her bosom were her own, and she had earned every one of them. Elsie Kettle liked to tell herself she had seen it all.

But the one thing she was not prepared for on that bright June morning was to look up from her ledger books and find the Widow Laughton staring down at her. She was so startled that she dropped her pen, blotting the page, and she cursed loudly.

"God Almighty, girl, how the hell did you get

in here? Look what you made me do!"

Once again Laurel found herself stammering, "I — the man outside said I could . . . That is, I knocked, but you didn't . . ." And then she let the words trail off, feeling like a fool for apologizing to the woman and so overtaken by her own surprise that she literally couldn't think of anything else to say.

In many respects Miss Elsie was exactly what Laurel had expected a bad woman to be like. Her voice was husky and coarse, and her language crude. Her face was painted and powdered almost to the point of grotesquerie, and her straw-yellow hair, which was dark at the scalp, was pulled up in an absurd tangle of curls on top of her head. She wore a loud yellow-and-black striped taffeta gown that was cut too low and too tight and the short sleeves of which did nothing to flatter the arms of a woman her age. When Laurel looked — and she made a point of doing so — she noticed with satisfaction that black silk stockings decorated the three inches of leg that were visible beneath the ruffle of the woman's gown. None of that was particularly surprising.

What Laurel did find disorienting was that the notorious madam of the most infamous brothel in Charleston should be found in such mundane surrounding as the windowless little office, furiously scrubbing at the blotch she had made on her ledger book. The surroundings, and the banal activity, were so inappropriate that Laurel was momentarily off balance — and irrationally disappointed.

Miss Elsie gave up on the ledger book and looked up at Laurel impatiently. "Well, don't just stand there with your mouth hanging open, girl. What do you want?"

Laurel recovered her dignity with an effort and determinedly made her tone easy and polite. "I have come to discuss a matter of business with you."

A smile pulled at Miss Elsie's bright red lips and she leaned back in her chair, laying one finger alongside her cheek in a speculative manner. "Is that a fact?"

Laurel nodded. "Yes, you see . . ."

"You're Jonas Sinclair's niece, ain't you?" Miss Elsie interrupted abruptly.

Laurel was somewhat taken aback, but recovered quickly. "Yes. As a matter of fact, that was what I came to see you about. You see —"

Miss Elsie chuckled. "I kinda liked that old geezer. Pity what happened; we miss him around here."

In spite of herself, Laurel blushed. She had a sudden vision of how Aunt Sophie would react to this conversation — or worse yet, how Caroline would — and her courage faltered. But she had come this far, and so much was at stake that she had no choice but to brazen it through. She began again, firmly, "Miss Elsie —"

Again she was interrupted. The other woman's tone was brisk and businesslike, but not unkind, and as she spoke she turned back to her ledger books. "I tell you what. Since I did like the old man and we got some history between us, I'll save us both some time and get right to the point. You ain't the first quality girl that's darkened my door over the years — and I could name you some names that'd take the starch right out of your corset. Right pitiful, some of them, and a real shame how quick a lady's ready to fall on her back when she ain't got nothing else to fall back on. But I ain't never hired one of them, and I never will. The fact is, a lady's a lady and a whore's a whore, and while you might be real good at organizing charity bazaars and settin' a tea table, there ain't one of you that knows how to do for a man where it counts — elsewise why would your menfolk be coming to me? Now you best get on back home before somebody finds out you're here. The way you look, parading around like a scarecrow, you're gonna start scaring off my customers."

Laurel listened to the speech with rising indignation and outrage and now she stepped forward and slammed her hand down deliberately on the face of Miss Elsie's ledger book. Her eyes were blazing. It was one thing to debase herself to the point of coming here, to have her intentions mistaken at every turn and to be paralyzed with dread of discovery by the wrong person, but to be told after enduring all that that she wasn't even fit to work in a brothel was beyond too much.

Over Miss Elsie's startled exclamation Laurel spoke sharply. "Now you listen to me. I did not come here looking for work. I did not come here to listen to your mangled philosophy about who

40

does and does not make a successful candidate for employment in your — establishment, and I most certainly did not come here to be insulted! I came . . ." She took a deep, deliberate breath. "To collect a debt."

Miss Elsie raised a thin, artificially shaped eyebrow. "Is that right?"

"That's right." Laurel removed her hand from the desk and stepped back, trying once more for a semblance of dignity. She folded her hands primly before her and made an effort to modulate her voice into what Caroline would approve of as a ladylike tone.

"You may recall," she went on evenly, "that about five years ago when the temperance ladies came through here and did quite a bit of damage to your place, my uncle was kind enough to lend you one hundred dollars for repairs. I should like for you to repay that amount now, please."

The expression on Miss Elsie's face went from irritation to disbelief to outrageous amusement. She chuckled; she laughed out loud; she slapped her knee in delight. "Lord, honey, if you ain't got one hell of a nerve! You march in here and expect me to pay you a hundred dollars just like that — and as straight-faced as you please, too! You're old Jonas' kin, that much's for sure. He always was good for a belly laugh when I needed it!"

Hot blood stung Laurel's cheeks and she clenched her laced fingers tightly. She said stiffly, "This is no laughing matter, I assure you. I dislike being insistent, but you leave me no choice. I will have that debt repaid."

Miss Elsie chuckled again and picked up her pen, dismissing Laurel with a shake of her head. "Honey, I paid that money back a long time ago. Now get on out of here before you start getting on my nerves. I got work to do."

Laurel should have been prepared for that, but she was not. For a moment she was so stunned she couldn't even think. Then she said sharply, "That's impossible. I've kept up with every penny that's come into that house for ten years and I know —"

Miss Elsie glanced at her shrewdly. "You never heard of taking payment in trade, sweetie?"

For a moment Laurel didn't know what she meant. When she finally understood, the breath went out of her body in a sickening rush and all she could do was stare. This had been her only hope, the last chance in a series of last chances. How could it be snatched away from her with a brazen laugh and lewd suggestion?

Her hands clenched tighter as she struggled to control the quavering of her voice. "I am not in the least bit interested in your notions of barter. All I know is that my uncle made you a loan of one hundred dollars in cash, and I am here to demand repayment. In cash."

Impatience mingled with the amusement on Miss Elsie's face. "And if I don't pay it, what're you going to do? Call the police?" She shook her head again and turned back to her books.

"I ain't got time to fool with you, honey. Now, go on."

Fury spun through Laurel in cold and helpless waves; she could hardly keep from shaking with it. After all this — the stealth, the degradation, the chances she had taken; having endured the contemptuous leers of the piggish little man outside and the laughter and insults of Miss Elsie herself; having cast aside her pride and risked her good name — only to be turned away in defeat with nothing to show for her trouble but a bruised ego and a sense of righteous indignation. It was unendurable. It was unthinkable.

In her lifetime Laurel Sinclair had learned to accept much unpleasantness and disappointment, but the one thing she had not learned was how to lose gracefully when her mind was set on something. And this was no time to begin. She stiffened her spine, lifted her head, and walked over to the sagging divan opposite Miss Elsie's desk. She sat down gracefully and spread the folds of her skirts around her, painting a pleasant smile on her face.

"I don't think I will be leaving just yet," she said. "It's such a lazy day and I've nothing much to do. Perhaps I'll just while away my afternoon here . . . and even into the night."

Miss Elsie lifted her head slowly, her eyes narrowing.

"I can only hope, of course," added Laurel, widening her eyes innocently, "that I don't scare *too* many of your customers away, because I intend to greet each and every one of them personally

— as a token of respect to their dear wives, of course."

Miss Elsie placed her pen on the ledger with a snap. There was no amusement in her face at all now. "Girl," she said coldly, "you can just forget whatever it is you heard about old whores having hearts of gold, because mine is pure iron as far as my pocketbook's concerned, and if you and your fancy petticoats ain't bustling through that door inside of five seconds I'm going to call my man and have you thrown out!"

"Oh dear." Laurel opened her reticule and took out a black lace handkerchief, with which she began to fan herself langorously. "Oh, no, I don't think you'd better do that. I don't think the Ladies' Temperance League would look too kindly on one of their own being physically abused while trying to bring the message of Jesus to the heathen. And I know you don't want any more trouble with the Temperance League."

For a long time the two women met eye to eye, Miss Elsie's expression hard and unyielding; Laurel's soft and sweet. And then gradually the harsh lines in the older woman's face began to relax, and a faint smile traced the curve of her upper lip. She sat back and regarded Laurel thoughtfully.

"You've got a head for business on you, little lady," she said, after a time.

Laurel's spirits leapt.

"To tell the truth, I've never had much use for women with a head for business," she finished flatly. "Too much competition."

Laurel said coolly, "How fortunate for you that I've never been interested in going into your line of business."

Miss Elsie chuckled, and the sound grated on Laurel's nerves.

"I hear you play poker."

Laurel was surprised, but she refused to show it. "That's right."

"Well, so do I." Miss Elsie got up and came around the desk. "Some folks think I'm right good. And I guess we're about to find out, because . . ." She leaned against the desk, one tasseled slipper crossed over the other, a taunting little smile playing with her lips. "I'm calling your bluff."

Laurel did not blink.

"That's right, Missy," she went on easily. "I call your Temperance League and raise with one mayor — who's not only a real good friend of mine, but a regular customer. And since half the police department owes me a favor or two, I reckon we can stand off anything the ladies of the church have to offer. Why else do you suppose they've left us alone all this time? Now . . ." She raised her finger to her chin and cocked her head, regarding Laurel speculatively. "The way I figure it, it wouldn't hurt me much to have you say hello to a few of my red-faced customers, but I reckon you wouldn't do as good when those same customers start spreading the word around about where the fine Miss Laurel Sinclair spends

45

her evenings. Between the two of us, it sure looks to me like you've got more to lose, and you've got two choices: either pay or play."

For another long and icy moment Laurel held the other woman's gaze. Then, with four generations of Sinclair and Beaulieu pride pulsing through her veins, she gathered up her skirts and stood. Head held high, she swept through the door.

CHAPTER
Three

Seth leaned one shoulder against the frame of the parlor door, sipped his coffee, and listened with interest to the exchange from the open door across the hall. He knew that the gentlemanly thing to do, considering what he had learned about Laurel Laughton's circumstances from the overheard conversation, would be to go to her home and wait for her there. In fact, that would be the only decent thing to do. But Seth had not been feeling very gentlemanly, or decent, lately. In fact, he was feeling downright wicked.

And curious. There was still too much about this whole situation that didn't make sense.

And so he listened intently, timed his move just right, and when Laurel Sinclair Laughton came striding through the door with her head high and her eyes blazing, he stepped right in front of her.

She collided with him; half a cup of lukewarm coffee splattered on the front of her gown. She gave a choked little cry of shock and dismay, and he caught her shoulders briefly to steady her.

She brushed ineffectually at the bodice of her gown while trying to move past him and uttering some muffled apology that sounded something like, "So sorry — didn't see . . . please excuse . . . I must go."

Seth said smoothly, "It was my fault." He produced a handkerchief from his pocket, at the same time moving unobtrusively toward the wall, blocking her escape.

As far as Laurel was concerned the worst had already happened, and colliding head-on with one of Miss Elsie's disreputable customers and having coffee spilled on her gown was nothing more than a minor inconvenience. A few moments ago the thought of actually meeting one of the debased men who frequented this place — the thought of meeting *anyone* here — had been her worst nightmare, but now she hardly noticed. She was churning with rage, humiliation and defeat, and all she wanted was to get out of here.

She took the handkerchief he offered with scarcely a glance and made a few absent dabs at her bodice. The stain against the black material was hardly noticeable, and not worth the trouble of lingering over. He was saying, "I hope you weren't burned. I should have been watching where I was going." And it occurred to her dimly — because she was far too upset to care — that he was standing rather too close, and seemed to be looking at her with an intensity that wasn't ordinary. As well he might, she reflected distractedly, considering who I am and where I am . . .

It occurred to her then that he might even mistake her for one of Miss Elsie's girls, and that notion alarmed her just enough to bring her back to her senses. "It's quite all right," she said abruptly, and thrust the handkerchief back to him. "No harm done."

She started to move past him, but he did not give way. It was then she realized her troubles had only begun.

She lifted her eyes to him slowly. Later she would recall that he was tall, and rather good looking with a sun-bronzed face which, contrary to the prevailing fashion, was clean-shaven. Laurel had always liked clean-shaven men. His hair was blond-tipped and curly, his build lean and rangy, straining at the shoulders of the brown tweed suit and tapering to a slim waist and narrow hips. She took in these details automatically and without much interest, for the only thing she really noticed about him at that moment was a certain indistinct but unmistakable aura of power about him, a kind of coiled strength which, to a less confident woman, might have been interpreted as threatening. He was smiling politely, but there was no warmth in his eyes. And he was blocking her way.

She lifted her chin coolly. "Sir, please let me pass."

His smile deepened, ever so faintly, at one corner. "Ah now, Mrs. Laughton," he drawled

49

softly, "I don't think you want to go out this way. You'll be walking right out on the street, and somebody might see you."

Startled, she realized he was right, and she turned quickly to go the other way. Then she stopped. Her heart, which had not lost nor increased its steady, furious rhythm from the moment she left Miss Elsie's office, suddenly gave a lurch of alarm and then seemed to settle with a sickening drop to the pit of her stomach. She turned back to the stranger, cautious and still with dread. "You know my name."

He tilted his head slightly toward the door across the hall. "I couldn't help overhearing," he admitted, with very little pretense of shame. "And I've got to tell you, ma'am, you put up a right fine fight. I thought you had her there for a while, myself."

Laurel's breath left her lungs in a single muffled puff, even as renewed heat flashed to her cheeks. It was one thing to have endured the humiliation and insult at the hands of a common woman like Miss Elsie, but to have a total stranger witness her degradation . . . and then mock her with it! Shame and fury tasted like bile in her throat and she barely managed to articulate the words. "That, sir, was a private conversation and none of your affair. Good day." She gathered her skirts to sweep away.

"Well, now maybe it wasn't," he agreed negligently. "Then again, I might just be able to help you out."

She stopped. She shouldn't have, she knew, and she knew it even more when she met the lazy gleam in his hooded eyes. Nonetheless, she stopped, tilted her head in a small gesture of condescension, and inquired, "Indeed? And how might you do that?"

"How would you like a chance to earn that money?"

It took Laurel approximately five seconds to understand his meaning, and that long only because she had never had experience with, or any reason to expect, that kind of proposition. At first she was so startled she didn't know how to react. Then her eyes flew wide, her nostrils flared, and her arm shot out to strike him.

He caught her wrist in an easy, but alarmingly strong, grasp before it came within a foot of his face. "Is this what I get for trying to help a lady out?" There was amusement behind the feigned surprise in his eyes and that only infuriated her more.

"You vile, despicable creature!" she hissed, trying to twist her arm away. "How dare you! Let me go this instant!"

He studied her with a relaxed, contemplative air, but his grip on her wrist was like steel. "To tell the truth, Miss Laurel, I've had my face slapped before and I reckon I could take it again, but if it's all the same to you, I'd rather not. At least not until we talk about this thing for a minute."

"Talk!" She almost forgot to struggle, and for

a moment incredulity and indignation left her speechless. And then it struck her, for perhaps the first time, that her circumstances held more than a hint of genuine peril — she was defenseless in a house of ill repute, held in the grip of a mocking stranger, and she had to fight back a surge of panic.

She held herself stiff and stern and looked him straight in the eye. She forced into her tone an authority which she was far from feeling at the moment and she said, "Sir, you have mistaken me. I am not . . ." She had to swallow. "I am not employed here. And if you don't release my arm this minute I'll scream loudly enough to bring the police no matter whose payroll they are on!"

A corner of his lips twitched and the glint of amusement in his eyes deepened to outright laughter as his gaze swept over her. "Meaning no offense, ma'am," he replied, "and not overlooking your, uh, obvious charms, I think maybe it's you who are mistaken. There's more than one way to earn money in a place like this, you know."

She stared at him. "What are you talking about?"

He released her wrist slowly, smiling. "I heard you say you play poker."

She was so surprised by that statement that she didn't even take advantage of the opportunity to run. "And?"

"And I thought you might be interested in a friendly little game."

Laurel thought, This can't be happening to me. The morning had started out to be as ordinary as any other in her life. Then, with no warning whatsoever, she had discovered her family was on the brink of penury, she had been held captive in a brothel by a mocking stranger who added insult to injury by as much as admitting that he did not exactly find her impossible to resist and now she discovered that all he wanted to do was play cards with her. Oh, if she could only give one good shake of her head and make it all disappear and find herself safely back inside the parlor of her house on Lamboll Street, looking back upon this as no more than a particularly fanciful daydream.

She rubbed her wrist absently. Though he had not really hurt her, she could still feel the imprint of his strong fingers against her flesh. No man had ever grabbed her like that before, and her heart still beat rapidly from the contact. She would be a fool to linger here even one more moment.

She said frostily, "I'm afraid your proposal is out of the question, sir. I don't know you." And once again, she swept up her skirts to go.

"My name is Seth Tait." He tucked his hat under his arm and gave her a small, careless bow. "Now you know me."

The smile he gave her was charming, and the challenge in his eyes was infuriating, but that was not what stopped Laurel. Miss Elsie had apparently heard the commotion in the hallway and had come to see what it was all about. Now she leaned against the doorway, surveying the scene with a wicked amusement dancing in her eyes which made Laurel's blood boil. One half-clothed shoulder was thrown back to better advertise her full bosom, and her gaze examined Seth in a leisurely, appreciative way. She glanced at Laurel with an expression that made Laurel want to claw her eyes out, for the last thing she could tolerate this morning was the pity of a whore.

Laurel turned deliberately back to Seth Tait. "I fail to see how a 'friendly game' can alleviate my circumstances, and I have no money for anything more serious."

"I'll be happy to stake you."

She looked at him closely, her precious concerns abruptly forgotten. "You would pay — just to play cards with me?"

He returned her gaze mildly. "Isn't that what men usually do in a place like this? Pay for the company of a woman?"

Laurel drew in her breath sharply. But her indignation was not quite as intense as it should have been, and the scathing words she should have retorted did not come easily to her tongue. Her mind was far too preoccupied with the novel, and completely intriguing, notion that a man would actually pay to have her sit across the table from him and play cards.

"You — your behavior is reprehensible, sir," she managed at last, but she made no move toward the dramatic exit which was her last chance to save her dignity — and her reputation.

"Well now Mrs. Laughton," he replied reasonably, "you meet a man in a whorehouse, you can't

54

exactly expect him to have the manners of a preacher, can you?"

There was a guffaw of laughter behind him, and Seth turned to meet Miss Elsie, sparing Laurel the necessity of a reply. Laurel was glad, because anything she could have said would have only made matters worse . . . and possibly destroyed her only chance to redeem this morning's sorry work.

She would not be able to say later that she had acted on impulse, without thinking, completely carried away by the moment — though that would have provided some solace. In fact, she thought about it as thoroughly as she ever thought about any rash decision, rapidly and single-mindedly and with a great deal of emotion.

Perhaps she would have reached a different conclusion had matters not gone so badly that morning, if she hadn't been so angry and still stinging with humiliation and defeat. Perhaps it might even have been different if the stranger hadn't rubbed salt in her wounds with his insulting impudence. And there was the money to consider. She could win, she knew she could. Years of observing Uncle Jonas's vices had not gone for naught, and there was more than one way to come out ahead when a man — or a woman — was desperate enough. She could win, and it would serve Seth Tait right. And she would have the delicious luxury of laughing in Miss Elsie's face on her way out.

Seth was saying, "You don't mind if we use your parlor for a quick game, do you ma'am?"

Miss Elsie chuckled. "I wouldn't miss it for the world."

She came into the parlor and removed a fresh deck from the drawer of one of the small tables. She placed the deck in Seth's hand, swaying close enough to brush her arm against his. "You just make sure it's a game of cards. Like the lady said, she don't work for me, and I wouldn't want to see a fine young man like you get in any trouble."

Seth replied soberly, "You've got my word on it." But there must have been something in his expression Laurel could not see, because Miss Elsie laughed, and caressed his neck with her fingertips before moving away.

Seth placed the deck in the center of the table and looked up at Laurel inquiringly. She hesitated only a moment, then came into the room and sat down, pulling off her gloves finger by finger.

Seth pulled out his own chair and took a seat. He reached into his pocket and placed a fifty-dollar gold piece on the table in front of her. "The lady deals," he invited.

Laurel looked from the gold piece to her opponent, masking her surprise — and her greed — with an effort. She removed the last glove and reached for the deck. "We're playing straights, if you have no objection, Mr. Tait," she said briskly, "and aces are wild."

It was Seth's turn to mask his surprise as she shuffled the deck with the crisp efficiency of a riverboat pro and began to deal the cards.

Seth was a man who lived by his instincts and

his instincts were singing him a chorus now. What had started out as a very simple and straightforward mission had somehow become very complicated, and it grew more so by the minute. Curiosity, he knew, could be a dangerous thing if it weren't handled properly, and he had trained himself to approach the unknown with caution. Something was very wrong here, and until he had a better idea what it might be, he was going to move very slowly.

He studied the woman across from him with coolly disguised curiosity. Her face was sharp, her mouth determined, and her jawline distinct. Her figure was slim — some might even call it angular — though its severity was relieved by the bustle of her gown, which made it difficult for him to tell what kind of hips were disguised by all that fabric, and by the swell of her bosom, which, to Seth's immense satisfaction, was impossible to disguise. He spent some time observing the shape of her breasts as defined by the black broadcloth with the wholesome and quite natural appreciation of a man who has not had a woman, nor even the desire for one, in several months, and found the experience altogether satisfactory.

It was not, Seth decided, that this Laurel Sinclair was a homely woman — he had come to the conclusion that there was no such thing as a homely woman east of the Mississippi — and she might even be called handsome under different circumstances. If her hair were undone, for instance, or if somebody could remove that perpetual little frown from between her brows . . . When those silver eyes of hers flashed with anger she was almost beautiful, making him wonder how her face would look, flushed and soft and well-kissed . . . No, he decided. She wasn't homely. It was simply that she was not at all what he had expected.

It occurred to Seth that he was at a distinct disadvantage when it came to approaching her. How could he find out how much she knew about her father and Colonel Ike without telling her more than he was ready to reveal? He realized with a mild shock that he had never even known the Colonel's last name. Out west things like that didn't matter, but here in the midst of civilization it was an acute handicap. And talking to Mrs. Laurel Sinclair Laughton would have been a whole lot easier if only he had had some place to start.

"Where did you learn to play like this?" he asked after a moment.

She didn't glance up from her study of her hand. "My uncle taught me. What will it be, Mr. Tait?"

Seth casually laid two cards on the table. "I thought maybe it was your husband."

"My husband didn't play." She dealt him two cards, and discarded one from her own hand.

Seth disguised his amusement as he watched her deal herself another card. "So, you are married then."

"I am a widow, as you can plainly see." She lifted her eyes. "Would you like to place a bet, sir?"

Seth silently pushed two five-dollar coins to the center of the table.

She had a poker face that would have stood her in good stead in any saloon in the country. That was only one of the things Seth was beginning to admire about her.

"As you can see, I don't have any change. But I would like to cover that and raise it twenty-five, please."

Seth lifted an eyebrow. "You do take your cards seriously don't you, ma'am?"

"That's the only way I know how to play."

"Lots of folks would say that's a dangerous habit."

She met his gaze levelly. "It's only dangerous, Mr. Tait, if you lose."

Seth returned his gaze to his hand.

Laurel watched him, trying to read something in a face that was as inscrutable as any she had ever known, and it occurred to her for the first time that he might be as good at this as she was. He might be better. The thought made her throat go dry and her stomach muscles tighten until they hurt.

If she had allowed herself to think about what she was doing for even a minute her courage would have failed her. This was not the same as playing for matchsticks with a bunch of garrulous old men whose only stake in the game was the company of a spirited young woman. It was hardly the same as passing the deck back and forth with Uncle Jonas while he beamed at her precocity and told long-winded stories about his salad days. She was playing poker for real money — money that wasn't even her own — in a place where she should not have been with a man she did not know . . . a man who, by his very presence here, had proven he was no gentleman and who had compounded that acknowledgment by insulting her more than once, a man whose quick, alert eyes missed nothing and revealed nothing. Yes, it was dangerous, but she couldn't think about that now. She had no intention of losing.

He hardly seemed to notice when Miss Elsie sidled up behind him and began caressing his shoulders with her hands. Laurel found that both embarrassing and irritating. What kind of man would allow a woman to make love to him so flagrantly while he was sitting across the table from a lady? The kind of man, she reminded herself grimly, who would come into a place like this in the first place. It was obvious, after all, that he hadn't sought out Miss Elsie's notorious crimson door for the sake of a cup of coffee.

He said after a moment, without glancing up, "I wonder, Miss Laurel, if you know a man they call the Colonel?"

"I know a great many colonels," she replied, somewhat impatiently. "Charleston is hip-deep in colonels." The tension was growing unbearable. "What are you going to do, Mr. Tait?"

He absently fingered some coins at his side. "Well, it's a hard decision," he admitted. "On the one hand, I don't like to take advantage of a lady. On the other, it would hardly be fair if I didn't give you a chance to pay back my stake. So why don't I just make it easy on you? I'll cover your twenty-five . . ." He pushed the coins forward. "And raise five."

Laurel's throat convulsed. If she stopped now, she would lose nothing except the money he had lent her. But if she proceeded . . .

He said casually, "This particular colonel sometimes goes by the name of Ike."

There might have been something familiar in the name, but Laurel was far too distracted to care. She replied briefly, "No. I don't know him."

She fingered her cards. She looked at the money in the center of the table. She did some rapid calculations in her head. The one thing she did not do was meet Seth Tait's eyes. Not until she had made her decision.

"Why don't we just make this simple all around, Mr. Tait?" she said pleasantly, and pushed the fifty-dollar gold piece forward.

She met his eyes without a flicker of expression in her own, and saw the same calculating blankness in his, though his lips were smiling. "Well, now. I guess that's plain enough." He covered her bet. "That's fifty dollars if you lose."

"But it's one hundred if I win." She laid her cards on the table with a smile. "Straight flush. That's what makes the game interesting. Isn't it, Mr. Tait?"

His expression did not change as he examined her cards. Still his eyes were lazy and alert, still that hint of a smile curved his lips. "I figured that was why you called straights at the start. That's what I would have done."

He looked from the cards to her, and the smile that traced his lips deepened, his eyes were lit with a spark of what appeared to be genuine admiration. "Congratulations, ma'am. You've got to be one of the smoothest little second-dealers I've ever seen."

Laurel gasped. Hot blood rushed to her face and for a moment she couldn't even speak. When she did it was in a voice so choked with outrage that the words were almost incoherent. "You — you *dare* accuse me of . . . of being a cheat?"

"One of the best," he complimented her graciously.

Laurel drew another breath, and this time managed not to choke on it. Her heart was pounding so furiously that her hands shook. But with an enormous effort, she brought herself under control. Gripping the table with both hands, she met his eyes. "Sir," she said deliberately. "Your accusations are beneath contempt, and I will not dignify them with a defense. The rules were clear from the outset. I will leave you with the money you advanced me, and take my winnings now please."

He chuckled, watching her across the table with unfeigned enjoyment in his eyes. "You've got nerve, lady, I'll say that for you."

But when, with a furious, impatient movement, she reached for the coins in the center of the table, he lifted a warning hand. "Just a minute if you don't mind."

Miss Elsie's eyes, Laurel's noticed, were dancing madly. She felt a cold sickness creep through the pit of her stomach as she sat back.

Seth laid down his cards. "Four aces," he said smoothly. "I believe that beats a straight flush."

Laurel felt the color drain from her cheeks. Her fingertips tingled and even her lips went numb. "But — that's impossible!"

He smiled. "I said you were *one* of the best. I was taught by an expert."

Times were changing, the Colonel kept saying, a man had to change along with them. He had made sure to teach Seth the ways of civilization, even when they were robbing trains and living by their grit and their guns, just so he could get along anywhere he had to. The trouble was the Colonel had taught him other things better, and Seth wasn't interested in changing.

Seth Tait liked life the hard way. There was nothing civilized about him, for all the reading, writing and fine manners the Colonel had forced on him. He was used to taking what he wanted and defending his right to do so coolly and dispassionately, the same way the Colonel and Augustus Sinclair had coolly walked away with thousands in gold all those years ago.

A miracle, the Colonel had said. His voice, filled with awe and wonder, drifted back to Seth in an instant, retelling the tale of more than twenty years ago.

"So Gus and me broke into that car, took out the guards — and found the gold. Yankee payroll gold. And we took it and never for a minute thought we'd done wrong.

"We weren't but about ten miles, cross country, from Chinatree. We had in mind to hide it there, with Gus's kin.

"But we got pinned down by snipers. Gus, he had the gold, and I tried to hold 'em off long enough for him to get away. I did, too. Then spent the rest of the war in a Yankee prison camp.

"Gus, though, he got through. Heard he made it back to the unit — then got himself killed three weeks later. He couldn't find me, of course. Never got a chance to tell me where he'd hidden that gold.

"After the war, I went back to Chinatree, but it'd been burned. His family had refugeed south. And Charleston wasn't too friendly a place for an ex-Reb in those days, I couldn't stay around to look for it. I got in some trouble, had to light out west, but I always meant to go back. Still do. It's there, just waiting . . ."

Miss Elsie burst into laughter, dragging Seth's attention back to the present. "I guess this just ain't your day, is it honey? Maybe now you'll learn to stay at home where you belong."

Laurel pushed up from the table, blind with fury, and whirled to leave.

"Uh, Miss Sinclair."

She turned back, her eyes blazing and her fists clenched so tightly that her nails stung her palms. Seth Tait collected his coins and glanced up at her mildly. "I believe you owe me fifty dollars."

"I owe you nothing, sir! You cheated!"

"It's not cheating," he reminded her reasonably, "when everybody's playing by the same rules."

"I don't have any money," she told him stiffly. "You knew that from the outset."

He pretended thoughtfulness. "Well, now, that is a shame. I guess we're just going to have to think of some other way for you to pay me back."

That was too much. Her head swam and her pulse throbbed, and if she had had the courage she would have spat at him. She gathered up her skirts and without another word stalked toward the back door.

Miss Elsie was still chuckling. "I like you, Mister." Her hand trailed along the back of his neck, teasing the inside of his collar, and the amusement in her eyes deepened into something a bit more seductive. "Tell you what," she murmured. "You come back sometime and we'll see what we can do for you. On the house."

"Why, that's real neighborly of you, ma'am." Seth stood and took his hat from where he had hung it on the back of the chair. "In the meantime, though . . ." He flipped a two-dollar piece onto the table. "Thanks for the use of the parlor."

He started to leave, and then noticed something lying on the floor beside Laurel's chair. He stooped to pick up a pair of black gloves, and held them thoughtfully in his hand for a moment before turning back to Miss Elsie. "Just one thing," he said. "You did pay back her uncle that money, like you said?"

Miss Elsie made a dramatic arch of her two thinly painted eyebrows. "You ought to know better than to ask a thing like that. Whores always pay their debts." And she grinned. "Just like gamblers."

After a moment, Seth returned her grin, and slapped the gloves lightly against his thigh as he went to follow Laurel Sinclair.

"You come back now, you hear?" Miss Elsie repeated her invitation.

"You can count on it," he tossed over his shoulder.

And then he heard a woman's scream.

CHAPTER
Four

Seth reached the back door just in time to see someone disappear around the corner of the building. His hand slapped for his gun and he swore out loud when he remembered it wasn't there. He dashed down the steps in two leaps and found Laurel Sinclair on her hands and knees in the dirt. The ragged sounds coming from her throat could have been sobs or, more likely, incoherent gasps of fury.

He took her shoulder and she flung her arm out blindly with a cry of rage and self-defense, striking him hard in the knee. "Take it easy!" he commanded, trying to fend off her blows. "I'm not going to hurt you!"

But she continued to flail at him, and when Miss Elsie appeared on the back steps he gave up struggling with her and ran after the man he'd seen fleeing around the corner of the building. After a few moments he returned, alone. The construction of Charleston houses was such that none of them faced the street; the assailant could have disappeared through any one of four surrounding courtyards or have even crossed the piazza and made it to the street to blend into the crowd. There was no sign of him.

Miss Elsie was helping Laurel to her feet, although Laurel was no more gracious to her than she had been to Seth. She alternated between brushing at the dust on her skirt and pushing the other woman's helping hands away, all the while muttering epithets beneath her breath. She looked pale and shaken, her bonnet was askew and her skirts were streaked with dirt, but the familiar v-shaped frown was in place between her brows, and except for a small tear in the shoulder of her gown and a streak of mud across her cheek, she appeared to be unharmed.

"What happened?" Seth demanded.

Laurel did not honestly know what had happened, and when she tried to think back she found it all was a blur. She had stormed out of the building, too angry to see straight, and suddenly rough hands had grabbed her and she was on the ground and she was still too shocked by it all to even be afraid.

"I started to turn the corner and someone shoved me from behind. Pushed me down." She was surprised to find her voice was shaking. That unsettled her so much that she clenched her teeth together and determined not to say another word. She wouldn't go into a state after the fact. She refused to break down now, in front of the hateful Miss Elsie and that arrogant Mr. Tait. She wouldn't start to cry, on top of everything else . . .

"Did you get a look at him?" Seth interrogated.

"No." She concentrated on scrubbing at a streak of dirt on her skirt. All she wanted to do was go home and forget this horrible morning. . . . No, first she wanted to find a way to make her hands stop shaking.

"Probably stumbled over some drunk left over from last night," Miss Elsie muttered in disgust. "Lord a'mercy, girl, what do you expect when you go sneaking down the back alley of a whore-house? You probably scared the poor bastard half to death." She turned a gaze on Seth which was completely lacking in its former hospitality. "Will you for God's sake get her out of here before she gets in any more trouble? Next thing I know she'll be setting the house on fire." With a switch of her heavily perfumed skirts she turned and stalked up the stairs.

Seth watched her close the back door and heard the firm click of the bolt, then he turned back to Laurel. She straightened her bonnet, adjusted the waist of her basque, and looked for all the world as though she had just experienced nothing more alarming than an inconvenient gust of wind. Seth removed her gloves from his pocket and handed them to her politely. "You forgot these."

"Thank you."

Her tone was calm and composed, but when she began to pull on the gloves Seth noticed her hands were shaking badly. A twinge of sympathy mitigated the admiration he felt for her, and he expressed it with a small shake of his head. "You've had a hell of a morning, haven't you lady?"

For once no sharp retorts were forthcoming. She paused in straightening the fingers of her gloves, released an unsteady breath, and met his eyes bleakly. "Yes," she replied simply.

That brief moment of vulnerability startled Seth, and unsettled him, because it was the one thing he had not expected from her and he was not certain how to respond . . . or even if he wanted to. But almost before he could examine it the moment was gone, and Laurel quickly turned her attention back to her gloves, as though embarrassed for the brief slip in her facade.

"Well," she said briskly, "thank you for your assistance, Mr. Tait, though it was rather too little, too late. I'll be on my way now."

Seth repressed a grin that was generated from an emotion he had not felt in a very long time: sheer delight. Laurel Sinclair was one woman who could keep a man on his toes.

He fell into step beside her. "You're not going to swoon, are you?"

"Certainly not," she scoffed. "I never swoon."

"Or cry?"

"I never cry either. It only makes matters worse."

"Good. Because you used up my handkerchief with coffee and I don't have another."

She paused at the edge of the courtyard, quickly checking the street, and then she turned to him. "Good day, Mr. Tait," she said firmly.

"I'll see you home."

"You'll do no such thing!"

He took her elbow in a light, but firm, grasp as she started to move away. "I'll see you home," he repeated in a tone every bit as determined as her own.

"Are you out of your mind?" She tried to tug her arm away with no success. "Do you think I'm going to let everyone in the world see me walking down the streets of Charleston with you? I don't even know you!"

There was a hint of genuine alarm in her tone as she quickly checked the streets again, and that amused Seth. An oxcart clattered by, and she sank back into the shadows as a group of ladies, parasols in hand, passed by on the other side of the street without glancing in their direction.

"*Please*, Mr. Tait." She looked up at him with eyes that were dark with distress. "Surely you can see it simply wouldn't be proper for me to be seen with . . . How would I explain you? You simply mustn't attempt to escort me home!"

"All I see," he told her with an utter lack of concern, "is that I'm not going to let you walk home alone after what just happened."

Laurel wanted to point out that his chivalry was misplaced, not to mention ill-timed, that she was perfectly unharmed, had no need of his or anyone else's protection and that his inappropriate

71

gentlemanly instincts could only do more harm than good — a fact which any *real* gentleman would have immediately comprehended. But there was nothing but stubbornness in his eyes and the set of his jaw was as strong as her own. It was apparent to her, as it surely must have been to him, that the longer they delayed at the edge of the courtyard the more chance there was of being seen by someone she knew, and that was one thing she simply could not have endured. Not today.

"Oh, all right!" Impatiently she jerked her arm away. "But for heaven's sake, at least get a cab. I don't want anyone to see us."

He threw back his head and laughed, startling Laurel so much that she forgot her anxiety in favor of a new surge of anger. "What are you laughing at?" she demanded.

"At you." His eyes were dancing. "You spend twenty minutes playing poker with me in a whorehouse, and now you're worried about what being seen with me on the streets is going to do to your reputation."

Laurel scowled with annoyance as he moved off, chuckling, but she had no answer to that.

Seth found a closed hack with very little delay, and helped Laurel into it quickly and without ceremony. Laurel gave the driver directions and leaned back against the cracked leather upholstery, closing her eyes briefly and allowing herself a small sigh of relief.

But no sooner had her muscles relaxed in the safety of the dusty-smelling carriage than an awful weakness swept over her as the impact of what had happened struck her for the first time. She had been *assaulted*. Right here on the streets of Charleston which she had walked in perfect safety all her life, someone had come from behind and used violence against her. Nothing like that had ever happened to her before; no man had laid rough hands on her; no one had ever meant her physical harm. She felt shaky and ill inside as the memory flashed before her eyes. She could have been killed, or — or raped, and now that it was all over she wasn't relieved at all. She was clammy with shock.

"Contemplating your sins, Miss Laurel?" drawled a soft mocking voice across from her, and Laurel's eyes snapped open.

She had been so involved in reliving the horror that she had forgotten the other occupant of the carriage. The sound of his voice shocked her out of her self-absorption and stung her into an immediate retort. "If you dare to suggest that what happened served me right —"

"Why ma'am, I wouldn't think of such a thing. Anybody can tell you're a fine, decent, upstanding woman —"

"And you are without a doubt the most ill-bred man I've ever met," she said tightly, clenching her fists against her skirts. "If you had half the sensitivity God gave a cornflower you'd see what I've been through and offer a little kindness, a little —"

"Sympathy?" That seemed to amuse him vastly.

73

"Lady, I've seen the way you take care of yourself and I've got to tell you, my sympathies are with the man that got away. He was probably running for his life."

She felt color rush to her cold cheeks and her eyes narrowed as she tried to think of something bad enough to call him, and then she realized something else. She was no longer feeling sick and terrified inside. He had succeeded in making her exchange her fear for anger and she looked at him closely, wondering if he had done it on purpose.

He lounged across from her, filling the carriage with his masculine presence. His hat was lazily balanced on one knee, and his legs were so long that his other knee brushed her skirts. She could not recall ever noticing such long legs on a man before, or such powerful thighs. Quickly she jerked her attention away from his thighs, but that did not ease the sudden rapid rhythm of her heart.

His face was shadowed and unreadable, just as it had been across the poker table from her, traced with the faintest hint of easy amusement . . . as though he knew a nasty secret he wasn't telling, or as though he was thinking things no decent man would think when he looked at her. And he *wasn't* a decent man, Laurel reminded herself. If he had been, he wouldn't have been in Miss Elsie's house in the first place. One glance at those wicked, too-perceptive eyes assured her that his motives were anything but kind. She must have been out of her mind to even consider assigning altruistic motives to his ruthless teasing. After all, hadn't he been the cause of all her troubles?

His next words only confirmed her opinion of him. He regarded her with that lazy, half-speculative light in his eyes and said, "I can't help wondering, though, what would make a fine up-standing young lady like you go begging at a whorehouse."

"I didn't go begging," she snapped. "I was collecting a debt. As you very well know," she added acerbically, "since you were listening at the door."

He shrugged. "Still, it must have been something pretty powerful, to push you that far."

She gave a small jerk of her chin as she turned to stare out the window. The carriage was weaving its way at an interminably slow pace through the traffic that crowded the narrow streets, stirring up the odor of manure and freshly hosed-down sidewalks. "Imminent poverty, Mr. Tait," she informed him, "is always a powerful motive."

"Hmm." The sound was noncommittal and unmoved. "Still, seems to me there might be an easier way to go about fixing that."

She replied coolly, and without looking at him, "Indeed. And I suppose you know just the way."

He appeared to think about that for a moment. "Well, for starters, you could have asked Miss Elsie for a job instead of a handout."

Her gaze jerked back to him. "You are a vulgar, disgusting man," she said through gritted teeth. "And I will not stay another moment in this carriage with you and be insulted. Signal the driver immediately."

He merely smiled. "No ma'am, I'm not going to do that. And you can't call me insulting for saying out loud what you were thinking."

That caught her off guard, and she closed her mouth on a retort so abruptly that her teeth clicked. How was she supposed to deal with a man who said every outrageous thing that came into his head, with no regard for decency or respect for ladyhood . . . and who had the most distressing habit of being right?

For there had been a moment, standing in Miss Elsie's parlor, when she had wondered what it would be like. Rushing out of the house this morning with desperation barking at her heels, hadn't she thought, even for the briefest of moments, that if worst came to worst . . . ? And in the end what had she done but barter her company — *herself* — to Seth Tait for a fifty-dollar stake in a poker game?

She brought her hand to her throat, rubbing it absently, and turned again to stare out the window. "Thank you for your concern, Mr. Tait," she said with as much dignity as possible, "but I don't believe I require the benefit of your advice."

He laughed, fully and with a kind of frankness that made Laurel understand why the Puritans had considered laughter a sin. The sound of it made her skin tingle and seemed to fill the carriage with vitality and maleness. Laurel tightened her hands in her lap and mentally urged the horses to move faster. How much longer could this horrid journey last?

"Come to think of it," he said after a moment, still chuckling, "I don't reckon that kind of work would do for you. So tell me, what kind of work would be called respectable for a widow woman like you?"

There seemed to be no way to avoid talking to him. Besides, there was a part of Laurel — that devilish, ill-restrained part of her that was always getting her into trouble — that wanted to talk to him, if for no other reason than to see if there was anything she could say that would shock him.

She turned back to him and replied, "They sew, or open bakeries, or fix broken china like my cousin Caroline or paint silly little watercolors that people buy out of pity and hide in their closets. I couldn't sew a straight stitch if my life depended on it, everything I bake falls flat, and I am much better at breaking china than mending it. Furthermore, you are quite right — I would be most unsuitable for the kind of work Miss Elsie offers. I have been married, and that was quite enough for me, thank you."

There, she thought with satisfaction. For the briefest instant she thought she saw a flicker of surprise in his eyes, but it was so quickly gone that she hardly had time to appreciate it. "Maybe," he suggested reasonably, "you'd feel differently if you were doing it for profit."

"Ha! Don't deceive yourself, Mr. Tait. Every

married woman does it for profit." And the minute the words were out she felt her cheeks go scarlet. She quickly jerked her eyes back toward the window again, but not before she saw that wicked amusement dancing in his. She had thought she was baiting him, but he had neatly trapped her into humiliating herself again. Dear Lord, how could she have ever been so foolish as to have gotten into this carriage with him?

She steeled herself for further mortification, for this man had already proven that there were no depths of vulgarity to which he would not sink. But all he said was, with only the faintest undertone of laughter to his voice, "I take my hat off to you, Miss Sinclair. I do admire a woman who says what's on her mind."

With all the courage she possessed, she turned to face him again, willing the heat in her cheeks to recede and her heart to stop pounding so. "Good," she said. "Then you won't mind when I point out that it's quite unseemly of you to express such an interest in my financial affairs. I really think this conversation should end."

"But I have a vested interest in your financial affairs," he pointed out. "You owe me money, remember?"

The carriage was very warm, and he took up a great deal of it. Everywhere Laurel looked she saw a part of him — a bronzed hand, a tightly muscled thigh, a broad shoulder. And suddenly she understood why that made her so uneasy. Aside from his crudity and his wicked eyes and the very obvious fact that he was no gentleman, he was the most outrageously attractive man she had ever met. That was a dangerous combination.

She swallowed hard, trying to still the nervous flutter of her stomach. She said sharply, "And I suppose you've concocted some base and depraved way for me to repay that debt, since I've already told you I have no money."

"Do you mean like selling your favors?" He gave a small shake of his head. "Well, I'll admit I've been thinking on it. But to tell you the truth, I'm not sure your favors are worth fifty dollars."

Laurel's mouth fell open and she drew in a breath for a reply she was, fortunately, not required to make. The carriage rolled to a stop just then, and Seth reached forward for the latch. She gathered up her skirts and was out of the vehicle the second he was on the ground, ignoring his offer of help and moving past him stiffly and without a word.

Seth paid the driver and absently took note of his surroundings. The tall, narrow yellow house, not much different from any other in Charleston, was surrounded by a wrought iron gate at street level and screened from its neighbors by two flowering magnolia trees. The flaking and peeling paint revealed bare gray boards in some places; but the brass door knockers gleamed, and the garden was immaculate. A false front door faced the street and opened onto a wide piazza which was situated to catch the faintest harbor breeze — a foolish vanity, since the houses were so tall and close together as to make the hope of any kind of air circulation futile.

Seth caught the garden gate she tried to slam against him, and he did the same with the door when she strode onto the piazza. "It is not necessary for you to see me inside," she said tightly.

"No trouble at all, ma'am," he replied, and followed her inside the house without giving her a chance to argue. Having come this far, Seth would let nothing keep him from seeing the rest.

At some point during the carriage ride — or perhaps even earlier, during the poker game itself — the reason he had first sought out Laurel Sinclair had faded to insignificance and had been almost forgotten. It was clear that Laurel and her family, teetering on the brink of poverty, could not possibly have recovered the hidden gold. That Gus had somehow turned the gold over to his family had been Seth's first theory, and the fact that he hadn't was encouraging news.

Seth followed her into the parlor and had his first real glimpse of what the Colonel used to call "genuine gentility." The carpets were faded and the draperies were threadbare; the molding around the ceiling was cracked and walls were in need of replastering in some places. Lacy little antimacassars covered the worn spots on the furniture and a shawl in once-brilliant colors of purple and blue was draped over the back of the spinet, the water-splotched silk and frayed fringe defiantly proclaiming days of past splendor.

Seth took in all of this in a glance because years

of living with a soldier on the edge of danger had trained him to be a quick and keen observer. But the real message of the room was more subtle, beyond the range of his physical senses, and within three seconds of entering the house he knew more about Laurel Sinclair than he could have learned from hours of questioning.

This was a place of quality, of objects carefully selected and lovingly treasured, of the kind of taste that could only be acquired through generations of culture. The patina might be dulled upon the woodwork, the portraits faded upon the walls and the mirrors cracked with age, but there was a certain arrogant splendor about it all which defied change. There was a world of tradition and permanence inside these walls which was as alien to Seth as the landscape of the moon, away of life wrapped up in words like aristocracy and lineage and breeding — words Seth had never understood until now. It amused him that a spitfire such as Laurel Sinclair should belong to such a place, but in an odd sort of way it made perfect sense.

She took off her gloves and her bonnet and turned to him briskly. Her hair, he noticed, was a rich dark color gleaming with hidden lights. It would be magnificent unbound.

"Very well," she said impatiently, "you've seen me safely inside. Now will you please leave before —"

But it was too late. From another room came a woman's gentle, musically accented voice, "Laurel, is that you?" And chiming in was another,

81

slightly higher and more breathless voice, "You see, Caro, I told you there was nothing to worry about. Here she is safe and —"

Both women entered the room at once and both stopped short, their eyes going first to Seth in surprise and curiosity, and then to Laurel. The dismay that crossed their faces when they took in her appearance was matched only by the impatience on Laurel's at the flurry that inevitably followed.

The younger girl came forward first, moving with a noticeable limp as she exclaimed in alarm, "My dear, what has happened? Your face, your gown —"

And the older, plumper woman clutched her hand to her throat and moaned, "Something dreadful! I just knew it! Something dreadful has happened and it's all my fault . . ."

Laurel said, "It's nothing, I'm perfectly all right . . . Auntie, don't you dare swoon!"

"Oh, Laurel, what happened? Look at you! I've been so worried about the way you rushed out of here and now —"

Seth stepped forward smoothly. "I assure you, ladies, there's nothing to be concerned about. Mrs. Laughton had a — small fall, but she's not hurt."

The sound of a male voice seemed to have an arresting effect on the flutter of feminine activity. Laurel glanced at him, and for the briefest instant something close to gratitude flashed from her eyes. The older woman recovered herself with remarkable alacrity and gave him an alert, curious stare; the younger woman's glance was more gently puzzled.

Laurel said, with obvious reluctance, "This is Mr. Seth Tait. He was kind enough to escort me home. Mr. Tait, my aunt Sophie Sinclair, and my cousin Caroline."

Seth bowed first to the older woman, then to the younger. Sophie said, "Tait? Do we know any Taits?"

Caroline came forward, a warm and welcoming smile transforming her plain face into something almost beautiful. "Mr. Tait. How kind you are to take such care of our dear Laurel. Welcome to our home."

Seth smiled at her and said gently, "It was no trouble at all, ma'am."

Sophie's small brow puckered with concentration as she insisted, "I'm sure we must know *some* Taits."

"No," Laurel said sharply, "we don't. He is a complete stranger."

Caroline spared a single troubled glance for her cousin's tone, then turned back to Seth. "You are new to Charleston, Mr. Tait? How lovely. Please, won't you sit down?"

Seth glanced at Laurel, having no intention of refusing the invitation and perversely anticipating her reaction. But before his eyes met hers his gaze fell on something else, and stopped there.

It was in the center of a small cluttered table, otherwise he would have noticed it before. Surrounded by a miniature vase of dried flowers, a painted fan, a conch shell filled with painted beads, an intricate needlework portrait of a shepherd and sheep, and a pair of gold-rimmed spectacles was a photograph in an elaborately carved gilded frame. The woman in the photograph was soft and lovely, wearing the hoopskirts and ruffles of twenty-five years ago. A man stood beside her.

Caroline repeated, "Mr. Tait?"

And Sophie chimed in with surprising energy, "Oh, yes Mr. Tait, where are my manners? Do sit down and tell us all about yourself. It's so rare that we have visitors from out of town. Laurel, run out to the kitchen and tell Lacey to bring some lemonade."

Seth looked up. "Thank you, but I can't stay."

The relief in Laurel's voice was evident as she said, "Of course he can't. We've already imposed on Mr. Tait enough —"

"Don't be silly, dear, the very least we can do to repay Mr. Tait's chivalry . . ."

Seth let the voices fade away as he walked over to the table and picked up the photograph. He stared at it for a long time.

"I see you're admiring Mr. Brady's photograph," Caroline said softly at his arm. "It's quite remarkable, isn't it? Aunt Iris was always so fond of it, though I believe it was considered somewhat of a folly at the time. It was taken just before the war."

Seth made himself put the photograph down and smile at her politely. "A handsome couple. Who are they?"

"Laurel's parents. It was taken on their wedding day."

Seth felt Laurel's gaze on him and he kept his face impassive. "Perhaps I should pay my respects."

"My parents are dead," Laurel said abruptly.

He kept his tone, and his gaze, level. "I'm sorry. A recent loss?"

A softness that surprised Seth came over her face as she glanced at the photograph. The muted glow in her eyes seemed almost like reverence. "My father died a hero to the Cause in the heat of battle," she said huskily. "I never knew him. My mother never recovered from her grief, and passed on only a few years later."

Caroline slipped an arm around her cousin's shoulders, and even Sophie was silent as the three women seemed to share a moment of tribute. Seth let the moment go on just long enough to become poignant, then he took advantage of it.

"A terrible loss," he said gravely, returning the photograph to the table. He looked at Laurel. "You must take a great deal of comfort from the fact that your father's sacrifice was to a noble cause."

Perhaps he overdid it, because there was a sudden flash of suspicion in Laurel's eyes. But her aunt Sophie, dabbing ostentatiously at her eyes with an embroidered handkerchief, declared, "Oh, sir, you don't know, you simply *can't* imagine what it was like. Those horrible Yankees, and what they did to us all! Our poor Gus, struck down on the field of battle, lingered for three days before the Lord finally took him to his rest. Why, his last letter to Iris was written on his deathbed, and when it finally arrived it was like a voice from the grave . . ." She muffled a sob in her handkerchief, then squared her shoulders bravely. "Of course, it was no more than any of our courageous boys endured, or their families."

A letter. The word set Seth's mind racing. A deathbed letter, perhaps a confession . . . But no. If he had revealed anything at all about the gold these women would not be living now in a half-tumbled-down house, and Laurel wouldn't be dunning the madam of a whorehouse for a debt owed a dead man. Still, Gus Sinclair had lived long enough to know he was dying; he might have left something behind.

Seth inclined his head toward the older woman solicitously, his thoughts carefully masked behind the smoothness of his tone. "You must have suffered terribly."

Sophie nodded indignantly, as though the offense had been committed hours, instead of decades, ago. "Why, the Pinckney mansion was destroyed right off, burned to the ground. It had stood for over a hundred twenty years till the Yankees came. They're no respecters of history nor of decency, either, let me tell you! They even burned the Congregation Church on Meeting Street and the Catholic —"

Laurel interrupted shortly, "It wasn't the Yankees that started that fire. Some slaves cooking on an open fire let their flames get away from them."

"It was the Yankees," insisted Sophia, "pure and simple." She turned back to Seth, her face flushed not only with indignation but now with a touch of pride as well. "The siege of Charleston was the longest in the war, you know, more than any city had to endure. Our beloved city held out until 1865."

Laurel said impatiently, "You weren't even here. You left right after the fire in 1861."

Seth's interest pricked. So it was true, Augustus's family *had* been gone by the time he had come back to the plantation with the gold. That part of the Colonel's story, at least, was holding up. He wanted to ask about Chinatree, but there was no smooth opportunity to do so. And at any rate, Laurel gave him no chance to encourage the conversation.

Laurel looked at him and she was once again the crisp, determined woman. "Really, Mr. Tait, you mustn't allow us to keep you. You've done quite enough and we must not take any more of your time."

The message implicit in her words as she moved toward the door might have amused Seth at another time. As it was, he hardly heard her. He was too busy thinking, wondering if there might not be something here worth his time after all.

Caroline said, "Oh please, Mr. Tait, we would never forgive ourselves if we didn't make some attempt to repay your kindness. Please say you will join us for supper. We do insist."

Seth did not even glance at Laurel. He smiled

at Caroline, because a man couldn't help smiling at eyes that anxious, and he bowed. "Thank you ma'am. I'd be honored."

He nodded to Sophie, who looked enormously pleased with herself, and to Laurel, who looked disgruntled. He wasn't interested at that moment in what Laurel Sinclair was thinking, or feeling. He was too busy making plans.

The Colonel had died at sunrise. Peach Brady held him in his arms and cursed God for making it take so long, and letting it be so hard, to die. But then, living had never been easy; why should dying be any different?

The irony was that after all these years and all the chances taken, snakebite should take the Colonel down. Peach had done his best to suck out the poison, but by the second day the wound had begun to fester, sending dark streaks toward the heart; by sundown delirium had set in and Peach knew there was nothing he could do but watch, and wait.

During the endless hours that followed Peach tended the fire to stave off death's chill. He sponged the Colonel's face with a bandanna wrung from an icy stream, stared into the night and thought about endings.

Just before dawn, the Colonel stirred. Peach went to him quickly. In the dull wavering glow of the fire he saw how old the Colonel looked; how sallow and wrinkled his face was, how gray his beard and how faded his eyes. From the time of his earliest memory the Colonel had seemed to Peach to be invincible, as ageless as the wind and as stern and tough as the oaks. Now he was frail and shrunken and old, and looking at him, Peach felt a stab of fear.

To cover it he began tightening and rearranging the blankets around the dying man, and the Colonel brushed his hand away. "Stop fussing with me, boy," he said gruffly, sounding so much like his old self that for a moment — a foolish, reckless moment — Peach felt hope flare inside him. But with the Colonel's next ragged, pain-choked breath that hope vanished. The old man's words were flat and weary. "There's not much time left and I've got some things to tell you."

Peach squatted beside the Colonel and his own muscles tightened in empathy with the agony that etched itself across the other man's face when he tried to speak. Peach said urgently, "Don't talk. Save your breath."

"It's my — goddamn breath," the Colonel gasped. "I'll do what I want with it."

Peach was silent, aching and burning inside, and for a time it appeared the Colonel would say no more. The brief effort had exhausted him.

Then he opened his eyes again and looked at Peach. Sadness and weariness seemed to have pushed the pain far into the background. He said tiredly, "Ah, boy. We've done some deeds together. And I reckon I'll burn in hell for most of them."

Peach wanted to say something but couldn't.

And the Colonel went on. "May God have mercy on my black soul, because of all the sins I've done the worst was what I did to you. Nobody can undo it now but you. Do you understand?"

Peach did not, but he nodded.

The Colonel frowned. "I made you an outlaw, boy, but you don't have to live that way now. You make something of yourself," he said harshly. "You've got a chance to be respectable now; you take it, do you hear me?"

"Yes." There was a thickness in his throat that interfered with his breathing, and Peach cleared it away. "I hear you."

"My kind of life's over, boy. You know that, don't you?"

This time Peach did know what he meant. He had heard those words, and that tone, before. It was goodbye to the old ways, the easy times. It was recognizing the advent of civilization with regret and relief.

Peach said, "Yeah. I know."

"You've got a name, a good name free and clear. I've seen to that. There's no law looking for Seth Tait."

Peach swallowed hard. "No. There's not."

"And you've got more. Chinatree . . ." The breath seemed to be going out of him fast. He was working hard to speak. "You remember . . . what we were going to do?"

At the word "Chinatree" Peach tensed, but he said nothing.

Now a flicker of triumph and determination

crossed through the Colonel's eyes, as it had so often before, then faded. "It's there," he said. "It's gotta be. And now . . . it's yours, boy. You go back east, back to Charleston, and you find it . . ."

The voice was fading and Peach moved closer, sitting on the ground and carefully lifting the Colonel's shoulders to his knees. The movement was reflected in the pain on his face, but even the pain faded into weary, determined effort as Peach put his arms around him and bent close. "I will," he assured the other man automatically. "I'll find it."

The Colonel's gray brows drew together and he lifted his hand, waving it weakly in the air until Peach caught it in his own and held it hard. "You go to Charleston," the Colonel repeated raspily. "You'll find it there. You'll find . . . everything there."

The Colonel's hand tightened with a surprising ferocity on his. "You go there," he said. "And do it — like we planned. Swear to me you'll go. *Swear.*"

Peach did not want to listen to this, but because he could feel the Colonel's life ebbing away with every second that passed and because there was a wild animal inside him wanting to rise up and claw and roar and fight death back with his bare hands if he had to, he said desperately, "Yes. I will. I swear."

"My saddlebags," the Colonel whispered. "Inside . . ."

After a moment, Peach left his side and went

91

to the saddlebags. There was a change of clothes, some money, lengths of rawhide and a handful of pegging strips, the usual paraphernalia of a traveling man. But at the bottom there was something else, and Peach drew it out slowly, coming back to the Colonel. It was a a faded, wrinkled picture of two men in Confederate uniform, and Seth had seen it many times before.

"Augustus Sinclair," the Colonel mumbled, touching the photograph. "He was the closest friend I ever had. He would've . . . would've wanted it this way."

A sort of peace smoothed out the lines in the old man's face, and settled in his eyes. Peach wanted to grab him and shake him and demand that he not give up; he couldn't die yet . . . not yet.

And then the Colonel said softly, so softly that Peach had to bend very close to hear. "He had a daughter, born during the war. Called her Laurie. You look her up, boy. I always thought . . ."

But Peach was not to know what it was he thought, for suddenly the Colonel looked at him sharply and demanded, "What's your name, boy?"

Moisture flooded Peach's chest and his throat, and burned in his mouth and eyes as he was suddenly transported back to a cobalt day and a field of poppies, and a big man's shining eyes and a booming voice declaring, "Well, by damn, I guess you are human after all! What's your name, boy?"

And himself responding with the first words he

ever remembered saying, in a voice that was small and clear and unafraid, "Seth. Seth Tait."

But now paralysis had overtaken the muscles of his throat and thickness clogged his mouth and it was a long time before he could answer hoarsely, "It's Seth. Seth Tait."

Faintly, the Colonel smiled. "Damn right. That's who you are. And don't you forget it."

He was gone, and suddenly there were a dozen things, a hundred, Peach wanted to say to him. His hands gripped the shoulders that were heavy and toneless as though with the force of his will he could infuse life back into them. He wanted to shout, he wanted to rage, he wanted to shake the Colonel and demand that he not give in to this foolishness; he wanted to beg him not to leave him. But in the end he swallowed the burning in his throat, and let the old man go. Seth dug a grave while the sun rose in quiet shades of pink and orange over the rim of the canyon, and covered it over with stones to keep the coyotes out. When the morning ended and the plain wooden marker was set in place, he stood over it for a long time, wanting to say something, wanting to feel something, but unable to do either.

Not one man, but two, were buried on that still cold morning. Seth Tait mounted his horse and rode off alone, headed east.

Now he was here, in Charleston, South Carolina, where it had all begun. And he had more than a job to do. He had a life to claim.

CHAPTER
Five

"But you weren't hurt?" Peter insisted urgently. He had stopped rocking midway through Laurel's discourse on the morning's events, and now he sat forward, both hands gripping the arms of the cane-backed rocking chair as he stared at her.

Laurel shook her head. Peter Barton was the only person she knew to whom she could tell the truth about her adventures and expect neither shock nor censure. "Only my pride. Not that that isn't injury enough, mind you."

They were sitting on the piazza, fanning away the heavy heat of the afternoon and waiting for the sun to go down with the possible promise of a harbor breeze. Peter was a regular guest for supper on Thursday nights, and Laurel was very glad it was Thursday. She had needed badly to talk to him.

Peter leaned back, relaxing a little. "Well, it served you right." A lecture! She *could* expect that now and again, but she could tolerate it.

Peter's sermons were never very long or very severe.

This one was even shorter than usual as he added with a small frown, "And that man . . ."

"Seth Tait."

Peter nodded thoughtfully. "Ah, yes. He's new in town. Been staying over at the Charleston Hotel."

Laurel was not surprised that Peter knew about him. Peter was a reporter for the *Gazette*, and it was his job to keep abreast of things. "A perfectly hideous man," Laurel said huffily, and the tempo of her fan increased with the words. "Utterly uncivilized and completely unfit for polite company. Of course," she felt obliged to add, however grudgingly, "he *did* dissemble for me with Aunt Sophie and Caroline, so I suppose he might be credited with some vestige of decency." Not that Laurel believed his discretion was in any way motivated by nobility. He could not have told the truth without implicating himself, and *that* would hardly have assured him of a supper invitation. She had no doubt that he would more than make up for his momentary lapse into civility when he returned this evening.

Just thinking about him made heat sting her cheeks again, so Laurel resolved not to think about him at all, though that was not an easy thing to do. As a matter of fact, she had thought about little else all day, for Seth Tait was not the sort of man one easily forgot. She might disapprove of him, and certainly he made her angry, but a certain element of excitement about him drew Laurel's thoughts back again and again like a moth to a flame.

"Do you know anything about him?" Peter asked.

"Only that he's rude, outspoken, and has absolutely no respect for ladies. Isn't that enough?"

Peter grinned. "Not for a reporter, my dear."

Fanning herself furiously with exasperation, Laurel found the effort making her feel even hotter. She folded her fan against the back of her hand with a sigh. "Well, you can find out whatever you want to know tonight. He's coming for supper."

Peter looked startled and Laurel turned down the corners of her mouth with wry resignation. "Don't look at me. It was Caroline's idea. You know she's never turned away a stray or a waif in her life and Aunt Sophie's just as bad. He sounds like a Southerner and he wears pants and he's still got all his teeth, so he must be husband material."

Peter looked disturbed. "The things you get yourself into," he mumbled. Then he looked at her. "Good Lord, Laurie, if I'd known you needed the money that badly I would've offered to marry you myself."

Laurel opened her fan again and began to stir the air listlessly. "Thank you, but you can hardly support yourself, much less a wife. Besides, I've given up on men as a way out of my difficulties.

They have an unfortunate tendency to die just when matters are at their worst."

"I don't know, I'm pretty healthy," Peter answered, not in the least rebuffed. "And you might want to reconsider your decision once I make my fortune."

"There are no fortunes to be made in Charleston, Peter."

He shrugged. "So I won't stay in Charleston. Maybe I'll go west, start my own newspaper —"

"Caroline would never leave Charleston," Laurel commented mildly.

"Well, who says she has to? She —" He broke off, coloring more deeply. "Confound you, Laurie," he muttered, "you've got no call to be messing in things that're none of your business."

"Caroline is my business," she reminded him, and then her expression gentled as she saw the genuine misery on Peter's face. The truth was, she did not think Caroline and Peter would ever make a match; Caroline showed not the faintest hint of interest in Peter other than as a family friend, and Peter was too backward about the whole business to ever work up the nerve to confront her. Laurel herself would welcome such an arrangement. Then there would be one person fewer for her to worry about; two, counting Peter. But Peter, generally a forthright and fairly rational young man, was completely lost when it came to his secret love, preferring to shield his adoration with jokes and shroud his ambition in grandiose plans and careless daydreams. Laurel felt sorry for him, and for Caroline, too, who would never know in what deep regard she was held.

"I'm sorry for teasing you, Peter," she said more kindly. "I really do wish you the best."

After a moment his lips turned downward in a reluctant rueful smile. "You'd better. If word of what you did this morning gets out, I will be the only friend you have, so you'd be wise to treat me nicely."

"So true," she agreed seriously. "Of course, if word ever got around I'd know exactly who to thank and then you *would* have to go west, young man, because there would be nothing left for you here, I assure you."

He grinned. "And since you wouldn't be received in any house in Charleston either, you'd have to come with me. Not altogether a bad arrangement."

"If you would only use that silver tongue of yours on Caroline neither one of us would be sitting here now. You'd be an old married man with four or five children and a piazza of your own."

His smile faded to wistful, and then as he shook his head, disappeared entirely. "Enough of this nonsense, Mrs. Laughton," he said sternly. "We've got more serious matters to discuss." A genuine frown drove away all traces of humor as he added, "I think we'd better talk some more with this strange man you've invited into your home tonight."

Seth Tait stood before the mirror, razor in

hand, looking but not seeing. His face was half-covered with lather and he was naked from the waist up, his galluses dangling around his hips, his feet bare. He was thinking about the Sinclair family.

Laurel Sinclair, if she were to be believed, had never heard of the Colonel, which eliminated the possibility, remote though it had been, that the dying Augustus had left a message for Colonel Ike with his family. She thought her father was a war hero; *everyone* thought he was a war hero. None of them had the faintest suspicion that Colonel Ike and Augustus Sinclair had committed perhaps the most daring robbery of the century. True, it was a wartime crime, but it was a crime nonetheless. And if any of these staunch southerners ever found out that the cache of gold, liberated from a Federal train, had never made it to the Confederate coffers where, by the rules of war, it rightfully belonged, the honor roll of the Confederacy would be minus one dead hero, to say the least.

The late afternoon sun streamed through the window, bleaching rectangles on the floorboards and turning the room into a steam kettle. Perspiration softened the lather on his face and caused it to drip down his neck, and with a sharp frown of irritation he lifted the razor again. His hand slipped, a spot of blood appeared on his jaw, and in a sudden surge of fury Seth flung the razor down.

"Damn it to hell!"

He realized he'd been angry since he'd set out on this journey — angry that the Colonel had left him, angry that the old ways were changing, and even angrier that to survive he'd have to change with them.

The fabled gold that the Colonel had talked about was his way out. Money would buy him respectability, a new identity, a new way of life. All the way across country on the train he'd berated himself for what he was doing: looking for fool's gold. But what other choice did he have? He'd promised the Colonel. That in itself was binding. But also he couldn't deny his hope that the money was there, that the Colonel had been right — that by some miracle hundreds of thousands of dollars were still there, buried somewhere, just waiting for Seth Tait to come along and claim them.

By the best of his calculations he was just over twenty-five years old and he'd already lived the lifetimes of a dozen men, but here he was at the end of the road waiting to start over. He had a name with no stigma attached to it, a head full of memories he could never talk about, a little money in his pocket and not much else.

And now he had the possibility of a fortune — and nothing stood between him and it but three starving women.

Had it ever occurred to the Colonel that Laurel Sinclair, or other survivors of Augustus' family, had as much right to the treasure as he did? Or even more? And there was the problem: If he told Laurel about the gold, she just might be the kind to turn him and the gold over to the police. She was cantankerous enough to do something like that. One never knew what southerners with their old-world sense of honor would do. Not that he could tell anyone about the gold without also telling how he knew about it, and that was one thing he could not afford to do.

He bunched up a towel in his hand, scowling at it fiercely. The Colonel and Gus had taken the gold. Of that there was no doubt. But the rest of it . . . speculations, ifs and maybes: *if* Gus had hidden the gold at Chinatree; *if* he had written his wife about it. *If* he had hidden the money somewhere else, *maybe* it had been found long ago and *maybe* it had been stolen again by persons unknown.

But what *if* the gold was still there, shining, untouched for over twenty years? Waiting. Waiting for him. And if the gold was at Chinatree, the Sinclairs were the key to its discovery.

The women should be easy to handle, especially the old lady and the one with the limp, Caroline. Laurel, now — she was smart, too damned smart for a woman, and gutsy too. She could be a help or a hindrance. It depended on how he handled her.

Still he couldn't get the picture out of his mind of Miss Laurel Sinclair Laughton begging at the whorehouse for money and trying to take care of Miss Sophie and Miss Caroline on a widow's pension. He kept seeing the shabby gentility of

101

the house, the brave front they put on, as though nothing had changed for thirty years.

"Damn it," he swore again. "Damn it to hell!" Close your eyes, he told himself firmly. Forget the women. They're not your concern. The Colonel kept the dream of the gold alive and he passed that dream to you. It doesn't belong to them. Despite the reasons he summoned up, he felt the softness rising in him again and as much as he wanted to push it away he couldn't. Not entirely.

He had been about twelve years old when his horse had stepped into a gopher hole and broken her leg. The animal was suffering, and even Seth knew the only thing to do was put her out of her misery. The Colonel had quietly put a pistol in Seth's hand and walked away. Seth had felt an awful helplessness welling up inside him; his hand had shaken, he had broken out in a cold sweat. Tears had started streaming down his face and blurred his sight. No power on heaven or earth could have made him pull the trigger.

At last he had flung the pistol into the dirt and run away, and when he heard the shot that ended the animal's life he had fallen on the ground and retched. Afterward he had wept, in misery and shame, silently and for a long time. At some point he had looked up and found the Colonel sitting beside him, quietly gazing off into the horizon.

To this day Seth did not know whether it was pity or sorrow he had seen in the older man's eyes, but when the Colonel had spoken the words had been flat and matter-of-fact, and they would stay with Seth forever. "You've got a soft streak inside you, son," he had said. "It's either going to kill you, or make a man out of you. I don't know which."

That was all. The Colonel got up and walked away and the incident was never mentioned again, but from that day on something inside Seth had changed. His first lesson in the ways of nature had not been an easy one, but it was well learned. Pity, mercy and compassion had no place in a land where life was cheap and death was lingering. The strong survived and the weak fell by the wayside, and Seth became what he had to be to survive.

With a grimness that bordered almost on obsession Seth practiced until he could shoot straighter and draw faster than anyone who challenged him, even the Colonel. He learned to take what he needed without questioning the right or wrong of it, and the only regret he ever felt was at times like this, when that softness threatened to creep through his good sense again.

His grip on the towel had grown slack, his muscles relaxing as his mind reflected. With fresh determination he tightened his fist and set his jaw, and after a moment he lifted the towel to dab away the slight trickle of blood on his chin. Laurel Sinclair was none of his business and was the last woman in the world who needed his pity.

If there was any gold, maybe he'd leave the

women a little. The Colonel would have liked that. As for him, he'd always liked San Francisco. Or maybe he'd go south to New Orleans, really start over. Maybe buy a saloon. Now that was something he knew about.

He picked up the razor and finished shaving with a firm, steady hand. There was one consolation in this whole mess, he decided, as he pulled on his shirt. Laurel Sinclair Laughton. If he had to spend another few weeks in this hellhole of a city, there were worse ways to pass the time than spending it with her.

Except for the clink of forks against slightly chipped china and the occasional rustle of a lady's taffeta sleeve, the silence at the dinner table was absolute. Two candles dripped puddles of wax into mismatched crystal saucers, the butter was turning into a milky pool in its dish. Laurel, choked to the throat in the stiff black taffeta, felt herself slowly going the way of the butter and the candles, melting away by inches.

It had been Aunt Sophie's idea to wear their Sunday taffetas in honor of their guest, just as it had been her idea to bring out the linen tablecloth, with its scorch mark tucked under a corner and its badly mended tear carefully turned out of sight. It had also been her idea to serve fried chicken, country ham and all the trimmings, when their usual Thursday night supper was Wednesday night's leftovers made into soup or, if the prices weren't too bad at the market, a little cold seafood. Another time Laurel would have read Aunt Sophie a lecture that would have sent the poor woman to her bed for such extravagance, but today she had enough on her mind without engaging in another battle with Aunt Sophie.

Silence had fallen abruptly, as silences often do at gatherings, allowing Laurel a precious few moments to fortify herself for the remainder of the evening. From the moment Seth Tait entered the house, the chatter and the flutter had been nonstop, perpetrated mostly by Aunt Sophie, of course, who couldn't do enough to see that he was comfortable and well entertained and made to feel welcome in their home. Caroline had overcome her timidity enough to do her part, but Laurel couldn't blame her for that. Caroline was gracious to everyone. And Peter, upon whom she had counted to keep the evening on an even keel, was so obviously ill at ease around the stranger that he only made things worse. Laurel, of course, had been on tenterhooks the entire evening, but so far Seth Tait had behaved with politeness and decorum, and not once had he referred to their previous meeting. She had almost begun to relax.

Laurel took advantage of the brief conversational lull to observe the two men across from her, and comparisons were inevitable. Both were about the same height, both had sandy-colored hair, though Peter's was a little darker, and both were reasonably pleasant-looking men. For all her life Laurel had considered one man to be very much like another with only surface distinctions, and that certainly held true in this case, for there was nothing in the physical appearance of either man to set one above the other. Then why was it that next to Seth Tait, Peter, who was considered quite handsome by most young ladies, practically faded into the woodwork?

The more Laurel studied the matter, the more she became convinced that the differences were not physical. Peter's face was a little softer, to be sure, and was marred by a light brown mustache; his shoulders were not quite as broad as the other man's nor his arms quite so well defined beneath the fabric of his coat, but those were all desirable characteristics for a young man about town and should not count against him. In fact, if it were a mere contest of physical beauty, Peter should by all reckoning come out ahead.

No, the appeal that Seth Tait generated — if appeal it could be called — was more intrinsic and less easily defined. It lay in the sharp planes of his face and the deep, outdoor color of his skin, the lazy alertness of his eyes and the way he had of smiling without smiling, always observing, always ready. He held himself with a natural ease and confidence that could not be learned or imitated, and his low drawl was smooth. Laurel realized suddenly that his simple unadorned masculinity was what was so uncommon about him. She had never known a man so purely masculine before.

Peter must have sensed something of the same quality, because his reaction to Seth was a cross between awe and carefully disguised antagonism — like a small dog who suddenly finds his territory threatened by a larger one. He knew a battle would be futile, but he couldn't help bristling at the invasion. Laurel found that amusing — and rather sad.

Laurel turned her gaze back to Seth Tait and found him watching her with a gleam of humor in his eyes, as though he knew she was comparing him to Peter and had no doubt as to how he had fared. As though to confirm her suspicions, he winked at her impudently.

Laurel held his gaze, refusing to flush. She smoothed her napkin in her lap and said pleasantly, "How dreadfully dull you must think us, Mr. Tait. We've rattled on and on about ourselves and haven't given you a chance to get a word in edgewise. Do tell us about yourself, sir. What brings you to Charleston?"

"Business," he replied. And when she drew a breath to continue the inquiry, he added firmly, "Personal business."

Laurel was undeterred. "Then you must have relatives here."

"Not exactly."

She tried again. "Where are you from?"

The gleam was still in his eyes, as though he recognized the challenge and enjoyed it. "Lately," he responded, "from Wyoming."

Sophie turned to Peter. "Didn't Henrietta Gibbs marry a Tait? I'm *sure* we know the family."

Peter smiled at her politely. "No ma'am, I don't

think so." He turned to Seth. "Surely you weren't born in Wyoming, Mr. Tait. No one is *born* in Wyoming."

The comfortable tone of Seth's voice did not alter, nor did his expression. "As a matter of fact, quite a few people are born there every year, Mr. Barton. Half-breeds and Indians, mostly, but still people."

Peter had the grace to look abashed. "Of course. I meant to say *white* people."

"Well, I reckon there's a number of them, too, but I don't keep count."

Seth began to butter a biscuit, and Laurel, irritated by his evasion, felt obliged to help Peter out. "Where were you born, Mr. Tait?"

Sophie's face puckered into a preoccupied frown as she suggested, "Perhaps the Atlanta Taits. Yes, that must be it. I'll get a letter off tomorrow morning to Dorothea . . . or is it Charlene?"

Seth glanced at Sophie, and then turned back to Laurel, who was waiting for his answer determinedly. "To tell the truth," he answered without a trace of shame, "I don't know much about my background. My folks were killed on the way west when I was just a tyke."

Caroline made a soft, involuntary sound of sympathy and Peter choked on a sip of water. Laurel could well imagine how he felt. Peter had been concerned about their bringing a total stranger into their home, and now it turned out that not only did they not know who Seth Tait's family was, but Seth himself did not even know. To someone as easily alarmed as Peter, that was disturbing news indeed. Laurel merely found it intriguing.

She said, "What do you do in Wyoming, Mr. Tait?"

"A little bit of everything."

Peter recovered himself enough to comment, "I understand there's quite a future in cattle ranching, Mr. Tait."

"True enough. But I'm in horses."

Sophie perked up. "We have friends in Kentucky who breed horses. Perhaps you know them — the Earlys?"

Seth smiled at her politely. "No ma'am, I'm afraid not."

"But surely you must. I understand they breed the finest quarterhorses in the country. He's a short man, rather round, balding, walks with a slight limp on his right side . . . ?"

"There's not much call for thoroughbreds out west," Seth explained. "We deal in mustangs, mostly, and break them as cutting horses." That much was true. He simply eliminated the fact that the last string of mustangs he had broken had been stolen.

At Sophie's blank look he elaborated, "For cattle work."

"Oh." Her tone, and her expression, were deflated.

Laurel pointed out curiously, "You said 'we.' "

A peculiarly shuttered expression came over

his face as he picked up his fork. "I used to have a partner. He's dead."

"My dears," Caroline interjected gently, "I'm afraid we are badgering poor Mr. Tait to death. You must forgive us, sir." She turned to Seth with a shy smile. "We must seem terribly ill-mannered, but we've never met anyone from the West before. I suppose all easterners find the subject fascinating."

Seth's face softened as he looked at her. "It's a hard land, ma'am. It makes exciting talk sometimes, I reckon, but it's not all it's cracked up to be."

"Well, I know Peter will find that disappointing." Laurel cast a teasing glance toward Peter, wanting to remove that uncomfortable frown from his face and draw him back into the conversation. "He's our local authority on the west and all things western."

Seth glanced at him without much interest. "Is that right?"

"Miss Laurel is exaggerating." Peter gave Laurel a carefully shielded look of reprimand and embarrassment, and his laugh was light and false. "I confess I have some interest in western lands, but most of my knowledge is confined to what I read in dime novels." At Seth's unresponsive gaze, his embarrassment deepened and he shrugged his shoulders. "Outlaw tales, mostly. You know, the James Brothers, Billy the Kid, Peach Brady and Colonel Ike . . ."

As though with the snap of an invisible string,

Laurel jerked her head toward Seth Tait. *Colonel Ike.* That was the name he had queried her about this morning. What in the world . . . ?

She saw Seth's fork pause briefly, infinitesimally, in midair before he lowered it to his plate again. He gave absolutely no other sign of recognition, and nothing changed on his face.

Laurel looked quickly at Peter. "It must be quite a treat for you to meet someone who might actually have run into those notorious characters, Peter. Rather than reading about them second-hand, you could write your own story about them from what Mr. Tait has to tell you."

Even that provoked no change of demeanor in Seth Tait, but his eyes, Laurel noticed, were very cool. Almost cold.

Peter's smile was condescending as he said, "I'm sure Mr. Tait doesn't have the opportunity to deal with characters like those. Just because a man crosses the Mississippi doesn't mean he's going to be on a first-name basis with every outlaw who ever made a name for himself." But there was a glint of eagerness in his eyes he could not quite disguise, despite his effort to keep his tone offhand. "However, I'm sure you are in a better position to hear things than we are in Charleston, Mr. Tait, and a little story about the goings-on out west might be entertaining to my readers."

"I don't know what I could tell you, Mr. Barton," Seth replied mildly, "except not to believe everything you read in books. There aren't too many outlaws left in my part of the country.

111

Schoolmarms and newspapers drove them out, mostly."

Sophie giggled nervously and even Caroline smiled. Peter looked as though he did not know quite how to take that, and before he could make up his mind Laurel spoke up.

"But you're being too modest, Mr. Tait! You must know all sorts of delicious gossip and are simply too shy to say so. What about this Peach fellow, and Colonel — ?" She looked inquisitively to Peter.

"Ike," Peter supplied, though he looked as though he wished he could change the subject.

Seth Tait saved him the trouble. "As far as I know, ma'am, they're both dead." He turned to Sophie. "Miz Sinclair, that was without a doubt the finest fried chicken I've ever had. I know cowpokes that would ride across two territories for a meal like that, and I'm one of them. Thank you kindly."

Sophie beamed and blushed. "Oh, Mr. Tait, you are a flatterer!"

"There's pecan pie waiting," Caroline said, "or fresh blueberry if you prefer."

"Thank you, ma'am, but I don't think I could eat another mouthful right now."

Caroline laid her napkin aside. "Well, then. Why don't we have Lacey bring some iced coffee into the drawing room?"

Peter went to Caroline's chair, and Laurel stood, making a show out of fanning herself with her handkerchief. "I do declare, I believe I will expire from heat if I don't take a breath of air. Mr. Tait . . ." She turned to him with her most charming smile. "Would you care to join me in a stroll around the garden?"

That nasty little smile played with his lips as he came around the table to her. "Miss Laurel, I'd be honored."

Laurel was aware of Peter's startled look and Aunt Sophie's flustered, uncertain expression, but she made her escape from the room before anyone could object. The moment they stepped through the French windows onto the piazza Laurel regretted her impulsiveness. There was a difference between being with Seth Tait at a brightly lit dinner table, with Aunt Sophie's chatter, Peter's awkwardness and Caroline's determined grace, and being with Seth Tait alone in the darkness. All of the uneasiness and suspicion she had tried to push aside for the sake of good manners at the table came flooding back, and that was not all.

With nothing more than the square of light from the dining room window separating her from the others, Laurel felt isolated, and the presence of the man beside her loomed like a physical force. That same masculinity that overwhelmed Aunt Sophie, intimidated Peter and caused Caroline to retreat into shyness was not lost on Laurel. He need do nothing but stand beside her and her heart beat faster, and she was not certain whether it was from fear or excitement.

He offered his arm to her and she ignored it, lifting her skirts a few inches as she started down

113

the stairs. He murmured, "Why do I have the feeling you didn't invite me out here for a romantic stroll in the moonlight?"

"Perhaps, Mr. Tait," she responded tartly, "because, despite evidence to the contrary, you do have some good sense after all."

"Sometimes," he admitted. There was the hint of a smile in his voice. "Not always where women are concerned."

Laurel took a breath and clasped her hands before her, determined to take control of the conversation before he did. Despite his rugged appearance and manners that were anything but urbane, he did have a certain smoothness of speech that could be deceptively charming. Fortunately, Laurel was not easily charmed.

She said matter-of-factly, "First of all, I think you should know that, while that was a fascinating tale you told about your orphaned past, I don't believe a word of it."

"Is that right? Why not?"

"It was entirely too smooth. Exactly like the plot of one of those horrible stories Peter is always reading, and just the sort of thing a man might make up to avoid answering questions about himself."

He began to chuckle, and the chuckle turned into a soft laugh of genuine amusement. Laurel darted a suspicious glance at him, and did not like what she saw. His face, silvered in the faint light of a quarter moon, was accented with shadowed planes that gave him a satyr-like look, and the laughter that glinted in his eyes was wicked — wicked and seductive and very annoying. Instinctively she stiffened herself against it. "I fail to see what's so amusing."

He turned the full benefit of that laughing gaze on her. "No ma'am, I guess you wouldn't." He sobered a little, but a telltale crease at one corner of his lips indicated he was still enjoying his own amusement. "The fact is, I *was* orphaned on the trail, and I don't know anything about my folks, and the one thing you picked to call me a liar on was probably the only truth I'll ever tell you."

Laurel frowned uncomfortably. There was something more than disconcerting about such unabashed frankness, and his steady, secretly amused gaze was making her skin prickle. At some point in the conversation they had stopped walking, and Laurel quickly picked up the pace again, holding her skirts away from the reach of a thorny rose.

"So, you admit you are a liar."

With his long, easy stride he had no trouble keeping up with her. "Among other things."

She was desperately curious to know what those other things were, but she knew asking would be futile. "Most liars have a reason for their lies."

"Most times it's easier than telling the truth. I try to do things the easy way whenever I can."

"I see." She glanced at him from beneath her lashes, hoping to catch him off guard. "You are a most curious man, Mr. Tait. For instance, when you mentioned Colonel Ike. What possible connection, I wonder, could you think I would have with a legendary outlaw?"

They passed beneath the shadow of a mimosa, and Laurel could not see his face, as hard as she strained. His voice, however, was perfectly casual. "I can't imagine."

"You must have had a reason for asking," she pointed out. Tension and frustration were tightening in her shoulders, for nothing in his posture or his tone gave a hint as to what he was thinking.

"I reckon I must have," he agreed. "But it's clean slipped my mind by now." And then he glanced at her, an odd look on his face that was somewhere between outrageous mirth and cautious disbelief. "Do they really write books about those fellows?"

"Of course they do," she responded, her irritation growing. "Do you read, Mr. Tait?"

"Whenever I get the chance. Headstones, mostly, or the labels off tomato cans. A little Homer or Plato if I can find it."

Laurel scowled, mostly to keep back a smile. He was the *most* peculiar man. "You are changing the subject, sir."

"Am I?"

"The subject," she reminded him deliberately, "was Colonel Ike."

"Oh, yes. I'll have to get my hands on one of those books one day. Sounds interesting."

Laurel stopped abruptly and turned to him. She felt like stamping her foot in impatience, and the only thing that restrained her was the certain

116

knowledge that such behavior should gain her nothing but more of his laughter. So she looked him straight in the eye and she said, "Very well, Mr. Tait, have your way for now. But I assure you this subject is not closed and I have a very long memory. We will talk about it again."

And to her surprise and consternation a flicker of something very much like sadness crossed his eyes. "Yes," he agreed softly. "I guess we will."

The night was warm and thick with the scent of jasmine and honeysuckle. In the shadows of the garden colors were faint and sounds were muted, and it was easy to forget that behind the high hedges and iron grillwork another world existed — one that was calm and orderly and, for Laurel, secure in its sameness. For there was nothing calm or ordinary about being alone with Seth Tait in this secluded place, and she felt far from secure when he looked at her in such an intense, thoughtful way. She felt as though anything might happen, and her heart beat faster in anticipation of it.

But then Seth started walking again, and his voice was as casual as the pace of his stroll as he said, "Tell me about this reporter friend of yours."

Laurel was disoriented and it took her a moment to match his negligent tone. "What do you want to know?"

He glanced at her. "Is he your beau?"

Laurel laughed, but it was more a nervous reaction than anything else. Again her pulses leapt with surprise. "Peter? Good heavens, no. Just an old friend." She returned his glance, aware that the gesture was coy and wishing it hadn't been. "Why do you ask?"

The knowing, frankly amused sparkle in his eyes was contrary to the mildness of his next words. "He doesn't seem to like me much."

Laurel felt unaccountably rebuffed. She did not flirt often, but when she did she was accustomed to the gentleman flirting back. "Peter thinks you are an interloper," she told him flatly, "a suspicious character and unfit company for gentlewomen. He also," she added somewhat triumphantly, "knows where I met you, which does not speak highly of your moral fiber."

"Or yours," he pointed out, and Laurel scowled.

"He must also know," Seth went on, "that I've kept your wicked little secret, so, while I may not be a gentleman, I think I deserve some credit for honor."

"That's a matter for debate," Laurel muttered, but relented reluctantly, looking at him. "I suppose I should thank you for that. It was — decent of you."

He bowed his head with a dry twitch of his lips, but his eyes were bold upon hers. "That makes two debts you owe me."

Laurel jerked her eyes away from him and increased her step. "Peter is right," she said shortly, "you aren't fit company for a gentlewoman."

"And what about you, Miss Laurel?" he inquired mildly. "What do you think of me?"

Laurel stopped, and turned. When she did she found herself standing toe-to-toe with him, her skirts brushing his legs and his face far too close. He did not back away, and neither did she. She looked him straight in the eye and she said quietly, "I think, Mr. Tait, that you are a dangerous man."

A slow smile traced his lips, and his eyes were lazily assessing her. "I think," he replied softly, "you're right."

She knew what he was going to do before he did it; there was no mistaking that smile nor the way his eyes slid slowly over her face to her lips and her throat and lingered on the swell of her breasts. Her breath caught and her heart hammered against her ribs, but she made no move to stop him as he took her shoulders and drew her against him.

His mouth covered hers with a swift, hot force, sudden and shocking and unabashed in its boldness. The kisses Laurel had known from other men had been gentle, hesitant, even shy, but always respectful and restrained. There was nothing respectful about Seth's kiss, and certainly nothing hesitant. He possessed her mouth as though it were his right to do so, invading her senses with dizziness and heat and leaving her weak.

He put his arms around her and pressed her close to his body, so that she could feel the hardness of his chest against her breasts and the power of his thighs against her skirts. She couldn't struggle; she didn't try. She was suspended and awash in sensation: the fever that burst upon her skin, the lights that danced behind her closed eyes, the roaring in her ears and the trembling of her muscles — helpless feelings, alien feelings, wonderful feelings.

His mouth moved upon hers, drinking and seeking, urging her to respond. And perhaps she did, for she knew nothing except instinct, the terror and the exhilaration of instincts uncontrolled and unexplored; a man's heat surrounding her, a man's strength embracing her, a man's lips boldly demanding and discovering hers.

It was he who ended the kiss, for she had long since lost the power to protest or push away. His hands moved to her arms, lightly supporting her, and his mouth left hers slowly. She opened her eyes and for a long time she could see nothing but shadows and moonlight, and his eyes, dark with desire, upon hers.

Her heart was pounding so painfully against her stays that even her vision throbbed, and she could not get her breath. Her limbs were watery, her legs barely able to support her weight. Her skin still stung from the rush of heat where his hands had touched her.

But gradually the world righted itself, her breath came more steadily, and she could see the faint sardonic smile that traced his lips. She stepped deliberately away from the support of his hands.

Her lips felt swollen and raw, and so did her breasts. She could not even look at him without a renewed rush of sensation coursing through her, as vivid in memory as it had been in actuality. But she straightened her shoulders, held his gaze, and said, "Shall we consider my debt paid, Mr. Tait?"

For a moment longer he looked at her, and then he laughed softly, shaking his head. "For one kiss? I don't think so, Miss Sinclair." She drew in a sharp breath, her eyes narrowing, but he lifted a warning finger. His eyes were still dancing. "Never sit down to the table," he advised, "without knowing what the stakes are."

Then he bowed politely, offering his arm. "Shall we rejoin the others?"

Laurel picked up her skirts and stalked away. She could hear him laughing softly behind her, but she did not look back.

CHAPTER
Six

Seth had been in places as fancy as Miss Elsie's — there were cathouses in Denver and Dodge City that made this one look shabby by comparison — but there was something about this establishment that made every saloon, whorehouse and dance hall he had ever seen seem like nothing more than an imitation of the real thing. The dust on the velvet curtains wasn't visible in the lamplight, the stains on the rugs were covered by shadows, the stale odors of smoke and perfume that he had observed that morning were replaced now by more vibrant, living scents. Business was brisk; drinks were being poured; cards were being turned, and the ladies were plying their wares; but all of it was done in an atmosphere of subdued refinement Seth found both puzzling and disconcerting.

There was laughter, but it was never shouted. There was piano music, but it wasn't boisterous. The women were as provocatively clad as any he had ever seen, but even in lace-trimmed chemises and silk stockings they managed to look modest. Maybe it was the honey-soft accents. Maybe it was the way the men, under Miss Elsie's firm supervision, behaved toward them — gentlemen even in a whorehouse. Maybe it was something about this town. Whatever it was, Seth found it intriguing, and vaguely pleasant.

It had been a long time since Seth had sat in a public place without constantly looking over his shoulder to see who might be stalking him, and it was a hard habit to break. Even though he was a hell of a lot more comfortable in a place like Miss Elsie's than he had been at the Sinclairs' supper table, and even though he had asked for Miss Elsie personally, his muscles still stiffened when he heard the soft step behind him, and felt the touch of a hand on his shoulder.

"Well, Mister, I gotta say, I never would've took you for a man of your word." Her hand slid down his shoulder and across his chest as she sat on the arm of his chair, grinning. "You did come back."

He caught her hand as it started to worm its way inside his shirt, forcing his muscles to relax as he returned her grin. "No offense, ma'am, but this is just a friendly visit. Buy you a drink?"

She shrugged and stood up, regarding him with speculative amusement. "If that's the best you can do."

She sat down at the table across from him, signaling to the bartender for the drinks. "So," she demanded easily, "what do you want from me that you think the price of a drink can buy?"

"What makes you think I want anything? Maybe I just want to pay you back for being so hospitable this morning."

The bartender brought the bottle — rye whiskey, like Seth was drinking — and Elsie poured her own. "Mister, I ain't no fool. You never gave something for nothing in your life. You and me, we're that much alike, and that's why I'm sitting here drinking with you instead of telling you to get out of my establishment and make room for paying customers."

Seth lifted his glass in a small salute, hiding his private smile. He knew he'd picked the right ally in Miss Elsie, but until this moment he hadn't realized that he liked the woman . . . and he liked her for the same reasons he liked Miss Laurel. It amused him to imagine the expression on Laurel's face if he were to ever point out how much she had in common with a whore, and for the sake of that expression he thought he just might tell her someday.

He said, "Information, a little advice. That's what I want, and I figured if there was one woman in town who could give it to me, it'd be you."

She nodded, studying him. "Well, that all depends, don't it? There's not much that goes on in this town I don't know about. Whether I want to talk about it is something else."

"I like a woman who can keep a secret."

Elsie regarded him steadily. "Yeah, I reckon you

would. Like why a certain man would want to pay a certain piece of riffraff five dollars to scare the daylights out of a certain Widow Laughton. Now that's a secret worth keeping, I reckon."

Seth said nothing. He didn't know why he was surprised, but he had to admit she had caught him off guard. He'd have to be more careful in the future.

He watched her drink, waiting, expressionless, for her to make the next move. She smiled.

"You are a cool character," she said approvingly. "And in case you're wondering, my price for keeping quiet is real reasonable. All I want from you is the truth. You tell Miz Laughton and everybody else in town what you want, but between you and me it's the truth. Deal?"

Seth regarded her, his expression curtained, for a long time. "Deal," he said finally. "As long as you're careful what you ask me."

Elsie laughed loudly enough to make heads turn, slapping her hand on the table. "Now you see? That's what I like about you!" She let the laughter fade into a warm, easy grin, gesturing with one hand around the room. "I got money," she went on conversationally, "more than just about anybody in town, I reckon. I got the mayor and bankers and police captains in my hip pocket. There's not much in this life I need right now, but you make me laugh. You make my ears perk up just when I thought there wasn't much in this old world I hadn't heard or seen, and it tickles the hell out of me, what you've got

125

in mind for that prissy pants Miz Laughton —
not that she won't give you a run for your money,
no matter what it is. So that's where I stand, just
so you know. I don't give nothing for nothing,
either, and what I'm getting out of it is . . ."
She lifted her glass, winking at him. "Just getting to watch. Fair enough?"

After a moment, Seth returned her salute, and
they drank together.

Elsie refilled his glass. "So what'd you pay that
boy to attack Miz Laughton for?"

"I wanted to meet her. I couldn't be sure what'd
happen when I got inside, so I made sure she'd
be indebted to me when she got out."

Elsie nodded, an admiring twinkle in her eye.
"I figured it was something like that. What'd you
want to meet her for?"

Nothing changed about his expression, but
Miss Elsie was one sharp lady. She said, "I reckon
that was one of those questions I should've been
careful about."

He replied, "Let's just say she's got something
I want."

Elsie murmured, "I'd give a lot to know what
that is." She sat back, tossing down another swallow of rye. "So what is it you think I can do for
you?"

Seth replied smoothly, "First off, you can tell
me how a man goes about impressing a lady of
quality in this town."

Elsie gave a hoot of laughter that pierced
through the muted murmurs and soft chuckles of

the parlor and, once again, brought stares their way. And, once again, Seth had to struggle with the habit of alarm that surfaced whenever attention was attracted to him.

She said, sobering with an effort, "Well, son, you *sure* as hell came to the right place!" She leaned back, propping her elbow on the back on the chair, dangling the glass from her fingers, affecting a thoughtful air. "Well, for starters, you don't go after the lady straight out. A spitfire like Miz Laughton, you wouldn't want to anyway. First you court her relatives, that's the way it's done. So you send the old dowager some candy or flowers, then you ask her permission to come calling." She grinned at him, eyes sweeping him up and down. "Not that I believe for a minute what you really want with Miz Laughton is to court her, or that a good-looking fella like you couldn't have figured out how to get to her without the candy and flowers. So just so's you don't waste the price of this drink, what do you really want to know?"

Seth smiled, linking his fingers lightly around the glass, watching her. "What I want," he said, "is the best game in town. High stakes, old money, solid players."

He could not tell whether the request surprised Elsie, or merely confirmed a suspicion. She nodded carefully, looking him over. "You got what it takes to play high stakes, do you?"

"Depends," he replied, just as carefully, "on what it takes."

She leaned back, topping off her drink, then

tossed it back with a neat twist of her wrist. She recapped the bottle, preparing to bring the conversation to a close. "In this town, it takes more than money. It takes connections. Because the best game in town isn't a game, it's a race. A horse race."

"A horse race, is it?" Seth tried to keep the satisfaction from his features, but he couldn't entirely hide the pleasure in his smile. He uncapped the bottle and refilled her glass. "Tell me about it."

After a moment of apparent debate, Elsie picked up her glass with a shrug and began to tell him. And for the next half hour Seth did nothing but listen, and learn, and plan.

Hugh Casom was tired. He'd been on duty all night because the night clerk — who was probably drunk or fighting with his wife or both — hadn't shown up. Hugh wished he had a cup of coffee and was thinking of stepping out of the hotel to the café across the street when Laurel Laughton came storming into the lobby of the hotel.

Miss Laurel was usually in a hurry, but this was more than that, Hugh realized. Under her hat, which she hadn't bothered to pin on straight, her hair was disheveled, with strands falling randomly along her forehead and neck. There were two bright spots of color on her cheeks, and her eyes — well, if there was such a thing as gray eyes blazing fire, Miss Laurel's were doing just that. Fatigue gave way to a new alertness as Hugh straightened his collar and prepared his officious

128

smile. But before he could so much as utter a pleasant "Good morning," Laurel Laughton strode up to the desk, braced her hands upon it and demanded, "I want to see Seth Tait."

Hugh blinked.

"Seth Tait," she repeated impatiently. "He is staying in this hotel?"

Hugh did not know what he found most startling: Miss Laurel's rudeness, or the fact that she had actually come calling on a male guest at a hotel. In all his years with the Charleston Hotel he could not recall anything like this happening, and for a moment he wasn't at all sure what the correct procedure was. He wished he had not been awake all night. He wished he had a cup of coffee.

One thing of which he was sure, however. No request, however bizarre, was an excuse for ignoring the amenities. So he smiled and said, "Good morning Miss Laurel. Always a pleasure to see you. How are you this fine morning?"

"In a great hurry and in no mood to pass the time," she replied crisply. "Thank you for asking. Mr. Tait?"

Hugh's smile wavered only slightly. "Why, yes, he's a guest here. Very fine gentleman, too, if I may say so." He settled back, preparing to express his opinions on Seth Tait and all his habits and, in the process, to finesse his way around to finding out just what his connection was with the Sinclair ladies, what the contents of the message was that he had delivered to them and who the mutual friend was, but Laurel didn't give him a chance.

"His room number," she demanded.

This time Hugh was so taken aback he literally didn't know what to say.

"For heaven's sake, Mr. Casom, I know perfectly well you're not hard of hearing so stop gaping at me. He *does* have a room number, doesn't he?"

"Why — why, yes, it's one-ten. But, Miss Laurel —"

"Thank you." She turned toward the stairs.

"Miss Laurel, wait! You can't go up there!" Hugh Casom scrambled out from behind the desk. "Let me call him down —"

"No, thank you. I'll find my way."

"Miss Laurel, this is a respectable hotel! You can't —"

But "can't" was apparently not a word in Laurel Laughton's vocabulary, and there wasn't much Hugh could do to stop her without causing a bigger scene than was already inevitable. So he just stood there wringing his hands, not knowing what else to do, hoping Miss Sophie would never find out, hoping his own *wife* would never find out, hoping against hope that Seth Tait might have already left his room . . . but not knowing what else to do.

Laurel's heels tapped like stilettos on the lobby's marble floors. She could feel Hugh Casom's desperate, shocked gaze on her back and that was only something else she had to be furious with Seth Tait for. By this afternoon it would be all over town that Laurel Laughton had gone to a

130

man's hotel room . . . which was no worse, she tried to justify, than going to a whorehouse.

It was not true that Laurel enjoyed scandalizing society for its own sake; the only time she ever defied social conventions was when those conventions inconvenienced her. Nor was it true, as some of the meaner-minded like to imply, that, being a war orphan, she didn't know any better. She knew perfectly well that no lady who cared a fig for the state of her reputation would walk into a public hotel and demand to know the room number of a man who was staying there. But where money was concerned a great many social expediencies had fallen by the wayside, and it seemed Laurel's reputation was doomed to be one of them.

The Charleston Hotel was the grandest in the city — indeed, many called it the grandest in the entire South. It stood four stories tall and covered an entire city block. It had resisted the ravages of war, fire and flood to stand like a memorial to days gone by, grander days, by far more opulent days. An upper and a lower piazza looked out over the street, with balconies surrounding an open courtyard. Laurel had once attended a wedding in that courtyard, and a charity ball in the elegant, hundred-foot-long dining room. She had never, of course, been up those stairs.

She decided that marching boldface into a brothel and brazening out an argument with the madam of the establishment must do a great deal for one's self-confidence, because even though her throat was dry she managed to keep her head high and her stride purposeful as she ascended the stairs. After all, she reasoned, once one had done that there was little left in life that held a potential for embarrassment . . . or so she thought until she knocked on the door of Room 110.

There was no answer at first, and she set her lips with a surge of renewed anger and raised her fist to pound again. The door opened and Seth Tait stood there . . . naked.

Or at least that was how it seemed to Laurel's first, incredulous gaze. She had seen men without their shirts before . . . or at least, as she thought hard to recall, she had seen *one* man. But Jonathan's chest, thin and white and almost hairless, seemed like that of a young girl in comparison to this man's. His musculature was broad and tight, knotted bands across the breasts and flat and strong downward to the waist. There wasn't the faintest trace of softness around that waist, and, flaring from his throat across his breast muscles, then narrowing down his abdomen until it tapered into his pants, was a thick mat of gold-tipped brown hair. His nipples were like smooth brown pebbles and the simple fact of noticing them brought a surge of heat to Laurel's cheeks. He had a towel around his neck and a smudge of shaving cream on his jaw, and the worst was, he didn't seem the least bit embarrassed. He did not even, as a matter of fact, seem surprised.

A slight lift of his eyebrow was his only acknowledgment that there might be anything remarkable about her sudden appearance at his door at eight o'clock in the morning; otherwise his expression was as mild as if he were greeting her across a tea table. "Why, Miss Laurel. How sweet of you to take the trouble to call. Come right in."

He stepped back from the door, and the gesture seemed like a challenge. But Laurel's only other choice was to conduct their business in the corridor, and she had no intention of doing that. She had no intention of even being seen with him, not dressed — undressed — the way he was. She stepped over the threshold.

"What kind of man opens the door without dressing?" she demanded, and made a determined effort not to look at him as he closed the door behind her.

"The kind of man who's expecting more hot water?" he suggested, and despite her best intentions, Laurel looked at him.

That was when she noticed for the first time that he was holding his arm at an odd angle behind his back, and when he turned to pick up his shirt he very casually, very smoothly, slid that arm around so that she could not see what he was holding . . . but not before Laurel got a glimpse, and a glimpse was all she needed. It was a pistol.

In a single smooth motion he concealed the weapon beneath the cushion of a chair and pulled on his shirt, not turning until it was buttoned to the waist. Laurel's mind raced and skipped over what she had just seen. What kind of man would even carry a gun like that, much less hide it behind his back when he opened the door? What kind of man frequented pleasure houses and engaged respectable ladies in high-stakes poker and then wangled supper invitations and sat down at their tables without so much as a blink of shame? What kind of man —

"And what brings you here this fine morning?" He turned, fastening the final buttons. He hadn't tucked the shirt inside his pants — it would have been obscene to do so with a woman in the room — but Laurel somehow found the suggestion of dishabille created by the shirt worn over his pants even more disturbing than when he had worn no shirt at all.

It was only that smooth-as-silk drawl, that small, knowing smile — that smile that seemed to insinuate he knew far too much about what she was thinking and where she was looking and worse, that he didn't mind at all — that jerked Laurel's attention back to the present and refocused her anger.

She said tightly, "I think you know that perfectly well, Mr. Tait." She reached into her reticule, produced a square of neatly folded bills, and tossed it toward him. Lacking weight, the bills didn't do justice to the venom behind her throw, and they fluttered to the floor only a few inches from her skirts.

Seth followed the money's progress with an interested expression. "Why, Miss Laurel, looks like you had a change of luck. Congratulations."

"The only change of luck I've had recently was when I met you, and that was all bad," she returned shortly. "And the next time you're looking for someone to be the recipient of your charitable impulses — or your twisted sense of humor, or whatever it was that persuaded you to slip that fifty dollars into my reticule — kindly find some other victim! I have enough problems."

With a twitch of her skirts, she turned toward the door.

His face was mournful as he bent to pick up the money, but the twinkle in his eyes was wicked. "So that's what I get for trying to mend my low-down, conniving, card-cheating ways. Spit on by the very model of Christian charity I asked forgiveness from."

"I wouldn't lower myself to spit on you! As for forgiving you . . . !" The dignified exit Laurel had almost made was ruined now, and she turned on him, eyes blazing. "How dare you try to humiliate me like that! Paying me off like some common —" She almost said the word, then choked and rushed on in a righteous fury. "No, you didn't even have the guts to do it in broad daylight, you had to sneak it into my purse — what were you thinking of? Did you imagine I wouldn't know where it came from? Did you think I wouldn't *care?* Well, Mr. Tait, I may not be able to afford many principles, but taking money from an unscrupulous, lying scoundrel like you is one line I haven't yet been forced to cross! Good day, sir!"

Once again she whirled for the door, and once again she was stopped — this time by the sound of his soft laughter. She turned, staring at him incredulously.

He scooped up the bills and tucked them casually in his pants pocket. "I guess it was worth it," he said, still grinning, "to find out just what lines you won't cross."

A lady would have demonstrated her outrage by the force with which she slammed the door behind her, and let it go at that. But a lady never would have entered his room in the first place, nor even come to this hotel, and curiosity was fighting an equally matched battle with anger. She reached for the doorknob, and curiosity won out. She turned back to him, scowling fiercely.

"What *were* you thinking of?" she demanded. "Why did you do it?"

"What?" he feigned innocence. "It couldn't be a simple act of chivalry?"

Laurel caught an unladylike snort just in time, but her expression served perfectly well to communicate what she thought of that excuse.

He leaned back against the lowboy with one elbow resting on its surface, regarding her with just the faintest trace of a speculative smile. "Well then, maybe I did feel sorry for the widow with a family to support. Maybe I wanted to make you mad. Maybe I wanted to square things between us . . . or maybe I just wanted to see you again."

The truth could have been couched in any one of those statements, or all of them — or none. But Laurel, with no more excuse than that she was, after all, still female, singled out only the last one. "Why would you want to see me again? What do you want from me?"

He smiled. "That should be obvious."

"Don't flatter yourself!" she snapped, and his laughter brought a surge of hot color to her cheeks.

She hated the way his eyes danced over her as he said, "I wouldn't presume, ma'am. What's obvious is that you're the only acquaintance I have in town and Charleston folks are pretty closed to outsiders. I was hoping maybe you could introduce me around."

Laurel didn't know which was more humiliating — to be the object of his vulgar attentions, or *not* to be. All she knew was that he was the most irritating man she had ever met, and her first instinct, after exclaiming incredulously, "Why should I?" was to stalk out without another word. But curiosity, once again, was her undoing.

So instead of whirling for the door, she took a single intimidating step closer to him. "Who are you?" she demanded quietly. "What do you want here? What do you want from *me?*"

The amusement left his eyes slowly and was replaced with thoughtfulness. But he didn't evade her gaze or shift away as she went on, "Why do you answer the door with a gun hidden behind your back? What are you afraid of? You claim you've got business here but you just said you don't know anybody but me. And what about this Colonel Ike you were asking about? What do you *want?*"

The silence was so long and so clear that Laurel could actually count her heartbeats. Seth's expression was absorbing, considering, as though poised on the brink of a monumental decision. A shaft of morning sun climbed over the windowsill and crept across the floorboard toward Seth's feet, and Laurel suddenly became aware of how filled with masculinity the room seemed, awash in the scents of shaving soap and leather. Those were scents with which she had been familiar all her life and to which she had never paid much attention before. Now she could not think of anything else.

Then Seth said, "I'm going to surprise you, Miss Laurel. I'll tell you the truth — or part of it anyway. I came here to find something, and you can help me. As for what I want from you . . . well, right now, it's real simple. I want you to get me an invite to the horse race the Jockey Club is holding Saturday week."

She gaped at him. As uncouth and unsophisticated as it was, she was capable of doing nothing else at that moment. Finally she managed, choking a little, "You want — *what?*"

"I want to make a bet on a horse." A note of dismissive impatience had entered his voice, as though he were unused to explaining himself and was getting tired of doing so. "This Jockey Club of yours is the fanciest outfit in town and they don't let outsiders in. You inherited a membership and you can get me in as your guest."

"You came all the way to Charleston to make a bet on a horse?" Her head was spinning. "You think you can just waltz in here and demand an invitation — that they would even let you — that *I* would . . . . What in the world makes you think I would want to help you?"

He smiled. "I helped you, didn't I? I kept your secret about Miss Elsie —"

"You vile, despicable creature, to think you can threaten me with —"

He held up a hand of protest. "I wouldn't think of it, and I'm hurt that you would accuse me. Nonetheless, you've got to admit I went out of my way for you yesterday, I even tried to return your money. The offer is still open by the way."

She gave a short, harsh laugh. "You think you can buy your way into the Jockey Club for fifty dollars? It will take more than that, believe me!"

"Which is exactly," he replied calmly, "why I need you."

"You are insane," she declared shortly. "I can't just bring a total stranger into one of Charleston's oldest and most exclusive clubs — a man I'm not even engaged to, a man my family doesn't even know!" But even as she spoke the words a secret, wicked part of her mind was envisioning the stir that would create and delighting in it. "It would scandalize the whole town."

"Which is exactly why you're going to help me," Seth said. Again that small, infuriating smile that knew too much and saw too much. "This might well be the biggest adventure of your career, and if you turn your back on a chance like this you'll never forgive yourself."

She didn't know which was more infuriating: his gall, or his uncanny perception. She compressed her lips tightly, however, on the stinging retort she wanted to make, because she had one more question to ask.

"This thing I'm supposed to help you find," she said when she was certain she could control her voice, "What is it?"

"Now that," he replied easily, "is a right interesting story. And I'll tell it to you at supper after the race Saturday."

Laurel's nostrils flared with a breath; she actually crunched her teeth together to bite back hasty words. "You," she managed at last, "are a liar and a cheat and I wouldn't have supper with you if you were the last man on earth."

She spun on her heel and jerked open the door.

"I'll be calling on you soon, Miss Laurel," he said pleasantly.

Her shoulders stiffened as though against a blow and her fingers tightened momentarily on the doorknob. "Then you'd better bring your gun," she retorted without turning. "And you can go whistle for your precious invitation to the Jockey Club!"

She slammed the door with a very satisfying crash behind her, but not before she heard again the infuriating sound of his soft laughter.

All the way home Laurel waited for the sense of righteous satisfaction that should have been the inevitable result of her noble gesture. All she felt was a mounting sense of irritation . . . and a kind of hot-pulsed excitement. She couldn't be sure whether it was due to anger or exhilaration. No man had ever been able to confuse her in such a manner before, and how dare Seth Tait succeed in doing so?

If there had been any way possible she could have resigned her conscience to keeping the money, of course, she would have. But she had known from the very beginning what Seth had only confirmed: the fifty dollars was nothing more or less than a down payment on a favor, and the last thing Laurel could afford was to be indebted to a man like Seth Tait.

Yet — and this was the most incredible part, the most infuriating part — the man absolutely refused to take no for an answer. He *still* had the audacity to assume she was at his beck and call, and Laurel would have dismissed him as a preposterous lout, she would have put him out of her mind and cut him dead if ever she happened to see him on the street again, except for one thing. *Why?* Why had he singled her out, what did he want from her, what could he possibly hope to gain by this determined, reckless pursuit of her attention? An invitation to the Jockey Club? It was absurd; there were two dozen people in Charleston who could have introduced him far more easily than she. And he had made it clear that he considered her physical charms quite easy to resist . . . but when Laurel remembered last night's kiss she wondered. When she remembered that kiss, in fact, she had to admit there was more than one reason why she couldn't put him out of her mind.

By the time her front gate came into view Laurel was soaked with perspiration and heaving from the pace she had maintained. She knew she was in for one of Aunt Sophie's tiresome lectures about how young ladies should deport themselves in public if she went in the house looking like that, so she paused to compose herself. Then she noticed the shiny black buggy drawn up at the carriage block and her heart gave an instinctive lurch of alarm. She didn't recognize the buggy, but it could have been Doc Weatherby's. Laurel had learned to be suspicious of anything she did not recognize, and to expect the worst until told otherwise. Heedless of her red cheeks and damp hair, she hurried up the steps.

The scene in the front parlor was almost as bad as she could have expected. The shutters had been drawn against the morning sun and the filtered gray light was dim and depressing. Sophie, in her frumpy pink morning gown with her old-fashioned lace cap askew, had collapsed into a petit-point chair and was sobbing into her handkerchief. Caroline knelt beside her in what Laurel knew was a painful position, patting her mother's hand.

Laurel jerked off her hat and tossed it toward a chair as she came in, not even noticing when it tumbled to the floor. "What?" she demanded without preamble. "What has happened?"

Cyrus Lars, vice-president of the bank, rose quickly from the shadows, his expression torn between relief at seeing Laurel and dismay as Sophie's sobs rose in pitch.

"Miss Laurel," he said, "I was just telling your aunt how sorry I am. If there were anything I could do, on my word I would, but it's out of my hands now. The government has rules about these things and I don't have any choice."

She knew that nothing good could come from the answer to her next question and her heart was beating so hard and so painfully that it was difficult to draw a breath. But nothing good ever came from avoiding the worst, so she demanded quietly, "What is it?"

Cyrus swallowed, his great Adam's apple bobbing, and shot another distressed look toward Sophie. Caroline's eyes, pained and helpless, met Laurel's.

Cyrus said, "It's about the note on the house, Miss Laurel. Your uncle borrowed five hundred dollars against it before he died and, well, the note was due over a week ago. I can give you thirty more days, but I'm afraid that's all. We'll have to foreclose."

Laurel's knees gave way abruptly and she sank to the sewing chair by the door. She couldn't take her eyes off Cyrus and her mouth was as dry as cotton, but she heard herself repeating, "Five — hundred dollars?"

He nodded soberly. "Yes ma'am. Here are the

papers, all right and legal, if you'd like to look at them."

Laurel took the papers he offered, but the writing on them looked like runic scribblings to her. She said hoarsely, "But — but how is this possible? We never knew — no one ever told us —"

"It was listed as a debit when the estate was settled," Cyrus pointed out in a slightly hurt tone, as though she had accused him of something dishonest. "Your aunt received a copy of the papers at that time."

Laurel turned her stunned, accusing gaze toward Aunt Sophie, who only sobbed harder.

She looked back at Cyrus, trying to think. "But — there's got to be something. Another loan, that's it. We'll just have to —"

He shook his head slowly. "Miss Laurel, you know I would if I could, but like I said there's nothing more I can do. Thirty days is the best I can offer you."

He picked up his hat, looked once more in Sophie's direction, and said, "I'm sorry." He bowed awkwardly, and saw himself out.

Caroline struggled to her feet, compressing her lips with the effort, and the expression in her eyes as she came over to Laurel was half pain and half fear. "Oh Laurel," she said softly, and then didn't seem to know how to finish.

The two women just looked at one another in a kind of stunned helplessness for the longest time, and all Laurel seemed to be able to see, in her mind's eye, was herself, flinging those bills at Seth's feet.

"It's my fault," Sophie sobbed tremulously, "all my fault."

Laurel looked at her dazedly, but could not even work up the energy, as she generally would have done, to agree with her. *Five hundred dollars.* Where in the world was she going to get that kind of money?

"We could take in boarders," Caroline suggested in a small, hesitant voice. "The Misses Mayfair have been doing it for years and no one seems to think the less of them. We could —"

"Boarders!" Shock dried up the last of Sophie's tears and she sat up straight. "Strangers putting their feet on my mother's cherrywood desk and burning holes in my French lace counterpane? Caroline, how could you suggest such a thing?"

"Mother I only —"

Laurel let the voices fade out. It didn't matter anyway. Boarders couldn't possibly earn them five hundred dollars in thirty days, not unless they took in the kind of boarders Miss Elsie did, who paid by the hour. The notion almost coaxed a hysterical laugh from her, and she had to force it back with an effort. Five hundred dollars. Could it be only yesterday — only this morning, even — that *fifty* dollars had seemed like all the money in the world to her?

She heard the distant sound of the door knocker, and the creak of Lacey's footsteps as she went to answer it. She thought dimly, What now? And she found it very difficult to even care.

Sophie broke off her heated discussion with Caroline when Lacey came in, bearing a small flat package. Her childlike temperament was instantly transformed from distress to delight as she tore off the wrappings, exclaiming, "My word! I wonder who it can be from? No one ever sends me presents anymore, and it isn't even my birthday! Oh!" Her eyes went round with joy as she lifted the lid of the distinctive gold box. "Chocolates! Girls, will you look at this! Real chocolates!"

"Who is it from?" Caroline asked curiously, and the shadow of a smile even began to cross her face as she took the box from her mother and examined its contents.

"There's a note." Sophie fluttered a paper in the air. "Oh, dear, you read it — I'm far too undone. Imagine, chocolates! Whoever could have done such a thing!"

Caroline returned the box to her mother, who promptly gratified herself with a bon-bon, and took up the note. "Dearest Madame," she read. "Please accept this small token of thanks for the generous hospitality you showed to a stranger in your home last evening. I would be most honored if you would allow me to return your kindness by taking you and your lovely family on a drive tomorrow, weather permitting. Your humble servant — Seth Tait."

Caroline lifted her eyes, and her eyebrows, first to Laurel, then to her mother, who giggled excitedly.

"I told you he was a gentleman!" she declared. "But of course he would be, being of the Atlanta Taits. Imagine that — candy *and* an invitation!"

"I think you have an admirer, Mama," Caroline said with a small, strained smile.

Sophie beamed a smile in Laurel's direction, past difficulties immediately forgotten in the light of present pleasures. "Not me, my dear, don't be silly! But our dear Laurel . . ."

As soon as she heard the signature on the note, everything else faded out for Laurel in a haze of red anger and disbelief. Seth Tait, who thought he could buy her with fifty dollars, who, even after their encounter this morning, had the arrogance to ply her aunt with candy and invite himself into their good graces *again,* whose biggest problem was how to waste his money on a horse race . . . Seth Tait was the last person in the world from whom Laurel wanted to hear at that moment.

But when Sophie made her insinuation, Laurel stood up and went over to Caroline, taking the note from her. She looked at it for a long time.

Caroline said hesitantly, "He does seem like a nice man. Perhaps — perhaps his writing to us is one good thing that has happened today."

Seth Tait, with his room in the fanciest hotel in town and his ready money and his penchant for gambling . . . was it only yesterday that Laurel had been in despair, trying to think of someone she knew who had money? But yesterday she had not known Seth Tait . . .

Laurel lifted her eyes from the note, a thought-

147

ful, almost calculating look in her eyes. "Yes," she murmured.

Caroline, who had seen that look on her cousin's face before, reflected a slight alarm in her eyes and she opened her mouth to question. But Sophie cut her off.

"Bring me my writing box, Caroline, and hurry! I must get a reply off right away. Of course we'll go driving with him, I haven't had an outing in I don't know how long! Won't this be fun, girls?"

Caroline hesitated, looking in some concern toward Laurel. But Laurel merely smiled, a cold tight smile that didn't quite reach her eyes. "Yes," she agreed quietly. "It certainly will."

CHAPTER
Seven

Laurel wasn't quite sure how they had ended up at Chinatree, nor whose idea it had been that the simple drive Seth had promised them should be extended to include a picnic lunch. She suspected Aunt Sophie was responsible for most of it, and tried to remind herself that anything that allowed her to spend more time with Seth was in her best interests. But she wasn't happy about bringing him to Chinatree.

He had hired an open carriage for the day, which allowed Laurel to sit up front with him while Caroline and Sophie shared the back seat. The fringed canopy danced jauntily as the carriage swayed over the rutted, overgrown drive that had once been the entryway to one of the most elegant plantations on the Charles. Like many of the oldest planter's homes, the house had once been reached by means of an avenue of oaks, and as Seth guided the horses into the dark tunnel of interlocking oak limbs Sophie chatted on gaily from the back seat about how it used to be, with pink and white crushed shells paving the drive and flame azaleas forming a border for the live oaks and black boys in short britches running ahead of the carriage, shooing away the peacocks that liked to wander onto the drive.

Laurel remembered none of this, of course. Chinatree had been burned by a renegade troop of Yankees in the winter of 1863, shortly after the Siege began and three months before Laurel was born. All she had of the legacy that should have been hers were her mother's memories and Aunt Sophie's tales, and the pictures she had formed in her mind. This was her special place, her secret place, and she was not entirely comfortable bringing a stranger here.

"Of course, Mr. Tait, you wouldn't have recognized it then," Sophie concluded with a sigh. "So much has been lost." She opened her fan and began to stir the humid air, putting on a wistful face. "So much."

"I can't imagine Mr. Tait is interested in any of it," Laurel said, "and why you wanted to come all the way out here I can't guess. There's nothing left but a graveyard. Hardly a fit place for a picnic."

"Oh, but it's such a pleasant drive," Caroline said. "And isn't it nice to get out of the city? I do believe it's cooler out here, don't you?"

"Not a bit," replied Laurel, peeling her shoulders away from the sticky back of the seat.

Seth shot her a grin beneath the brim of her

hat. "I hope I'm not putting you out too much, Miss Laurel," he said — but softly, so that the other two couldn't hear over the sound of the wheels.

An uncomfortable little frown gathered between Laurel's brows. Had it been so long since she had wanted to attract a man that she had forgotten how to simper and fawn? Or maybe she had never known. She knew that a sharp tongue was not the best way to impress a man from whom she might — possibly, one day — want a favor, but neither, she was sure, would Seth Tait respond to insincere flattery and mealy-mouthed compliance. Besides, she didn't have to impress him. He had his own agenda; all Laurel had to do was stay out of the way until she found out what it was and devised a method by which to turn it to her advantage.

Still, she admitted grudgingly, "Maybe it is a little cooler under the trees."

Seth laughed, and laughter from Seth Tait never showed Laurel to advantage. She felt her neck grow hot with the meaningful looks directed on her from the back seat, and her frown darkened.

If, a year ago, anybody had told Seth that he would be driving three respectable ladies dressed in mourning weeds around the South Carolina countryside in a hired carriage he would have thought they were crazy. Even now, he had to wonder how sane he was in planning the trip.

He had heard too much about Chinatree not to want to see it, and he supposed that in itself was a good enough reason for the seven-mile excursion out of town. The Colonel believed the gold was buried on Chinatree and it was as good a place as any to start looking. If he was going to do this thing, after all, he might as well do it right.

He knew the house had burned down during the war; that fact, the Colonel had said, was why Gus had decided to steal the gold instead of turning it in to the Confederate army. He wanted his family to be provided for after the war. What Seth hadn't counted on was how big the place would be, and what twenty years of abandonment could do to it.

He had been on ranches out west that were the size of some eastern seaboard states, but he had always thought farming in the east was on a much smaller scale. They had been moving through the green, mossy-smelling tunnel for fifteen minutes now and there was no end in sight. And everything was so lush and overgrown, so dense and thick and *green*. He couldn't stop thinking in terms of western lands, where a marker left in the desert could remain untouched for centuries, where open spaces gave a man room to think and where he could look up and see trouble coming while it was still a mile away. He couldn't see anything here, not even the end of the tunnel.

He gestured with the buggy whip toward the fringe of what looked like gray hay that festooned the trees overhead. "What's all that? I see it everywhere I look. Something an animal dragged up there?"

Laurel cast him an amused look. "It's Spanish moss. It's pretty common around here. Some folks think it's romantic."

"Do they now?" He did not return her gaze, but kept his face tilted slightly upward, studying the moss. "Sounds like some mighty odd folks."

Laurel tried not to smile, but in the end couldn't help it. "You really are a duck out of water here, you know," she told him frankly. "Whatever brought you east must have been pretty important."

He turned a smile on her, slow, easy and natural. He was handsome enough to take one's breath away when he smiled. "Maybe I just came out to see the scenery."

Laurel had to look away in order to keep her composure. "And what do you think of it so far?"

Seth's smile widened into a grin. "You're not very good at this, you know."

She looked at him sharply. "What?"

"Being polite. Not that I mind. I like it better when you say what you think, lets a fellow know where he stands."

Laurel looked away with a deliberate lift of her chin. The man was impossible. "I don't have the faintest idea what you're talking about."

"What I think about the scenery," Seth went on in an easy, conversational way, "is it's too green, and too thick, and too close together. It's a wonder you all don't choke, just trying to breathe the air."

Laurel turned her head until she was almost

looking over her shoulder, but she still had to raise her hand to her mouth to hide a grin.

"Oh, Laurel, look, your mother's roses!" Aunt Sophie sat forward excitedly. "I was afraid the frost might have gotten them this year. Oh, Mr. Tait, I wish you could have seen the gardens back in the old days. Laurel's mother had the greenest thumb in two counties. You know, Caroline, we should take some cuttings back . . ."

Sophie chattered on and Seth let her voice fade into background noise as the green tunnel opened up at last, on what it seemed he had waited all his life to see. And what he saw was nothing but a ruin.

A set of wide, curving steps led onto an invisible veranda. One chimney stood straight and tall in the middle of an empty field, another, several yards away, was half-crumbled. A twisted tree shaded the hearth of what must once have been the kitchen, and a few graying boards and a collapsed roof identified another outbuilding. The grass was knee high, shrubbery choked with weeds, the stone borders of the flower beds overgrown with trailing vines and littered with debris. Looking at it, Seth felt an almost overwhelming sense of dismay, and sadness.

There was nothing here but memories and ghosts and, though logically Seth had not expected anything more, he was still irrationally disappointed. As for where the money might be buried . . . even if there had once been markers, they were long gone now. He wouldn't even know

154

where to begin to look.

He drew the horses up beneath the shade of a sweet-smelling tree and for a moment just sat there, letting the desolation which seemed to be a symbol for this whole wild scheme start to work its way into his bones. He had wanted to see and now he had seen he might as well turn around right now and start back. He could spend a lifetime digging and not happen upon the right spot.

But then his old stubbornness took hold again, a kind of contrary determination to not be cheated out of what was rightfully his — not by time, or his own lack of imagination, or death itself. The gold was here; the Colonel had been sure of it. And maybe Seth didn't know where to start to look, but somebody did . . . maybe one of these women, maybe one of those old goats like the ones at the Jockey Club. Augustus Sinclair had left a letter; maybe he'd left more than that. It was up to Seth to find out.

Besides, he didn't have anyplace else to go.

He climbed to the ground and, with a smile, turned to help the ladies out.

Laurel wondered what Seth thought as he looked around the ruins of the hopes of the South; she always wondered what outsiders thought. She wasn't old enough to remember it ever having been any different, any more than he was, but she had heard the stories. Her head was full of stories, and she liked to fantasize. That was why this was her special place. This place reminded her that life had once been different;

and when she came here, somehow, no matter how bad things were, she was able to believe that things might one day be different again.

She watched as he bent his head attentively toward Aunt Sophie's ramblings, and was surprised by the gentleness with which he assisted Caroline over the uneven terrain. He asked alert questions and seemed genuinely interested in the stories Aunt Sophie had to tell . . . which wasn't entirely impossible to understand, Laurel supposed. A man with no family, no history . . . *If indeed he had no family, if anything he had told them about himself at all was true.*

They found a spot under the huge magnolia tree that had once shaded the eastern gallery, and Seth cleared away the broken branches and fallen flower pods while Laurel stood by with the blanket and Sophie and Caroline walked toward the graveyard to pay their respects. Seth watched their progress.

"Are both your folks buried here?" he asked.

"My mother's buried in St. Mary's," Laurel replied. "They never recovered my father's body."

"I thought you said he died in a hospital, that he wrote a letter home."

"A field hospital," Laurel said, snapping out the blanket and allowing its folds to spread across the ground. "A lot of men were buried where they fell when the hospitals were attacked. It was really hard on my mother, though — his last letter had included his burial instructions, and it was a final request she couldn't fulfill."

It was as though he had known, somehow, that the clue was there, and he had just been waiting for her to say the words. That was what was in the letter. *Burial instructions.* What safer way to let his wife know where the gold was buried than to make sure she would find it when she buried him? Back in those days they wouldn't have hired undertakers or grave diggers; trusted servants or family members would have taken spade to earth for the final rites. It was the *only* way, in war time, that Augustus could be certain the gold would end up in the hands of those he loved.

The money was in the graveyard. It made perfect sense.

Seth bent to straighten the corners of the blanket, and his face, carefully schooled in hiding his deepest emotions, revealed nothing. "That's a pity. But what did he have to send instructions for? Didn't he have a plot already in the family cemetery?"

Laurel shook her head. "That's the odd part. He didn't want to be buried in the cemetery — and the way Aunt Sophie tells it it's probably just as well he was never shipped home. There would've been at least a double funeral if mama had tried to bury him where he asked her to."

Seth kept his voice as casual as possible. "Oh, yeah? Where?"

They were both on their hands and knees, spreading out the wrinkles in the blanket, and when Laurel made a turn, sweeping the blanket with her hand, Seth's face was only inches from

157

hers. Another man might have looked ridiculous in that position, but Seth Tait never looked anything but masculine, calm and in control. He was far too masculine, in fact, to be that close to her, and Laurel frowned a little, sitting back on her heels. "This is a ghoulish subject. How did it ever get started, anyway?"

"Just curious." He sat back, resting his arm across one upraised knee in a stance that expertly disguised his impatience. He had holed up for weeks at a time in an empty arroyo, lain motionless for hours behind a clump of sagebrush while sheriff's deputies searched within six feet of him; he knew how to wait. He simply preferred not to.

She lifted her hand to smooth back a straying strand that was tickling her neck, and she realized too late that the gesture was a nervous one. She said ungraciously, "Well, your curiosity is unbecoming and anyway I don't know. It's in the letter — something about where they first met, but I haven't looked at those letters for years."

That was all he could expect to learn right then and it was enough. She still had the letter — letters, so there was more than one — and everything he needed to know would be there. All he had to do was find a way to get the letters, and that would take some thought. He had never had to steal anything as simple as a letter before.

He was sitting close to her — at least as much by accident as by design — and he smiled as she shifted away. "I'm making you nervous," he said.

Laurel started to make an automatic protest but knew it would be pointless. "You always make me nervous," she said shortly, brushing the residue of crushed leaves off her skirt. "It's like being in the same room with a trained bear — he might be wearing a chain, but you still never know what he's going to do next."

Seth laughed, a full and hearty laugh that made his eyes dance and caused Laurel to shush him anxiously and look around for her aunt.

"Not so loud — will you hush? It's not decent! Now look what you've done — Aunt Sophie is coming over. She's going to think you're —"

"What?" The laughter faded but left its sun-sparked residue in his eyes. "Having a good time at a picnic with a pretty girl? Courting you, maybe?"

There was a moment when Laurel didn't know what to say; when, looking at those gently lit, dancing eyes she *felt* like a girl, sparking the best-looking boy in town. But it was only a moment, and she recovered herself quickly. "I'm not a pretty girl, and you're not courting me. Now, behave yourself."

He looked at her for a moment thoughtfully, still smiling. "Well," he said, as Aunt Sophie's shadow bore down on them, "I reckon you're right about one thing. You're not a pretty girl. You're quite a woman."

She met his eyes, but she couldn't be sure what, if anything, she saw there. And maybe it was best, because just then Sophie came fluttering up, fanning herself breathlessly as she exclaimed, "I do declare. Laurel, I've never seen such a mess! We've got to hire some boys to get out here and clean off those graves. It's the good Lord's own disgrace the way we've let them get grown up like that! What will people say?"

Seth stood up to help Sophie sit down, but before he did he winked at Laurel most irreverently. And because he caught her off guard, she couldn't stop her own grin as she stood up to take Aunt Sophie's other arm.

The picnic lunch was another one of those extravagances Laurel would have raised the roof about if it hadn't happened to serve her own purpose. Sophie had asked Lacey to bake a whole ham and fry up a pullet, but that was only the beginning of the feast. A pan of rolls, a dozen pickled eggs and as many baked apples, a chess pie and blackberry pie . . . Laurel watched in dismay as dish after dish was set out on the blanket. There was enough there to supply a church social and still have leftovers, and more than once Laurel resisted the urge to look over her shoulder for the extra guests. Perhaps she should stop wondering what it was Seth Tait wanted from her, and look no farther than her own table.

But she did wonder about him, and in more ways than one. Since yesterday, the most important thing she had wondered about him was: How much money did he really have?

It amazed Laurel how her relatives could so quickly forget the wolf at the door and blithely go on a picnic as though nothing else mattered. But then again, why shouldn't they? They knew Laurel would think of something, Laurel always did. Laurel would take care of them, just as she always had.

Just how she was going to take care of them this time Laurel wasn't sure yet, and more than once in the past twenty-four hours she had been seized by that panicky little catch in her chest that suggested maybe this time she wouldn't be able to do anything at all. Seth Tait was the only idea she had, and she wasn't even sure if he *had* five hundred dollars. And even if he had, how did she imagine she was going to persuade him to lend it to her? She barely knew him.

And yet . . . he was pursuing her. He had as much as admitted yesterday that she had something he wanted. If they could arrange a bargain . . .

First she had to find out what she had to bargain with, and then she had to somehow convince him it was worth five hundred dollars. Oh, she hated this kind of maneuvering and deception, and she was no good at it at all. Things would be so much simpler if she could just deal with him face to face like a man.

When the last of the food was packed away, Aunt Sophie settled back with a ball of tatting and Caroline with a book. Laurel didn't know whether to throttle Aunt Sophie or thank her when she suggested, without any effort at subtlety at all, "Laurel, why don't you show Mr. Tait around? A nice walk after the meal will do you good."

Another time Laurel would have shot back any one of a dozen replies: that a walk in this heat was more likely to destroy one's health than benefit it, that there was nothing to see but weeds and snakes, that Mr. Tait did not look any more energetic than she felt. But as much as she would have liked to she could not afford to miss this opportunity.

So she tolerated the mocking twinkle in Seth's eyes, and even managed to smile at him as he offered his hand to help her to her feet. It was a big, work-roughened hand that sent a little wave of heat through her with its touch, and she dropped it as soon as she was standing. Ignoring the arm he offered, she plopped her sunbonnet on top of her head and walked toward the house, tying the black ribbons as she went.

Seth said, "Is this a race?"

"Sorry." Laurel checked her stride. "There's still a lot of rubble around here; be careful where you step."

He shot her an amused glance. "I should be telling you that. How long has it been since you went walking with a man, Miss Laurel?"

"Two nights ago," she replied promptly. "I walked with you in the garden."

"And did it a lot better, as I recall."

Laurel drew in her breath for a retort, but thought better of it just in time. Holding her skirts in one hand to avoid the worst of the burrs and grass seeds, she walked in silence for a time.

The air was hot and heavy, pulsing with the drone of cicadas and syrupy with the scent of magnolia and jasmine. But except for the occasional ripple of grass as some small creature scuttled out of their way, nothing stirred, not even a breeze. They moved around the shell of the building, skirting the crumbling steps, through the remnants of a long-forgotten flower bed, past a small statue, so chipped and scarred and overgrown with moss that its original shape was no longer discernible. After a while Laurel could almost forget Seth's presence, lost as she was in the heavy stillness and thoughts of the family she'd lost.

His voice was quiet and mellow, not intruding into the moment so much as blending with it. Still the unexpected perception in his words startled Laurel. "You didn't like me coming here, did you? You don't like anybody coming here but you."

What was even more surprising was that Laurel felt no urge to evade or dismiss the question. She answered naturally, without thinking about it all, "There's not much left in this world that belongs to me but this, Mr. Tait. I know it's not much to look at . . ." She made a deprecating gesture with her wrist. "But what it represents is more than I can ever expect to have, and everything I might have had . . ." She glanced at him, suddenly embarrassed. "I know it sounds silly. You wouldn't understand."

"No," agreed Seth slowly. "I reckon I wouldn't, seeing as how I never had much more than a horse and saddle to call my own my whole life. Something like this . . ." He looked around a little, shaking his head as though in wonder at it all. "Something this big, this important leaves its mark on the land. And I guess if I'd ever been connected to something like that, even a little bit, I'd feel like you do. I'd want to protect it."

Yes, Laurel thought, *protect.* That was how she felt about Chinatree — secretive, private, protective. She had never been able to explain that, even to herself, but Seth understood.

They walked along in silence for awhile, but it was a new kind of silence, companionable and at ease. Seth picked up a fallen willow branch and absently whipped the grass at his side as they moved along. Bare-headed under the sun, his hair glinted with copper and gold highlights, squint lines radiated from his eyes. Laurel found herself looking at him more than she had intended to.

"I never thought before how it would be not to know who your folks were, or where you came from," she said after a time. "It must be an empty feeling."

"Sometimes," he admitted. "Most times you don't think about it. Most times it doesn't matter."

For a moment Laurel thought about that, then smiled dryly. "Maybe you've got the best deal after all. Sometimes I think I'd be a lot happier if I didn't have to remember who I am and where I come from all the time. Lord knows I'd get a lot more done."

Seth chuckled, his eyes twinkling as he glanced

at her. "I just bet you would."

They had reached the far side of the house, where the column of a fallen portico, almost overgrown with vines, formed a natural barrier. It was shady there, and deep-summer quiet. Seth gestured with the willow branch, gazing around.

"Do you ever think about rebuilding?"

She gave a surprised little laugh. "Rebuild Chinatree? Do you know what kind of money that would take?"

But his expression was thoughtful as he looked over the landscape. "I don't mean like it was. I don't guess you could ever do that. But start over. Put up a little house, some cross fencing, raise horses. That's what I would do, if it was mine."

Chinatree, a horse farm! Laurel did not know how to adequately express her incredulity, so she didn't even try. She said instead, "Sometimes the past is best left undisturbed, Mr. Tait."

He just smiled. "Do you think so?"

There was something about that smile, about the dark amusement in his eyes, that she couldn't quite interpret, and it disturbed Laurel. She drew a breath. "Why did you ask us on this outing?"

His expression relaxed into easy, amused lines as he replied, "Why did you accept?"

"That's simple. I can't afford to offend anyone who might turn out to have money."

His eyes danced as he tossed the willow branch away. "So it's back to money again."

"There are two kinds of people in this world, Mr. Tait, the rich and the poor. When you're poor, the only kind who matter are the rich."

"And you think I'm rich."

"You'd have to be, to gamble at the Jockey Club."

"Maybe I'm just too lazy to make money any other way."

She looked at him frankly. "Maybe you are."

"There are men who would gamble their last dollar for the chance on making ten. I reckon you know that."

"Yes. The minimum bet at the Jockey Club is two hundred dollars."

His face was impassive. "I didn't think the Old Guard had that kind of money anymore."

"This is Charleston, Mr. Tait," Laurel said crisply. "We have a reputation for picking ourselves up by our bootstraps. Fortunes have been lost since the war, it's true, but fortunes have also been made — in cotton mills, factories, and from strangers who like to throw their money around in private clubs."

He grinned. "So if I was third-generation Charlestonian, I could make a bet for two hundred dollars and nobody would lift an eyebrow."

Laurel replied coolly, "I wouldn't be surprised. Those are the rules. Are you interested?"

She could feel her heart beat, waiting for his answer. Two hundred dollars was a lot of money. Only a fool would take a chance on losing it if that were all he had. In Laurel's opinion, only a fool would take a chance with that kind of money no matter how much he had. Of course, it wasn't *five* hundred, but if he could afford to lose that much he must have more . . .

Seth said, "What time?"

Laurel released a breath she was not aware she had been holding. "Ten o'clock."

He nodded. "I'll call for you at nine."

Laurel's heart resumed its normal rhythm. She wasn't really any the wiser than she had been before, but at least there was a chance. And Saturday . . . she would find out Saturday, after the race. She would hold him to his bargain.

Seth said, "How long has your husband been dead?"

"Three years."

"Are you going to wear black the rest of your life?"

She was taken aback by the personal comment, and didn't have a ready reply. She glanced at him quickly, but did not linger to try to interpret the expression in his sun-narrowed eyes. "It would be proper," she answered, somewhat stiffly. "Besides, my uncle died last year."

Seth nodded soberly. "That's a shame."

She was about to murmur some acknowledgment for his sympathy when he added, "A handsome woman like you shouldn't go around dressed in black. It makes you look like a scarecrow, and doesn't do a thing to stir up a man's interest."

Laurel's breath left her lungs in an astonished huff, and she turned on him. "Honestly, you are the most impossible man! How I dress is none of your affair and I'll thank you to keep your opinions to yourself! As for stirring up your interest, that, I assure you, is the last thing I want to do!"

His slow, thorough grin only added another degree to the heat that scorched her cheeks, and he turned too, so that they were face to face, and close enough to touch. "It wasn't my interest I was talking about, Miss Laurel. It's been stirred up since the moment I met you."

She wanted to back away but pride wouldn't let her. The heat of the sun and the heat of her own body pulsed around her, the drone of insects was low and far away. She said, a little hoarsely, "You flatter yourself, sir, if you think for one minute —"

"I don't think anything. I just know what I like."

And slowly, without taking a step closer or changing his expression or moving his eyes from hers, he lifted one hand and tugged at the strings of her bonnet. She wanted to jerk her head away, to whirl indignantly and leave him standing alone in the shadow of a fallen portico, to stalk away and not look back. She didn't move, not when, with a single arching motion of his hand, he pushed the bonnet off her head, not when it tumbled to the grass at her feet, not when his fingers cupped her head and not even when, with a slow subtle pressure, he drew her closer.

His fingers spread over her cheek, his thumb caressing her chin, tilting it upward. His face was so close it was a blur. Heat radiated from his fingertips, flowing like lava into Laurel's muscles and bones. She could feel a tightness in her stom-

168

ach, a heaviness in her breasts, and her heart was pounding hard. She couldn't move her face away, or even her eyes. And she didn't want to.

She whispered hoarsely, "Why are you doing this?"

There might have been the faintest curve of a smile at the corner of his lips, she could not tell. All she could see was the shape of them, full and near, and all she could feel was his breath brushing across her face like a secret, warm and intimate. He said softly, "I'm not sure I know the answer to that myself."

Both hands came up then, holding her face. His fingers were like iron, but his touch was gentle. His eyes were clear and dark and seemed to pin her with their thorough, probing power. He said, "Maybe it's because I never met a woman like you before. Maybe it's because we're so much alike, you and I, more than you realize. Maybe it's because I never knew a woman who needed kissing as much as you do."

And then he kissed her, and Laurel didn't know whether she would have stopped him if she could have, because after the first startled breath it was too late to try. He filled her with his taste and his strength; he made her limbs go weak and her head spin, but a kind of triumph blossomed inside . . . an exhilarated yearning, a powerful hunger she couldn't control. She kissed him back; she clung to him, her fingers tightening on muscle and sinew, her mouth tasting him shamelessly, her will merging with his until everything faded away except what they took from each other, and gave to one another.

His hands were on her waist, pressing her close. She could feel the strength of his chest against her aching breasts and the hardness of his pelvis pressing into hers in a way that should have shocked her, but instead only sent a surge of dizzying heat through her, of mindless triumph. The sensations that filled her were unlike anything she had ever known before, or even guessed were possible with a man. This was the way it was meant to be, the way it should have been, this was what she had been missing all her life.

Perhaps it was that realization, the simple knowledge of how deep was her desire for him, that penetrated the fog and brought back her common sense . . . or perhaps it was he who moved first. Laurel only knew that when their lips parted, when his hands moved from her waist to her arms, tightening there for a moment before stepping away, when her body felt the absence of his — it was as though she had suddenly been pulled back from the edge of an abyss. Breathless, dazed, for a moment she could not comprehend what had happened to her.

His hands moved up her arms, to her shoulders, then back again. His eyes moved over her face, her neck, her breasts, and they were dark as though with fever. His face, too, had a faint flush beneath its natural brownness, and his voice was husky, a little breathless. "Are you afraid of me, Laurel?"

Her heart would not stop pounding; the whole

world shook with its rhythm. Her fingers were wrapped around the lapel of his coat, and she made herself release them. She whispered, "No." It wasn't him she feared; it was herself.

Once again his eyes went over her, searching, probing, hungry. He released her arms slowly, his fingers pulling away as though by force. He said, "You should be. I'm a liar and a scoundrel and I'll ruin you if I can."

Without his support Laurel's legs threatened to buckle; she stiffened them deliberately, tightening her hands into fists with the effort. She managed a breath that was almost steady, and she held his gaze. "You said yourself we're too much alike, Mr. Tait," she said. "Maybe you should be afraid of me."

They stood for a long moment, eyes locked, inches apart but not touching. Then Seth smiled, and bent to pick up her bonnet. "Maybe I should," he said.

He handed Laurel her bonnet, and waited while she replaced it with fingers that did not tremble too much. Then, with a small bow and a sweep of his hand, he gestured the way back to the others.

Caroline knocked lightly on Laurel's door that night after her mother had retired. The door was halfway open and at Laurel's absent answer she came in and then — acutely aware of her mother's open door just down the hall — she closed the door behind her.

"Laurel," she said, a little uncertainly, "I just

wanted to talk to you for a minute while mother's asleep. I know how worried you are and it must seem as though we're not trying to be any help whatsoever . . ."

Laurel looked up from her study of her wardrobe, an absent frown on her face. "Hmm? What?"

"About the five hundred dollars." Caroline twisted her hands together. "It's a lot of money and I know you don't think I have much more sense about money than mother does, but I've been thinking, Laurel, and there's only one thing to do. We have to sell the house. We can get a great deal more than five hundred for it and —"

The frown vanished from Laurel's face in a moment of astonishment, and then she said dismissively, "Don't be ridiculous. We can't sell the house. Where would we live?" She turned back to the wardrobe and took out one of her three summerweight black gowns, holding it up to herself for inspection in the pier glass opposite. This gown was a bit more fashionable than the others, with three-quarter-length sleeves and a well-padded bustle and oversize bow in back. She sometimes wore it to church.

"That's just it," Caroline said eagerly. "With the money we had left over we could buy a smaller house, outside of town."

"What do you think?" Laurel interrupted, pressing the gown flat across her abdomen and turning for a profile. "Could we dye this some other color? And don't we have some lace somewhere that isn't black?"

172

Caroline looked as startled as if Laurel had suddenly suggested they go rob a graveyard. But she recovered herself quickly, and reached forward to take some of the material between her thumb and forefinger. "I — I suppose we could try to bleach it out, and then put some color back in. Maybe a brown, or a navy."

Laurel narrowed her eyes at the mirror, as though trying to picture the color, then shook her head. "Lavender," she decided, "or puce. Something with a little warmth in it, for heaven's sake."

Caroline made an obvious effort to keep her tone neutral as she said, "Are you putting away mourning, then?"

"I am for Saturday, anyway." Laurel gave her reflection in the mirror one last critical inspection, then tossed the dress on the bed. "I'm going to the Jockey Club."

She turned back to the wardrobe, rummaging around in the bottom. "I'll have to do something about a hat, too, I suppose, and gloves. Surely Aunt Sophie has a pair of white gloves put away somewhere? Wasn't there ever a time when we didn't wear black?"

She turned, and burst into laughter at the expression on Caroline's face. "For heaven's sake, Caro, stop gaping! I've surely done more shocking things than accept an invitation to the Jockey Club in my lifetime. I'm technically a member, you know, and the last time I heard it was a perfectly respectable organization."

"I — I'm sorry. It's just that you don't usually care for — that is, you're not usually interested in —"

"Respectable things?" Laurel's eyes twinkled. "Well, I suppose you're right, but I'm making an exception in this case. I don't suppose there's anything to be done about my shoes." She lifted her skirts a little and peered down at her scuffed black lace-ups. "We'll lengthen the hem and maybe nobody will notice."

"You're not" — Caroline cleared her throat — "going alone, are you?"

"Don't be silly. That's one thing even *I* couldn't manage." And she turned, pretending to straighten the wardrobe, hiding her expression. "Seth Tait is escorting me."

Caroline kept her tone carefully unrevealing. "I see."

There was a long silence, and eventually Laurel was forced to turn and face it. She smiled at her cousin. "Go on."

"Oh, Laurie," Caroline said, her eyes tight with distress, "I wouldn't presume to criticize, and please don't take this wrongly, because I'm sure Mr. Tait is every bit the gentleman, and he's certainly been nothing but generous with all of us, it's just that — well, we do know so little about him. I wouldn't want you to entertain false hopes when he might turn out to be completely unsuitable . . ."

Laurel did not know whether to laugh again, or cry, or embrace her cousin. But she was far more touched by Caroline's concern — misplaced though it might be — than she would have expected to be, and she stepped forward, taking the other girl's hands. "Don't waste your worry on me," she told her gently. "I assure you, Mr. Tait is perfectly unsuitable in every way imaginable except one . . . he has money. And I know exactly what I'm doing."

But far from reassuring her, Laurel's words only caused the anxiety in Caroline's eyes to deepen. "Oh, Laurie, you wouldn't —"

"Hush," Laurel said firmly, and emphasized her words with a squeeze of the other girl's hands. "Don't worry. I'm going to take care of things." She leaned forward and kissed her cousin on the cheek. "Now go on to bed and don't think about it any more. And in the morning ask Aunt Sophie about the lace, would you?"

After a moment Caroline managed a smile, murmured goodnight, and left the room. But she did not go to bed. And she could not stop worrying. She spent a long time pacing up and down, agonizing over her decision. Then she sat down at her writing desk, took out paper and pen, and before she lost her courage, wrote:

Dearest Peter,

I loathe intervening in the affairs of another, but you have always been such a good friend to the family, and I know how fond you are of our dear Laurel, and I don't know where else I might turn for help. Please understand that what I am about to ask of you is prompted only by my deep love for my cousin and greatest concern for her well being. Perhaps it is wrong of me, but I am somewhat concerned about the stranger in town, Mr. Seth Tait . . .

CHAPTER
Eight

Saturday dawned crisp and fair, a welcome change from the hot muggy days of summer in Charleston. Seth rented a buggy and called for Laurel shortly before nine in the morning. Of necessity the race was being held early before the sun began beating down and sapping the energy not only of the horses but of the spectators.

Laurel was waiting for him on the piazza. She had spent most of the previous day and all of the morning listening to her aunt whine and wring her hands over the impropriety of Laurel going out with a gentleman alone, and she knew the only way to avoid more of the same was to wait for Seth outside. If he came to the door they would never escape Aunt Sophie.

Sophie had been more than cooperative until she had learned of Laurel's intention to attend the race unchaperoned. She had lent her considerable dressmaking expertise and fashion sense to the project of Laurel's gown, and the result was a striking dress of rich, warm purple trimmed with gold braid and — in concession to Laurel's widowhood and in consideration of the fact that they could not find another shade — black ribbons. Sophie had recovered Laurel's best bonnet, and Caroline had found a gold silk scarf in an attic trunk. The fringe from that scarf now adorned the parasol she carried, and formed stylish tassels on her lavender gloves. When Laurel looked at her reflection in the mirror what she saw was bold and stylish and guaranteed to turn heads. For a moment she was so taken aback by her own appearance that she almost yearned for the security of her old black garb. She hadn't worn anything pretty or fashionable since her wedding day; and seeing now what the rich color of the gown did to her skin and how the gold bonnet brightened her eyes, she remembered what it was like to be a girl, when nothing mattered more than being pretty, and being pretty was the best feeling in the world.

She started quickly down the steps when she heard the buggy pull up. Seth was already dismounting, and when he saw her he stopped, and she knew once again what it felt like to be pretty, when pretty mattered. His hat came off; his eyes surveyed her slowly from head to toe; and by the time she reached him, he was grinning in a way that made her blush.

"Well now ma'am," he drawled, "don't you look fine? And quite an improvement if I may say so."

She didn't look at him. "The Jockey Club has always been a fashionable place. Let's hurry and get out of here before Aunt Sophie sees you."

He feigned shock. "You wouldn't want me to do anything behind your aunt's back would you? Doesn't she approve?"

"She treats me like a sixteen-year-old with my first beau," Laurel replied impatiently. "And unless you want a chaperone dogging your heels all day you'd best stop jabbering and help me up so we can go."

Seth laughed softly and helped Laurel into the seat, but Laurel didn't relax until they turned the corner and left the house behind. It wasn't just Laurel going riding with a man that Aunt Sophie objected to, although she was still ridiculously old-fashioned about things like that; it was their destination. The Jockey Club simply wasn't what it used to be, she had wailed over and over, with Yankees and carpetbaggers and the white-trash rich and what she euphemistically termed the "money changers" — as though betting on horse races was something that had been invented since the war. While it might be acceptable for a lady to attend in the company of her husband or a male relative, it simply wouldn't *do* for Laurel to be escorted to such a place by an unattached male, a virtual stranger. Who knew what she might be exposed to, or what kind of vulgarity she might stumble upon without a knowledgeable man — or at least a female chaperone — to protect her? At the very least, Sophie had entreated desperately, she might ask Peter to accompany them . . . and that was where Laurel balked. The last thing she wanted, besides a chaperone, was to have Peter along, watching her every move. The entire point of the outing was to engage in large-scale wagering, and Peter's presence could inhibit Seth as easily as Aunt Sophie's.

"It wasn't easy to get you in today, Mr. Tait," she said after a time. "I mean, while I can get you through the gates on my credentials, getting into the inner circle is quite something else again."

He slid her an amused glance. "Now Miss Laurel, I know you can get just about anything you set your mind on. Still, I'm obliged."

"I certainly hope so. Aside from everything else, my reputation will be in tatters after today."

"And I know how much that means to you."

Though his face was sober, she could hear the subtle mockery in his voice, and it rankled.

"You'll be introduced to a Colonel Boatwright," she said stiffly. "He was a close friend of my uncle and when I mentioned I had a friend from out of town —"

"A rich friend."

"That helped," she admitted. "A lot of the old families don't have the money to bet but the men go anyway just to remember the way things used to be. And to sweeten the purse — well, they have to invite outsiders. Even some Yankees."

"If they're rich enough?"

She scowled. "I really don't see what you find

so amusing about it, Mr. Tait. Your money might buy you a place in the betting circle but it won't buy you a membership in the Jockey Club — you can ask any rich Yankee about *that*." She caught the edge of her temper before it got out of hand and was annoyed with herself for defending an institution she didn't care a fig about. What was it about Seth Tait that made her want to argue with him no matter what he said?

She took a breath and went on, in a much more neutral tone, "Some of the business men of Charleston will be here today, I imagine. The owners of the lumber mills and phosphate mines, ship owners, those kinds of people."

"All the high rollers, eh?"

But once again his faintly mocking tone spurred her temper and she snapped, "You are the most vulgar man! This isn't a poker game, you know. It's a horse race. The sport of kings."

He chuckled, shaking his head. "You sure do take things seriously. Why, back where I come from, all it takes to make a horse race is a starting place and a stopping place and a hat to throw the money in."

Her smile was faintly superior. "Well, you'll find it quite different here. Of course, it's not like the old days. I never got to see it, but I've heard the stories of how the Jockey Club was before the war. Back then the races were only for the first families of Charleston, the real blue bloods. I couldn't have gotten you in then no matter how much money you had."

"Well, aren't I lucky that times have changed?"

She ignored him. "I understand the festivities surrounding the race were even more exciting than the race itself. There were huge dinner parties and a grand ball. I can imagine how all the ladies must have looked in their silks and satins with the big full skirts and the men in their dinner suits. The halls decked with flowers, the chandeliers sparkling . . ."

Not until she felt Seth's gaze on her did Laurel realize how wistful her voice sounded, and she quickly jerked herself out of the reverie. She went on, more matter-of-factly, "Of course, during the war and after, the old race course at Washington Park was destroyed, and the stands. Aunt Sophie said the stands were quite remarkable, one for the Jockey Club members and a special one for the ladies, covered to keep out the sun, and one for the public, too. All kinds of refreshments were served and there was bunting and a band. It must have been grand."

Seth was still looking at her, and there was no mockery in his tone at all as he agreed quietly, "It surely must have been."

They left the city and drove along an unpaved road which gradually became more congested with carriages and horsemen.

"We're almost there," she said. "The old Preston place. They hold the race here now."

Following her instructions, Seth turned in through a pair of sagging fences and stopped the buggy. Before them were carriages arranged in a neat semicircle, facing an oval race course of hard-packed grass. After all her vivid descriptions and admonitions to Seth about his casual attitude, Laurel felt a little embarrassed to see it all now through his eyes. It was, after all, hardly more than a starting place, a stopping place, and a hat to collect the money in.

"No stands," she said, forcing nonchalance into her tone. "These days I guess we just watch from our carriage."

"No stands, no bunting and no band," Seth agreed, but even though she looked at him sharply, searching for some sign of irreverence, his expression was very reserved — almost disappointed.

He guided the buggy along the line formed by the others, found a space, and pulled up. Laurel looked up and down the row, nodding to acquaintances, steeling herself for the scandalized looks of matrons. There were a few men but most of the carriages held women, shielding themselves from the sun with their brightly colored parasols. She heard the high whinny of horses and noticed a corral over behind some trees. It didn't take much imagination to figure out where the men were.

Laurel looked at Seth. "If you want to watch the horses run, you can stay here. If you want to participate, we'd better go find Colonel Boatwright."

He grinned as he came around the buggy to help her down. "How did you get so bossy, anyhow?"

"Experience, Mr. Tait. Experience."

She unfurled her parasol when she was on the ground and, because everyone was already staring anyway, she took Seth's arm, holding her head high and smiling and bowing in the direction of the most openly curious.

Seth said, "I can't help but notice most of the ladies are in their carriages, and I'll just take a wild guess women aren't allowed in the betting area. Is this one of the things that's going to do your reputation in?"

"It doesn't matter. They're all gossiping like crows over a carcass the minute we pass by. Let them." She smiled broadly and lifted her hand to a group across the way. "I've done worse."

"That I know for a fact," Seth murmured.

Laurel ignored him. For the sake of what this day could mean to her she could endure more than a few snide comments.

They left the carriages behind and moved across a grassy area where men were gathered in knots, smoking, talking and gesturing broadly. The barnyard smell was more pungent here, mixed with the odors of rum and cigars. Laurel lifted her arm as a familiar form came into view. "Colonel Boatwright," she called. "Over here!"

A tall man with iron gray hair and a slight limp broke away from one of the groups, coming toward them with hands extended. "Why Miss Laurel. Aren't you a picture?" Beaming, he grasped her hands and kissed her cheek. Then he turned to Seth. "And this must be your friend, Mr. . . . ."

Seth extended his hand. "Seth Tait, sir, and pleased to be allowed to participate in your little race."

"Glad to have you, sir. Any friend of Miss Laurel's . . ." He smiled at her. "Well, her family and I go way back. Way, way back."

He clapped a hand on Seth's shoulder. "Come on over here son, let's have a look at some of this horse flesh." Then he hesitated, glancing at Laurel. "Now, Miss Laurel, I know you don't want to be hanging around a dirty old stable, so why don't you just let me get one of my boys to walk you back to your carriage?"

Laurel knew perfectly well that the real reason he wanted her out of the way was so that he could talk to Seth about the betting procedures, and he didn't consider it proper to do so in front of a lady. Men were such silly creatures; they had actually convinced themselves that gambling — much like certain unsavory things that went on in places like Miss Elsie's — was something women had no idea even existed.

She gave him an overly sweet smile and twirled her parasol so that the fringe danced. "Now, Colonel, you know better than that. You're not going to be able to get rid of me that easily when you know I just find everything about horse racing fascinating."

The colonel cleared his throat uncomfortably, and, out of his view, Seth winked at her. It was such an unexpected gesture that Laurel almost laughed out loud, and caught herself just in time.

"Yes, well . . ." The colonel offered his arm. "Come along, then. Mind those pretty skirts."

Seth couldn't help but notice that, despite the colonel's reluctance to take Laurel into what was apparently an exclusively male domain, the greetings she received from the men — young and old alike — were a great deal warmer than those she had gotten from the ladies in their carriages. More than once he observed a pair of male eyes following her in a way that, while far from disrespectful, made him wish irrationally that it was his arm she was clinging to, not the older man's.

Six beautiful horses trotted restlessly in the paddock, and Seth let out a low whistle of appreciation when he saw them. There was Arabian blood in all of them, he could tell.

"Well, I see you appreciate good horses." The colonel sounded pleased.

Seth leaned against the top rail, his eyes moving over the assortment in a practiced, expert way. "I know something about horses," he admitted. "Raised some myself out west." But his rangy little quarter horses had nothing in common with these elegant, fine-boned mounts. They might almost have belonged to a different species.

"We lost much of our finest breeding stock during the war," the colonel said, "valiant steeds who served in battle. I remember my own Harvest Moon. Won the Jockey Club race back in '59 and then was shot out from under me at Atlanta. But that was another world and time, and we all did what we had to do."

"It looks like a few good lines made it through," Seth said.

"Some of the breeders managed to save some good horses for us in Kentucky. But, sir, I can prophesy that racing will never be the same here in Charleston as it was thirty years ago."

Seth glanced at Laurel, who, careless of her fancy dress, was leaning against the rail and studying the horses with an avaricious eye. "What do you think?" he asked her.

"If I had two hundred dollars," Laurel replied, almost without thinking, "I'd put it on that little chestnut over there."

There was a moment of startled silence, in which Seth turned away to hide his grin, and then Colonel Boatwright burst into laughter. "Miss Laurel, you are a caution in this world! Now come on out from here before you get that pretty dress dirty and let us menfolk conduct some business."

Laurel could have sworn with frustration as the colonel led her away. She had wanted to see exactly how much — if anything — Seth could afford to bet, but there was nothing to be done about it now without making a scene, and that wouldn't do Seth or herself any good. So she managed to smile and allow Colonel Boatwright to turn her over to one of his sons, but as hard as she strained she could not see what was going on as he returned to Seth.

Colonel Boatwright's tone was all business. "Somebody will take your bet in that tent over there." He indicated the tent a hundred yards or so to the right. "The odds are posted and there's a floor bid of two hundred dollars."

Seth smiled dryly. "So I was told."

"You've got . . ." The other man pulled out a pocket watch and glanced at it. "About fifteen minutes to look 'em over and make your choice. I'll meet you inside the tent."

There were only two horses that Seth would seriously consider. One was a bay, a big strong horse with a deep chest and wide nostrils, the sign of a good sprinter. But the track was just over a mile long, and the winner would need staying power as well as speed. The other horse, a chestnut, was smaller and daintier with long tapering muscles and straight, strong forelegs; he could go the distance but might not have the speed. Seth stepped into the betting tent and checked the horses' colors against the odds. The bay, riding under blue and red, was Saladar and his odds were two to one. Almost a sure thing. The chestnut, whose colors were gold and purple, was a longer shot at ten to one, and the track talk was he had never been proved.

In his pocket Seth had two hundred fifty dollars and some change. If he lost, he wouldn't have enough left to pay his hotel bill for another week. But it was going to take more than two hundred fifty dollars to stay in this town as long as it would take to find the gold, to spread around the kind of money it would take to get into the places he needed to go. And Seth had never been the kind of man to walk away from a risk.

He stepped outside again and walked to the paddock fence, studying first the bay and then the chestnut.

"So you like my horse?"

Seth turned to see a tall man beside him, elegantly dressed, holding a silver cup with a sprig of mint sticking out. He smelled of bourbon and bay rum.

Seth turned back to the horses. "I like both the bay and the chestnut."

"Saladar, the bay, is mine and he's going to win the race." He extended his hand. "Keith Peterson. I own Peterson Phosphate."

Seth hesitated before taking the proffered hand. The other man had given him no reason to dislike him, but a smart man didn't need a reason. There was something oily about Peterson that made Seth immediately distrust him. "Seth Tait," he said after a moment. "I'm new to town."

"You must know someone," Peterson said, "to be invited here. It's like pulling hens' teeth to get these old Rebs to invite anyone new. Of course, I have the inside track since my horse is going to win."

Seth knew then which horse he was putting his money on. "Yours is a nice animal," he said, "but I like Johnny Reb."

The other man took a swig of his mint julep. "You must have money to burn, Mister. That animal'll be left in the dust by the first turn."

Seth said, "Maybe."

189

The other man watched him through narrowed, amused eyes. "Are you a gambling man?"

Seth smiled. "That's the name of the game."

"How'd you like a bet on the side?"

Another time, another place, and he wouldn't have hesitated. He had, in fact, been unconsciously setting Peterson up for this from the moment he had walked up. But at the last moment he remembered the contempt in Laurel's voice when she spoke of the Yankees and the phosphate miners, and some instinct warned him that even if he won he would lose by association with this man. And Seth had learned to listen to his instincts.

He said, "Thank you kindly, but I don't gamble with strangers."

He turned and walked toward the tent. Colonel Boatwright was watching from the doorway, and there was approval on his face.

The odds on Johnny Reb hadn't changed. Two hundred fifty dollars, and fifty of that he wouldn't have if Laurel hadn't thrown it back in his face . . .

He put his two hundred on the counter, then covered the money with his hand before the clerk could take it. "Wait," he said.

The colonel frowned, and the clerk looked impatient. "Window closes in four minutes, Mister," he said. "Make up your mind."

Seth took out the last fifty and placed it on the counter. "All on Johnny Reb," he said.

The colonel slapped him on the back as Seth received his ticket, chuckling. "Sure do hate to

190

take your money, son, but you shouldn't have let that Peterson rile you. He might be a son of a bitch, but he's got the fastest horse on the track, and you're never going to see that two-fifty again."

Seth just smiled. "I reckon that's why they call it horseracing."

Seth arrived back at the carriages just as the horses were lining up at the starting gate. Laurel was pacing up and down impatiently, the braid on her parasol flashing. "Well?" she demanded. "What took you so long? Did you get in?"

"Remind me to ask why you're so interested in how much money I make — or lose." Seth took her elbow to help her up into the buggy.

"Don't be insulting. Naturally, I'm interested, after having gone to so much trouble on your behalf. All I asked was —"

"I bet my last sou," Seth informed her, "on Johnny Reb."

"Oh, fie! Nobody bets his last dollar on a horse race!" But she looked at him uneasily. "Do they?"

Seth just grinned as he climbed up beside her.

A feeling of excitement swept the spectators as the horses lined up at the starting gate, mounted by small jockeys in their colorful costumes. Laurel stood up in the carriage, holding her hat, squinting into the sun. "Which one is Johnny Reb?"

Seth gestured toward the line. "Purple and gold."

Laurel turned slowly to look at him. "The color of my dress."

"Well, a man looks for luck wherever he can get it."

His tone was nonchalant and so was his expression, but a little thrill went through Laurel nonetheless. He had picked her horse, and her colors. They were in this together.

An anticipatory hush fell over the crowd and drew Laurel's attention back to the gate. "They're almost ready to start," she said, her voice low and tight with excitement. "Come on, Johnny Reb."

Seth cast her an amused look but she didn't notice. The starting pistol cracked and she grasped his wrist as the horses shot from the gate, thundering around the track into the distance. The dust of their wake shimmered like gold in the sun.

"I can't see!" Laurel cried, bouncing on her tiptoes. "Who's ahead?"

Seth, like everyone else, had gotten to his feet at the sound of the starting pistol, but the dust obscured his vision just as it did hers. "I'm not sure," he said tightly. "I think . . . It looks like Saladar's leading on the quarter turn."

The horses disappeared around a stand of trees. Laurel realized she was still gripping Seth's arm. She withdrew her hand but couldn't stem the excitement. Anxiety over Saladar's position only heightened the intensity that was already so thick in the air. People were shouting, waving their hands; ladies who would not have otherwise have raised their voices above a murmur were whipping off their hats and cheering their favorites on. It was heady, delirious, exhilarating, and at that moment Laurel could understand why a man *would* bet his last dollar on a horse race.

"Here they come!" someone shouted from another carriage.

The horses had rounded the half-mile turn and were plunging toward them down the track. Saladar was in the lead with a black horse in second and then in third was Johnny Reb, gold and purple rippling in the wind.

"There he is!" Laurel shouted. "Run, Johnny, run." She knew she was behaving in a most unladylike like way, jumping up and down and shouting at the top of her lungs, but so was everyone else. Even Aunt Sophie would have done a bit of shouting, Laurel thought, if she had been here; the wildness was so contagious.

She could feel the tension in the muscles of the man beside her as though it were her own. "He's making his move," Seth said softly. "I knew he would. Come on boy, run for it."

The jockey was standing in the saddle, bending low over Johnny Reb's mane. They were at the three-quarter-mile marker and the chestnut was gaining on the black. Johnny Reb passed him and then was in a dead heat with the bay.

Laurel glanced at Seth and saw his face was as hard as stone. She looked back at the horses. No, she thought, Reb's made his move too late. He's not going to be able to pass the bay . . .

But she was wrong. And so, from the look on Seth's face, was he. Neither of them had even begun to guess what kind of heart the horse had. In the last tenth of the mile, the jockey used the whip for the first time and Johnny Reb swept over the winner's ribbon with more than a head to spare.

The roar from the crowd was wild and disbelieving, but Laurel hardly heard it over the sound of her own screams of joy. "You won! We did it! You won!" Her arms were around him and she didn't know how, nor did she care. She heard his laughter in her ear and he squeezed her so hard she thought her ribs would crack.

Belatedly, she wriggled away, gasping with laughter and delight. "People are staring! Stop! Let me go before we both fall!"

He let her go just long enough to spring to the ground, then he grasped her waist and swung her down beside him. "How much?" Laurel demanded. "How much did you win?"

Seth stared at her for a moment, then burst into laughter. "You're not only greedy, you're shameless. A lot," he told her. "I won a lot." Taking her elbow, he started leading her through the crowd toward the tent.

"Well, I do think I have the right to know," she said, keeping her voice as restrained as she could. "After all, it was my horse, and my colors."

And your fifty dollars, Seth thought, amused.

He stopped and looked down at her. "The odds were ten to one," he said. "I put down two-fifty."

Arithmetic had always been one of Laurel's best skills, and she had the figures almost instantly; but it was a moment before she could speak the words. "Then that means —"

"Twenty-five hundred dollars," Seth said. Then he grinned. "And yes, it was my last dollar."

He offered her his arm again, but it was a moment before Laurel could lift her hand to take it, or trust her legs to move. She kept thinking about all that money; she kept seeing it in different-size piles, in various denominations, in all kinds of shapes and sizes and ways of distribution. And she knew it would be a very long time before she could think about anything else.

CHAPTER
Nine

The simplest thing for Seth to do, perhaps even the smartest would have been to take his twenty-five hundred — minus, of course, the five hundred that rightfully belonged to Laurel — and call himself ahead of the game. New Orleans couldn't be any hotter than this place, and a man could make quite a start for himself in New Orleans with two thousand dollars. Or San Francisco . . . there was a town. It was always cool in San Francisco.

Two thousand dollars was a lot of money, more than he had had on him at one time in quite a few years now. With that kind of grub stake there wasn't much he couldn't do; he could make life easy on himself for a change. The average man would be more than satisfied with a piece of change like that jangling around in his pocket.

But Seth wasn't the average man, and he had never done anything the easy way in his life. Two thousand dollars was a lot of money, but it wasn't a quarter of a million, which was roughly what

Seth expected the gold would amount to when uncovered. Of course, uncovering the gold at all was a long shot, but then so had Johnny Reb been. Seth knew that the smartest thing to do would be to quit while he was ahead, but the truth of the matter was that he simply did not know how. And leaving town now was not a serious option. He was enjoying his life as Seth Tait. He liked being respectable — at least partly so. To his surprise he'd liked driving the Sinclair ladies out to Chinatree, three fine ladies of the Old South under his temporary care. He'd liked having dinner in their dining room amid the heirlooms and family mementos. This whole new world was somehow familiar to him. Something about the past spoke deeply to him, and he hadn't expected that at all.

Walking into the Jockey Club's inner circle with Laurel on his arm, he'd felt proud and respectable. Respectable. The feeling was addictive, like drinking fine bourbon or pulling off a perfect robbery. There was a thrill to it, a heady rush of victory knowing that he was playing the part of an upstanding citizen and getting away with it. The funny thing was that it came so easily to him. Was this what the Colonel had wanted for him when he sent him back east? A life so different from what he'd known back then that he couldn't even have imagined it? If that's what the Colonel had intended, he'd done a good job preparing Seth for it, because nothing had ever come so easily to him in his life.

And there was Laurel, of course. She was a big part of it all, not only in the doors she opened for him but in the challenges she issued. She made it easy, and she made it hard. The best things in life were always that way.

Tonight he was going to give her a share of the money he'd won on Johnny Reb. Despite the incident over the fifty dollars, he had a feeling she would accept money from an honest horse race. How he knew that he couldn't say; it was just one of those instincts he was beginning to develop about her. Five hundred dollars would be a bonanza for the impoverished Sinclairs, and she and her family would be neatly off his conscience.

Conscience? He smiled wryly. Conscience wasn't usually one of his concerns. Maybe that was just a part of becoming respectable, and that was definitely Laurel's fault. He probably should stay away from her, but he needed her. Or rather, he needed the letter she had that would lead him to the gold.

Seth called for her in a cab a little before six. The sun was still bright and slanted blindingly through the waxy leaves of magnolias and tupelos that surrounded the little house on Lamboll, perfuming the hot air so heavily that it was hard to breathe. As he let himself onto the piazza and lifted the polished brass knocker on the weathered front door, Seth reflected that of all the strange situations he had found himself in, choking in this heat in a coat and tie just for the sake of calling on a woman and drinking sherry in a musty little parlor with her aunt was surely the strangest.

Laurel did not appear immediately, and it didn't occur to Seth until later that such was the proper protocol for a young lady and her suitor. It amused him to realize he was being treated like a suitor, almost as much as it amused him to think of Laurel as a proper young lady. Still, there was something appealing about it as well, just as there was something appealing about the dark hot room with its clutter of scarred heirlooms and battered treasures. He couldn't say he truly understood it, but he recognized, in a dim and uncomfortable way, the value of things like traditions and heirlooms — and memories.

Sophie chattered in that lively, schoolgirlish manner of hers about the old days of the Jockey Club and the gentlemen she had known whom she naively assumed were now close acquaintances of Seth's as well since he had been a guest of the Jockey Club. She talked about the grandeur and the pomp and the elegance with apparent ignorance that anything had changed. Though he had heard many of the same stories from Laurel that morning, Seth was not bored. He found, somewhat to his amazement, that he liked listening to the older woman talk; he liked her silly little aphorisms and her dulcet tones and her dimpling cheeks; he liked being able to relax and do nothing but nod and smile and occasionally murmur, "Yes ma'am" and to drink wine as smooth as silk and just as harmless. It occurred to Seth that the reason for that might have been that the only times he had felt safe enough to relax completely in years, perhaps in his whole life, were those moments he spent under the roof of the little house on Lamboll.

Within twenty minutes Laurel came down in the company of her cousin, looking impatient and a little put out and even prettier than she had looked that morning. The gown was the same, a deep rich purple that brought out the fire in her eyes and made her skin look like alabaster, nipping in her waist and adding a saucy thrust to her profile with its prominent bustle. But in the place of the wide bonnet she had worn that morning was a little scrap of lace and dried flowers that could hardly be called a hat; it was perched atop a gleaming upsweep of dark hair which was, apparently, the cause of Laurel's ill temper. Before they knew he was looking, Seth saw Caroline turn Laurel toward the mirror in the hallway and make a few quick adjustments to the hairdo. Laurel swept up a peacock-colored paisley shawl and strode into the room, buttoning her gloves, as Seth got to his feet.

"I'm ready," she announced, barely glancing at him.

Seth bowed, his eyes glinting with appreciation as they swept over her. "Miss Laurel, you look lovely."

Laurel gave him a suspicious glance, then bent to kiss her aunt's cheek. "We won't be late, auntie."

A look of uncertain consternation came over Sophie's face and she fluttered her handkerchief around her face. "Oh Laurel, I just don't know if I can approve. A young lady dining alone in a public place with a gentleman . . . I just don't know what people will *say*."

Laurel replied impatiently. "First of all, I'm hardly a young lady; and even if I were, times have changed since you were a girl, Aunt Sophie. As for what people will say, I'm sure they have much better things to discuss than where and with whom I dine; and if they don't, we can only feel sorry for them, can't we? Good night, dear."

She bent to kiss Sophie again and the older woman looked too dazed to reply. Seth bowed to her, and then to Caroline, and, taking his cue from Laurel, didn't linger.

Seth caught her arm as she strode down the walk. "Whoa, there. Nobody's after you; I checked."

Laurel looked a little embarrassed as she slowed her stride, and Seth kept his hand lightly on her arm. "I'm sorry you had to wait," she said. "Those two *will* make such a fuss about everything."

"I didn't mind; a man likes to think a woman's making a fuss for him. And you *do* look nice."

Seth had never had much chance to use flowery flattery and did not have a vast repertoire of compliments, but Laurel looked so surprised and so secretly, absurdly pleased that he immediately wished he had used a stronger word than "nice." She looked elegant, striking, bold enough to take a man's breath away in her purple dress and lush, bright shawl and with her dark hair gleaming. She looked as though she should be with someone important, proud and confident and as rich as polished silver. When Seth looked at her he almost felt a moment's disorientation, as though this grand-looking high-spirited woman could not possibly be with him, followed by a stab of fierce possessive pride because she was, and it was right that she should be. But he didn't know how to tell her that and wasn't at all sure he wanted her to know it.

Laurel avoided his eyes as he helped her into the cab, and only when they were under way did she recover herself enough to inquire, "Where are we going?"

"The hotel dining room, if that's all right with you." He couldn't resist adding, in a voice that was as bland as he could possibly make it, "I was assured it was a perfectly respectable place to take a lady for supper, but considering the source I could have been misinformed."

Laurel inquired curiously, just as he had expected, "Who was your source?"

He grinned. "Miss Elsie."

Laurel stared at him, shock and outrage warring in her eyes and mingling with — again as Seth had expected — no small amount of curiosity. "You went to — you asked *her* — you had the audacity, the impudence, to ask the advice of a . . ." She swallowed the word. "On what would be the proper way to entertain *me?*"

He replied, just for the sake of the expression on her face, "I'm a stranger in town. I have to ask someone. Was she wrong?"

Laurel continued to look at him as though he were some alien and fascinating form of beast she could not quite decide whether to admire or fear. The battle between offended dignity and rampant curiosity was so plain in her expression that it was all Seth could do to keep from laughing out loud. At last it was the curiosity that won out, and she said, "What were you doing there, anyway?"

Seth replied, eyes twinkling, "I don't need Miss Elsie to tell me that's *not* the kind of question a lady would ask."

Laurel's cheeks went scarlet. She jerked her eyes away, and she didn't speak to him again until they entered the dining room of the Charleston Hotel.

It was every bit as elegant as Laurel remembered it, and even more so because this time she was entering as a paying guest, not a volunteer at a charity booth. This time the tables were fragrant with flowers and draped with heavy linen instead of cheesecloth, and they were glittering with candles. And this time she was entering on the arm of a man who made heads turn. The looks the two of them garnered sent a curious thrill of excitement through her.

She knew that word of her latest indiscretion — marching up the stairs of this very hotel to Seth Tait's room — had no doubt spread quickly and expected that eyebrows would be raised when she appeared in the hotel dining room on the arm of that very man. And she knew that she looked fine in her purple gown and bright shawl, and Seth Tait was, by anyone's standards, a good looking man. Still, it was the *way* people looked at them that set her heart beating a little faster with an odd sense of pride and triumph.

The dining room of the Charleston Hotel was filled with the wealthy, the well-traveled, the interlopers and survivors; they were brash or they were refined, but they were all comfortable with their positions. When Seth and Laurel walked in, however, they were suddenly no longer comfortable. Conversations broke for a split second. Eyes were raised and then quickly lowered and conversations resumed a little too hurriedly. What Laurel saw in those quick stares was not only curiosity, but the smallest, almost undetectable trace of fear . . . almost as though they were looking at a wild animal encountered unexpectedly on a familiar path. It took Laurel a moment to realize it was Seth who caused those looks. Seth, who with his smooth, graceful movements and his long, tight muscles and his cool, alert gaze was as out of place in the over-dressed dining room as a tiger in the marketplace, who entered a room and took command. Yet it felt natural to be on his arm, sharing in the looks he received — neither one of them belonging and both of them enjoying it. The pleasure that swelled within her as they were escorted to their table was heady.

Why, she thought, a little dazed with all that was rushing through her head, we're two of a kind, just as he said. It doesn't seem possible, and no one would believe it if I told them, but it's true. He smiled at her a little as she was seated, a cool, dry smile that, on any other man, would have flustered or annoyed her. Laurel met his eyes, and her heartbeat lost its excited pace, settling into a steady, certain rhythm. She looked at him, and she felt confident; not comfortable or relaxed or even at ease, but sure. She looked at him, and though the thought had not yet consciously formed, she must have known even then what she was going to do.

Supper was very strange. Laurel was not sure she had ever been served dishes so elegant, but she hardly tasted what she ate. Under most circumstances she could not have thought of a greater treat than to be able to spy on the rich and nouveau riche, but she was scarcely aware of the people who shared the dining room with them that night. She wasn't even sure whether or not she and Seth talked, and if so what was said. There was a queer tightness in her stomach, a heat in her hands, a kind of quivering in her throat — all the symptoms of impatience, nervousness, and intense concentration.

She was more annoyed than she might otherwise have been when, as the iced coffees were served, Keith Peterson came over to their table. She hadn't even noticed he was in the restaurant, but Seth didn't look surprised. Neither, however, did he rise, as a gentleman would have done, or even pretend to be gracious when Peterson said, a little too loudly, "Well, Mr. Tait, looks like your instincts paid off. Doing a little celebrating, are you?"

Laurel couldn't help noticing how Seth, even seated, looked bigger and more powerful than the other man who was standing. And he barely glanced at him as he replied, "I hope you didn't bet on your own horse, Peterson. That's not good business."

The stain of color in Peterson's cheeks was more explicit than a reply, but his smile remained fixed. "Win or lose, it's all in a day's work," he answered. "Maybe only one of us walked away with money in his pocket, but both of us ended up in the same place tonight, didn't we? So I wouldn't be getting too uppity about it if I were you. You never know when you might need a friend." He nodded to Laurel, said, "Ma'am," and walked away.

Seth frowned after him, looking as though he wasn't sure whether or not he had been insulted. "What did he mean by that?"

Laurel made an elaborate brushing gesture at the sleeve of her gown. "That man always makes me want to wash my hands. What? Oh, he was talking about the party, I suppose. After every race the Old Guard Jockey Club has a reception. They might have to let people like Peterson into the club, but who they invite to the party is another matter altogether."

Seth's eyes were shaded as he looked into the tall dark glass of coffee. "I see."

Laurel lifted one shoulder. "It's really a pathetic little affair — lemonade and cookies and a string trio that couldn't carry a tune in a bucket, but I guess it's their way of keeping the old days alive — and keeping people like Peterson in their place."

Seth said, without looking at her, "I guess you got an invite to this party."

Laurel sipped the coffee, concentrating on the luxury. It was dark and rich, and good coffee and ice to cool it with were two things Laurel could not afford. "Why yes, I think I did."

"But I didn't."

The off-handed reply she had been about to make died unspoken, and Laurel looked at him more carefully. An unexpected understanding — or what she thought might be understanding — was beginning to dawn. She said, "Does it matter?"

He looked at her. Behind the eyes that were almost opaque there was the faintest trace of a lingering disturbance, as though he were thinking about something other than his words implied. "The way you were talking this morning, not much else does matter in this town besides who you are and who you know and where you get invited."

Laurel's impulse was to laugh, but she repressed it quickly, knowing that if she did laugh he would too and the subject would be dismissed.

She didn't want to dismiss it.

She said instead, "I wouldn't think a man like you would care about things like that."

The curve of his lips was faintly bitter — so very faintly, in fact, that she later thought she might have misinterpreted the gesture — but his voice was perfectly bland as he replied, "How do you know what kind of man I am, Miss Laurel?" Then he tasted his coffee, made a slight face, and put the cup down again. "Besides, sometimes knowing the right people is the only way to get what you want. Being cut out makes it harder to get to know those people."

And that was it, the opening she had been waiting for. "And what is it you want, Mr. Tait?" she said.

The smile relaxed, becoming speculative and thoughtful as he looked at her. He was silent for so long that Laurel felt compelled to add, "You promised to tell me if I got you in the race. I expect you to be a man of your word."

"Oh, yes ma'am," he assured her, "you can count on that."

His drawl was soft and low and there was a subtle gleam in his eyes that made her pulses beat just a fraction faster.

"I want a lot of things," he went on. "I'm just sitting here wondering which one you'd be likely to enjoy hearing about."

Laurel kept her tone even. "How about the one that brought you to Charleston? What do you want here?"

He gave a dismissive half-shrug, but his eyes, his smile, never left her. "That's easy. What I want is a home, a place to belong. What I came here for was to find it."

Laurel was not so gullible as to believe that and she could tell by the glint in his eyes that he didn't expect her to. The frown of annoyance was creeping to the surface before he even finished speaking — and suddenly it stopped. Because there was a moment — just the briefest fraction of a moment — when she thought she saw something in his eyes or heard it in his voice, and she did believe him. Just for a moment.

But even as she registered that fragment of truth she was sly enough to realize that letting Seth know what she had seen would be an enormous tactical error . . . at least at that point. So she shrugged elaborately and lifted her coffee glass. "Well, if you're not going to tell me the truth I suppose there's nothing I can do. But I did keep my side of the bargain, Mr. Tait, and I believe you owe me something for that."

He murmured, "My undying gratitude wouldn't be enough, I guess."

She gave him a controlled little smile. "You guess correctly."

"Well, let's see if I can afford your price."

Laurel couldn't believe he was making it so easy for her — and at the same time she had never imagined it would be so difficult. She was certain she had had to make more humiliating requests, entered into touchier negotiations, and endured far more discomfort for the sake of her family over the years, but at that moment nothing had ever seemed more difficult than looking into Seth Tait's lazily twinkling eyes and steeling herself to ask him for money.

She took a sip of her coffee; with all the courage she possessed she held his gaze. She said, "I'd like to arrange a loan, Mr. Tait. Five hundred dollars."

Earlier in the evening Seth had thought about easy ways, and if he had been a believing man this would have been a sign as to exactly how he should handle the matter of Miss Laurel Laughton. He had the money in his pocket, wrapped in a piece of white paper to keep it separate from the rest, and he had had some vague notion of giving it to her here in the hotel dining room so she couldn't refuse without making a scene. Five hundred dollars was set aside for her in his coat pocket. She had just asked to borrow five hundred dollars. Why couldn't he do things the easy way?

He leaned back in his chair, regarding her with thoughtful amusement. "I'm not sure a woman who can go from fifty to five hundred dollars in debt in less than a week is such a good risk. Looks like those principles of yours were a little more expensive than you reckoned on."

An angry stain of color touched Laurel's cheeks and her jaw tightened. "Insults are cheap, sir, and if that's all you have to offer . . ." She gathered up her skirts in preparation to stand.

He lifted his hand in a lazy gesture of deterrence. The enjoyment in his eyes was shameless and complete and Laurel withstood it without blinking. Let him, she thought. Let him laugh, let him make fun, let him get whatever satisfaction a man like him gets from a situation like this and let it be at my expense . . . only let him say yes.

He said, "I didn't say we couldn't talk about it. But that's a lot of money, and I need to know some things."

Laurel's heart gave a cautious little skip of hope, but she kept her voice calm. "Naturally. I'll answer whatever I can."

Seth reached into his pocket and felt the packet of money. His fingers slid over it and withdrew a cigar instead. "What's the money for?"

"Apparently my uncle had some outstanding debts of which I was unaware when he died. One of them was a lien against the house, which is due in thirty days. The amount is five hundred dollars."

Several things went through Seth's mind then; most prominent among them was the memory of Laurel as he had first met her, arguing with a whore for the sake of a hundred dollars. A flash of anger went through him that wasn't entirely rational, and he thought, She wasn't meant for this. What would Augustus Sinclair think if he could see what his daughter had been reduced to, begging from a whore and bargaining with a thief? What would the Colonel think?

And was any of it Seth's problem?

He fingered the cigar, realizing in a vague way that it probably wouldn't be proper to light up in a place like this, with ladies present. That was just a little something else he had picked up from the Colonel, along with table manners and good grammar and a passable penmanship. It occurred to him suddenly that the Colonel was the only real gentleman he had ever known, and Seth wasn't sure how smart it would be to rely on his instincts in a situation like this when those instincts had been taught to him by an outlaw. Still, he wondered what the Colonel's advice would be to him now.

He was almost certain that even the Colonel would have told him to take the money from his pocket, pass it quietly to the lady under the table, and speak not another word.

Seth said, "Then I reckon you'd be offering me a mortgage on the house, as collateral."

The residue of uncomfortable color that still stained Laurel's cheeks drained abruptly. Collateral. She could not believe she had forgotten something as important as that. Collateral meant, as she very well knew, that if she were unable to repay the loan — and how in the world did she think she could? — he would take the house. She hardly knew this man and what she did know was not to his credit; how could she risk the very roof over their heads with him?

She said quickly, "No. The house — it isn't mine to mortgage, it belongs to Aunt Sophie. I couldn't do that."

He nodded soberly, tapping the end of the cigar on the table. "What, then?"

The words were out before she knew it. "Chinatree. I could offer you Chinatree."

There was a kind of quickening in Seth's eyes that sent a shaft of dismay through Laurel, an alertness that was gone as quickly as it had appeared, leaving nothing in his expression but bland indifference. "I didn't know it was for sale."

"It's not," she said harshly. Her fists tightened under the table. "I meant as collateral."

The amusement came back into his face. "The way you handle money, it amounts to the same thing. But a broken-down cemetery and a yard full of weeds and snakes? I don't think so. Don't you have anything I could use?"

A calmness stole over her as she played her last card. "Yes," she said quietly. "I have a great deal, I think."

He lifted an inquiring brow. "Like what?" He reached for his coffee glass, then frowned, muttering, "How can you drink this stuff? You reckon I could get it heated up?"

Laurel took a breath. "Like your own membership in the Jockey Club. Like an invitation to parties even the governor of the state can't get into. Like acceptance, respectability. A home."

Seth's expression was amused, but his eyes were interested. He had forgotten about the waiter he had started to hail. He said, "I don't know which to ask first — how, or why. Matter of fact, I'm not sure I really want to know the answer to either of them."

Laurel folded her hands atop the table and held his gaze. "The why should be obvious. Money. You have it; I need it. As for the how . . . it's really quite simple."

She drew a breath, but she didn't really need the fortification, or the time to reconsider. Her voice was amazingly calm as she finished, "You'll merely marry me."

For the longest time Seth simply looked at her. He did not blink, or smile, or change his expression in any way. Laurel, for her part, didn't even breathe, nor did she feel capable of it. There had been a moment, when the words left her mouth, that she had been terrifyingly certain he would laugh, and she thought she would die if he laughed. Now she realized this dead-faced silence was much worse. Her courage deserted her beneath the quiet gaze of those steady eyes, against the unchanging features of this stranger, beneath the power he exuded. She must have been mad. She surely hadn't meant it. How could she have thought this would ever work?

But when he said, at last, in the mildest of tones, "Is that right?" Laurel didn't back down. There was still some steel thread of desperation within her forcing her to hold on, insisting it could work.

She nodded, once, and said, again quite calmly, "Men and women have married for less worthy reasons, I don't doubt. I have something you want and you have something I want. It seems like a perfectly reasonable partnership to me."

Though his expression was still masked, his tone was too pleasant not to be disguising amusement. "The last time the subject came up," he reminded her, "it seems to me you said you'd never marry again."

She replied flatly, "The last time the subject came up I wasn't about to lose my home."

He looked down at the cigar, which he still balanced between his fingers, and the easy tone of his voice seemed forced as he said, "You'd throw away your whole life for five hundred dollars?"

"Without that five hundred dollars," Laurel replied evenly, "I won't have much of a life, now will I? Besides," she felt compelled to add, "It's more than that. It's —"

He glanced up at her. "The other two thousand."

Laurel swallowed hard. "Yes," she admitted, "in part."

"It's not going to last forever," Seth pointed out. "And I wasn't lying when I said that was all I had. What happens when it's gone?"

"You'll get more," Laurel told him without flinching. "Men like you always do. And as I said, that's only part of it."

She fully expected him to ask what the other part was, and she could feel a panic starting because she wasn't at all sure she could explain it, even to herself. But he didn't say anything. He simply looked at her, and there was no amusement in his eyes now at all. His eyes, in fact, held all the warmth and animation of a shaded swamp, and just looking at him caused the prickle of a chill to touch Laurel's spine. Then he said, very quietly, "I think you're serious."

Laurel would have answered, but abruptly, her throat was too dry. And she did not have to say anything; the truth was in her eyes.

Seth replaced the cigar in his pocket, and once again his fingers brushed the packet. Enough, he thought. It's gone far enough. For once in your life do the right thing, and it just might turn out to be the easiest thing too . . . He withdrew two bills, enough to pay for the meal, and laid them on the table. Then he stood up and came around to Laurel's chair.

Laurel's heart started to pound the moment she felt his hands settle the shawl on her shoulders. It couldn't have been his touch, brief and charged though it was; it must surely have been a delayed reaction to the incredible thing she had just done. Or it might have been a glimpse of his face — its strong lines and hard planes a reminder of the power of his masculinity, the shuttered expression a graphic sign of how little she knew about him. When he offered his arm — a belated gesture, almost an afterthought — Laurel was embarrassed because her palms were damp.

He did not say a word, except to the driver when he instructed him to stop as they approached The Battery. Laurel, who by this time was in a quandary of uncertainty and regret, was shocked; she had expected him to deposit her on her front doorstep like a naughty child who had wandered too far from adult supervision, and she was trying frantically to find some way to salvage both her dignity and, possibly, the proposition as well.

His hand was hard on her elbow as he guided her away from the carriage and toward the parklands that overlooked the bay. His step was measured, but Laurel could feel the tension in his muscles, the coiled strength in his fingers. And though she refused to be intimidated by him, there was something very natural and very female within her that reacted to such silent, effortless masculinity with a whisper of fear.

They were not the only strollers. Night had not fully fallen, but the twilight was rich and the shadows soft and deep. The ocean was like an indigo scarf dropped carelessly on the ground, rippling in the wind, and though the night was still sultry, the breeze brought the faint taste of fish and salt that felt cool on the skin. Occasionally a carriage would creak slowly by, and now and then a scrap of murmured conversation would be carried across the way, or perhaps a snatch of laughter. But for the most part they were alone. Seth did not speak for a long time.

After a while he stopped and lit up the cigar. The odor of sulfur and tobacco was pungent for a moment, then was carried away by the breeze. He said, "You don't even know me. I could turn out to be a wife beater."

It was such a relief to hear his voice, his tone casual and unconcerned, that Laurel's nervousness left her in a rush. She replied, turning to face him levelly, "I'd like to see you try."

After a moment he smiled. "Maybe I'll run off and leave you in a month's time. How would you feel about that?"

"As long as the note on the house is paid," Laurel replied practically, "I suppose I wouldn't feel much about it at all. But I don't think you'll do that."

"Why not?"

He touched her arm lightly, indicating the path that curved near the stone wall overlooking the ocean, but he didn't touch her again as they started walking.

Laurel said, measuring her words carefully, "If it were that easy for you to walk away from whatever it was that brought you here, you would have left already. Besides, I think you do want what I can give you."

"Respectability?" The ashes of his cigar made a fleeting red arc as he flipped them toward the sea. "If you have enough money you don't need respectability."

"But if you don't have it, money will never be enough."

Seth glanced at her, amusement glinting in his eyes. "So with you at my side, you're saying I could have both."

Laurel lifted her chin a fraction. "Possibly."

"It never occurred to you that if you married me you'd probably be giving up what little respectability . . ." he emphasized the word slightly, "you have left?"

"I don't know why you say that. You're not a Yankee or white trash, which puts you way ahead of the pack as far as the Old Guard of this town are concerned. As long as you don't already have a wife hidden away out west somewhere, I can't think of any reason why marrying you would be anything less than acceptable."

Seth murmured, "No, I don't have a wife already. But somehow I don't think even that would stop you."

Laurel thought about it for a moment. "No," she admitted. "As long as I didn't know about it beforehand, it wouldn't matter at all."

They had moved around the path to a place where the natural curve of the stone wall formed a recessed alcove. A small bench had been set there, and during the day it would be a pleasant place to sit in the shade and catch the ocean breeze. As the last rays of the sun were absorbed into the sea, however, the little alcove became a dark, shadowy spot, secluded from the path and almost invisible to the passing eye. Laurel was sure they had arrived in this spot by accident, just as she was sure that if she turned and tried to retrace her steps now Seth wouldn't let her. So she turned, with a studied nonchalance, and leaned against the wall to look out over the bay. Seth stood close, resting his arm atop the wall so near to hers that their fingers brushed. Her heart-beat accelerated, but only a little.

After a moment Seth tossed the remnants of his cigar over the wall, and he said, "Maybe respectability's not all I want from you, Laurel." He turned, looking at her. "I don't know what your ideas are, but as far as I'm concerned a marriage is a marriage, in every sense of the word."

Now the pace, and the weight, of Laurel's heart increased noticeably. She tried to tell herself it was influenced by hope, because he had spoken as though he were ready to agree to the marriage, but she knew it was more than that.

She, too, turned away from the wall to look at him, and when she did she discovered their chests were only inches apart. She had to take a step backward to look up at him, and she felt as though that small backward step put her at a definite disadvantage. Her heart was beating very hard now.

"Naturally," she said in her most detached, most modulated voice, "I realize that you are somewhat attracted to me — I dare say I wouldn't have had the courage to make my suggestion if you weren't. And it's not as though I were a maiden. Of course I understand what marriage means and —"

"What about you?"

There was a certain roughness to his voice and he took a step closer. The aroma of cigar smoke and leather teased her senses, overwhelming her with masculinity. It was little wonder she was flustered, but she hated the stammer in her voice as she replied, "I — I don't know —"

"What do you think about me? Because I'll be damned if I'll share a bed with a woman who'd be just as glad to shoot me in my sleep. And seeing as how you've already said it's my money you're after, maybe I shouldn't be putting ideas in your head."

She stared at him in the grainy shadows, her embarrassment momentarily forgotten in her astonishment. "Certainly I'd do no such thing! And it's not just your money, it's . . ." Now she was stammering again, but she could not retreat beneath the intensity of his gaze. His eyes had an almost animal quality, reflecting hidden lights and pinning her beneath them, and she couldn't back away. "I think — I think we would suit together, better than most. We think alike. You're not shocked by me and whatever you do to shock me — well, I think I can learn to live with it. I hope you don't expect me to say I'm fond of you because I hardly know you, but I do enjoy your company — most of the time — some of the time, and I think I could *learn* to be fond of you . . . and there's no point in pretending that I find you physically repulsive, because you know you're not, and that I don't, not that such things matter . . ."

At some point he had placed his hands on her arms, and as she spoke he moved closer until now his face, his mouth were only a fraction of an inch from hers. Laurel's back was pressed into the stone wall, she couldn't move any farther. Seth said, "I'm glad." And he brought his mouth down on hers.

The movement should not have, but it caught

her by surprise. Her gasp of pleasure was caught by his mouth and a hot rush of surrender began deep in her abdomen and spread upward; she welcomed it. And then, between the space of one breath and the next and without any warning at all, he did the most astonishing thing: he pushed his tongue inside her mouth.

The sensation was so shocking, so heated and evocative, that Laurel was for a moment as helpless as a fly in amber; muscles weak, head spinning, paralyzed with the intense strangeness of the feeling. And then a shaft of alarm penetrated, a thin thread of common decency; she lifted her hands to his chest and tried, though without much real energy, to push him away. His hands closed on hers firmly, holding her still, his thighs pushed hard against hers, and his tongue explored the inner recesses of her mouth in a slow and thorough imitation of the mating act which should have been obscene, which certainly was obscene, but somehow it didn't feel so to Laurel.

He took her breath away, he left her helpless and mindless and dazed to the very fiber of her soul. He filled her with uncertainty and expectation and tiny, wavering threads of fear — fear of him, fear of herself, fear of what was happening between them. Her breasts ached, there was heat low in her abdomen, and this intimacy that he forced upon her — no, that she accepted willingly, even hungrily — changed something deep within her, and that frightened her too.

Her lips were raw and swollen and she could

still taste him inside her when he moved his mouth away. The roughness of his cheek abraded hers, scraped across her sensitive lips, and his hands were hard on hers. His breathing was harsh and uneven, and he whispered, "Shall I marry you Laurel? Is that what you want?"

Her heart was pounding with such a force that she thought she would be ill. Only the gripping strength of his hands on hers, only the fact that her body was pinned between his and the wall, kept her on her feet. Almost without volition she moved her parted lips across his face, tasting the roughness of his skin, the salt of his perspiration, the heat that flamed from him. And she whispered in a gasp so broken and breathless she thought he couldn't hear, "Yes." Again, "Yes."

His hands tightened sharply and he lifted his head, looking down at her with such burning intensity that she had to focus through the daze; she had to look back at him. He said softly, "I'm not a gentleman. You know that. If I'm your husband I'm going to act like one, and maybe you won't always like the things I do to you."

Laurel made herself hold his gaze until her breath was almost even, and then she answered, "You once said — I might like it if I was doing it for money."

There was a suspended moment in which the words echoed with the cold dead sound of pennies falling into a deep well. Seth's hands released hers, and he stepped away. And then, incredulously, Laurel saw the faint, dry upward curve of his lips, and he shook his head slowly. "What kind of woman did I get myself tangled up with anyway?"

Her heart started beating again. "Maybe . . . you should ask yourself what kind of man you are, to do so."

He looked at her without replying for a long time. Then he said, "Tomorrow morning, will you change your mind?"

Laurel's throat went dry, and all she could do was shake her head.

"A week from now?" His tone was sharp and his eyes narrowed as he looked down at her through the filter of darkness. "What about if somebody leaves five hundred dollars in a potted plant on your front porch next week, will you still want to marry me?"

Laurel knew she should think about that, she knew her whole future hinged on the answer to that, but she couldn't think at all. His heat was still on her skin and his taste was still inside her mouth and all she could do was blurt, "What do you want me to say? Yes, I think I would — I don't know! I shouldn't but I think I would . . ." She pressed her fingers to her temples, half turning away. "Why ask me that, it doesn't matter!"

"No." His voice was odd, and quiet. "It doesn't."

He turned for a moment and looked out over the sea. Laurel saw his hand reach inside his coat and linger there for a moment. He brought out a cigar, and studied it as he spoke. "You could make things easy for me. Maybe I could make things a little easier for you too. I reckon it wouldn't be the worst deal I've ever struck."

And then he turned. The expression in his eyes was severe, and his lips were tight. "But don't expect too much from me Laurel. And you've got to promise to remember, whatever happens, that this was your idea."

Now that the moment was here a strange calm stole over Laurel, just as it had in the restaurant when she had known what she had to do. Her heartbeat was steady and sure and her breathing was almost normal. She searched Seth's face in the shadows without any trepidation whatsoever. "Does this mean we have a bargain?"

There was a moment when she thought that, after all, he would say no. And then that familiar, dry ghost of a smile appeared on his face again, and he tucked the cigar back into his pocket. "Yeah," he said, "We've got a bargain. And may God have mercy on both our miserable souls."

CHAPTER
Ten

On the long train trip across the country Edgar Cassidy had plenty of time for reflection. One of the things reflected on was how oddly patterned, almost deliberately ironic, life was.

A twenty-year search had ended three weeks ago at a wooden marker on a desert grave. A hat, a saddle, a holstered gun were all that remained of the man who had tormented Cassidy for most of his adult life, who had been his quest, his obsession, his reason for living. The way Cassidy figured it, he had missed Colonel Ike by less than two days. All these years of searching, and he had lost by only a matter of hours. When he found that grave in the desert, when he read the crudely carved words on the marker and knew what they meant, he had wanted to scream his rage to the heavens, he had wanted to fling himself down and tear away the dirt and stones with his bare hands. He had even thought, for one brief and fierce moment, of turning his pistol on himself.

It was over, and he had lost.

Only it wasn't over. He realized that when he learned that Peach Brady had disappeared. A man was dead, his partner gone . . . the conclusion was obvious: Colonel Ike had not taken his secret to his grave.

Nothing else would send a seasoned outlaw like Peach Brady hightailing it back east, and that was exactly where he had gone, even though it took a while for Cassidy to pick up his trail. Brady had made a career of dodging the law, picking his hiding holes and learning how to lie low; and there wasn't a man in the west who could cast a shorter shadow when it was necessary. But going back east was a mistake. Brady was in Cassidy's territory now.

Edgar Cassidy reached into his pocket and took out the folded poster. Nobody had ever taken a photograph of Colonel Ike or Peach Brady — the old colonel was too smart for that — but the descriptions of them were accurate enough. Once he had figured out what Brady was up to, he hadn't had much trouble tracking him across the Mississippi. The big bonus had come, of course, when he discovered on a hotel register in St. Louis the name Brady was using now. Tait. Seth Tait. At that point Cassidy became firmly convinced that his theory was right. Colonel Ike had told his partner about the gold. And Peach Brady was going back for it.

That was where the pattern came in, the grand irony, the strange and magnificent plan that mastered the universe. For Peach Brady hadn't just disappeared. He had gone home. The search had brought Edgar Cassidy full circle — back to Charleston, South Carolina, where it had all begun.

Caroline heard the door knocker but did not allow herself to be distracted from her work. The morning room where she sat had been transformed from a once pleasant little parlor into a storehouse of makeshift shelves, sandbags, paints and chemicals. But it was at the back of the house, away from the flow of traffic, and the light was good. Though her mother often fussed about the mess she made, Laurel did not begrudge her the space, and Caroline was most content when hidden away in her little cubbyhole, hard at work.

Distantly she heard Peter's voice, greeting her mother and asking for her, but Caroline's concentration was intense as she carefully molded a mixture of zinc oxide, potassium and silicate over the long crack in a delicate china saucer. Out of the corner of her eye she saw Peter enter the room and stand quietly watching her, but she dared not look up to even smile at him. The smallest shift in the amount of pressure she applied to the fissure now could mean another hour's work. She smoothed the putty-like glue out until it blended into the original china finish, adhering as it began to harden to hold the two pieces together. When the consistency of the material became too dry to manipulate, Caroline carefully placed the edge of the saucer upright in a box of sand, where it would finish drying and, later, be sanded and repainted. With a small sigh of satisfaction she wiped her hands on the heavy workman's apron she wore and turned to Peter with a smile.

"Come on in, Peter," she said, "I'm finished here for a while."

The small shake of his head was filled with admiration as he shifted a box of paint pigments from the faded green loveseat and sat down. "It always amazes me," he said, "your patience."

"With that kind of work one has to be patient," she replied simply. "There's no choice." But then her smile took on a slightly wistful, almost bitter tinge as she added, "But that's true about a great many things, isn't it?"

Peter frowned a little, uncertain what she meant. And not knowing how to respond, he came to her work table, examining the chipped teapot awaiting attention and the matching saucer in the sand box. "The Old Guard trying to hold on to the past?" he remarked lightly. "Some Charleston Grande Dame trying to save the last vestige of the family's heirlooms?"

Caroline shared his smile. "Mrs. Connel's whole set of Old Paris china is almost gone. She was telling me her husband ordered it from France right before the war. They buried it when the shelling began and hardly lost a teacup, but over the years her grandchildren have done more damage than the Yankees. Of course she can't pay much to have it repaired."

"Of course not. And so you give yourself away."

"Now, Peter," she chided gently, "don't scold. You know I get a great deal more pleasure than money from what I do. There's satisfaction in knowing I'm helping people hold on to their memories, preserving the past."

"And most of those people you're talking about would be a lot better off if they'd forget the past and pay a little more attention to the future."

"Now you sound like Laurie."

"Who, I've always said, is probably the most sensible woman I've ever known. Which is why . . ." He took a paper from his pocket and unfolded it with a meaningful look. "I found this note from you so puzzling. What in the world has this Seth Tait done to have gotten you so upset?"

Caroline sighed. "Oh, dear. I was afraid I was doing the wrong thing. I'm not upset, Peter, truly I'm not, and he hasn't done anything untoward that I know of. I'm sure I must be making a mountain out of a molehill but I simply didn't know who else to ask. Sit down, won't you, and let's talk?"

Peter knew it was difficult for Caroline to get up and down and equally uncomfortable for her to look up at him while he was standing above her. He immediately cursed his own thoughtlessness and resumed his place on the loveseat. Caroline turned in her chair to face him, her hands folded tightly atop her apron-covered lap.

"Please don't misunderstand, Peter," Caroline said earnestly. "I have nothing against Mr. Tait. He's really quite charming and he's been so good to us —"

"The man hardly knows you," Peter said sharply. "I hardly think it behooves him to be 'good to you.' In fact, if you ask me his entire behavior has been a little out of line for a gentleman, which Seth Tait obviously is not."

Caroline looked distressed. "Then you have heard talk — about Laurel and him. That's what worries me, Peter. You know I would never question Laurel's judgment or motives and she has been taking care of all of us for so long that I wouldn't dare to presume, but . . ." And now her cheeks went deep red. "There *are* unscrupulous men about who — who prey on unsuspecting females, and Laurel seems quite — well, taken with Mr. Tait's charm, which as I've mentioned is considerable, and I can't help worrying."

Peter did not know which he found more astonishing: the fact that Caroline even knew about unscrupulous men and the designs they might have on innocent women, or the image of Laurel Sinclair as an unsuspecting female. But he had heard talk — most particularly about the outcome of the Jockey Club race; and even without Caroline's note, he had intended to have a stern talk with Laurel about her behavior. He could not forget what Caroline didn't even suspect: how and where Laurel had really met Seth Tait. Peter had no doubt that Laurel had some scheme brewing regarding Seth Tait, but whatever it was had gone far enough if it was worrying Caroline.

He said gently, "Laurel has always been able to take care of herself, Caroline. I really don't think

231

there's any need for you to worry."

But the troubled frown on Caroline's brow only deepened. She looked down at her hands. "I think . . . well, I think Laurel is interested in him."

"In what way?"

"In a romantic way." Caroline looked up at him, distress darkening her eyes and tightening her hands in her lap. "Peter, she's made a point of going out with him without a chaperone. People have seen them together at the horse race and afterward, alone in the hotel dining room. I know people are talking. Mama even heard the gossip at her Wednesday Bible meeting. But that's not what bothers me; people have always talked about Laurel, and she doesn't care — sometimes I think she even enjoys it. It's the way *Laurel* talks about him, and the way she looks when he's around . . . and the way he looks at her."

Caroline's voice fell on this last, and her eyes dropped. "The color in her cheeks was so bright it almost looked as though one could warm one's hands over it. She finished in a muffled tone, "I know you must think I'm the silliest fool who ever lived, and forward as well to be speaking to you of such things, but sometimes, where a gentleman is concerned, even the most sensible lady isn't always — sensible."

It took a moment for Peter to find his voice, mostly because he was fighting the urge to leave his seat and close the distance between them, to clutch her hands fiercely and assure her that the last thing he thought her to be was silly, or a fool

. . . and because he was wondering if it were possible, even by the remotest stretch of the imagination, that Caroline might sometimes feel less than sensible when she thought of him, and was wishing that she would meet his eyes, so that he might read the truth.

But he allowed himself that foolishness for only a minute. Caroline had come to him for help, she needed something that only he could give, and that in itself was more than he could have dared ask for. He had an excuse to see her, to be with her, and even though he was sure her concern for Laurel was misplaced, he wasn't at all averse to doing what he could to discredit Seth Tait.

He said gently, "I do think you're worrying unnecessarily about Laurel, but the way that man appeared out of nowhere and suddenly attached himself to her, to all of you really . . ." He frowned a little. "To tell the truth, I've been a little suspicious of him myself from the first."

Caroline looked relieved. "Then you don't think I'm being foolish?"

Peter smiled and reached forward to pat her hand. "How could I think you're ever foolish about anything? Laurel might not thank either of us for interfering, but I know you're only doing it because you love her."

A new color came into Caroline's cheeks as she glanced down at his hand, which now covered hers lightly and didn't move. She murmured, "And you do too. Love her, I mean."

Slowly, Peter withdrew his hand, and sat back.

"Yes," he admitted. "Laurel's always been like a sister to me."

Caroline glanced up at him, but whatever expression was in her eyes was too fleeting for him to read, for she quickly looked away again. Peter could see he had made her uncomfortable and he cursed himself for it. He went on in a brisk, businesslike tone, "The fact is, as soon as I got your note I put some wheels in motion. I'd like to know a thing or two about this Mr. Tait myself. There are ways to trace people like that, and I have the contacts to do it, but it may take some time."

When Caroline smiled at him, looking so grateful and relieved, Peter hoped it would take a very long time indeed.

"Oh, thank you Peter. I knew I could count on you. And you don't think it's too bad of us, do you? Will Laurel be very angry?"

"Laurel," he assured her, "will never find out. And you know she would do the same or more if she were worried about either one of us."

That thought had apparently not occurred to Caroline, and it seemed to cheer her enormously. "You're right, of course. Peter, you *are* good to help me like this!"

Impulsively, she extended both her hands to him, and he was quickly on his feet, helping her up. "Now let's find Mama and persuade her to join us for lemonade outside. It's cool in the back garden and Lacey made some tea cakes this morning."

That was where Laurel found them a half hour later: in the back garden, sipping lemonade in the spattered shade of a mimosa. She was somewhat taken aback at Peter's presence, but then decided it was just as well. She might as well get it all over with at once, and Peter, she well knew, would cause her the most trouble.

Seth had wondered whether she would change her mind, and perhaps he was right to do so. Laurel had awakened the morning after the incredible events at the Jockey Club — and the even more incredible ones on the Battery afterward — in a prickle of cold sweat, almost breathless with the impact of what she had done. If there had been another way — if someone *had* left five hundred dollars under a flowerpot at that moment — Laurel was sure she would have backed out. But no miracle was forthcoming, and as she had lain there with the yellow shafts of sunlight creeping slowly over her rumpled cotton sheets, trying to imagine what it would be like to have a man's long muscled form sharing that bed with her — then quickly trying not to imagine — the prickling shock and dread gradually left her and was replaced by something which, even at this moment, she couldn't quite define.

An hour earlier she and Seth had gone to the county justice to arrange for the marriage ceremony, which would be a week from Monday in his office.

"It would be so much nicer," Sophie was complaining as she sipped her lemonade, "if we could have a bit of ice, but Laurel has cut our order down to twice a month. It just doesn't last in this heat."

Laurel took a deep breath and strode out into the garden. "With any luck, Auntie," she announced brightly, "it won't be long before you'll be having ice every day. And Caro can pack up all those broken teacups and send them right back to their skinflint owners. Afternoon, everyone. Peter, good to see you. Is there an extra glass?"

At first Sophie started guiltily at the sound of Laurel's voice; now she looked alarmed. Everyone was staring at Laurel as Sophie echoed weakly, "Ice every day?" And then, decisively, she thrust her palmetto fan toward Caroline and declared, "It's the heat. Cool her off, Caroline, open her collar."

Laurel laughed as she sank onto the weathered wicker settee next to Peter. "Nonsense. Though I *will* take some of that lemonade, even if it doesn't have any ice. . . . Thank you, Caro, it looks good." She accepted the glass and sipped from it, hiding a grimace at the warm acid taste.

Peter demanded, "Well, don't just keep us all in suspense. What did you do, rob a bank? Or maybe you had as much luck at the Jockey Club the other day as your friend did."

Laurel glanced at him, her eyes narrowing shrewdly above the rim of her glass. "In a way," she admitted, "I did."

"For heaven's sake, Laurel," Caroline insisted, "do be plain! Talking about ice every day and

236

my giving up my business — why, you'd think we'd inherited a fortune!" Then, with a daring flash of hope in her eyes that stabbed directly at Laurel's throat, she added, "We didn't, did we?"

Laurel's fingers tightened on the glass and her voice was so bright it was almost brittle as she replied, "Better than that." She squared her shoulders and looked Caroline, then Aunt Sophie directly in the eye. She couldn't quite manage Peter's gaze, yet. "I'm marrying a fortune," she said, "a small one anyway. And its name is Seth Tait."

And before the stunned silence could turn to horror she went on in a practical, easy tone, "There's no point in being coy about it; you'd find out sooner or later. It'll be a week from Monday. We would've done it sooner but that was the only time the justice had open —"

Sophie recovered herself enough to gasp, "Find out? Find out? You make it sound like a crime!"

And Peter exploded beside her, "It *is* a crime!" He set his glass down on the rush-covered table with a thud that almost toppled it. "Blast it Laurel — I'm sorry, Miss Sophie, but I can't allow —"

"Peter, please!" Caroline cried. "Laurel, you can't be serious! You wouldn't marry a man you've only known for a matter of weeks —"

"Marriage!" gasped Sophie, sinking weakly back against her chair. "Our Laurel — marriage . . . oh, Caro, my fan, my salts, quickly . . ."

Laurel got to her feet impatiently. "For heaven's sake, Aunt Sophie, it's nothing to swoon about!

I'd think you would be happy. You're the main reason I'm marrying the man."

Caro stopped in the act of swinging the fan back and forth before her mother's face and raised stricken eyes to Laurel. Peter stood stiffly behind her. And Sophie, forgetting she was in the midst of a swoon, brought herself up short, looking pleased. "Well, I did always like Mr. Tait," she admitted. "And he's always been more than generous with us —"

"Mother!" Caroline said in a strangled tone. "Laurel is not for sale! She is not marrying the man just so he can bring you candy and flowers!"

Peter's mouth tightened, but he said nothing. Laurel, catching the blaze of disgust in his eyes, refused to be bowed.

She said coolly, "She's right, Caro, and there's no use pretending. Seth Tait is a good catch and if I don't get him someone else will. And frankly I can't think of anyone else in this town who needs what he has to offer more than we do."

"A good catch?" Caroline looked desperately from Laurel to Peter. "How can you say that? You don't know anything about him, you've no idea of his character or his family or — or —"

"I know enough," Laurel interrupted shortly. "I know he's got money and we need it. And if being willing to support this ragtag family and broken-down house isn't a sign of a man's good character, I don't know what is."

Caroline's eyes were dark with anxiety and her voice sounded near tears. "But — you make it sound like a business! Laurel, it's a marriage, and it shouldn't be like that! Mama, tell her!"

But Sophie had abandoned her vapors and looked, for once in her life, almost thoughtful. "In the old days," she said, "back in our grandparents' time, all marriages were business arrangements. One family wanted another's land or house, daughters were married off, dowries were bought and sold. And many of those marriages turned out quite happily. It's important to know what one expects from the start, I think. Of course," she added quickly, aware of the stares from her daughter and Peter, "Laurel has known her young man for such a scandalously short time, but things aren't the way they used to be, are they? And with such a shortage of eligible gentlemen — those from good families, I mean — I do think some leniency must be given, some things simply overlooked. Perhaps there won't be too much gossip."

"Mama, for the love of heaven!" Caroline cried. "Who cares about the gossip when Laurel is throwing her life away — and she's doing it for us!" She turned to Laurel, the tears all but overflowing now. "You know you'd never consider such a thing if you didn't have to take care of us. If I weren't such a burden and if Mama —" She turned angry eyes on her mother. "If Mama could keep two pennies in her pocket! Whatever happens to you will be our fault, all of it!"

Laurel reached for Caroline's hand but she jerked away, shielding her face to hide the tears. "Caroline, you don't understand . . ."

And Sophie said, looking at Laurel very oddly, "It's true, isn't it? You wouldn't be marrying Mr. Tait if — well, if I had managed Jonas' money better. If I hadn't been so improvident, if —"

"We can't build our lives on 'ifs,' " Laurel said sharply. Then, more gently, to both Caroline and Sophie, "It's nothing to make a fuss about. Everything will be better when I'm married, I promise. Please don't worry."

Caroline turned desperate, pain-filled eyes on her and looked as though she would have said more, but Peter stopped her.

"Caroline," he said quietly, firmly, "I think this has all been a bit of a shock for your mother. Perhaps you'd better take her inside."

Caroline hesitated, but Peter's meaning was clear. After a moment Caroline helped her mother to her feet and the two women went inside.

When they were alone Laurel topped off her glass with the bitter-tasting lemonade to give her hands something to do, and she said, "All right, give me your lecture and go away. I have things to do."

Peter replied quietly, "Laurel Sinclair Laughton, are you out of your mind? You don't just up and marry a man you've barely known two weeks, a stranger off the street —"

"Oh, for heaven's sake, Peter," Laurel cried angrily, turning on him, "don't you stand there telling me what I can and can't do! You don't have the first idea what it's like —"

"How rich can he be?"

"Rich enough!"

When Peter took a step toward her, Laurel jerked away, her eyes blazing, but her anger couldn't hold up for long against the hurt and concern in Peter's eyes.

He said, "Laurel, I told you before if money is the problem we can work something out. I'll do whatever I have to . . ."

Laurel pressed a hand to her temple and said tiredly, "Peter, I know you mean well, but you can't help. I know what I'm doing, I promise."

"How *can* you? For the love of God, Laurel, you met the man in a —" He looked around suddenly, as though afraid of being overheard, and lowered his voice. "In *Miss Elsie's,* have you forgotten? What kind of man goes to a place like that, did you ever think about that?"

Laurel looked at him curiously. "Yes, I have wondered. Why *do* men go to places like Miss Elsie's, Peter?"

He looked for a moment utterly astonished, then he flushed scarlet. "How in the world should I know? Ask your — your fiancé, he seems to be such an expert!"

"Maybe I will," she murmured, causing Peter to stare at her again.

Recovering himself, Peter said sharply, "you've done some crazy things in your life Laurel, and I've laughed as hard as you have about most of them; but this is no game! You're bringing this man into your home — into Caroline's home, and Miss Sophie's — you're agreeing to be his *wife* . . . What if . . ." And again a flush of scarlet touch his neck and he lowered his voice painfully, "What if you have a child?"

Laurel touched her throat, half-turning from him. "I hadn't thought of that," she murmured. And then, in a stronger voice, "Maybe I won't. Oh, Peter, I can't worry about everything. Let me solve one problem at a time, won't you?"

"I can't let you do this."

And finally, exasperated, she had had enough. "You can't stop me. You can't even make me reconsider. I am going to marry Seth Tait a week from Monday, and that is that."

He looked at her for a long time, soberly. "Your final word?"

"My final word."

Peter dropped his eyes. "There never was a man — or a woman — alive who could go up against you when you'd made up your mind. But I had to try."

And then he looked at her, and his eyes were filled with regret. "I know you've got your reasons, Laurel, and I know you're too smart to do something like this without thinking it through. I wish I could give you my blessing, but I can't. I'm sorry."

When he had gone, Laurel stood alone in the garden, releasing a deep sigh of what should have been relief, but what felt more like fortification for what was to come. Because Peter was wrong — she hadn't thought this through. And she was only now beginning to realize what an enormous risk she was taking.

CHAPTER
Eleven

One of the things that made Edgar Cassidy such a good lawman was his ability to change, chameleon-like, according to his environment, and to do it so effortlessly, so instinctively that even he hardly noticed he was doing it. Had he been walking into a hotel in Denver or Dodge City he would have done so in boots and open vest, his jaw unshaven, a fine film of trail dust coating his skin and his clothing. He would have surveyed the room and made a quick, accurate assessment of the likelihood of trouble, then he would have walked up to the desk, presented his Pinkerton identification and the wanted poster for Peach Brady, and asked his questions. That was the way things were done out west.

But in Charleston, South Carolina, a less direct approach was called for, and he donned his Eastern persona as effortlessly as he reached for his celluloid collar and freshly brushed bowler hat when he dressed that morning. And, just as naturally as a chameleon changed its skin and Edgar Cassidy changed his clothes, he was able to adjust his thinking, to slip into the mind of his quarry when it was called for. That was the other thing that made him such a good lawman.

He didn't waste his time skulking around the docks, the shantytowns and the riverfront saloons where it might seem to the average man that an outlaw like Brady might be found. Cassidy hadn't studied Brady's habits as well as he might have, but he knew Colonel Ike better than he knew his own mother. Colonel Ike had a hankering for fine things, a taste for luxury that he indulged whenever possible. He wouldn't have slept with the rats and the fleas when there was a fine hotel in sight, and Cassidy had a notion that an appreciation for creature comforts was only part of the legacy Colonel Ike had given his adopted son.

Peach Brady had changed his name, even changed his appearance to the extent of shaving off his mustache and cutting his hair; he had left behind the territories where he was known and he had a little money in his pocket. He wouldn't have any notion that anyone would be looking for him in Charleston; he'd have no reason to hide. If Cassidy knew him, and he thought he was beginning to, the first thing Peach Brady would have done upon arriving in Charleston would have been to check into a hotel.

Unless, of course, the Colonel's instructions had been so precise and the circumstances had been so simple that all he had to do was ride out, dig up the gold, and leave without ever spending a night in the city.

By noon on the first morning of his search, it was beginning to look very much as though Brady had done just that.

The trail, by the time Cassidy arrived in Charleston, was almost three weeks old, which, for a city that got as much traffic as Charleston did, was very nearly cold. There was no way to trace his movements from the time he had alighted from the train — nor even to be sure, in fact, that he had left the train, or even made it this far. All Cassidy could do was to make inquiries, systematically, at every hotel and guest house in the city, beginning with the ones he thought most likely to appeal to a man like Brady, then moving upward toward the more expensive.

He approached the desk of the Charleston Hotel with as much outward confidence as he had the six-room "Clean Rooms" facility near the train station, though inwardly he was beginning to fear defeat. There were other avenues he could try, of course, and he had every intention of doing so, but he was beginning to wonder whether Brady had made it this far after all . . . or whether he had already found the gold and fled.

He tipped his hat to the short, round-faced fellow behind the desk. "Afternoon, friend," he said pleasantly. "My name is John Brooks, farm implements and supplies . . ." He flashed a small white card toward the clerk but repocketed it before the other man had a chance to read it.

"And I was told to meet a fellow here by the name of Seth Tait. You probably know him, good looking man, tall, light-haired . . ."

Hugh Casom was nodding and smiling before the other man even finished speaking. "Why sure, I know Mr. Tait. Fine fellow, always pays his bill on time. We'll miss him around here."

Only years of professional training, often in life-or-death situations, allowed Cassidy to keep his alarm hidden. "Miss him? Has he checked out already?"

"Not yet, but I imagine he'll be doing it pretty soon." And suddenly Hugh's face cleared. "Why, you wouldn't be here for the wedding, would you?"

Cassidy hardly missed a beat. "Getting married, is he?" He chuckled. "Well, that's good enough reason to miss our appointment, I guess, though you'd think he would've mentioned it. I'd like to meet the lady who finally snared him, though; she must be quite something. A local girl is she?" And all the time he spoke the words came as though from someone else's mouth; his mind was working furiously, projecting, calculating, speculating.

Hugh said, "Well, the truth is it was all a little sudden-like. Close to being scandalous, some folks say." And he leaned forward confidentially. "Mind you, the Widow Laughton is from one of this town's first families and not a word of shame has ever been associated with that name, but she can be a little wild sometimes. Not that I'd be one to speak out of turn, you understand . . ."

Edgar Cassidy nodded sympathetically and leaned his arms on the desk to listen.

"Well, that wasn't so bad, was it?" Laurel said brightly. "At least as weddings go." Her voice was as tight as a piano wire, her smile as brittle as glass.

She sat straight and tall beside Seth in the hired carriage, her hands folded primly in her lap, her neck so rigid that not even the feathers on her bonnet swayed. She looked as though she would break if he touched her.

A small smile curved Seth's lips. "I wouldn't know. This is my first time. You're the expert."

Laurel darted a quick look at him to determine whether or not he was teasing. "It was fine," she repeated firmly. "Quick and to the point."

"Very business-like."

"Exactly."

In the end, Aunt Sophie had overruled her decision to be married in front of the county justice. A small, unpretentious wedding was right and good, she had agreed, as befitted Laurel's widowed state and the more recent loss of her only male relative. But no Sinclair in the history of the family had ever taken the vows before anything less than a fully ordained minister of the gospel and to do otherwise now would be like not being married at all. It would be worse than living in sin, it would be sacrilege; none of them would ever be able to hold up their heads in public again.

In the end it had been easier to give in to Sophie's rantings than to argue with her.

Marriage by a preacher, however, was not enough. No, there had to be an announcement in the paper — "Do you want people to think we're *ashamed?*" Sophie had insisted — and even a small wedding party afterward. From the simple signing of papers Laurel had first envisioned — painless, efficient and impersonal — the whole thing had gotten completely out of hand, turning into something very much like a real wedding. And Laurel had not been able to meet Seth's eyes since she had walked into the pastor's study that afternoon.

The whole thing had been a nightmare: The minister's wife banging out the wedding march on an out-of-tune piano, Aunt Sophie sniffling into her handkerchief, Caroline acting as her maid of honor and trying to smile through her tears. Laurel wouldn't have been surprised — nor would she have blamed him — if Seth hadn't even shown up, but he had, standing strong and sober beside her through the whole thing. She imagined he had even made the correct responses to the minister's questions — her heart was pounding so loudly she couldn't be sure — and when the minister said "You may kiss the bride" he had turned to her, lifted her gloved hand to his lips, and kissed her fingers politely. Aunt Sophie had burst into sobs.

Even now, Laurel couldn't help making comparisons between this and the wedding she had had with Johnny. The church had been decorated for Christmas with banks and banks of poinsettias, candles gleaming like a million stars against the old stone walls and dancing in the stained glass. Her dress had been of white satin with a six-yard train, and she had worn a lace veil trimmed with white satin rosebuds that draped below her knees. She had been so young then. But the white dress and the veil and the ceremony at the altar hadn't particularly blessed that union. Aunt Sophie had sobbed at that wedding too. And Laurel was just as married now as she had been then.

That was what she had not counted on.

Laurel swallowed hard and concentrated on the passing view from her window. "I'm sorry about all the fuss and feathers. I know that wasn't part of the bargain."

"No," Seth agreed mildly, "it wasn't. But looks to me like we did leave out one little thing that was."

She turned to him with a question on her lips and he caught her chin in his fingers and kissed her.

He meant it to be a hard kiss, a kiss of mastery, even a punishing kiss — and he wasn't even sure why he wanted it to be so except that he couldn't forget the way his heart had stopped, just for a minute, when she had walked into the pastor's study in her soft gray dress with its fragrant corsage of lilacs on the shoulder, and how she had been too embarrassed — too miserable and ashamed — to even meet his eyes while she said the words that made her his wife. And he was angry, because he hadn't expected the soft un-folding of sweet possessive pride when she walked into the room, and he hadn't expected to stand before a preacher and make promises he had no intention of keeping, and he hadn't expected to be so confused by the trappings that surrounded him . . . piano music and flower petals, women crying and words in a newspaper: *Mrs. Jonas Sinclair is pleased to announce the marriage of her beloved niece, Laurel Sinclair Laughton, to Mr. Seth Tait.* . . . Tradition, pride, certainty. He hadn't expected it to mean so much. He hadn't expected it to be so real.

And that was why, when he took Laurel's face in his hands, his fingers were hard and his kiss was bruising — until he felt her gasp of surprise and the weakening of her muscles, her instinctive surrender . . . and the anger was gone in a wave of heat and desire that he could not control and he kissed her because he wanted to kiss her, be-cause she was Laurel and she was his. And because it was too easy to forget, when he kissed her, what was important and what wasn't, he broke away abruptly.

He held her face still between his fingers while the haze cleared from his vision and the tight-ness from his skin, but it was a moment before he could speak. Even then his voice was a little husky. "Just so you don't forget your part of the bargain."

His hand released her chin and Laurel's fingers touched her lips automatically — as though to hold the kiss that was already fading, or perhaps to soothe away the soreness he had left. She said, in a tone that was perfectly steady, "I haven't forgotten. You've kept your word. I'll keep mine."

At Seth's insistence, they had stopped at the bank as soon as they left the minister's house, and he had paid off the note in cash. Laurel felt as though she, too, had been bought and paid for, which he had no doubt intended. It will be worth it, she assured herself, dropping her hand from her lips and closing it in her lap. Already it was worth it. The house was theirs, free and clear, and if that was all Seth ever did for them, the marriage vows she had made before God and the people she loved would be worth it, and tonight . . . her heart was beating wildly and she could still feel the imprint of Seth's strong fingers on her face, his heat and his muscles and the passion of his kiss. Yes, even tonight would be worth it.

The carriage rocked to a stop before the Lamboll Street house. The day was gray and weepy — fittingly so, Laurel reflected — and the windows gleamed with lamps lit against an early twilight. Other buggies already lined the street, although it wasn't as bad as it could have been — for every name Sophie added to the list of those who simply must be invited to the wedding supper, Caroline had quietly marked off two. The result was a quiet affair consisting only of the closest friends and neighbors, but it was still too much for Laurel.

"I apologize for all the bother," she said to Seth

when he came around to help her down. She indicated the house and the surrounding evidence of company. "I know it can't be the kind of thing you like."

"You promised me respectability," Seth replied. "Isn't this part of it?"

"Yes," Laurel said, a little uncertainly. "I suppose it is." And then she looked at him, her hand lingering on his strong, broadcloth-covered forearm as she stepped onto the carriage block. "You're a very odd man," she murmured.

And then, quickly lowering her eyes, she preceded him up the drive onto the piazza.

Laurel opened the door and stepped into the parlor, then let her breath out in a long stream. "Oh Caro," she whispered. "It's lovely."

The shabby little room had been decorated with candles and bowls and vases of white magnolia, their leaves shining velvet soft in the light. The draperies were tied back with garlands of laurel — symbols of good luck — and rose leaves and sprigs of jasmine formed a runner in the center of a long table where a small collection of wrapped gifts had been arranged. A clutch of pathos tightened in Laurel's throat at the sight, and it was a moment before she could speak.

"It's beautiful," she whispered, and drew Caroline into her arms. "Thank you, it's more than . . . it's perfect."

Caroline could not keep the wistfulness out of her smile as she stepped back a little, patting Laurel's cheek. "I may not approve of this marriage, Laurel, but I *do* approve of you. I want you to be happy, that's all."

She noticed Seth then, standing a little behind Laurel but close enough to have heard every word. Her cheeks went a miserable mottled red, but she met his eyes bravely, and extended her hand. "Welcome to the family, Mr. Tait," she said.

"Miss Caroline." Seth bent over her hand, and Laurel had to admire the fact that his face showed neither amusement nor impatience.

Sophie moved in then, her handkerchief clutched in her hand, full of tearful embraces and soggy sentiments, and that initiated a whole stream of well-wishers. For the next several minutes Laurel did nothing but kiss cheeks and embrace lavender-scented shoulders and smile until she thought her face would crack.

There was a familiar voice in her ear and she turned to greet Peter. "Oh, Peter." Her pleasure was genuine. "I'm glad you're here."

"I wouldn't have missed it." But he didn't smile, and his lips were cool against her cheek. His eyes were on Seth.

"Congratulations, Tait. You know she's much too good for you."

"I know that," replied Seth, shaking his hand. "But more important, so does she."

Seth's smile was easy and his tone light, but even Laurel could feel the tension that crackled between the two men. She was grateful when Sophie broke in with a flutter of her handkerchief, "Come now, there's wedding cake and blackberry wine in the dining room. Laurel — Mr. Tait — you must do the honors."

The dining table was covered with a lace cloth and lined with magnolia blossoms which wilted in the heat and filled the room with their cloying scent. Glass bowls, filled with oil and topped with lit wicks, covered every available surface. The wedding cake leaned slightly on one side and was spare of frosting on the other, but all of Aunt Sophie's finest had been brought out for the occasion: Spode dessert plates, hand-cut crystal glasses, every unstained and least-mended napkin in the house. The knife with which to cut the cake was tied with a white ribbon, and two decanters of blackberry wine flanked it.

Seth took up a decanter of wine and began pouring as though he were born to the role of host. Laurel sliced the cake with unsentimental efficiency and hands that were slightly damp on the knife.

"And now a toast," said Sophie brightly.

The silence rang.

Laurel put the knife down and looked up at Seth helplessly. The curve of his lips was reassuringly cynical as he lifted his glass to her. "To my beautiful bride," he said. "May this marriage bring her everything she hoped for."

There were murmurs of relief and approval and the clinking of glasses. Laurel, unable to withstand the wicked amusement in Seth's eyes a moment longer, turned quickly back to the cake.

Peter put his glass down without drinking and walked away. In a moment Caroline followed him.

"Sorry," he muttered, noticing the concern in her eyes. That was one toast I can't drink to. Wasn't there any way you could delay this . . . this farce?"

She shook her head. "She was determined, and you know there's no reasoning with Laurel when she gets like that. The house note was due . . ."

"And he paid it."

Caroline nodded, and Peter's lips tightened with repressed anger and impotence.

Caroline said hesitantly, "Your investigation — any news?"

Grimness entered his tone. "Only that no one in Wyoming has ever heard of him."

Caroline looked unsettled. "Wyoming is a big state."

"With very few people," Peter pointed out, "and most of them know — or at least know of — everyone else. Particularly the ranchers. If he really is in horses, like he said —"

"He never really indicated that he had a real ranch. Perhaps he exaggerated, or we misinterpreted . . ."

"Or maybe he just plain out lied."

Caroline's hand touched her throat. "Oh, Peter," she said miserably. "Perhaps it's best not to know. Laurel is married now for good or ill, so we might as well put a pretty face on it."

"It's not over yet, Caroline."

"But —"

"Maybe he told the truth about his folks dying on the trail west. It seems plausible enough — after all, lots of southerners went west after the war and a lot didn't make it. If that's the case there's a good chance there would've been some mention of it in their hometown newspaper, and every newspaper keeps copies of its weeklies."

Caroline looked awed. "But — going back twenty years?"

Peter nodded. "Some might even have copies before the War. All I have to do is start looking."

"But — where? How can you possibly look in every paper in every city in the country?"

He smiled indulgently. "First of all, I won't do it. I'll send out telegrams to some editor friends of mine, and they'll make their copy boys do it. And it won't be every newspaper in the country. I don't think Seth Tait picked Charleston off the map; he must have some business around here. So I'll start with the *Gazette*, then the Savannah Dispatch, the Atlanta *Journal*, and the smaller papers around those cities . . . process of elimination."

Impulsively, Caroline reached for his hand. "Oh Peter, you're such a good friend. What would I do without you?"

Again his lips tightened in an inner struggle with pain. "If I were a good friend I never would have let this happen — not to Laurel, not to you."

Her eyes were wide and her voice gentle. "Peter, you did everything you could —"

He shook his head harshly. "No, I didn't. I

should have seen this coming, I should have stopped her. I should have robbed a bank to get her money or tied her up to keep her from marrying the man —"

Her fingers pressed the top of his hand. "Peter, you mustn't torment yourself. We don't know that Mr. Tait isn't perfectly respectable, and —"

With a sudden surge of courage that seemed to catch Peter off guard as much as it did Caroline, he covered her hand swiftly with both of his. "Caroline, I can't let you stay here with that man in the house. Laurel has chosen her path, but you are too fine, too fragile to be exposed to whatever he may turn out to be. If I were any kind of a man I would have taken you away from here long before now, but —"

"Peter, please!" Her voice was strangled, her cheeks drained of color and her eyes dark with distress. "I must — I must beg you not to speak to me so." She tried to tug her hands away, which, in a moment of desperation, he wouldn't release. "And if you persist . . ." The words faded into a miserable whisper as spots of color crept back into her face. "I'm afraid I must ask you to leave!"

Peter released her hands as though stung and felt a rush of heat singe his own neck and jaw. "My apologies, of course, Miss Caroline," he muttered. "I was overcome — with anxiety for you all. Please forgive me."

She managed a stiff smile, but did not meet his eyes. "Excuse me. I should help Mother serve."

Peter's hand tightened into a helpless, frustrated fist as he watched her move away from him with her halting, dignified gait.

Seth observed the interchange from across the room. He had observed a lot in the short time he had been at the party, in the way he had of noticing things, and he was surprised at how much it interested him.

"So that's the way it is," he murmured.

Laurel looked up at him quickly. "The way what is?"

Seth gestured with his wine glass. "Your boyfriend, and Miss Caroline."

"He's not my boyfriend," Laurel snapped.

"That's good to know. You're married to me now, and I'd hate to have to shoot him."

Belatedly, Laurel noticed the lazy twinkle in his eyes, and she forced her muscles to relax. "I wouldn't think it would matter to you one way or another."

"Oh, it matters," he assured her softly. The glint in his eyes was not so much amused now as speculative, and it made her heart tighten and skip a beat. "You're mine now, and I aim to hold on to what's mine."

Laurel's tone was even. "As long as it's convenient, of course."

For a moment something unreadable flickered across his eyes, then was gone. He smiled. "Of course."

He glanced over her head and murmured, "And speak of the devil . . ." He gave Laurel a slightly mocking bow and moved away.

When Laurel turned around, Peter was approaching her. His face looked tight and strained and he spoke stiffly. "I'm leaving now, Laurel. I wanted to say goodnight."

"But not congratulations?"

His face darkened. "I think you know that's too much to ask."

"Oh, Peter, you are the stubbornest man! Why don't you accept the fact that what's done is done and make the best of it?"

Peter mumbled, "That's just what your cousin was saying."

Laurel's eyes widened in a mixture of amazement and exasperation as she understood. "And you argued with her? Over *me?* Something that's none of your business, I might add — or hers!"

"If it's not my business, I don't know whose it is," he shot back. "She depended on me to keep you out of trouble and how can she respect me when I couldn't even keep you from making the biggest mistake of your life?"

"That's the most absurd thing I've ever heard."

Peter looked away miserably. "If I'd gotten hold of my gumption sooner it might never have come to this. I might not make much of a husband, but at least without Caroline to worry about you wouldn't have been quite so desperate . . ."

"Now's a fine time to think of that."

He looked at her sharply. "There's no need to mock me, I feel bad enough as it is. At least I would have gotten her out of the house before you brought *him* here."

Now all traces of humor left Laurel's face. "You're talking about my husband, Peter, whether you like it or not. And I don't think I like what you're implying."

"You might like it," he told her coolly, "a lot more than the truth. And I will find out the truth. I promise you that. It's the least I can do — for both of you."

He leaned forward and kissed her on the cheek, then bowed and departed. Laurel looked after him, puzzled, but he didn't look back.

If respectability, acceptance, a feeling of belonging were the things Seth really wanted from Laurel, he would not have been disappointed that night. Silver-haired ladies turned out in their finest bowed and smiled at him. Doc Weathersby drank a toast to him. The police chief called him "son." Cyrus Lars, to whom Seth had only moments ago proven his credit-worthiness, clapped him on the back and declared him to be the man of the hour. Seth had to hide a smile in his wine glass when he tried to imagine what the Colonel would think if he could see him now, drinking with a banker. Drinking with a banker, laughing with a lawman, married to a lady. There were moments when Seth almost expected to wake up and find someone else had stolen his body and was experiencing these unlikely events in his name. And there were other moments when it all seemed so perfectly natural, so right, that he couldn't think why any of it should seem strange.

He hadn't meant to seek Caroline out, but when he found himself standing directly beside her he could hardly walk away. She was, among all the people he had met since coming to Charleston, the one person who could still make him uncomfortable — perhaps because there was something about her innocence that constantly made him feel guilty. It was odd how he could look a banker or a policeman boldly in the eye without a qualm, but before a small brown-eyed girl he still felt as though he should try to hide.

For a moment she looked as uncomfortable as he felt, and then she noticed the empty glass in his hand and said quickly, "Some more wine, Mr. Tait?"

He knew he should have allowed her the opportunity to escape — and himself as well — but he didn't. "No. It's fine." He looked at her steadily. "Thank you for the party, Miss Caroline. I know you don't approve of me, but this was a mighty fine thing you did all the same."

Caroline's cheeks colored but she did not evade his gaze. "I'm sorry you had to overhear that," she said. "I admit I don't know you well enough to approve or disapprove of you, but I can't approve of a marriage that takes place on such short acquaintance . . . and for such unworthy reasons."

She dropped her eyes on the last, and Seth said quietly, "So. She told you."

"Laurel doesn't often keep secrets from the family." She looked at him again, her eyes large with apology and sincerity. "Please understand, Mr. Tait, it isn't that I dislike you, it's that I love my cousin so much. She has spent her life taking care of Mama and me and we owe her more than I can say. The thought of anyone hurting her . . ."

Seth did not know what to say. He looked down at his empty glass.

Then Caroline said softly, "Do you love her, Mr. Tait? Everything would be different if you did . . ."

Seth looked at her, startled. And then he couldn't look at her anymore. "I admire Miss Lau— my wife a great deal."

Caroline smiled sadly. "That's not the same as love."

Across the room Seth saw Peter bow to Laurel and start for the door. He said softly, "I reckon you'd know about that, ma'am."

Caroline caught the direction of his gaze and blushed furiously. "I'm sure I don't know what you're talking about."

Seth smiled at her gently. "Yes ma'am. But if you did, I reckon you'd agree that what you call love isn't always a simple thing."

"No," she said quietly, and dropped her eyes. "It's often mistaken for other things . . . like pity."

"Now Miss Caroline," Seth said smoothly, "I don't know why any man alive would ever think to pity you. You're one of the strongest women I've ever known, and the only reason you don't realize it yourself is because you've always had Laurel to take care of you. I don't think she was doing you any favor."

Caroline raised startled, incredulous eyes to him, but he merely bowed. "Thank you again for the supper party, ma'am."

Laurel was talking to the undertaker's wife when Seth touched her arm lightly. "It's late," he said. "We should go."

Laurel turned to him, surprised. "Go? Go where? What are you talking about?"

He tucked her arm through his and drew her a little away, his smile a little dry. "This may not be much of a marriage and I might not be much of a husband, but we still deserve a wedding night. And we're going to spend it at the hotel."

Laurel's first inclination was to argue with him, and that was when it came over her: *Married*. Married meant that she did what she was told, particularly in a matter like this. It was a strange and shocking sensation, but even more so was the feeling that followed: a hot wave of something like embarrassment mixed with anticipation mixed with nervousness and dread. *Hotel.* Her wedding night would not be spent in her own high tester bed with its plain white coverlet and utilitarian mosquito netting, awkward as that might have been, but in a hotel room. *His* hotel room. There was something scandalously lascivious about that, even sinful — and yet the prospect did have a certain appeal. Had Seth made the arrangements to spare her — and Caro and

Sophie — the embarrassment of leading him to her bed? Laurel had not given much thought to the exact procedure when bedtime came, but trust a man to consider all the details.

She could feel the heat in her throat and her hands and she was sure he could see it in her face; his eyes were mocking her. She looked away. "I — I'll have to go pack a bag."

"Your aunt has already done it."

She looked at him sharply, but he just smiled. "If you want to have any of my money left over for spending you'd better not keep the carriage waiting much longer. I'm paying for it by the hour."

Laurel did not remember much about their departure, or the drive to the hotel. The night clerk greeted Seth with a big smile and called him by name as he handed him his key, and then, with a shy, darting glance at Laurel, said, "Evening, Miz Tait." It was several seconds before she realized who he was greeting.

Seth took her arm and led her toward the stairs. Neither of them noticed the man who stood up from the deep settee on which he had been reading the newspaper. He watched them climb the stairs until they were out of sight, then he folded the paper beneath his arm and left the hotel.

CHAPTER
Twelve

The room looked no different from the last time
Laurel had visited it, when she had come storming in to fling Seth's money so magnificently back
into his face. It seemed ironic to think of that
day, how awkward she had felt to be in a gentleman's hotel room, how shocked and almost giddy
she had been when he had come to the door without his shirt; and though she knew it wouldn't
have changed anything, she couldn't help feeling
that everything might have been different if she
hadn't chosen nobility over practicality for the
first time in her life at that particular moment.

Johnny had carried her over the threshold of
his father's three-story Georgian home. Seth
didn't bother, and Laurel was glad. She felt foolish enough . . . and awkward, and uncertain, and
even a little scared. She had felt all of those things
with Johnny too, but one thing she had not felt
with him was this pulse-quickening, hot-cold
anticipation, the fluttering in her stomach that

felt like anxiety, the tingling of her skin that felt like excitement. The door closed with a soft click behind her and she was alone in the room with this stranger. Her husband.

He set her small valise, freshly brushed and aired for the occasion, by the door. Laurel glanced in his direction but couldn't quite meet his eyes. She walked over to the mirror above the low dresser and unpinned her hat. She took off her gloves, finger by finger, and arranged them neatly atop one another, thumbs matching, on the dresser. She heard Seth moving around behind her, but she did not look to see what he was doing. She took off the corsage of wilted lilacs. When Seth spoke, the sound of his voice was so close it made her jump.

"Here." He had two glasses in his hand and he held one of them out to her. His eyes reflected amusement at her nervousness. "Don't ever accuse me of being an inconsiderate husband."

Laurel took the glass, sniffing it cautiously. "What is it?"

"Good Kentucky sipping whiskey. You'll like it."

"Ladies don't drink spirits." She eyed the glass skeptically, but did not return it.

"You'll like it," Seth repeated, and crossed the room to lounge in the chair beside the door. He gestured to her with the hand that held his own glass. "Stop fussing with yourself and sit down. Relax."

There was no place left to sit but on the side

of the bed, but even under the circumstances Laurel was reluctant to make herself that comfortable. She did not want to project a sense of intimacy that she was far from feeling for this man who was her husband for the sake of convenience only, and she didn't want to give him ideas . . . which was, of course, ridiculous. He was her husband and he could have as many ideas as he wanted.

Thus resigned, she sat delicately on the edge of the bed and took a swallow of the whiskey. Her eyes watered, her throat burned; she gasped and coughed.

Seth's eyes danced lazily. "I said *sipping* whiskey." He demonstrated. "Try it again."

Because the whiskey was the only liquid available to soothe her fiery throat, Laurel did, sipping this time. She found, to her surprise, that it actually had a taste, and the burning sensation this time was more of a warm glow. She cleared the hoarseness from her voice and said, "It's — interesting." She took another sip.

Seth smiled. "I believe a woman should be able to enjoy a drink with a man now and again. But I'd appreciate it if you'd quit before you get tipsy. Somehow the notion of a wife who gets drunk on her wedding night doesn't seem like much of a compliment to the bridegroom."

Laurel tried not to blush, and took another sip — cautiously.

Seth glanced down at his own glass, and the mirth was gone from his eyes when he looked at her again. His posture was easy — shoulders back in the deep chair, one ankle resting on his knee, the glass dangling casually between his fingers — and so was his voice. But his expression was sober. He said, "I don't want any misunderstandings. You're probably wondering what kind of man you've got yourself hooked up with and I guess it scares you some — I can't think of any other reason why you'd be sitting there as stiff as a dressmaker's dummy, like you'd break the bed if you put any weight on it."

Laurel drew a quick breath to protest but he overrode her, his voice mild but firm.

"I can't say that I blame you, and you probably have good cause to be worried. You'll find out sooner or later I don't know much about how to treat a lady, I don't even know what you expect. We come from two different worlds as far as that goes. But . . ." His eyes held hers solemnly. "I'm just a man, and I'm not going to make you do anything you're ashamed of or don't want to do and I'm not going to hurt you. I don't want you to be afraid of me, and I never had much respect for men who kept their women that way."

A lady would have blanched at such frank talk, or at the very least denied to the heavens any knowledge of what he referred to. But Laurel was relieved. She had heard obliquely of all sorts of perversions — men who, for example, liked to watch their wives undress in full lamplight — and she was glad she would not be subjected to any such ordeals. Seth Tait was the epitome of the

268

mystery that was male, but at least now she knew where she stood. Her first wedding night would have been a great deal more comfortable if Johnny had been quite as frank.

She smiled a little into her glass, remembering Johnny with his skinny white chest and his fumbling, earnest attempts at romance . . . his adoring gratitude afterward and his embarrassed insistence, in the morning, on pretending nothing had passed between them the night before. It had all been rather furtive and distasteful, and she had no reason to think it would be any different with Seth. But somehow she did.

She looked up at him. She wasn't tipsy, but the warm feeling was spreading through her limbs and perhaps it loosened her tongue as well. She wasn't sure she would have felt quite so comfortable with Seth at that moment if not for the whiskey. She said, "As long as we're being frank with each other, my friend Peter suggested I ask you something, and now seems to be as good a time as any."

"I'm not real sure I like the way this is starting out, but go ahead. Ask."

"Why do men go to whorehouses?"

His eyes flashed momentary startlement, then narrowed in slow amusement. "I think you'd better give me that glass."

"Don't be absurd. And don't patronize me; you know what I mean. I asked Peter but he said you were the expert."

"Dirtying my name behind my back, is he?"

Seth murmured, lifting his glass. "I might have to shoot him yet."

"I thought at least you were one man that would answer."

"And I thought you were one woman who would at least *know* the answer."

She frowned. "I don't mean that. Everyone knows *that*. I mean — even married men go." She looked at him, simple curiosity darkening her eyes. "Why?"

Seth looked for a moment as though he were debating whether to laugh or take her seriously, whether to answer or dismiss her. Then he shrugged. "That's a complicated question. Ask a dozen men and you'd get a dozen answers, I reckon."

He saw the impatience in her eyes and he relented. After another sip of whiskey he said thoughtfully, "Most men don't have any women friends. A woman they can just sit down and talk to, you know. Sometimes it's good to just be with a woman you don't have to pretend with."

Laurel nodded slowly. "I understand. All the same, I'd appreciate it if you would refrain from visiting Miss Elsie now that we're married."

His eyes glinted. "Jealous, Mrs. Tait?"

"Not at all," she replied with dignity. "It simply wouldn't look proper, that's all, and we have enough to live down without adding your personal habits to the list. Besides . . ." She took another sip of the whiskey. "We get on well enough, don't you think? I don't see any reason why I can't be your friend, even if I am your wife."

Something odd came over Seth with those words, something midway between surprise and wistfulness and a slow, welcome certainty. *Friend.* For all his life, the Colonel had been Seth's only friend, and the concept of having this woman as a friend was almost as alien as having her as a wife. And yet both notions were gradually starting to feel comfortable, and perhaps that surprised him more than anything else.

He set his glass aside and came over to her, sitting beside her on the bed. He touched her face with his fingers, guiding it toward him, and he kissed her lips lightly. He kept his eyes open, watching her, and so did she. He smiled.

She said, "May I ask you something else?"

He didn't remove his fingers from her face, nor his eyes from hers. "Might as well."

"The way you kissed me the other night — did you learn that in a place like Miss Elsie's?"

He took the glass from her fingers and set it on the table by the bed. His thumb teased the corner of her lips, causing them to part. He tasted her lips with the tip of his tongue, drawing her lower lip inside his mouth; he traced the shape of her teeth and the sensitive inner flesh. He covered her mouth with his and Laurel sank into his embrace, her lips parting wider, welcoming the taste of him inside her.

The heat took over, the weakness, the spinning sensation inside her head. When he released her she was dimly surprised to find her arms around his neck, her head resting against the pillows, his hands supporting her back. She whispered breathlessly, "You — may as well know Miss Elsie said I wouldn't make much of a pleasure woman."

His lips touched her face, her throat, and every caress was like a brand. "It's a good thing I didn't marry Miss Elsie then, isn't it."

His hands slid up her body and threaded through her hair, dislodging hairpins, spreading the rich dark locks across the pillow. His eyes were a conflagration of lights and darks, his breath warm and slow on her face. Laurel's throat grew tight, looking at him and knowing the purpose in his eyes, feeling his touch on her skin and the long, luxurious stroking motions his fingers made through her hair. She whispered, "Should I — should I undress now?"

He touched her lips with his. "No." His fingers moved down and expertly unfastened the buttons on her collar.

One by one the tiny buttons on her bodice gave way to the slow, lingering manipulations of his fingers. With every loosened button Laurel's heart beat loud and harder until she thought it would explode. She closed her eyes, thinking it was somehow the ladylike thing to do, but then she wanted to see his face, to look into his eyes. But heat and breathlessness blurred everything as he pushed aside the material of her bodice and gently tugged at the drawstring of her chemise. Her breasts were exposed, and he lowered his head, placing long slow kisses there.

It was at that point that everything spun out

272

of control for Laurel. Arrows of desire flamed from the touch of his lips and stabbed at her abdomen; a red haze formed behind her closed eyes. Her hands tightened on his shoulders, a moan of pleasure escaped her throat. Pleasure. She had never imagined it could be so with a man.

At some point she recalled he sat up and blew out the light. She remembered the layers of her clothing falling away to the welcoming curtain of darkness; her fingers fumbling with the tapes of her bustle and petticoat, his breath brushing like a caress across her naked skin. And when she turned into his arms again she felt his bare chest pressing hers, the silky texture of hair brushing her breasts, muscles strong and tight as he enclosed her in his arms.

There were times when Laurel was convinced that some other woman lay in Seth Tait's arms; it surely couldn't be she behaving with such wanton abandon, surrendering so completely, enjoying so thoroughly and needing so intensely. The sensation of his unclothed thighs, strong and firm, pressed against hers brought no shame to her; the touch of his fingers on her secret parts ignited flames of desire. Her own hands roamed restlessly over his form, plunging into the thick silkiness of his hair, molding the lean muscles of his back, shaping his ribs and his arms and his taut, spare waist.

There was none of the sense of resignation or endurance with which Laurel had resolved to accept the evening. When he moved above her she shifted to welcome him, her arms winding around him, her mouth open to taste his. His invasion of her body was slow and thorough, filling her with the strength and power of him, drawing a cry of pleasure and need from her even as he began to move inside her. The need built, spiraling into ever-tightening circles of passion that caused her to cry out, clutching him to her, as an explosion of pleasure more intense than anything she had ever imagined racked her body.

A lifetime of heartbeats and gasping breaths, of heated caresses and dazed, hungry kisses passed before Laurel became aware of the lifting of Seth's weight, the loosening of his arms from about her. Her throat made an instinctive sound of protest and she reached for him. He shifted away but in only a moment was with her again, drawing her into his arms, dropping kisses into her tangled hair.

Another lifetime followed, of distant awareness, penetrating warmth, of the simple wonder of being held against him, wrapped in the familiarity of a body she now felt she knew as well as — better than — she knew her own. How strange it was, she thought, that this ordinary act of marriage should change so many things. Worlds had opened up for her that she never had known existed. A stranger had been transformed into a lover, and that lover was now the whole of her world, all that she knew or ever wanted to know. And yet it was all so sudden, too sudden, too intense to be real. How could it be real, what she was feeling as she lay in his arms in the aftermath of the most intense, the most shocking and moving, experience of her life? How could she trust any of her senses when he had turned her whole world upside down?

It was all too much to think about, and all she wanted to do at that moment was feel.

Seth pushed his fingers through the hair at her temples, tugging the veil-like strands from her face. She felt his kiss on her cheek, and the curve of his smile. "So, Mrs. Tait," he murmured huskily, "how do think you're going to like being married this time?"

She smiled secretly into the curve of his shoulder, and snuggled more securely against him. "I think," she replied, "in time, I could learn to tolerate it."

"Hmm. And how much time do you reckon that'll take?"

Laurel lifted her face, and her arms, to him. "Only," she whispered, "another moment."

". . . and that was when old Cody jumped up and said, 'Coyote, hell! That wasn't nothing but Shortie, trying to cross that cactus field in the dark without his boots!' "

Laurel burst into laughter. "Is that a true story? That can't be a true story. I think you're making half of this up."

Seth just smiled and reached for the cigar he had extinguished half an hour earlier.

It was almost dawn, and the last two hours had

been spent listening to Seth's outrageous stories of life in the west, or telling her own stories about the absurdities of Charleston society, or caressing each other, or holding each other, or simply feeling good with the silence. Neither of them had slept, and Laurel had learned something else new: it was possible for a man and a woman to make love more than once in the course of a single night. She was beginning to wonder, in fact, if there was any limit to how often it could be done, because just when the silences lengthened, just when she started to grow drowsy in his arms and thought surely he must be tired, too, the prickles of desire would begin to stir and swell, and, impossible though it seemed, each time they made love was better than the time before.

But that was not the most important, or even the most startling, thing Laurel learned that night. What amazed her even more than the act itself was how easily and completely whole lives could be changed because of it. Before she had married Seth she had admired him, it was true. And there was certainly no use denying now that she had always found him extremely handsome, exciting, mysterious, intriguing. There had even been things she liked about him. But now . . . now she could laugh with him. Now she could tell him things she would not even have shared with Peter and know that he neither judged nor censured her; he simply understood. It was as though once the physical barriers were lowered all the others were too, and in a few short hours Laurel had grown closer to Seth Tait than she had ever been to another human being. And that, she supposed, in the final analysis was the essence of marriage.

He was leaning back against the headboard of the bed, wearing his trousers and nothing else. Laurel, wearing her rumpled nightdress, lay on her stomach at the foot of the bed, her chin resting on her folded hands, looking at him. She wanted to touch him, to feel the familiar texture of his skin beneath her fingers, the muscle and sinew, the silky dusting of chest hair . . . and she would touch him, soon. Perhaps the most wonderful part of being married was knowing that there was always later, and anticipation only heightened the pleasure.

She said a little wistfully, "It certainly does sound like an exciting life, out west. Won't you miss it?"

His hand hesitated for only a fraction of a second as he brought the match to the tip of the cigar, but his expression didn't change. "Maybe we'll take a trip out there sometime, and you can see for yourself."

Laurel smiled, both with pleasure at how wonderfully married that sounded, and with sadness because of its impossibility. She shook her head. "You know I can't do that. Aunt Sophie, Caroline . . . I can't leave them. And they'd never leave Charleston."

His eyes narrowed briefly against the haze of cigar smoke, and his expression was sober. "You might be surprised at how well they'd get along without you if you gave them a chance."

Laurel laughed a little, but it was a strained sound. "Neither one of them could draw a bucket of water if I weren't there to turn the crank." She couldn't quite keep the anxiety out of her voice as she added, "I guess you didn't realize you were marrying my family when you married me."

He hesitated, studying the tip of his cigar. Then he said quietly, "There were a lot of things I didn't realize, I reckon." And before she could question, he said, "Do you ride?"

Laurel blinked at the abrupt change of subject. "Why, of course. English saddle, side-saddle . . ."

He grinned, "How about plain old western saddle? I'm going to get you a horse. Me too. There's a red gelding down at the livery I've got my eye on, and a pretty little bay for you. I reckon I ought to get a buggy for the ladies, too. Confound if I can understand how they can walk anywhere in this heat."

Laurel sat on her heels, her hands pressed together like a child restraining her wonder on Christmas morning, and the brightness in her eyes was magnified suddenly by a sting of tears which she quickly blinked away. "No," she shook her head firmly. "No, I can't let you. Two horses and a team — why that's five hundred dollars at least, not to mention what a buggy would cost . . . Seth, are you out of you mind?" The delight that had flooded her face only a moment ago had now been replaced by horror. "No, absolutely not. You'll be bankrupt in no time at that rate —"

Seth grinned and stretched out an arm, catching the sleeve of her nightgown and drawing her to him. "Why don't you let me worry about that?"

But Laurel shook her head again, her frown distracted. "I have to worry about it. You don't know what it's like, being poor . . ."

"I've reached in my saddlebags for flour and come up with dust plenty of times."

"— having people depending on you, scraping to make ends meet, and just when you think you're finally in the clear something else happens . . ." She shook her head again adamantly. "No, I have to worry about it, and I can't let you throw your money away, Seth. We have to be careful."

Seth realized then how very much he preferred the delighted child who had so briefly welcomed news of his gift to the anxious, frowning woman he saw now. And he wanted, with a desperate intensity that startled him, to take that frown out of her eyes forever, to bring back the little girl.

He settled one arm firmly about her shoulders, holding her close. "You don't hold the purse strings anymore, Laurel," he told her, not unkindly. "And I'm buying you the bay."

He could see the effort it cost her to bite her tongue, and he wished there were some way to make her believe that she didn't have to worry, that she could relax now and lean on him, that he would take care of her. But he didn't have the words, and he wouldn't have known where to begin if he had. Perhaps that was because he had never, in all his life, wanted to take care of anybody before, or needed to.

And then he felt her forcibly relax her muscles, and she smiled up at him. Her hand opened against his chest, spreading tendrils of warmth and desire, and she said, "Tell me some more of your wild life in the west. I don't care if you did make them up, your stories are better than those dime novels of Peter's. Are you sure you don't know some about Colonel Ike and Peach Brady? Peter would probably print them in his newspaper."

There was a moment when everything froze within Seth; even his hand, reaching to extinguish the cigar, froze in midair. The present clashed against the past and he was caught in the middle. And then the world, which had momentarily been knocked sideways, slowly righted itself.

Seth answered quietly, measuring his words, "Yeah. Matter of fact, I do know one story. Maybe I'll tell you sometime. But now . . ." He stretched over her to extinguish his cigar, and lowered her to the pillow beneath him. "I think maybe we'd better send a note round to your aunt's house telling her not to expect us back today."

Laurel draped her arms around his neck, closing her eyes on the pleasure of his touch. "That," she sighed, "sounds wonderful."

A long time later, holding her in his arms, Seth kissed her fingers and whispered, "How do you feel?"

Her reply caught at his heart.

"Safe," she murmured, and snuggled closer to him stretching her arm across his chest. "I feel safe."

CHAPTER
Thirteen

"Of course you understand, Mrs. Sinclair," Edgar Cassidy said with a smile, "I would never ask you to part with your heirlooms, nor even consider it. But you would be surprised at the treasures you have hidden away in your attic, castoffs and forgotten scraps of what you might consider junk but which might, in fact, be turned into a handsome profit — under the right guidance, of course."

Sophie sighed elaborately as she looked at the card he had given her. Before them was a tea tray set with sugar cookies and cooling cups of tea — she so rarely had visitors from out of town that Sophie felt it was the least she could offer. And Mr. Cassidy had come, of course, with the most excellent of recommendations. Sylvia Clark of Richmond and Dorothea Montgomery of Atlanta had both used his services, and, according to Mr. Cassidy, had done so to their great advantage.

"Oh, I don't know, Mr. Cassidy," she said.

"I'm such a flibberty-gibbet about business . . . I wish my niece were here, but —" She dimpled and blushed a little. "She's away on a brief honeymoon."

"My congratulations then. If you would prefer that I talk to her — or even to her husband, if you have no other male relatives — I would be pleased to come back whenever you say. I expect to be in Charleston for several weeks, calling on other clients —"

He looked as though he was preparing to go, and Sophie said quickly, "No." Her face grew thoughtful. "Now that I think of it, perhaps it would be best if Laurel didn't know anything about this at all."

Mr. Cassidy smiled. "I understand. You'd like to use your profits to buy her a nice wedding present, I expect. Well, you can certainly count on my discretion."

It was the word profit that finally swayed Sophie; that in combination with his suggestion about talking to Laurel's husband. She couldn't forget Caroline's angry accusations that Laurel wouldn't have been forced into such a scandalous marriage if she, Sophie, were not so reckless with money, and that hurt. Though she could hardly raise the objections to the marriage that Caroline did — Mr. Tait, after all, was *such* a nice man — she did not ever want it said that she was taking advantage of Laurel, or living off the charity of a stranger. The attic was filled with boxes and parcels she hadn't looked at since she was a child and it would be *so* nice to have money of her own. Money that she had earned.

She smiled at Mr. Cassidy. "I shall start searching the attic this very afternoon. Now, do finish your tea, Mr. Cassidy, and tell me about yourself."

Two days later Seth and Laurel checked out of the hotel. He had given orders that her bay and his roan should be saddled and brought up, and Laurel had rushed outside while he paid the bill, eager to examine her horse. Seth was glad she had gone ahead because he didn't want her to see the foolish grin on his face as he watched her through the long window in the lobby; he didn't want her to guess how much pleasure it gave him to see her happy.

People nodded and smiled at him as he moved through the lobby, and some of them called him by name. He returned their greetings, struck by the sudden realization that he was leaving this hotel for the last time. He was going home . . . with his wife.

It was an odd feeling. Less than a month ago he had been loath to leave his room, awkward at having to move around town without his gun. Now it felt perfectly natural to do so. Mere weeks ago he hadn't been able to set foot outside the lobby without scanning every face for danger and every street corner for hiding places. Now he tipped his hat to strangers on the street. Now there weren't, in fact, too many people who were strangers to him.

He wasn't the same man who had checked into this hotel a month ago. He had come here alone, but he was leaving with a wife. Though neither of them had meant to make it a real marriage . . . somehow it was already more real than he could have ever guessed it would be. He was responsible now, not for one woman but for three, and he didn't mind that. And Laurel . . . how could he think about changes without thinking about her? She was funny, she was tart, she was open and she was smart. Even the stunning passion that he had discovered, buried like a hidden jewel deep within her, was only part of the whole experience that was Laurel. She made his head spin; when he was with her, nothing seemed impossible and nothing mattered except that he always be with her. He had never known a woman like her before; he couldn't imagine ever being with anyone but her, and he supposed he must have known that even when he agreed to her terms for marriage. Laurel. She was the reason he wasn't the same man he had been when he had checked into this hotel.

He was still watching her through the window, trying not to smile too obviously, as he settled up his bill.

"It's been a real pleasure having you, Mr. Tait," Hugh Casom said, beaming as he offered his hand. "I wish you and Miss Laurel all the luck in the world, and that's the truth."

"Thank you." There was still enough of the cynic left in Seth to wonder, as he shook the other man's hand, how much of those good wishes were prompted by the extra ten dollars he had added to the money he passed to Hugh.

"Now don't you worry about your bags, I'll have a boy get over there with them inside the hour," Hugh assured him.

"Appreciate it." Seth turned to go.

"Oh, by the way, did that friend of yours ever find you?"

At that moment everything changed again.

Seth had taken perhaps five steps toward the door. He could see through the window that Laurel had already mounted and was waiting for him impatiently. She had insisted on a sidesaddle, and her skirts trailed gracefully over the horse's flank. The skirt was forest green, and she wore a matching green hat with a yellow feather that she had admired in a shop window the previous day. He had bought it for her because it amused him to hear her fuss about the money . . . and it made him happy to see her eyes light up when she put it on. He looked at her for one long moment, drinking her in, letting the impression linger on his brain, because he knew when he looked back at her nothing would be the same.

He turned back to Hugh, his face perfectly impassive. "Someone was looking for me? Who?"

Hugh frowned. "Brewster? Johnson?" His face cleared. "Brooks, that's it! John Brooks. Some kind of salesman, claimed he had an appointment. Course it was the day you were getting married, so I told him, I said . . ."

Seth let Hugh's voice drone on, his expression frozen in pleasantness, nodding now and then to indicate attention, his subconscious mind registering and storing details even as his conscious mind was busy planning his next move.

Because he really hadn't changed at all. He was still Peach Brady, and somebody was looking for him. He had come here for one thing, and every minute he delayed brought his pursuer a step closer. He was crazy to have ever thought he was safe here. He couldn't afford to make that mistake again.

Laurel was still waiting for him when he went outside; her eyes were still dancing in the sun and her wit was still sharp and the feather on her hat was still bobbing jauntily in the breeze. But Seth was aware of a sense of loss as he mounted and turned his horse toward what was — for the time being, anyway — home. Because he had been right. Everything was changed.

It was not difficult for Seth to find what he needed. The difficulty arose when he realized that what he needed was not what he expected.

Laurel's bedroom — his bedroom too, now — was simply furnished; almost Spartan in its utilitarianism. It was a big room, with those floor-to-ceiling sash windows that were so prevalent in Charleston, which made the sparseness of its furnishings seem all the more stark. Aside from the bed made with its neat white counterpane and a wardrobe in which a few dresses, mostly black, hung, there were a chest of drawers, a small lamp table, a single chair and a trunk. It was plain that all the good furniture had either been sold or moved downstairs over the years, and what remained were only the necessities. The single decoration was an amateurish painting of a house, field and gardens, done in bright bold colors with a myriad of tiny details, most of which were undecipherable. The painting bothered Seth, seeming familiar to him somehow, until Laurel caught him staring at it and explained it was a depiction of Chinatree in its glory days. Her mother had painted it.

Laurel was out of the house, doing the marketing, and Seth had led the other two women to believe he was going with her. Instead he went back upstairs to their bedroom and closed the door. He felt no qualms about what he was doing, and only part of it was because Laurel was his wife. The other part was because he had done worse in his lifetime. Much worse.

He opened the lid of the trunk to mounds of tissue paper. When he folded back a few layers he realized that there was a wedding dress inside — from her first marriage, obviously. The neat, careful way in which it had been packed suggested more practicality than sentiment, and Seth moved it aside with as much care. There weren't many other items in the trunk — a few pieces of heavy crystal which he presumed had belonged to her mother, some leather-bound volumes on agriculture that were stamped with the name

"Augustus Sinclair," a carved wooden box containing a single strand of pearls and a locket with a strand of hair in it, the last of her mother's jewelry. Seth felt strange, opening that locket. He knew the hair belonged to Augustus Sinclair, and the prickle on the back of his neck felt like a hand reaching from the grave to touch him.

On the bottom of the trunk was a packet of letters tied with a faded blue ribbon. It was that simple.

He rearranged the contents of the trunk, took the letters over to the chair by the window, sat down and began to read.

He had intended only to scan, moving quickly through the years until he found what he wanted, but phrases kept catching his eyes: "Beloved, to return to you again . . ." ". . . The sweetness of night, when I can dream of you . . ." And he found himself reading whole sections, finally entire letters. The picture that emerged was one of two people deeply in love, tender and sincere, disturbingly vivid.

"And yet in the midst of the slaughter I can close my eyes and I am at Chinatree at dusk, the air perfumed with jasmine and the sweet hum of the tree-frogs, rocking chairs creaking slowly on the verandah. I reach across and touch your hand . . ."

"My deepest sorrow, beloved, is not for us, for we have known more joy in our short time together than surely two people ever deserved, but for our darling Laurel, who will never know the legacy that is rightfully hers. This war is lost, my love, and has been for months now, but we have lost more than a way of life. We have lost the only thing that any of us can ever hope to give our children: the future."

"You mustn't fear for me. I have too much to come home to to let a Yankee cannonball get in my way now."

And finally, the last letter. It was in a different hand and had obviously been dictated. "I know this is the letter you hoped never to receive and I hoped never to write, but perhaps we both knew from the beginning it was destined. I have reason to believe Ike —" Seth's heart jumped when he saw that name "— is dead, or else he would be bringing this message to you. I have trusted him with so much already, just as he has trusted me, that I would gladly trust him with this last request. But alas, it is not to be. I have to rely, my darling, on your devotion, which I know to be certain, and the probability of this missive reaching you, which is not. Do this for me, and know that I will rest easy forever more in the knowledge that my life, and my love for you both, has not been in vain: Bury me now beneath the bench where we sat on a twilight evening so long ago and I stole my first kiss. Have only family present at the ceremony. And accept what I give to you with my last breath, and all my love. Do this, and I die easy. To you, my only love, I leave the promise that I have done what I had to do. To our beloved daughter, Laurel, I leave the future."

The door opened with a soft click, and a shadow fell over Seth. Laurel said uncertainly, "Seth?"

He looked up at her slowly, then back at the letter in his hand. "He loved you very much."

Laurel came into the room, a puzzled frown troubling her brow as she unpinned her hat and tossed it on the bed. "Are those my father's letters?"

He did not have to school his face into innocence. The contents of the letters had left him momentarily too disturbed for pretense. "Do you mind?"

"Why — no, I suppose not, but, for heaven's sake, where did you find them?"

"I was looking for a place to put my extra shirts," he replied absently — a facile lie that he had prepared in advance just in case.

Laurel tossed her gloves on the bed beside her hat and came over to him, smiling. "I haven't looked at them in years. When I was a little girl they used to make me cry."

There it was, the final proof if ever he had needed it, that the gold did exist. *I have done what I had to do. . . . accept what I give to you. . . .To our beloved daughter, Laurel, I leave the future.* It was so plain a blind man could see it. He had buried the gold, just as the Colonel had said, on Chinatree, and he had chosen a place that only his wife would know about. He had left the clues as clear as daylight in his last letter. And the gold was still waiting there, after all these years.

To our beloved daughter, Laurel . . .

Seth stood up and moved before the window, taking the letter with him. So tell her. They were married, what was hers was his, there was no reason to keep the secret.

Yet there was every reason. A man like Peach Brady could take half a million in gold and disappear with it with no one ever the wiser. If a woman like Laurel Sinclair — Laurel Tait — should suddenly fall into the possession of a fortune in gold coins, every investigator, lawman and banker in the country would converge on her. In order to claim the gold, Laurel would have to leave this place and that she would never do.

Seth felt a surge of anger for the father who, in meaning the best for his child, had in fact left only the worst. But he couldn't blame Augustus. If Laurel's mother had been able to follow the instructions in the letter, it would have been the best. Twenty years earlier, in the upheaval of war, no one would have questioned a fortune quietly squirreled away; and if they had, there would have been few agencies in place to follow through. Twenty years ago they could have used that money to quietly invest in a business, to rebuild Chinatree, even to go west. No, he couldn't blame Augustus.

But he could blame the Colonel. All these years he had known about the gold and he had never done anything about it. He had claimed to be such a good friend of Augustus Sinclair — didn't he care that his family was starving while a fortune in gold lay buried in the backyard? Even in the end, he had sent Seth back for the gold, made him promise to go back for it, and he had known about Laurel. He had known that Laurel Sinclair, the legitimate heir to the fortunes of war, was still living and in need, and he had forced Seth to make this decision.

Seth's fist tightened on the letter until the paper crumpled and threatened to tear.

Laurel touched his arm lightly. "It must be hard for you," she said softly, "not knowing. We're both orphans, but at least I have memories of my mother, and these letters from my father. I know that they loved me."

Seth glanced down at her, then back out the window. He forced his hand to relax on the letter. "I wonder sometimes," he admitted, without meaning to. "I wonder who my parents were and what they were like . . . and what I might have been like if they had lived. It's not an easy feeling, when you're not sure who you're supposed to be."

Laurel nodded, and rested her cheek briefly against his arm. "Still, you were lucky. You did have a chance to grow up."

"Yeah," Seth agreed slowly. "The man that raised me tried to do what was best for me, I reckon. But I'm not sure he ever knew what was best."

He glanced down again at the letter in his hand, and he had to make the final admission to himself. He couldn't tell Laurel about the gold because he was Peach Brady. Because Peach Brady was a thief and outlaw who had come three thousand miles to rob her of her inheritance and, though Laurel might understand many things, she would never forgive him for that. He wanted to do what was best for her, but he couldn't change who he was.

And the best thing he could do for her was to get on with what he had come here for, and get out of her life.

He gave her a smile as he turned, smoothing out the wrinkles in the letter before returning it to the stack on the chair. "You pa sure was fond of your ma. It's funny for a man to be able to write down things like that. He even wanted to be buried underneath the bench where they first kissed."

"Oh, is that where it was? I remembered something like that."

He kept his back to her as he straightened up the stack of letters. "You ever go out there, looking for that bench?"

"Goodness, no! It would have rotted away long before now, and everything is so grown up it would be impossible to find where it used to be. It's silly, anyway. Why would anyone even care?"

He grinned, returning the letters to her. "I thought women were supposed to be sentimental about things like that."

She shrugged. "Not this woman." But her eyes were veiled as she returned the letters to the trunk. "It's not as though Chinatree could ever be the way it was."

"You'd like that, wouldn't you?" Seth said, with sudden perception. "To rebuild it, just like it used to be."

Again, Laurel shrugged, but the faint tinge of wistful color in her cheeks gave her away. "That's impossible. It would be stupid to try even if I did have the money, which I don't and never will." She turned to him with a quick, dry smile. "It would be smarter to try to turn it into a horse farm."

It was hard for Seth to look at her then, and to return her smile. But he did it. He had done harder things in his lifetime.

He said, "Listen, I remember your aunt complaining about the shape the cemetery was in. I was thinking I might go out there and start cleaning it off."

Laurel looked surprised. "There's no need to do that. No one ever goes out there to see it."

"It would make your aunt happy," he replied casually, "and give me something to do. I'm used to working outdoors."

Laurel stepped forward and looped her arms around his neck, smiling as she tilted her head back to look at him. "You know," she said, "sometimes I think you're a lot nicer than you pretend."

He drew her close and rested his chin atop her head, mostly so that she could not see his face. "I wouldn't count on that," he answered quietly. "I wouldn't count on it one bit."

Caroline was in the parlor when Peter came in, mending a man's shirt in the morning sun. She looked startled when she noticed him and then a little embarrassed.

Peter's first words were short, and held a touch of the bitterness of self-reproach. "I thought Laurel's grand sacrifice was going to solve all your money problems, but I see you've been forced to take in sewing now, on top of everything else."

Caroline blushed, but the tilt of her chin seemed a little defiant. "Don't be silly, Peter. It's . . . this is Mr. Tait's shirt."

Peter was dumbfounded. "You're mending Seth Tait's shirt?"

She turned back to her work, her tone defensive. "Well, you know Laurel knows nothing about sewing and he lost a button —"

"And he had the gall to ask you to fix it?"

"Not at all." The needle that flashed through the fabric had an impatient rhythm, and her voice held a touch of asperity. "I noticed he'd lost a button and offered to sew it on for him. After all, he's done so many nice things for us, it seemed a small enough gesture of thanks. I really don't see why you're so interested, Peter."

Peter sat down in a chair opposite her, controlling his expression, and his tone, with care. "It sounds as though you're changing your tune about the mysterious Mr. Tait, Caroline."

"I guess I've gotten to know him," she said simply. "He's not like I thought he'd be. He's, well, kinder and more thoughtful. And I've never seen him behave as anything other than a gentleman. He treats Laurel with the utmost consideration and hasn't given any of us reason to doubt his affection for her."

"A real saint, I can see." Peter made no attempt to disguise his sarcasm.

"Oh, Peter, don't be cynical, it's most unbecoming. Maybe this marriage can work out between him and Laurel." And then her face brightened as she looked at him. "He gave her a little horse! Did you know that? She's thrilled over it."

Peter muttered, "Riding around like a circus performer, she'll be killed. She doesn't need to be encouraged in her foolhardiness."

"And he saved the house for us," Caroline went on, "but you know that, and he's paid Mama's back dues at the Carillon Club so she can take friends to lunch there, and do you know he has spent almost every day for the past two weeks out at the cemetery, cleaning off the graves? Only last night he was insisting that I stop mending china —"

Peter got to his feet angrily. "It's none of his business, Caroline, what you do. He married Laurel, not you —"

Caroline's eyes twinkled mildly. "Why, Peter, what a silly thing to say. You sound jealous."

"I'm not jealous," he returned shortly. "Are you?"

"Am I what?"

"Going to give up your china repair just because he says you should?"

"Of course not." Caroline calmly folded the shirt and returned it to her sewing basket. "I do it well, and my customers depend on me."

Peter paced to the window and back again. Caroline took out another piece of mending. "Do sit down, Peter. You're wearing me out just to look at you."

Peter stopped and looked at her. "I guess I am jealous, Caroline," he said quietly. "I've been the only man in your life since your father died — and in Laurel's and your mother's too, of course . . ." He broke off, and then corrected himself firmly, "No. In *your* life. And now Tait has forced his way in —"

"Not forced, Peter," Caroline corrected gently. "He's family now."

Peter took a breath. "I know it makes you uncomfortable, Caroline, but I still think that you and I . . ." The look of pleading in her eyes almost stopped him, but then he forged determinedly on. "That we can be more than friends. If you'll let me —"

"Peter, you know how I feel about that." She dropped her eyes, her hand tightening on the garment she had brought out to mend. "I'll never . . . well, I couldn't let myself be a burden to — to anyone. I'm very contented with my life as it is and I want to keep it that way, living here with Mama, running my little business . . . and keeping you as a friend if I can."

"That isn't what I want."

She looked at him sadly. "We can't always have what we want, Peter."

He looked as though he wanted to say more, then stopped himself. He ran his fingers tightly through his hair. "You are a frustrating woman, Caroline."

"I'm sorry Peter."

His voice was quiet and heavy. "Not as sorry as I am."

He resumed his seat and pulled out a letter from his pocket. "I guess I might as well tell you, I have a letter from Savannah about Tait."

Caroline dropped the mending and clasped her hands together, the sad, uncomfortable expression in her eyes vanishing immediately into excitement. "How extraordinary! Oh, Peter, do tell! What does it say?"

He didn't raise his eyes from the paper, though he knew its contents by heart. "It's from a lawyer, Rankin Legare. He saw my ad in the classified — I ran it in all the big cities from Richmond to Savannah about Seth Tait, in addition to asking my editor friends to check their morgues for information on the family. You know the kind of thing, anyone knowing anything about the past or family of. . . . This lawyer, it seems, knows all about the Tait family. They're from near Savannah it seems, went west just after the war, mother, father and child, and were never heard from again."

Caroline drew an excited breath, her eyes glowing. "So this lawyer can put Mr. Tait in touch with his relatives!"

Peter shrugged. "I assume so, but what he was really more interested in was me getting in touch with Tait and telling him about some railroad shares his granddaddy left him. Not a fortune but certainly worth a pretty penny now." He raised his eyes to Caroline at last. "So it seems Tait is an heir of some sort. He might just turn out to be the answer to Laurel's prayers after all."

"Oh, that's wonderful news," Caroline said. "Not about the inheritance, though I'm sure that will be welcome too — but to find his family after all these years! I'm sure he'll be . . ." And then broke off, noticing Peter's dark, glum expression. "You don't think so."

"There's still something fishy going on, Caroline," he said tightly. This isn't the whole story about Tait, I feel it in my bones. Maybe he's related to these people in Savannah. Maybe he killed the real Seth Tait out west."

"Peter, no!"

Her horrified tone made Peter wish he had curbed his imagination — or at least his vocalization of it. Still, he insisted stubbornly. "We really don't know, Caroline. There's a lot about Tait we don't know, like his life out west —"

"Peter, please, don't start that again. You already checked on that and —"

"Obviously not closely enough. I'm going to keep on trying."

"Oh, Peter." Dismay, mingled with more than a touch of anxiety, colored Caroline's tone. "Let it alone, please. Seth and Laurel are married, it's over and done. And now this inheritance — why it seems like a fairy tale. Too good to be true."

"Exactly, Caroline. It's all too good to be true and I don't believe any of it."

"Well, I for one do. Happiness is something Laurel deserves, and Mr. Tait, too. So listen to me, Peter." She leaned forward a little, almost as though she were going to reach for his hand — but she didn't. "I'm begging you to forget about our investigation. We've found out all we want to know."

Peter said nothing.

And then she did reach out her hand, and touch his fingers lightly. "Promise."

He could not have denied her anything at that moment, and she knew it. "All right." The words were heavy with resignation. "I promise I won't send out any more inquiries on Seth Tait."

She smiled, sitting back again. "When are you going to tell him?"

Peter frowned. "I'm not," he said flatly. "I don't like the man and I'd be the last to give him good news." He stood and dropped the letter onto the settee beside her. "You tell him; he'd probably be more likely to believe it coming from you than me, anyway."

He turned to leave, then noticed the newly framed photograph on the table. He picked it up. "There they are, the happy couple." Laurel and Seth, dressed in their wedding finery and frozen in time with the stiffness only a photograph could convey, looked back at him from the painted china frame. He put it down beside the one of Laurel's parents, a preoccupied frown on his face.

Caroline said, "It's lovely, isn't it? And it was so generous of you, Peter, to arrange to have it taken. What a lovely wedding gift."

He couldn't quite meet her eyes. "It didn't cost anything. The photographer works for the paper."

"Still, I know Laurel appreciates it." And she smiled. "And don't pretend you're not sentimental about weddings. The photographer told me when he brought our picture over that you had asked for one too."

Peter glanced at her quickly, then away. He picked up his hat. "Just as a memento of Laurel, nothing more."

"Oh Peter, that's very sweet of you." Her smile was soft and benevolent. "That's the Peter I know, the loyal friend, not the cynical reporter who looks for bad deeds where none lie."

Peter paused at the door, and looked back. "You know your problem Caroline? You see good in everyone, and that can be dangerous."

Her soft words followed him. "No more dangerous than seeing bad everywhere!"

Peter let himself out and walked down Lamboll Street. The sunlight dappled on the cobblestones through the live oaks and the smell of magnolia and crepe myrtle was heavy in the air. More and more his meetings with Caro were leaving him feeling frustrated and angry. He loved her — he had always loved her — but even when he was working up the courage to tell her so, she wouldn't give him a chance. She was so sure she'd be a burden to any man who cared for her, but didn't she realize how much care she took of others? He didn't know how to convince her. It was something she had to realize herself; simply telling her wasn't going to make her change.

And now there was another obstacle between them. That damn Seth Tait. Every bone in Peter's body was convinced that there was more to Tait's background than ancestors in Savannah and railroad shares in a lawyer's office. A hell of a lot more. But Caroline was equally convinced that Tait was full of righteousness and good will. What would she think if she found out what he'd done with his photograph of the newly married couple — that even now copies were circulating among federal marshals and prominent citizens in every major city in the west, in hopes that someone might be able to recognize the face, if not the name.

Peter only hoped that by the time he got the answers he sought, it wouldn't be too late.

CHAPTER
Fourteen

A man was watching the house from across the street when Seth and Laurel entered. To the casual observer this might have meant nothing at all: a middle-aged man in a summer-weight coat and wide-brimmed straw hat taking a leisurely stroll down the street should signal no alarm, and certainly there was no evidence that he was watching the house. Seth's eyes were trained to see what the ordinary man could not; his instinct was honed to recognize the signs. The house was being watched, and his time was running out.

They had spent the afternoon with Colonel Boatwright and some of his cronies, talking horses. Laurel never lost an opportunity to keep her end of the bargain by introducing him to Charleston's first citizens, opening doors he couldn't have opened for himself and making him feel accepted. Sometimes he found himself getting so wrapped up in it all that he forgot none of it mattered any more; sometimes he actually was able to introduce the subject of Augustus Sinclair and the war years, in some vague hope that he might gain a clue as to where, exactly, the gold had been buried. He never succeeded, of course.

He couldn't stay here much longer. If it hadn't been for Laurel he would have left weeks ago, the moment he'd found out somebody was looking for him at the hotel. The gold was there and it was at least part hers. He owed her that much — and the Colonel. He couldn't just walk off and leave her with nothing. He didn't know how he was going to be able to leave her at all.

Some day he supposed that these last few weeks in Charleston would seem as if they had belonged to another man. He'd look back on the time that he had talked like a gentleman and married a lady and kept his gun holstered in the top drawer of a bureau that was older than most roads in this country, and it would seem like a story he'd heard that had nothing to do with him. But right now it felt like the most real, the most important and true, thing that had ever happened to him. And he was so tired of running.

Caroline was waiting for them at the door, her color high and excited and her face tight with a mixture of anxiety and eagerness. "Laurel — Mr. Tait. I'm so glad you're back." Her voice was breathless. "Did you have a nice visit?"

Seth could not resist moving beside the narrow window and lifting the lace curtain a little to glance out, while Laurel replied, "If you only knew how silly that sounded, Caro. I don't think you'd be called a sinner for using my husband's first name. Yes, it was nice, but *breathlessly* hot, don't you think? I can't recall the weather ever being this bad, even in August."

The man was still there. He had taken a seat on the bench that surrounded a fragrant mimosa in front of the Castleburys' garden gate. A visitor, waiting for the Castleburys to return. Or a federal marshal, watching the house.

"Laurel," Caroline said, "may I talk to you — both?"

That was when Seth noticed the odd tone in her voice, and it was reflected in her face when he turned. He said, not too sharply he hoped, "Is something wrong? Did something happen while we were gone?"

Caroline touched her throat in that way she had when she was nervous, and the uneasiness in her eyes seemed to deepen. That guilt that Seth always felt when she looked at him burned like a brand inside his chest, and every instinct he possessed was ringing alarm.

"Yes," she said, "in a way. . . . Could we all go into the parlor and sit down?"

Laurel cast a puzzled glance toward Seth, but Seth's eyes were turned toward the view from the window, where the man still sat, watching and waiting.

As soon as they entered the parlor Caroline turned and blurted, "I have a confession to make."

"You? A confession?" Laurel's eyes were twinkling. "Let me see if I can guess what it is. You've stolen from the collection plate at the church? No? Then you must have forgotten to feed the birds in the garden. Or maybe you took two pieces of cake instead of one."

"Laurel, please," Caroline said unhappily. "I'm serious."

Laurel sat down on the sofa and patted the place beside her, indicating Caroline should join her. Seth remained standing by the door, and Caroline's eyes were on him.

He managed a smile. "I can't imagine what you could have to confess about, Miss Caroline."

She took a deep breath, obviously drawing on her deepest resources of courage. And she said the words that Seth must have known all along she would say.

"It's you, Mr. Tait."

As though from a distance he heard his own voice, calm and polite, holding just the right note of surprise. "Me?"

"Yes." She dropped her eyes. "I did something foolish and unforgivable, something that I now regret, and it concerns you."

Seth's alarm became mitigated by mystification, but it was Laurel who spoke. "Seth? What on earth are you talking about, Caroline?"

Caroline glanced at her cousin and then, with an obvious effort, made herself meet Seth's eyes again. She pressed her hands together in front of her. "When you began courting Laurel I was worried because we knew nothing about you, and so . . . and so I asked Peter to investigate you."

"Caroline!" Her voice was shocked and angry, and Laurel started from the sofa.

Seth took a step forward and placed his hand on her shoulder, but his eyes didn't leave Caroline's. And his voice was dangerously quiet. "Investigate," he repeated. "Investigate in what way?"

Caroline twisted her hands together nervously. "First he sent telegrams out west to Wyoming, but no one there had heard of Seth Tait."

Laurel jerked away from Seth's restraining hand. "Caroline Sinclair, I'm ashamed of you! How could you?"

Seth felt his muscles relax fractionally. He said, still holding her gaze, "Go on."

"Then he put classifieds in some of the eastern papers, asking about you and your family."

"That was clever of him," Seth said.

"He just thought that since you'd come east you might have some connection. Well, anyway, it paid off." She reached into her pocket and took out a folded paper. "He got a letter from a lawyer in Savannah . . ." She lifted her eyes to him and her expression was anxious and apologetic. "And I hope this makes up for the horrible thing we did. We've found out about your family." She held out the letter.

For a moment he just stared at her. Then he said, "It's probably not the same people."

Caroline nodded, still holding out the letter, her eyes almost pleading now. "This lawyer describes a family who went west with their son Seth about the time you described, and who died on the trail but left no trace of the child. . . . How many families can there be whose circumstances match so exactly?"

Seth's heart was pounding, and it was with a surprising effort that he lifted his arm to reach for the letter. A hundred fantasies, a thousand, of who his family might have been were about to dissolve into smoke. The truth was within his grasp, and it was a truth he had never expected to find.

Go to Charleston. The Colonel's voice. *You'll find — everything there.*

"I'm not sure I want to know," he murmured.

"Yes you do." Relief and cautious pleasure were in Caroline's voice as he took the letter. "It's good news. The lawyer can tell you all about it — you'll probably want to go there and talk to him in person. And there's more news, Seth. Your family was one . . . well, of some substance. Your grandfather left you some railroad stocks . . . ."

Laurel twisted around to look at him, and Seth's eyes met hers.

"Probably worthless," he said.

"No, the lawyer doesn't think so. In fact . . ." Caroline broke off, pressing her fingers to her cheeks, "but I should be ashamed of myself, telling you this when it's really yours to read and find out. He — the lawyer — wants you to contact him as soon as you can, so perhaps you'd better send a telegram." And once again anxiety came into her eyes. "Are you very angry? Do you hate me?"

"Hate you?" Seth's voice was a little dazed, and so was his expression, as he looked at her. "No, I don't hate you."

She smiled and came over to him, touching his arm lightly. "I am happy for you — for both of you." She looked at Laurel, and then back to Seth. "You've found a wife and a family. You're a blessed man."

And hesitantly, shyly, she kissed him on the cheek, then left the room.

He turned his eyes to the letter. He read it over and over again. The names of his parents, their brief and tragic history. A house on Pickett Street that had reverted to an uncle . . . an uncle. He had relatives, living, who remembered his parents, who remembered *him* . . . who knew who he was. The railroad shares. A small fortune in stocks, and it was his by legal right.

Laurel said softly, "Seth . . ."

That was the first time he realized she was standing beside him, her hand clutching his arm, reading the pages with him. Her tone, and her expression, were as stunned as he felt.

What's your name, boy?

He looked down at the letter again. "Says here . . ." His voice was a little hoarse. "That the stocks 'should provide a reasonable yearly income.'" And they had been there all the time, legally his, waiting for him to collect. He had emptied pockets on trains belonging to companies in which he owned shares. He had robbed banks and rustled horses and he had come all the way back here to cheat a widow out of her only inheritance . . . and all the while the stocks had been there, waiting for him.

Laurel said, in a half-whisper, "Yes."

But her eyes were wide and questioning, and she did not seem to be thinking about the stocks. Seth couldn't meet those eyes for long.

The enormity of the truth began to unfold before him, and it was hard to take it all in. He had money now, real money, the kind he could claim in the open and spend without shame. *Laurel* had money now. No more scraping for pennies and bargaining at the market for yesterday's fish. He could take care of her. He didn't need the gold.

But this letter contained something more important than the money. His identity was there. He didn't have to run anymore, he didn't have to hide. *What's your name, boy?*

He had a past that was unsullied and a name that had never been abused. He was Seth Tait. No one could prove that he wasn't, and the future was anything he wanted it to be.

"Railroads," he murmured, and almost smiled. "Who would have ever thought I'd turn out to be respectable?"

"Yes," Laurel agreed unsteadily, still watching him. "Who would have?"

He could see her shoulders tighten as she added, "I guess — I guess you don't need me anymore."

For a moment the significance of the words

didn't register, and when they did — when Seth understood that odd, anxious look in her eyes — he wanted to laugh . . . and then he couldn't even smile. Because suddenly, intensely, he knew exactly what he wanted the future to be. And he knew the only way he could have it was to get rid of the past.

He wanted to crush her to him, to hold her tightly one more time, to tell her things he should have told her a hundred times a dozen nights ago. But all he said was, quietly, "I need you, Laurel. Now more than I ever did."

And he made himself walk away from her, toward the window. The parlor windows faced the garden, not the street, so Seth could not see whether or not the man was still out there. He knew he was, though; he could feel it. Wouldn't someone always be out there, watching, waiting?

It was a long time before he spoke, and when he did it was without turning around. "You took a big risk with me. I could've turned out to be anything. Your cousin knew that, so did your reporter friend. That letter might not have brought such good news. You really took a chance."

Laurel forced a smile, but her voice sounded brittle. "Well, it paid off didn't it? Now I'm married to a railroad heir."

Seth said, still without turning, "Why did you do it, Laurel?"

She couldn't answer. Her heart was pounding so hard it was difficult to even draw a breath, much less form the words . . . the right words, the true words. Something was wrong, she could see it in Seth's eyes, in the muscles of his body, the lines of his face. Everything was changing between them and he had closed her out. She wanted to reach him, she wanted to help him . . . she didn't want to lose him. But she couldn't even speak.

Late afternoon light slanted through the windows, filtered by the jungle growth of the garden outside. Seth stood as still as a silhouette, looking out. His voice was quiet but strong, and curiously without emotion. "It's no secret that neither one of us went into this marriage for the ordinary reasons. And for me . . . hell, it was just a game. I never meant it to last more than a few months. I guess you knew that."

Laurel's heart was beating so painfully that it closed up her throat. She gripped the back of the sofa for support and she wanted to speak, she wanted to stop him from speaking, but she couldn't.

"I always told myself you knew what you were getting into," Seth went on. "That's what I liked about you, a sensible woman, always had your eyes wide open . . . but you didn't know what you were getting into. You couldn't have. And now I've got to tell you and this is where it gets hard, because . . ." He turned then, and looked at her. "It's not a game anymore, Laurel. I don't know how it happened or when — maybe it was there from the beginning — but I'm not looking to get out in a few months anymore. I'm not pretending to be married to you anymore. I want it to be forever."

Relief weakened Laurel's legs and flooded her eyes. "Oh, Seth," she whispered. She took a faltering half-step toward him.

But he shook his head sharply and said, "No. You just listen. Because what I'm going to tell you you're not going to want to hear, and it's going to change everything. But you need to know it."

He turned back to the window. His words were almost a monotone. "I told you some things about the man that found me on the trail, and raised me. But I didn't tell you the most important part. I didn't tell you why I came here."

"He died a few months back, I told you that. And he sent me here. He was a friend of your father's, Laurel. His best friend, you might say. They served together in the war."

Seth heard her soft gasp of surprise but he didn't turn.

"Toward the end, I guess, when they both knew the war was lost, they happened upon a Federal payroll train. To make a long story short, they made off with the gold, the two of them. Hundreds of thousands of dollars' worth. But they got separated, and it was your father that ended up with the gold. He buried it on Chinatree, then died before he could go back for it. Apparently he thought the Colonel was dead too, because he never could get word to him about exactly where the gold was buried. The Colonel hightailed it out west, and he never was able to get back here to look for the gold. So when he died, he sent me."

He stopped, but didn't turn around. Laurel's head was spinning. Her breath came unevenly but she hardly noticed. Her fingers dug into the upholstery of the sofa. She said, with difficulty, "No. You're mistaken. My father — was a war hero. He wasn't a thief. He couldn't have . . . have done what you said."

Then Seth turned. The setting sun etched his features in harsh relief, and he looked very tired. "I never much believed the story either till I got here. Then I realized it all fit. When I heard about the deathbed letter your father wrote I realized the Colonel had been right all along — the gold was buried on Chinatree. And the only way I'd ever have a chance of finding it was to get close to you."

"So you married me for my money." Her voice strayed, on the last word, toward the sharp edge of hysteria, and she pressed her finger to her lips as though to hold it back.

Seth agreed quietly, "Seemed like a fair trade."

Laurel gave a violent shake of her head and turned so abruptly from him that her skirts whirled about her ankles. "No! No, you're wrong! My father wasn't a thief. This — This Colonel of yours lied — *you're* lying! There is no gold; if there was do you think we would have lived like this all these years, half starving, turning our clothes until they were threadbare, scraping for — ?" Her voice broke unexpectedly and she had to grit her teeth to continue. "He wouldn't have let us live like this! If there was gold, he would have told us!"

"But he did," Seth insisted. "That last letter to your mother — he told her where the gold was buried! Beneath the bench where they first kissed, remember? If she had been able to follow his instructions she would have found the gold when his grave was dug and everything would have been different."

No. Everything within Laurel repeated that single word over and over again until she could hardly think for the sound of it. No, no, no, no . . .

"You're lying, Seth Tait," she said hoarsely. "And so was this — this Colonel you keep talking about." He had to be lying, he had to. It couldn't be true.

"I asked you about him when I first met you. He was the reason I came to Charleston, and he knew your father."

His voice was low and calm, and that core of quietness made the unimaginable seem real.

"My father could never have been involved with a thief — a criminal. Never." But her voice was more of a stunned whimper than the outraged protest she intended it to be.

"It happened, Laurel. It's true. They took the gold, your father buried it at Chinatree —"

"Never!" She brought her hands to her ears. "I won't listen to any more of this filth!"

"Your father, Augustus Sinclair, buried the gold

316

at Chinatree," Seth repeated quietly. "That's the truth. I know it, Laurel, and you've got to believe it too."

For a moment she almost did believe. How could she not, when he seemed so sure? Her hands fell slowly away from her ears, and she stared at him.

And then, without warning, the anger welled up in her again. "You were going to steal it!" she cried. "This gold you said my father took! You came here for the gold, only the gold . . ."

"At first," he admitted. "But later, after we . . . I wanted to find it for you. That's what I've been doing at Chinatree, trying to find the spot —"

"You married me because you wanted the gold." Her voice was ragged and hoarse, dry with shock. "You married me because of some lies a criminal told you about my father, and that was all!"

She clenched her fists, her eyes glittering like chips of ice, her face white, her voice low and shaking. "Get out of my sight, you lying, cheating, son of a —"

"I never lied to you."

"You used me!"

"Just like you used me."

"I believed in you," she said hoarsely, her fists tightening at her sides. "I trusted you, I thought you — you were my *husband,* no matter how it started, and I —"

He took a step forward, his face torn with pain. "Laurel —"

"No!" She flung up a hand to ward him off, her eyes wild. "No, you stay away from me. I don't ever want to see your face again. I won't listen to any more of your lies! Just get away from me!"

"Not until you listen to me. Not until you hear the rest."

"There's more?" The ragged edge of hysteria had taken over her voice now and she did not try to control it. "You expect me to listen to *more?* Well I won't, do you hear me? I don't have to and I won't! All I want is for you to get out of here — just *get out!*"

She picked up her skirts and fled up the stairs. Before Seth's foot touched the bottom step the bedroom door slammed, and he heard the bolt click.

The office of the Charleston *Gazette* was on Broad Street in a narrow old building that had seen better days. It was hot in summer and cold and drafty in winter; when the windows were opened as they were now to catch the humid summer breeze, noise from the streets below wafted across the city room and its crowded rows of desks. But the reporters and editors seemed oblivious to the rhythms of life that flowed from the streets. The city room had its own noisy energy — the heavy throbbing of the presses on the floor below, the shouts of "rewrite!" and "copy boy!" from the editor in his tiny cubicle of an office, the calls of the reporters back and forth as they worked and reworked their stories for the next edition.

Peter Barton hadn't grown up wanting to be a reporter, and that certainly never was his parents' plan for him. His father Lucias had expected his only son to follow him into the family business and become a partner in Barton and Co. Cotton Brokerage. But then Lucias hadn't known at his son's birth, shortly after the firing on Fort Sumter, that the war would change everyone's life, and that most plans made before Robert E. Lee's surrender would never come to be.

Lucias had gone off to fight for the Confederacy and in 1865, with one leg shot off but lucky to be alive, had returned to a city in desperate circumstances. Charleston was in turmoil; the crops had been burned by Yankees, renegades or withdrawing southern troops; and the cotton brokerage business never recovered. Lucias counted himself lucky to find work as a clerk with a shipping firm.

The Bartons were as well connected in Charleston as the Sinclairs and bore their change in status with the same grace and courage as other families in their situation. They didn't complain and they did the best they could.

His family managed to give Peter a year at the university, and Peter returned to Charleston determined to work hard, save up a nest egg and then go west and find adventure and a fortune. His personality combined a lively imagination, a penchant for daydreaming, and more energy than he knew how to handle.

He'd fallen into newspaper work because the job was readily available. Reporting paid little, required long hours and was usually frustrating, but Peter took to it like a bear to honey. Newspapers flourished in Charleston after the war, with nine papers vying for readers' subscriptions. The *Gazette* wasn't as influential as the *News and Courier* with its influential editorials and its serializations of great literary works by the likes of Thomas Hardy and Mark Twain, but it was lively and not afraid to take chances.

Peter liked that about his paper; he was good and he knew it. All he needed was a big story, something spectacular to make his name and reputation. Maybe that was why he was so fascinated by the Seth Tait story — if indeed it was a story at all. He'd developed instincts, good ones, over the past five years, and all his reporter's intuition told him there was more to Seth Tait than a lost family in Savannah. As he sat at his desk going over one more time the file he'd set up on Tait, he mentally pushed away Caroline's objections to his inquiries. Caroline needed to understand that she was part of the reason he was pushing so hard. If he broke a big story on Tait, he'd solve two problems at once: Get rid of the man for good and save Laurel from heartbreak down the line, and maybe impress Caroline enough that she'd see Peter for the man he really was, a man who could take care of her quite wonderfully.

"Hey, Barton," someone called across the room. "You just got a telegram from someplace in Wyoming. About somebody named Peach Brady."

Laurel sat on the edge of her bed, her arms wrapped tightly around her waist as though to contain pain, her lips pressed tightly together against the horrible, racking, agonizing sobs that wanted to break through. What a fool she'd been. She had thought she was so clever, so in control . . . and all the while he'd been laughing at her. He'd told her he wanted respectability, roots, a home. And all the time what he'd really wanted was gold that he wasn't even sure existed. But he hadn't cared. Marrying her had been nothing more than a convenience.

She was a fool who had somehow, stupidly, without in any way being prepared for it, blundered into love with him. And that was the final insult, the ultimate indignity. She had fallen in love with him and he had rewarded her with betrayal, just as had every man she had ever known . . . even, as it turned out, her own father.

No! Not her father. Dear God, not her father. Not the illustrious Augustus Sinclair, scholar, gentleman farmer, hero to the Cause. He couldn't be a common thief. Not while the Confederacy for which he fought lay gasping in its death throes, not while his men were starving on the field of battle, not her father. He was a man of honor, of principle, a man whose only concerns

321

were for his family, his home, his way of life. *And who might do anything to protect them?*

The little voice spoke up insidiously, a snake hissing in the grass. She tried to block out the words, but the harder she tried the louder they grew. His last thoughts had been of his family and their welfare. His last letter . . .

The letter that Seth had married her to get. The pleas for her mother to bury Augustus in a certain spot, the warning to have no one but family present . . . the words of a dying man, she told herself — a man dying in pain, not knowing what he was saying. He wasn't writing about the gold. He wasn't.

But what if . . . what if it were true? What if her father and the Colonel had stolen the gold? What if he had buried it and now years later that legacy of cowardice and deception had come back to tear her life apart?

There could be hundreds of thousands of dollars buried there. She thought about all the years of suffering and doing without and scraping to get by — the money had been there, hers, and she had never known it. And Seth, whom she had foolishly trusted, whom she had almost begun to believe cared for her as much as she cared for him — he had known it was there, and not only had he kept it a secret from her, he had planned to steal it from her.

She gripped the bedpost until its carved pattern cut into her palm and she ground her teeth together to keep from screaming. She wanted to throw something, she wanted to hit, to destroy, to tear apart just as her world had been torn apart in these last few minutes. Why had he told her *now?* Now, when everything could have been so perfect, when they should have been celebrating, when it should have been the beginning of a new life together.

But that was easy to understand. He didn't need her anymore. He had a family in Savannah, railroad shares, and he didn't need her. He had only stayed as long as he thought she could help him, however unwittingly, find the gold. But he hadn't been able to find it. Laurel wanted to believe it didn't exist, but even as her mind clung to that thought, deep down inside she knew: Seth Tait might be a liar, a thief, a reprobate who'd used her and mocked them all, but he was no fool. He believed there was gold at Chinatree and he believed the clue was in Augustus' last letter.

She was staring straight ahead, her vision blurred with anger and pain, and gradually the object on the wall opposite her came into focus. She stood slowly, staring at it.

The gold was buried beneath the bench where her parents had first kissed. But that bench was long gone, and no one would ever guess where it might have been. All the landmarks were gone, burned, rotted or overgrown. Nothing remained of the way Chinatree once had been . . . except memories. And Laurel's mother had committed those memories to canvas.

There was a soft knock on the door, and Seth's voice. "Laurel."

She ignored it, walking slowly toward the painting.

The doorknob rattled. "Laurel, I'll go if you want me to. But not until I finish what I have to say. Open the door."

She took the painting from the wall. Her mother had not only preserved her memory of the bench where her husband had first kissed her — it was easy to discern, among the hundreds of other tiny details crowded onto the canvas, by the cherubic rendering of Cupid which hovered above the bench — she had honored her husband's last wishes in the only way she was able. Next to the bench was a macabre detail that would have been shocking had it been noticeable to the casual observer. But there were so many small details in the painting, all of them out of proportion and out of perspective, that it was impossible to notice every one of them. Laurel had looked at the painting a thousand times and never noticed this one. It was a small, dark tombstone planted in the grass, and her father's name was inscribed upon it in letters so infinitesimal as to be almost unreadable. What she could not do for Augustus in fact her mother had done in the painting, and the long-ago bench was preserved in time.

Laurel knew exactly where the gold was buried. She had walked across that very spot a hundred times.

Sophie had been drawn from the dining room where she was supervising the laying out of the evening meal when she'd heard the shouting from the other part of the house. Most alarmingly the voice had sounded like Laurel's, and although Sophie couldn't hear the whole argument, muffled as it was by the heavy cypress walls, she could still catch a word now and then. But now there was no mistake — Seth was definitely pounding on Laurel's bedroom door and shouting.

At first she tried to calm her alarm by telling herself it was only a lovers' quarrel, a newlyweds' silly spat over hurt feelings or misunderstood words or maybe even a disagreement over how much Laurel had spent on a new hat. But, of course, Laurel hadn't bought a new hat recently, and this sounded more like the shelling of Charleston than a lovers' tiff. Sophie motioned the cook back into the pantry with a firm hand, but she herself stayed transfixed at the bottom of the stairs. When she heard Laurel's door open, she moved away, but she had only gone halfway across the hall when Laurel came flying down the stairs, cheeks aflame, eyes blazing like coals.

"Laurel, dear, can I —" But Sophie hardly had the words out before Laurel pushed by her down the back hall that led to the stables.

"Laurel . . . Laurel!" Sophie pattered after her. "What is it? For heaven's sake, where are you going? What do you —"

"I'm going out to Chinatree!" Laurel called

without looking back. "Just leave me alone!"

"Chinatree!" Sophie was at the back door now, shouting across the courtyard. "On horseback? But you don't have a hat! Are you mad? Laurel, it's almost dark — come back here! You haven't had your supper! You can't —"

Laurel had already disappeared into the stables, and Sophie sagged against the wall, out of breath.

She turned gratefully when she heard Seth's steps, and caught at Seth's arm as he tried to brush by. "Mr. Tait, thank heavens! You must stop her. She's going to Chinatree and she doesn't even have a hat!"

Seth tried to move on but she tightened her grip, pleading. "Whatever you quarreled about can be remedied, but you simply can't let her —"

"I won't," Seth said grimly, and pulled away.

Just as her fingers dropped she heard the pounding of hoofbeats and saw Laurel on the back of her little bay dash wildly down the alley, hair flying, riding astride.

"Oh dear heavens," Sophie gasped, pressing a hand to her breast. "Look at that! Will you just look? What will people say?"

Seth replied tightly, "Before it's over, I'm afraid there's a hell of lot." And he pushed out the door toward the stables.

Edgar Cassidy had been undecided, but only for a moment. His first impulse had been to follow the woman and Brady on their headlong dashes from the house, but his carriage would be no match for their horses. He bridled his instincts and instead knocked on the door of the Sinclair house. Miss Sophie would tell him all he wanted to know in the batting of an eye.

He was surprised that it was Sophie herself who opened the door. "Laurel, thank . . ." She fell back when she saw Edgar Cassidy standing there, and he was quick to lend a supporting arm. Sophie's hair had come loose from its bun and strands fell wildly about her face. Her cheeks were flushed and her eyes glistened as if she'd been crying.

"Miss Sophie — is something wrong?" Cassidy felt a lightning-fast tingle of triumph. Something was happening, something important, and it could only be to his benefit. "I hope I haven't come at a bad time. I waited until I saw your niece leave the house —"

"What? Oh — oh, no, I mean, yes!" She looked at him distractedly. "Oh, Mr. Cassidy, perhaps this is a bad time. My niece and her husband just had a terrible quarrel and now she's run off and it's getting dark and they haven't had their supper, either of them!"

Cassidy tightened his grip on her arm and led her to the parlor. The last thing he wanted to do was be dismissed now. "But surely it's nothing to concern yourself with. Perhaps a glass of water?"

Sophie collapsed on the worn velveteen sofa and wrung her hands. "I told her, I told her not to go. But I've never seen her in such a state. She said she was going to Chinatree, of all places!"

Cassidy formed a polite smile. "Chinatree? I'm afraid . . ."

She waved a dismissing hand. "The old plantation, it's all burned down now. And way out in the country, with dark coming on . . . !"

"Would you like me to take my carriage," he offered, "and go after her?"

Sophie looked at him for a moment, the tears welling up again. "Oh, you *are* a kind man! But no . . ." She dabbed at her eyes with a balled-up handkerchief. "Mr. Tait has gone after her, but they were both so — I can't describe it. So *passionate!* It was really quite frightening, and I just can't think what could have happened to bring this on!"

Without asking, Cassidy went to the sideboard and poured a small glass of sherry for Sophie. She took it with trembling hands and downed it in one draught.

"Miss Sinclair, I really can't say how sorry I am to see you so distressed. We'll dispense with business for today, but you simply must allow me to stay until you're feeling better."

She raised her hand in feeble protest.

"No, I do insist." He sat across from her, smiling persuasively.

"Oh, you are too kind." She gulped back tears. "This has always been such a quiet household, it truly has. But — Laurel was almost hysterical. I could hear her screaming about lies and gold . . ." She looked up at Cassidy, tilting her head like a plump little bird. "Why would they be shouting about gold? And then Laurel came down, not even properly dressed for riding, and then Mr. Tait, looking like the devil himself."

Cassidy kept his smile in place, but his eyes were narrowed with rapid thought.

"Riding through the streets in her house dress with no hat and her husband chasing her," she fretted, "why it's no better than white trash. People like us don't carry on like that, Mr. Cassidy, and I hope you understand . . ."

The doorbell chimed for the third time that day.

Edgar stood quickly. "Allow me, Mrs. Sinclair. You're in no condition to handle any more crises," Cassidy said, and crossed the parlor. But before he could reach the front door, Caroline had already opened it, a worried look on her face.

"Peter . . . Chief Henderson. What —"

The group surged the parlor, the men making apologetic half-bows toward Sophie, whose head was lolling back on the sofa. "Miss Sophie," Henderson said formally, "we're sorry to burst in like this but we need to talk to Seth Tait. Is he at home?"

"No, no," Sophie said weakly. "He and Laurel have just left for Chinatree."

Peter's face mirrored his alarm. "She's gone alone to Chinatree with Tait?" He shot a quick look at the chief.

Sophie straightened, shooting a defiant look at Peter. While she might criticize her family to her heart's content, no one else was allowed to do so in her presence, a fact which Peter should have known very well. "They are married after all," she said icily. "Not that I can imagine it's any of your business. Why do you want to talk to Mr. Tait, Chief Henderson?" she said. "Perhaps I can give him the message."

Henderson looked embarrassed and regretful. "I'm afraid not, Miss Sophie. It's a personal matter."

He turned to Caroline and bowed. "Sorry to disturb you, Miss. Miss Sophie. We'll just go on out to Chinatree and see if we can't get this thing straightened out."

"And we'll bring Laurel back," Peter added grimly, "safe and sound."

Caroline put her hand on Peter's sleeve. "This is frightening me," she said, caught up in the intensity of Peter's voice. "What's going on? Please tell me —"

"You'll know soon enough, Caro," Peter said quietly. "Until then —"

Just at that moment Cassidy materialized out of the shadows of the room where he'd been watching intently. "Mr. Cassidy," Sophie said, "I'd almost forgotten." Then remembering her manners, "Do you know these gentlemen?"

"Only by reputation," Cassidy said, reaching in his pocket.

"I'd like to introduce myself. I'm Edgar Cassidy, Pinkerton Agency, New York City." He passed an identification card to the police chief. "I think I can be of some help on this case, and I'd like permission to accompany you to Chinatree."

"Case? Pinkerton? But you . . . you were . . ." Sophie struggled to get up from the sofa and then fell back in defeat. "Caroline," she whispered. "Get my smelling salts and get them now. I'm sure I'm going to faint."

Caroline stood frozen, looking from her mother to Peter, more terrified than she'd ever been in her life. "Peter, please, tell me . . ."

He unwound her fingers from his arm reluctantly, giving them a reassuring squeeze before letting go. "Do what your mother says, Caro, and no more questions, not now. We have to get going." He looked at the police chief, and then added quietly, "God help us all, you'll both know soon enough what's going on."

CHAPTER
Fifteen

Laurel's lungs were bursting by the time she entered the tunnel of live oaks that lined the drive to Chinatree; she felt as though she had run every one of the past seven miles on foot. She leaned low over the neck of the heaving little bay; she was sorry to press so hard, but she didn't slow down. She didn't know why she was running anyway. Seth was right behind her; she could hear the pounding of his horse's hooves above the sound of her own. He could have overtaken her at any time, but he hadn't; there was no need. He knew where she was going. And even though Laurel knew she couldn't outrun him she had to try, because what she was really running from was much bigger and much more frightening . . . but she couldn't outrun that either.

The air was hot and still, and inside the tunnel it had a greenish cast. The effect was other-worldly, muffling, disorienting, and for a moment it almost seemed as though nothing that had happened over the past few hours was real. Caroline had never gotten that letter from Savannah; Seth had never found out about his family; he had never told her why he had come here and she had never learned about his lies. Her father was not a thief; there was no gold; and she was not even now rushing toward the spot where it was buried.

But respite from the truth was only imaginary and all too brief. It *had* happened. She burst out of the tunneled drive and onto the twilit grounds of Chinatree, tugging on the reins so sharply that her horse skidded. She could see a pile of gardening tools propped up against a twisted tupelo and she slid off the horse, holding her skirts high to keep from tripping, and ran for them. She wasn't even sure why she was running until she heard Seth's voice behind her — close behind.

"Laurel, damn it, stop! What are you trying to do?"

Laurel reached the tools and grabbed one of them, a short, heavy-handled scythe. She whirled on him, bracing her feet and gripping the weapon, ready to swing. "Stay away from me!" she gasped. "I mean it!"

"Laurel, for God's sake, listen to me!"

"Do you think I'd believe anything you tell me now? Do you think I even *care?*"

He kept walking toward her, though slowly, and every step seemed pained and measured. The wind had tousled his hair and his face was shadowed in the twilight, sad and lined. "Is that it then?" he demanded quietly. "Are you going to kill me with that thing?"

Her hands tightened on the handle. "I won't kill you," she replied, breathing hard. "But I promise I'll hurt you if you don't *stop right there.* You're not going to win, Seth Tait. You've lied and cheated and used me and everyone in my family but you're not going to win!"

"Just what the hell are you going to do, Laurel?"

"I'm going to find the truth, something you're obviously not acquainted with. I'm going to find out if there's any gold or not. I know what the letter means, Seth, and I'm going to find out if my daddy was a hero or a traitor. You can't stop me."

"For God's sake, Laurel, nobody said your daddy was a traitor! You've heard what it was like in the South near the end of the war. Your father wanted the money for you and your mother, for your family, can't you see that? He was just trying to take care of you, like he always had. He did it out of love for you and your mother."

Laurel fought back the sudden bite of tears in her eyes. "Then I have to know, Seth. If what you've said is true, if the gold is there, then by all that's holy I'm going to have it and no one is going to stop me."

She thought she saw, in the uncertain light, the briefest flash of impatience cross his face. He kept coming toward her. "And then what?" he demanded. "How are you going to explain suddenly coming into a fortune in gold? What's going to happen when you try to spend it or take it to the bank? That gold is part of the federal treasury, Laurel. You don't think they're going to let you keep it, do you?"

He was trying to confuse her, and she angrily shook off the temptation to consider his words. "That never seemed to be a problem for you!"

"No, because I wasn't going to stay here. Because I know places to go where nobody asks questions and places to hide where nobody ever looks. Is that what you want? Is it?"

She hesitated, fighting the truth behind his words, denying it as long as she could and growing angrier and more confused with every moment. "Shut up!" she burst out. "You're lying again, you think you can trick me into trusting you, but you can't. The *only* thing I can trust is what I can see for myself, and if that gold is there, it's mine! It's mine and I intend to have it, do you understand that? You can't stop me!"

"For God's sake, Laurel, look at yourself!" He stopped then, and spread his hands. "Look what it's done to you — to both of us! I don't want the gold! I don't want to know where it is, I don't even want to know if it ever existed, it doesn't matter anymore! Don't you see that? I came back here because I promised, and then when I met you . . . I think from the beginning the main reason I wanted to find it was for you, so that you would be taken care of. But we don't need it now. Let it be, Laurel!"

She wanted to scream at him, to cover her ears

and blot out his lies . . . lies that she wanted to believe, lies she couldn't help believing because she needed them so badly . . . and because she could see, deep within his eyes, that they weren't lies at all.

With a muffled cry she flung the weapon down and turned blindly to run. In only a moment his arm snatched hers, overbalancing her, and she went down, his weight pinning her to the ground. He turned her over but her fists flailed at him, her feet kicked and she screamed out her help-lessness and rage. She wanted to hurt him as he had hurt her, she wanted to hurt him because she couldn't escape him, because she loved him and even now she couldn't stop.

She could see the desperation in his eyes, the need and the pain that was as great as her own. He dodged her wild blows, he caught her hands, he pinned her legs beneath him but she broke away again, cursing him hoarsely, until he stopped her cries with his mouth. She lifted her-self to him, pressing herself into him and losing herself in him, drinking of him as desperately as a moment ago she had fought him, as love and hate blurred for an instant into one and then the hate disappeared altogether leaving only love, and need. And desperate, desperate sorrow.

"Laurel," he whispered hoarsely against her neck. His arms were so tight around her that they hurt. "Don't you know how much I love you? I never wanted to, I never thought I could, but I never had a choice . . . just like I never had a choice about hurting you."

Her face was wet with tears. "Oh Seth, why didn't you tell me about the gold? Why did you lie to me?"

He lifted his face and looked down at her. His own face was ravaged, his eyes dark with a pain so deep that it hurt Laurel, just looking at it. "Oh Laurel, I had to."

He pulled her to her feet, holding her shoulders to steady her. Her throat was dry and her limbs were trembling; she had to hold on to his arms for support. He looked at her intently, and his gaze seemed to go through her soul.

He said, "The man who raised me, who told me about the gold — his name was Colonel Ike."

She stared at him. Peter had talked about Colonel Ike and a man named Brady. All the time it had been in the back of her mind, a fuzzy, blurred connection . . . but it was a connection she couldn't quite make. Or perhaps was unwilling to make.

His eyes closed slowly as though against a long, sharp pain. "Oh, Laurel, don't you understand yet? Don't you know who I am?"

"No," she whispered. And even though it was all beginning to come together, much too clearly, much too fast, still she repeated, "No."

He opened his eyes, looking at her sadly. "I couldn't tell you about the gold without telling you how I knew. And I guess — since I came here all I've been trying to do is forget how I knew."

He lifted his hand, as though to smooth a strand of her tangled hair, then let it drop again uncertainly. His tone was heavy. "What I told you, as much as I told you, was true — my folks did die on the trail, and my name is Seth Tait. But I didn't know my name for years after the Colonel found me and he had to call me something." He looked away briefly, then back at her.

"One other thing I told you was true, Laurel, though I didn't mean for it to be, or even know it was, at the time. I did come back here to find my home, my family, to find out what I could be . . . something I could never do out west. The gold was just an excuse. Look." With a gentle pressure on her shoulders he turned her around. "Look what I've been doing out here all these weeks. I didn't realize it myself until just now. I thought I was looking for the gold, but I wasn't."

Through the lengthening shadows of twilight Laurel was able to see quite clearly what she had been too distraught to notice before. The weeds and undergrowth had been cleared away to reveal a smooth, level yard. The crumbling fence around the graveyard had been righted and repainted, the graves cleared of debris and weeds. Crumbled bricks, remnants of wooden pillars and collapsed walls had been hauled away. The brook that used to wander through the garden had been cleared out and now ran freely again. The face of an old sundial, long buried beneath the rubble, had been righted and set in place again. Seth had not been searching for the past. He had been clearing way for the future.

Laurel turned back to him, aching and unsure, loving him more than ever and terrified that that was not enough.

Seth said, "Here my name is Seth Tait. I have a home, and a family, and it even turns out I've got a past, and money to build a future on. That's why I don't need the gold. But out west my name is Peach Brady, and that's why I couldn't tell you about the gold when it might have made a difference. And that's why it's too late for us now."

He must have heard it long before Laurel did — the sound of hoofbeats, coming up the drive. There was no need for speculation or reasoning it out or denying the inevitable; she knew what those approaching riders meant and she could feel the time that was left to them ticking off with each beat of her heart.

She gripped his arm. "Seth, it's not too late for us, it doesn't have to be! I know where the gold is, my mother — she left a clue, too, even if she didn't mean to! We can get the gold and we can run away —"

He shook his head shortly. "Do you think I haven't wanted to ask you to do that? A dozen times since I realized someone was after me here, and it was only a matter of time . . . I kept thinking, if only I could find the gold, I could

339

take you with me even if I had to kidnap you — Mexico, Canada, even Europe . . . But you can't leave this place, your family. And . . ." With a simple, final gesture of his hand he indicated their surroundings. "I guess in my own mind I knew I wasn't going anywhere either. It's home, and I'm tired of running."

She caught his sleeve. "Seth, don't be a fool! It doesn't matter what you've done in the past, it's what you do now that counts! You were trying to help us, I see that now, and even — even lying to me was just your way of protecting me."

She cast a desperate glance over her shoulder and she could see them now, silhouetted against the dark tunnel like Stygian sentinels. There were three of them, and one of them she recognized by his uniform. Police Chief Henderson. She shook Seth's arm. "Seth, for God's sake, get to your horse! Run! I'll tell them — I'll tell them something, I'll keep them here. Just *go!*"

But he didn't move. He just looked down at her, a gentle smile in his eyes even behind the sorrow. "I'm sorry, Laurel."

"We need you, Seth — *I* need you! You can't just give up!"

He kissed her tenderly on the forehead. "Laurel," he said quietly, "Leave the gold. It's only going to bring grief to whoever touches it. And whatever happens, you're still Seth Tait's wife. You'll be taken care of."

She looked at him helplessly, desperately and it seemed in that moment all of him was imprinted on her soul — the shape of his brow, his wind-tossed hair, the pain in his eyes, the touch of his fingers, hard on her arms, the whisper of his breath . . . Seth. Hers for too short a time, the only man she had ever loved. And now it was too late.

Not until they turned into the tree-lined drive leading to Chinatree, until he saw the two horses loosely tethered and knew that it wasn't a wild-goose chase, that Seth Tait was here, did Peter actually believe what had happened within the past two hours. Seth Tait was Peach Brady, notorious outlaw of book and legend. He had known from the beginning there was something not right with Tait but he had never expected anything like this . . . never imagined it could be this big, this important, this real.

And then he saw Laurel, and for the first time since his dash down Meeting Street to the police station on the corner, he thought about what the truth might do to her, what it might do to Caroline and Miss Sophie. Seth Tait was Peach Brady, a famous and notorious criminal, and Peter had tracked him down. Breaking this story would be his own ticket to fame and fortune. At the same time publishing it in the *Gazette* would bring ruin and shame to the people he cared about most in the world.

Peter tried to reconcile the two conflicting issues. He had to tell the world about Peach Brady; it was his duty. Yet a twist of fate made his doing the right thing, which would bring him the recognition that had always been out of reach, hurt not only Laurel but Sophie and Caroline. He struggled to convince himself that eventually all of them would be grateful that he'd ferreted out the viper in their midst, for how long would any of them be safe with a man like Peach Brady living in their house? He had no choice. They would simply have to understand that.

They drew up in the shadows of the ruined chimneys of Chinatree. Nearby two horses were tied to a low-hanging limb, and less than five hundred yards away stood Laurel and Seth, unmoving, watching them in the twilight.

"You'd damn well better be right about this, Barton," Chief Henderson said. "I got to tell you, I don't feel easy in my mind about any of it."

Peter felt the muscles tighten across the back of his neck. "It's not me," he said shortly. "It has nothing to do with me. I'm just reporting what that sheriff in Wyoming telegraphed."

Cassidy drew up his horse beside Henderson's. "It's him, Chief," he said quietly. "I've been chasing him, and his partner Colonel Ike, for a long time."

Henderson glanced at him and then away. His voice was heavy with resignation as he said, "I reckon we'd better move in, then."

"Are you armed, Chief?" asked Cassidy. "I have a gun myself if you need me."

The chief looked at him sharply. "I'll be handling this, Cassidy, no need of your gun. I let you come along as a favor. I suggest you remember that."

"With all due respect sir, that man is a notorious criminal, a gunfighter. You don't know what he's likely to do —"

"With all due *respect,*" returned Henderson shortly, "I've sat down at that man's supper table and I'm not going to go pulling a gun on him without cause. I want this to go smooth and easy and I don't want Miss Laurel hurt. God knows the heartache of this will be enough for her." He nudged his horse forward.

At the chief's words Peter felt his own heart constrict into a tight, hard knot. The man *was* a criminal. But try as he might, Peter could not think of one thing Seth Tait had done since coming here that warranted his arrest. He had kept a roof over the Sinclair ladies' heads. He had garnered Caroline's admiration. He had made Laurel happy.

Still, he was a wanted man in Wyoming and Peter wasn't responsible for that. He was responsible only for a criminal's capture. Tightening his lips, Peter urged his horse after those of the chief and Cassidy.

Laurel watched them approach, her hand tightening on Seth's arm. "Please," she said urgently. "Seth, I'm begging you — go. I'll come to you, wherever you say, only go now before it's too late!"

He smiled faintly. "And be shot in the back? That's not the way I picture meeting my Maker."

He sobered. "That's not the way I want you to remember me."

"Seth —"

"No." He lifted his hand then, firmly smoothing away a smudge of dirt on her cheek. There was no smile on his lips now, or in his eyes. "I know about living on the run, Laurel, and it's not what I want for you. For us."

And that was it. When Laurel looked up, Chief Henderson was dismounting and coming toward them. Behind him was another man Laurel didn't know, and Peter.

Peter.

Seth said, "Good evening, Chief." He glanced over Henderson's head and the corner of his lips tightened in the beginnings of a smile. "Barton."

Chief Henderson looked uncomfortable, but he met Seth's eyes . . . and he kept his hand on the butt of his gun. He said, "Seems there's a warrant out for your arrest in Wyoming, Tait. I've come to take you in."

Seth just nodded. "I'm not armed, Chief. And I won't put up a fight."

"That's good." Henderson sounded sad. "We don't want any gun play around Miss Laurel. I'm going to have to put these cuffs on you."

Seth stepped forward and held out his wrists and then Laurel couldn't stay still any more. She grabbed Henderson's arm. "Chief — Jack," she pleaded, "how can you do this? You know this is a mistake, it has to be! You can't . . ."

His eyes were filled with genuine regret. "I

344

have to do my job, Miss Laurel, much as I wish I didn't sometimes. I am sorry." He looked at Seth as he snapped the handcuffs in place. "You too, Tait. I never would've figured . . ."

But he let the words trail off with a shake of his head as he led Seth away.

Laurel wanted to cry out, to run after them, to fling herself on Seth and refuse to let him go. She wanted to shout reassurances and promises, to tell him everything would be all right, she would do something, anything, whatever it took to set him free. But she didn't have the breath, and she didn't trust her voice.

She watched through a hot blur of tears as the chief helped Seth to mount his horse, then took the reins and turned both horses toward the drive. Seth did not look back.

Distantly she heard the squeak of leather and jingle of bridle as someone dismounted, and foot-steps approached her.

"Come on, Laurel. I'll see you home."

Laurel jerked away when Peter touched her shoulder. The haze of grief left her, the mind-numbing loss was stripped away, and as she looked at Peter, everything congealed into stark cold clarity. "You," she said slowly, hoarsely. "It had to have been you. Caroline told me you were investigating him but she didn't say . . ."

"She didn't know," Peter admitted. He couldn't quite meet her eyes. "I just got the telegram this afternoon. Listen, Laurel, I know this hurts you now, but in the long run it's for the best."

Laurel drew back her arm and struck him across the face, so hard that he staggered back.

"How dare you," she breathed, low and ragged. "How dare you assume to know what's best for me. How dare you interfere where you don't belong. How dare you stand there now and look me in the face —"

"For God's sake, Laurel, he's an outlaw!"

"Is he?" she cried. "What has he ever done to you, Peter? Did he go behind your back digging into your past? If he had he might have found a pretty thing or two, mightn't he? Did he pretend to be your friend while sneaking and lying behind your back —"

"Laurel, I didn't —"

"Get out of my sight!" She pushed him hard in the chest. "Go on, get your story, that's all you cared about in the first place isn't it? Well, it's yours. You have it, but that's *all* you have! Go on, get away from me!"

Peter looked torn and miserable. "Laurel, I can't leave you out here alone."

Contempt and fury laced every word as Laurel replied, "If you're still here by the time I'm in the saddle I won't be responsible for what I do." Laurel picked up her skirts and pushed past him.

Peter hesitated, his expression agonized, and then Cassidy spoke up quietly behind him. "Perhaps it would be best if you went on ahead, sir. I'll ride with the young lady."

For another moment Peter lingered, then he

swore softly to himself. "I guess I can't do anything but harm here." He swung into the saddle. "I'd better go prepare Miss Sophie and Miss Caroline for what's happened."

Cassidy waited until Peter's horse had cantered down the drive before he turned his own horse around. Laurel had reached her horse but had not mounted; she stood with her forehead pressed against the horse's neck, perhaps hiding tears, perhaps near collapse. Cassidy dismounted respectfully a few feet from her and walked the rest of the way.

When she heard him approach Laurel straightened, injecting strength into her muscles, her mind working frantically. Judge Casper. He was an old friend, and he had liked Seth the few times he'd met him . . . Judge Casper would listen to her. He would help her. He had to.

Cassidy said, "Can I help you, ma'am?"

"Not unless you know a good lawyer." She grabbed the pommel and prepared to mount.

"As a matter of fact I know several, but I'm afraid none of them can help your husband now."

She looked at him sharply. "Who are you?"

He reached into his pocket and took out a leather identification case. "I'm Edgar Cassidy, with the Pinkerton Detective Agency. I tracked Peach Brady all the way from Wyoming."

Laurel stiffened. "Then I have nothing to say to you."

He smiled. "I can understand your feelings ma'am. I don't have anything against Brady myself, and if you'll excuse my saying so, there's got to be a lot of good in a man who could command the loyalty of a woman like you."

Laurel stared at him.

"Personally," Cassidy went on, "I always figured it was his partner, Colonel Ike, who was responsible for most of what Brady got blamed for. And with the Colonel dead, why I figure all Brady wanted was to come on back east and make a new life for himself. Looks like he had a good one, too." He shook his head. "It's a shame."

Laurel's voice was tight with suspicion. "Then why did you follow him back east? What are you doing here?"

"Do you mean with those other two?" He gestured back the way Peter and the chief had gone and smiled again, faintly. "Well, that was just lucky coincidence. I'm not interested in Peach Brady's crimes, that's not my case. No, it was the Colonel I've been tracking all these years — and a federal payroll of stolen gold."

Laurel's heart began to pound, slow and heavy. She tried to keep her face still, but he must have seen something in her eyes because he smiled gently.

"He told you about it, didn't he? I thought he would have. You see, that's all I'm here for, ma'am. To interview Peach Brady about that gold." He glanced at the sky. "And I reckon I'd better be getting on with it. It's nearing dark, so if you're ready to go I'd be pleased to ride back to town with you."

But Laurel didn't move. She stood there, gripping the reins, desperation pulsing in her veins. "What are they going to do to my husband, Mr. Cassidy?"

"Well, first they'll have to extradite him. It's long and involved and expensive. But since Brady — or Tait — has committed no crime in South Carolina, he sure can't be tried here."

Laurel forced the next words. "And then?"

Cassidy lowered his eyes briefly. "Frontier justice is swift and harsh, ma'am, and some of the things Brady's charged with are federal offenses."

"Do you mean — hanging offenses?"

For a moment he didn't answer, and then he said, "Of course, I'll be glad to put in a word for him if Brady is willing to cooperate in my investigation. Finding that gold would mean a lot more to my employers than hanging one outlaw — one who's already shown he's trying to go straight."

Through the daze of horror Laurel grasped on to one phrase. "Your — employers?"

"The U.S. Treasury Department, ma'am," Cassidy said. "Some say the longest arm of the law."

He turned toward his horse, adding, "Of course, he might not even know where the gold is. In which case I couldn't help him at all."

"Wait," Laurel said sharply. She pressed her fingers to her temples, trying to think.

Cassidy looked back at her.

"What if," she said, "What if you had the gold — all of it. Not just the information, but the actual gold . . . what could you do for my husband?"

His eyes narrowed as he looked at her. "Ma'am, do you know something you should be telling me?"

She held his gaze. "Answer my question."

For a long time he seemed to be debating. It seemed like a lifetime to Laurel. Then he said, "Deals are made all the time. If the only way we could get the gold was to give Peach Brady an amnesty, I imagine it would be a simple enough thing. Of course, you realize we couldn't even consider anything like that until the gold was actually in our possession."

Laurel let the reins drop from her fingers and walked over to the pile of tools Seth had left stacked together; from them she selected a shovel. Cassidy followed her as she crossed the yard to a gnarled spreading oak, circled to its east side, and took three steps out from its trunk. She handed Cassidy the shovel.

"Start digging, Mr. Cassidy," she said.

"No, Mrs. Tait. Or should I say Mrs. Brady?" Smiling, Cassidy withdrew a pistol from inside his coat pocket. "*You* start digging."

CHAPTER
Sixteen

The jailhouse was a big, square, unpretentious building on the corner of Meeting and Broad which served both as police headquarters and holding area for prisoners. Thirty or so prisoners swelled its ranks that night, mostly drunks and wife beaters, and Seth's entrance caused quite a stir.

He was put into a cell with six other men, two of whom were snoring drunkenly. The others regarded him with a mixture of suspicion and skeptical admiration. One, a toothless, whip-cord thin man of indeterminate age, grinned at Seth, studying him unabashedly.

"Well, look at you." His voice was as thin as his body. "What's a clean-looking fella like you doing here? Rich, too. Look at them boots. You get caught in the wrong bed, did you?"

"Something like that."

The cots were full and so was the floor. Seth stood by the iron door, resisting the urge to put his hands on the bars.

"Who?" A big man in a dirty flannel undershirt and baggy trousers sat up, scowling. "Who you talkin' about?"

"Don't you pay attention to nothing? This fellow here, plain he don't belong here. Look at them boots . . ."

Seth wondered, for perhaps the last time in his life, what the Colonel would think if he could see him now. Somehow, throughout all they had been through, all they had done, and despite the fact that he had always known what he was doing and what he deserved, Seth had never really believed it could end like this. Behind bars. The fetid smell of iron and urine and unwashed bodies filling up his nostrils, the air thick with hopelessness, shadows of fear circling and lighting and circling again like lazy black flies. He had never thought it would come to this. Not once.

Laurel, quiet and clean, was a lifetime away from this place, like something that might have been but never quite was, something he almost had but couldn't quite reach. The little house on Lamboll Street. Real silver on the table and chipped china in the cupboard. Peeling wallpaper and faded rugs and generations upon generations of memories . . . home. Something else that was never quite his.

"Say." The skinny man, braver now, stood close to Seth, thrusting his face forward to make himself noticed. Seth could smell his perspiration and sour breath, but there was no belligerence in the face — more like curiosity, mixed with sympathy. "What d'ya figure they're going to do to you, fella, now that they got ya?"

Seth looked out the cell toward the empty corridor where a single uniformed sentinel stood guard. "Hang me, I reckon."

Hang me. He had never expected that, either. He should have, but he never had.

The silence in the cell was appropriately reverent. Then the big fellow spoke up. "You done something worth hanging for?"

Seth looked at the opposite wall, stone blocks that were scarred and water-stained. This was a dismal place. No medieval dungeon could have been more oppressive. "No," he answered quietly, after a time. "I can't think of a thing."

Then he raised his voice a little. "Sergeant."

The officer turned his head, then approached cautiously. He stopped a good ten feet from the bars, regarding Seth suspiciously. "What do you want?"

"Paper, and a pen," he answered, "and somebody to be my witness. I need to make a will."

The officer's eyes narrowed. "You're the one wanted out of state, ain't you? What makes you think an old outlaw like you's got anything to leave anybody anyhow?"

"I don't," Seth replied tiredly. He couldn't resist the urge any longer. He put his hands on the bars, closing his fingers around them. "But Seth Tait does. Ask the chief. I've got a right to make a will. And I want it done here, in Charleston.

Before . . . before they ship me back west."

The officer looked uncertain. "Well, I'll ask. But it don't seem regulation to me —"

He broke off, staring, as the bars beneath Seth's hands suddenly shifted. Seth felt it, but he did not have time to look because it was not just the bars that were moving. The cots that were bolted to the wall began to swing, the floor beneath his feet shuddered, metal hinges squeaked and scraped. A sudden fierce lurch threw Seth sideways but he held on to the bars and righted himself in time to see the Sergeant, with astonishment stamped on his face, plunge backward onto the floor as though shoved by an invisible hand. He dropped his rifle and it skittered across the floor toward the cell and then, incredibly, slid backward again. People were shouting. Metal was screaming. There was a low, crashing, rumbling noise in the distance and Seth turned to see his cellmates, terror stamped on their faces, tossed in a tangle of arms and legs on the floor. He tried to push away from the bars but the ground shifted and plunged beneath him, flinging him back. People were screaming now, trying to run, trying to crawl, but it was too late. Seth lifted his arm to shield his face as a long, groaning crack appeared in the opposite wall, and stones and mortar began to collapse inward.

The ground was hard and thick with grass and roots, and the digging was slow. Laurel's back ached and her arms ached but she kept digging

— not because she could feel Cassidy's gun on her but because she was waiting for her moment, gauging the distance, gathering her strength. Not now, but soon, she would position the shovel as though to dig but bring it out instead, catching Cassidy broadside across the middle or, if she could manage it, the head.

She paused, bringing her sleeve across her face to push back escaping strands of hair, leaving a streak of mud. "You lied," she said. "You're not a Pinkerton agent. I should have known that. I would have known that if I hadn't been thinking about — about Seth and what had happened. The Pinkerton Agency doesn't know about the gold. The government doesn't even know about the gold. Nobody ever knew about it but my father and Colonel Ike, and the people they told."

Cassidy smiled tightly. "And one other person — the man they stole it from. I was on guard duty that night, you see, and I've never forgotten, never given up. I was just a private and even though it was wartime, even though the whole train was wiped out, I was too ashamed to go back and report that I'd let two confederates steal the payroll. Because that's what I did, you know." His voice tightened with bitterness. "They pulled their guns on me and I blubbered like an idiot, I turned it over to them. I was eighteen years old. And I never forgave myself. I deserted the army, let them think I was dead. I've been lying ever since, lying and chasing a man called Colonel Ike, and the life he stole from me."

His eyes came back to her as though from a long distance. "If anyone deserves that gold, I do. Not you. Not Peach Brady. I've spent my life looking for it. It's mine."

And then he smiled thinly. "But I didn't lie about being a detective. I had to make a living while I was hunting down my dream, and Pinkerton had everything I needed to do both. Keep digging."

"It's dark. I can't see."

It was past nine o'clock and twilight was more than grainy — it was thick with shadows. Cassidy looked uneasy, but he ordered sharply, "You don't need to see. Just dig."

"It's not here. Maybe I was wrong —"

"You were sure enough when you thought it would get that precious outlaw of yours out of jail."

And Laurel saw her chance. "There isn't any gold!" she sobbed. "There never was, it was all a lie, a filthy, rotten lie . . ." She raised the shovel as though to fling it down in frustration, and she could see the startlement on Cassidy's face as she pivoted at the last minute to swing the shovel on him. He raised his pistol in the same instant and fired.

Laurel hit the ground hard and she thought she was shot. There was a roaring in her ears, a terrible rumbling, crashing sound, and the trees overhead were bending and twisting wildly. That's when she knew she wasn't shot because Cassidy was on the ground too, and when she tried

356

to push herself to her feet she couldn't because the earth itself was moving.

That was when the world went crazy. She got to her knees, gripping the trunk of the oak for support. In the distance she heard the terrified high-pitched whinny of a horse. Cassidy got to his feet, staggering drunkenly, flailing his arms for balance, and Laurel could see — she could actually *see* — the ground swelling and buckling beneath his feet. And then, with a horrible ripping noise, a fissure opened up in the three feet of ground that separated her from Cassidy. Laurel screamed and pressed herself backward against the tree. The fissure traveled like a forked-tongue snake, opening up earth in its wake, and Cassidy stared at it, mesmerized. When he began to run it was too late; the fissure swallowed the earth beneath his feet and Cassidy with it. Then it sealed itself raggedly and was no more.

Laurel could hear herself screaming. She screamed and screamed until she was hoarse and all that came out of her mouth were silent gasping sounds. The tree to which she was clinging began to shake, flinging her backward. Mutely she stared as it swayed, and leaned, and she gathered her skirts and ran as the two-hundred-year-old oak slowly pulled its roots out of the ground and fell with a crash that deafened her. Laurel sank to the ground and prayed.

She didn't know how long it lasted. A minute, an hour. A lifetime of horror. Finally everything was still. She opened her eyes. Even in the dark she could see the devastation, and what she couldn't see she could remember. Cassidy, swallowed alive, buried forever with the gold he had spent his life trying to find. Great rips and bulges scarred the ground, trees were overturned, the horses . . .

She stood slowly, turning around, trying to get her bearings in the dark. She had to get home. She had to get somewhere it was safe, away from here, just away from here . . .

She stumbled along, feeling her way in the dark, tripping over uprooted saplings and mounds of earth, terrified of falling into one of those fissures, of being sucked down to the center of the earth as Cassidy had been. Judgment Day, she thought, it's Judgment Day for all of us, it has to be. Oh Seth, I'm sorry, I should have trusted you, I should have believed in you, I should have been with you . . .

Through the tunnel with its crushed and shattered trees, climbing over piles of them, scratching her face and her hands and circling hundreds of feet around them. It went on forever. She could never find her way back to town like this, in the dark, with all the landmarks destroyed. She had to get back. She had to be with Seth, she had to tell him.

Suddenly she heard a sound, and she froze. "Please," she whispered.

A crashing in the brush. Her heart stopped. A soft whinny and she closed her eyes, weak with relief. She stumbled toward the sound until she could make out in the dark the shape of her own bay, standing in the shadows of the woods. She grabbed the reins, whispering "Good girl, oh beautiful girl."

Suddenly the earth shook again. The horse bucked and tried to rear, but Laurel held on tight to the reins. Terror made her rigid; she wanted to scream but she hadn't any breath; all she could do was hold on and prepare to die.

Then it was over. The earth was still again. The bay stood heaving and trembling at her side; the reins were wrapped so tightly about her hands that she could feel the sting of blood. But she was alive.

She rested her face against the horse's mane and wept.

When Seth regained consciousness he thought he had died, after all, and this was hell. He could hear the moans of the tortured and smell the smoke and flames. He couldn't see and he thought it was because it was dark or he was blind, but when he wiped his arm across his eyes it came away wet and sticky and he realized his face was covered with blood. A falling chunk of mortar had cut a gash in his scalp; there was a lot of blood and considerable pain, but the wound did not appear to be mortal. He sat up carefully, dislodging chunks of stone and rubble, testing his arms and legs. His head swam and he experienced an alarming surge of weakness, but it passed. Gradually his eyes focused.

The night was lit with a flickering orange glow and the air was thick with smoke and dust. Gradually he realized that it wasn't the jail that was on fire, but the world outside . . . a world clearly visible through the collapsed outer wall. He got to his feet, half-stumbling, half-climbing over rubble that was waist high in places. Once his hand brushed over a body and Seth thought the prisoner was dead, but then he heard a moan and the figure struggled to his knees. It was the big man who had spoken to him earlier. He was dazed but otherwise unharmed. Seth helped him to his feet and watched him stumble through the collapsed wall into the world outside — a world that was, no doubt, turned just as upside down as this one was.

Seth found three more of his cellmates. The others had either escaped already, or were hopelessly buried beneath the rubble. He could hear cries from other parts of the building, and somewhere outside the faint, almost pathetically inadequate clang of fire bells. He hesitated, bracing himself against the half-fallen wall, trying to get his breath and clear his head. *Laurel.* He had to find Laurel. Miss Sophie, Caroline . . . the world had gone crazy. People were screaming; shouts for help, moans of agony. He pushed away from the wall and stumbled back toward the inner building.

The cell door sagged on its hinges and he pushed through easily. One end of the corridor was blocked, but at the other there was a gap in the stone wall big enough to drive a wagon through. Seth climbed through and emerged onto more chaos.

Another long cell was filled with prisoners, and they had not been so lucky. Some were pinned under cots and fallen rubble, others had been injured in the panic. They beat against the bars, they pried at the window with wooden legs torn from the cots, they screamed at Seth and stretched their arms through the bars, tearing at his clothes as he passed. Seth pulled away from them, pushing forward. He heard a muffled moan and moved toward the sound. A man lay on his side on the floor, half-buried beneath the fallen lintel from the doorway that separated the cells from the barracks. Seth knelt beside him.

It was Chief Henderson.

His face was ash white and drawn with pain, but his eyes registered recognition when he saw Seth. "My pocket," he whispered. "Cell keys. Get them."

Seth turned his attention to trying to lift the lintel that trapped him.

"No!" Henderson grabbed for his arm. "Listen — to me. This place could go at any minute. All those prisoners — trapped. Get the — goddamn keys!"

Seth hesitated, then the earth began to shake again. He bent over Henderson as the ceiling rained mortar and the support beams creaked ominously. The rumblings subsided, but the howls of terror from the cells had only increased. Seth looked at Henderson for another moment, then searched the other man's pockets until he found the keys. He ran to open the cell doors.

He did not know how many of the prisoners would survive the stampede for freedom. He did not know if any of them would survive if the earth heaved again, if the building started to crumble before they got out. He fought the tide, making his way back to Henderson.

The chief looked surprised. "You — are a crazy man. Get out of here."

Seth put his back to lifting the beam. "Your legs. Can you move them?"

"Don't be a fool, man. Another tremor could finish this place. Get out while you have a chance."

Seth tightened his muscles, lifting with all his strength. The beam lifted a fraction. He felt the shift of weight as the chief tried to pull free. "Hurry! I can't —" He redoubled his efforts, his head bursting.

"I'm out!"

Seth let the beam collapse.

The chief struggled to his feet, and then leaned against the doorframe beside Seth, both men gasping. At last Henderson raised his head. He held Seth's eyes for a long time. Then he said, "Let's get out of here."

Laurel awoke to the sound of angry chattering and for a moment she thought perhaps she'd died and heaven was inhabited by a troop of vociferous squirrels. Slowly she opened her eyes and focused. On a tree lying at an angle across two others, three gray squirrels voiced their obvious displeasure at the wreckage around them. Laurel struggled to a sitting position, every bone in her body aching, and took in the scene. The squirrels, alarmed by her sudden movement, scurried off into the underbrush, still chattering, while Laurel rose to her feet and looked around in wonder and in awe. Trees were torn from their roots and tumbled about, rocks had been flung from the earth and were heaped in untidy piles; it looked as though the world had been turned upside down, and Laurel was surprised — almost suspicious — to find herself still alive.

Snatches of the night came back to her like someone else's nightmare. She had ended up leading the mare, afraid the horse would step into a newly opened hole and fling Laurel over her head, or break a leg and force Laurel to leave her suffering. The night was blindly dark and terrifyingly still — except for those times when the earth shook again, flinging her to the ground and pelting her with falling rocks and limbs. She had lost the road somehow. She remembered finally, after one particularly terrifying tremor, covering her head with her arms and curling herself into a ball, determined not to take another step . . . and that way she had stayed, sleeping fitfully, throughout the night.

She was thirsty and achy. Her throat felt like sandpaper and her head throbbed, but she was alive. She heard the jingle of bridle and saw her horse, standing not far from where she had dropped the reins last night, nibbling grass beneath a tree. And the road — gutted and broken, strewn with limbs and heavy branches and overturned boulders, but still a road — was no more than a hundred feet away.

She had to get back to Charleston. The morning was so quiet here it was possible to close her eyes and believe that nothing had happened at all. Already the birds were rebuilding their nests, the squirrels looking for food. But had Charleston survived? Had the same devastation struck the city? And if so, Caroline, Sophie . . . Seth. What had become of Seth? *Oh, God, let Seth be all right.* Caroline and Sophie — how would they cope, who would take care of them? How frightened they must be. She had to get to them and she had to find Seth.

She caught her bay's reins and led her to the road, then, forcing her aching, battered muscles, Laurel mounted. She lifted the reins and nudged the horse into a careful walk. "Come on, girl, we're going home . . . if we can find it."

CHAPTER
Seventeen

By late afternoon Laurel reached the city. All around her were scenes of devastation and tragedy — houses whose chimneys had toppled into the streets, sidewalks upended and broken. Families were camping outside, trying to cover with quilts and blankets what few possessions they'd rescued. There was noise and confusion and heartbreak, certain to be followed by death and disease and pestilence. It's like something out of the Bible, Laurel reflected in dazed horror as her horse picked its way carefully through the rubble. She thought of the plagues that had tormented Charleston — first the war and then the cyclone of '85 and now this . . .

She stopped twice to get water for herself and the horse, and at the second house the old man who showed her to the horse trough insisted that she take some food — a slice of corn bread and a piece of ham. When she demurred he said, "At a time like this what's mine is my neighbor's. It's the only way we're ever going to pull through this."

She wolfed it down, grateful for the first food she'd had in almost twenty-four hours. He smiled at her and told her to slow down — whatever she was looking for was either standing or not, and hurrying wouldn't make any difference.

When she asked him if he'd heard anything about the buildings beyond Broad and Meeting streets, he'd shaken his head. "Don't know. News travels slow. I just hear it's bad all around. We're all sleeping in the streets tonight — safest place to be if the shaking begins again."

"I pray that it's over," she said fervently. "Surely it's over."

"That's for God to know — but whatever, we'll survive. Charleston always survives, Miss. You know that."

Laurel nodded as she climbed on the tired horse and headed it toward Meeting Street.

The old man was right: Charleston always managed to survive, but at what cost? What about the people she loved, the people who needed her to take care of them? And Seth . . . there were things she hadn't said to him and needed to say. So much had happened since she had awakened in his arms yesterday morning and even when she had thought the worst was over, there had been even more. But even until the moment they had taken him away, even as Cassidy was holding a gun on her, forcing her to dig for the gold that had brought nothing but misery and loss from the moment of its taking — even then, she had expected to see Seth again. But now . . .

The deeper she rode into the heart of the city, the more apparent and frightening the damage was. Houses packed close together had tumbled one upon the other; garden walls and chimneys had fallen, blocking the streets so that Laurel had to detour through yards and along alleys, often losing her way and spending precious time trying to find a familiar street that would lead her home. Church steeples lay shattered in the streets, stained glass lay in shards, glittering like jewels in the dust in the late afternoon sunlight. A great church bell lay cracked in the street, a cross lay broken on the ground.

Farther down Meeting, Hibernian Hall was still standing though its marble portico lay in pieces in the street. The building, as perfect in its conception as a Classic Greek temple, was a symbol to Laurel of what Charleston had always been, and the sun reflecting off the hall's columns gave her hope that she would find her home and family still intact. St. Michael's seemed undamaged and that too gave her heart a lift. The old man had been right — Charleston was surviving, Charleston would endure.

Half a block farther at the corner of Broad and Meeting she swung down from her horse and led it through the jostling crowd. The streets filled: police, city workers, firemen, and the beginnings of some kind of militia were all shouting, giving orders. City Hall and the Courthouse seemed to have suffered little damage.

Trembling, she hurried toward the Main Station, the police department and jail, on the corner of Meeting and Broad where Seth would have been taken if he had made it this far. She did not know whether to hope he had been safely inside the building, or to hope he had escaped. When she saw the shape the building was in she knew, with a cold stab of terror in the pit of her stomach, what to hope.

Huge granite blocks that made up the building were dislodged, and there were holes in the wall as though from cannonballs. Windows were shattered, the roof was sagging . . .

"Oh dear God," she whispered. "Seth . . ." Could anyone have survived that? Could anyone still be inside? She slid off her horse and started toward the building.

The policeman who was guarding it stepped out and stopped her. "Sorry ma'am, that's off limits. You can't go in."

"But my — my husband was in that jail." She looked past him desperately. "I've got to see him."

He shook his head. "Well, you won't find him there, ma'am. The jail's been evacuated."

"Evacuated?" Hope flared. "Then the people who were inside — they're all right? Where did they go?"

He looked at her sadly and kindly. His face was streaked with dirt, his eyes tired, gray hair matted. He smelled of perspiration and smoke, and his uniform was torn and filthy. But he had not forgotten his position; he was still a servant of the people.

He said, "I have to tell you, ma'am, that some of the prisoners were killed. But we think most of them made it through."

Laurel felt the blood drain from her cheeks. "Do you know . . . who survived?"

"No ma'am . . . we just don't have any idea. Not yet. I'm sure if you come back in a day or two . . ."

Abruptly, Laurel's knees buckled, and she sagged. The officer stepped forward quickly, catching her arm.

"Are you all right ma'am? Do you feel faint? Maybe you should sit —"

"No," she whispered. And then more strongly, "No." She braced herself against his arm for a moment, and straightened. "Thank you, I'm fine." She took a breath. "Where's the chief, can I see him?"

"He's coordinating the militia, ma'am. I haven't seen him since last night."

"Then he's all right?"

"Yes ma'am, though I hear it was pretty close going . . ." He stopped, apparently thinking better of detailed descriptions, and cleared his throat. "Are you sure I can't get you some water, ma'am? You look mighty pale."

"No, no I'm fine." With another breath, Laurel turned for her horse. "I have to go home." And she clamped her lips together abruptly, grasping for strength. "If I have a home. Have you heard anything about Lamboll Street?"

"No ma'am, I haven't. But you can't cut down Broad."

She took up the horse's reins. The streets were too littered for riding, and she would have to lead the animal the rest of the way. "Why not, what happened there?"

"At the News and Courier building, the quake knocked some of the big granite blocks off the coping — they hit the sidewalk and then the street . . . broke all the water mains. Street down there is flooded. Just cleaning it up this morning."

"Thank you," she said dazedly, and turned, tugging on the reins.

She turned down Ladson, her steps growing heavier and her heart more empty with every block. All around her the gardens were ruined, wrought iron fences and gates twisted, chimneys toppled. She passed people standing forlornly gazing at their houses, women crying . . . old people looking lost.

Slowly and more slowly she plodded along, afraid of what she might find. Seth. Seth was probably dead, dead in the quake. Sophie and Caroline, they could be dead too. How could she bear it if she lost them all? How could she?

At the corner she stopped and took a long shuddering breath. The house was standing. The chimneys were gone and the windows were shattered and the piazza was sagging . . . from the side it looked as though a giant hand had taken a swipe at it, but it was standing. She rushed toward it, dropping the horse's reins.

Her neighbor came down the street just as she opened the gate. "Don't go in there, Miss Laurel," he called. "It might not be safe. The fire department said to stay out of the house until a fireman could go in with you."

"But Aunt Sophie and Caroline —"

"They're fine, but worried to death about you, I'll warrant. They're all down at the Battery."

"At the Battery?" Her heart started beating again. They were alive!

"That's where the relief tents are set up. You'll find them there."

"They must be frantic," Laurel said quickly. New energy flowed through her veins as she thought about how terrified they must be, all alone and helpless. "I've got to get to them."

"Miss Laurel, there's no need to try to take that horse any farther. Part of our stable is still standing, we'll put her in with our animals."

Laurel turned over the reins and hardly remembered to call thank you as she picked up her skirts and hurried toward the Battery.

It can't be real, she thought, when she finally reached the area. It was like a circus or a carnival, except in place of heady excitement there was frantic activity. A tent city had sprung up along the Battery, and hundreds — no, thousands — of people were milling about, some intent on business, it seemed, others wandering about as if seeking something — or someone.

Laurel had no idea where to begin. Almost

rudely she pushed her way through the throng, studying each face, hoping to recognize someone in the crowd, looking for one face in particular. When a hand fell heavily on her shoulder she spun around expectantly. "Miss Laurel, I'm glad you're safe."

"Colonel Boatwright!" She almost wept for joy at seeing a familiar face. "Caroline — Aunt Sophie? Have you —"

"They're fine," he said, "just fine. They're over at the kitchen — that's the big white tent with the blue flag."

"Thank God," she breathed. "Thank God."

"Of course they're nearly crazy with worry over you," he added. "Wanted me to form a search party, but we can't form search parties for half the folks in Charleston." He looked grim for a minute, then forced the thought aside. He pointed to a ribbon on his chest. "I'm part of the temporary militia. We're keeping law and order, watching for looters, helping lost children. You might ask that husband of yours if he'd help us out — he looked like a man who could handle himself."

The pain that stabbed at her must have been visible on her face, because Colonel Boatwright was immediately solicitous. "Miss Laurel, I'm sorry. He isn't . . . ?"

She shook her head in fierce denial, swallowing back the weakness. "I — it's just that I can't find him. I'm looking for him. Is there any list of casualties anywhere? I'm afraid —" Tears came to her eyes, tears of fear, exhaustion, pain, and she couldn't fight them back.

"I think they're compiling one down at City Hall," he answered kindly. "I'll be working down that way and if I hear anything I'll let you know. Now you go over to the kitchen and get yourself something to eat. I'll find you, and Miss Laurel, don't worry. Mr. Tait will be fine."

Laurel nodded and walked away. How could he be fine? How could anyone be fine after this?

The kitchen was a large tent with a long trestle table blocking the open front flap. Standing there with several other women was Sophie Sinclair, dishing up bowls of soup to the weary survivors waiting in line. For a moment all Laurel could do was stand and stare. Sophie was wearing one of her best dresses. Laurel remembered that last night had been prayer meeting at the church, and at the time of the quake Sophie and Caroline would have been on their way home. The dress was dusty and stained, but that didn't seem to bother Sophie at all as she efficiently dished up the food with her plump little hands, saying something personal to each person who passed in front her. But what was most remarkable to Laurel was Sophie's headgear. She wore tied around her head like a turban, a bandanna, a cotton hand-kerchief such as maids and field hands wore. It was an amazing sight — her frail, scatter-brained aunt standing over a soup pot serving the public. But what was even more amazing was that Sophie looked years younger.

Sophie looked up and caught Laurel's eye. "Thank God!" the older woman cried. "Thank God. Here, Miz Boatwright, you finish up, I must go to see my niece." Sophie made her way around the table and clutched Laurel in her arms. "Oh my Lord, we thought you were dead. We were so worried. When Peter told us he'd left you at Chinatree we feared for your life. I tried to get the militia to go out there but they said there was too much to do here. Oh, child . . ." She embraced her hard, weeping.

"I'm fine. I'm fine . . ." Laurel held on tight, tears burning her eyes. "I was so worried about you."

"About me? About me?" Sophie seemed startled, and the tears dried up. "Why in the world, child, would you worry about me? Why if there's anyone who can take care of herself in a crisis it's certainly Sophie Sinclair."

Laurel was too amazed to respond.

Sophie went on, "God was with us last night. We were just leaving the church — we had gone to pray for you and Seth, you know, after all that had happened — and then the earth started to shake. We rushed back into the sanctuary and flung ourselves on the floor. Oh, I thought I might have a heart seizure right then and there! The whole earth shook, but the walls held. Glass was shattering and the candelabra crashed right down into the main aisle — well, I've never seen anything like it." Sophie stopped to remember. "Not even the shelling or the hurricane. This was the biggest adventure in my life," she said almost proudly. "Then as soon as the aftershocks were over we came straight down here; we sat up all night — all of us," she added. "And then this morning, we started getting things organized. Those who could go home did and brought food and dishes and sheets —"

"Have you been home?"

Sophie for that moment looked her age. "I was too afraid," she admitted.

"It's all right," Laurel assured her quickly. "The chimney fell and the windows broke, but otherwise, it's fine."

"Where's Caroline?" Laurel asked, "Is she here?"

"No, she's over at the hospital —"

"Over at Roper Hospital? Was she hurt?"

"Not at Roper," Sophie explained. "The quake hit the hospital pretty bad so all the patients were evacuated. No, we have our own hospital tent. Caroline's over there — and she's fine," she added quickly. Then she chuckled. "You'd be surprised how fine."

Then she stopped and looked around. "I thought Mr. Tait would be with you. Has he joined the militia? He's not letting you wander around alone?"

Laurel did not know whether to feel relief or anxiety over the fact that no one had seen Seth. If he had escaped from the jail he would be fool-ish to stay here; he could have long since gained his freedom. *But oh please, let him have stayed here,* she prayed. *Let me see him just one more time* . . .

She swallowed hard and tried not to let her aunt see her fear. "I — I don't know where he is. We got separated."

Her aunt patted her hand. "Well, you stay with me now honey. I know he wouldn't want you wandering around with all this riffraff on the streets, and the men have got enough to do without worrying about their womenfolk."

Laurel said, "I — I have to see Caroline. Just to make sure . . ."

A familiar voice called out, "Miz Sophie, we need you back here. Somebody's got to tell me if these damn biscuits are done or not."

Laurel and Sophie both turned to see a tousled strawberry blond head sticking out of a flap in the tent.

"Miss Elsie?" Laurel said in disbelief. It took her a moment to recognize the madam without her lavish makeup.

"Well, Miss Laurel — or should I say Mrs. Tait?" She grinned. "Earthquakes make strange bedfellows."

Sophie stared at her niece. "You know her?"

"We've met," Laurel said vaguely. "What's she doing here?"

"Coming, Miz Elsie." Sophie waved at the other woman, and then whispered to Laurel. "She donated lots of food — and almost all the sheets for the hospital, and she and her . . . 'friends' offered to staff the kitchen." She raised her hands in a gesture of defeat. "What else could we do but say yes in this time of crisis?"

"Miz Sophie." The voice came again, more demanding now.

"I must go," Sophie said. "Those women in the kitchen don't know baking powder from flour. I'm the only one who can organize them; now run along, Laurel, and see Caro."

Feeling more dazed than ever, Laurel turned in search of the hospital tent. If Seth were injured, perhaps he would be there.

"Caroline Sinclair," Laurel said to a tired-looking nurse who was leaving the hospital tent. "Is she here?"

"She's with Dr. Broussard," the nurse responded. "He has a temporary office out back."

A stab of alarm went through Laurel and she hurried toward the doctor's office. She arrived just as Dr. Broussard was giving Caroline's shoulder a pat.

"Well, Miss Laurel," he said, "I was just telling your young cousin she needed some rest, but she refuses to stop."

Caroline's face lit up as she saw Laurel and the two women ran into each other's arms, embracing fiercely.

The doctor said, "I wish I could hire your cousin to work for me, Miss Laurel. She's got the natural instincts of a nurse."

"Because I know what it's like to be ill," Caro said a little shyly, pulling reluctantly away from Laurel's arms to address the doctor.

"More than that," Broussard replied. He pulled

out his pocket watch. "I've been here since midnight last night. I think I'm going to find my wife and children and sit down and eat with them — that is if Miss Sophie has any food left."

"She does," Laurel assured him.

"Then I'll bid you ladies goodbye — and Miss Caroline, sit down now and then."

"But not until we get the sheets boiled," Caroline answered.

He gave a wave of his hand and a wry shake of his head. "You're in charge."

Laurel held Caroline at arm's length, noticing the smudges beneath her eyes. "Darling, you look so tired. You must sit down."

"I feel fine. I feel wonderful. I've so much energy, Laurel, because there's so much to do. Right now I've got to hunt up some big old pots — like the kind Lacey used to make soap in. We're going to heat up water and start washing some of the soiled sheets and towels. They have to be absolutely sterile, and the nurses — well, they're so busy with the patients, I've taken on a lot of responsibilities —"

"I'm so glad to see you, Caroline. I've been so worried about you!"

"Well, I'm fine, but look at you. You look like you need some rest. Have you eaten? No, I thought not." Taking Laurel's hand, Caroline pushed aside a sheet that was used as a screen and pulled her cousin forward. "Come on in here and let me clean you up, and then we'll send someone to bring you some food —"

Laurel, shocked into docility, sat down and let Caroline sponge off her face and hands. "Now where is Mr. Tait?" Caroline asked. "I guess he's helping the militia?"

Laurel swallowed hard. "I don't know. We got separated at Chinatree. I've been looking and looking. He may be hurt — or worse."

Sympathy shadowed Caroline's eyes, and was quickly replaced by encouragement. "Well, he's not here," she said. "I have a list of all the patients, and he's not among them. But I'm sure Mr. Tait is fine, Laurel. He's probably worried out of his mind looking for you right now."

Tears welled in Laurel's eyes. "I don't know. Oh, Caro, I'm so scared."

Caroline put her arms around Laurel, drawing her head onto her shoulder. "There, there, Laurel, you know you're being silly. Mr. Tait can certainly take care of himself, and he would be very annoyed if he knew how you were carrying on about him. I know how you love him, dear, and how scared you are, but making yourself ill with worry won't accomplish anything. He loves you, and he will come to you as soon as he's able."

Laurel raised her swollen burning eyes to Caroline. "He loves me . . . you really think so . . . ?"

"Of course he loves you. Why I knew the minute he stepped into our parlor — and so did you. You're just too stubborn to admit it, just like you won't admit how much you love him."

"I do love him," Laurel answered softly, "but it may be too late to tell him."

"Now stop it right now. Stop that kind of talk, Laurel Sinclair Tait. Thinking the worst won't solve anything. We have to believe in the best." She got to her feet and clasped her hands together briskly, looking down at Laurel. "Now if you aren't going to go get some food then you need to get to work and help me around here."

"Whatever you say, Caroline," Laurel replied almost meekly.

She and Caroline looked at each other and smiled. Caroline said, "I know, it's a miracle isn't it? Here I am taking care of you and all these people at the hospital and . . . Peter."

"Peter!" Stunned, Laurel realized she hadn't even thought to ask about Peter. "Is he all right?"

"He is now. Oh, Laurel, it was awful. He was helping evacuate the hospital and part of a wall fell down on him. He was trapped for a while, until someone pulled him out."

"How badly was he hurt?"

"His arm is broken, and a couple of ribs, the doctor says, but he'll be all right. But when I saw them bringing him in on that stretcher and he looked so pale . . . it made a lot of things very clear to me, Laurel. It took a great deal of doing, but finally I see what's important and what's not. You and Mama and Peter — and Mr. Tait, of course. You're what's important in my life. My family."

Laurel's eyes flooded with tears again, but she tried to smile. "You don't need me, Caro. I always thought you did, but I think you manage much better without me. And I'm so proud of you."

Caroline's eyes shone shyly. "Your husband — Mr. Tait said much the same thing to me once. I didn't understand him then, but I do now."

She closed her hand around Laurel's. "Now will you visit Peter? He didn't tell me what happened yesterday at Chinatree, and I'm not sure I want to know; but I know he's been beside himself with worry. He blamed himself for leaving you alone. Please come, Laurel. It would mean so much."

Their progress through the aisles lined with cots and pallets was slow, for everyone seemed to have a word for Caroline and she stopped to return each greeting or answer each request.

"Hello Miss Caroline."

"Did you get word to my wife yet?"

"Please — some water . . ."

"I'm leaving now, Miss Caroline. Thank you . . ."

Peter was in an area reserved for those not very seriously injured. His pallet was on the floor — cot space being reserved for those more desperately in need — and he was sitting up, his shoulders propped against the wall. There were plaster-covered scratches and burns on his face, and his arm was in a sling. He looked pale and exhausted, but his eyes lit up at the sight of Laurel.

"Laurel!" He reached for her hand. "Thank God. I can't tell you — thank God!" He squeezed her hand tightly, looking up at Caro. "You *are* a miracle worker!"

Caroline smiled as she knelt beside him, smoothing his forehead with a tender gesture that could not be mistaken for anything other than what it was — the touch of a woman in love. "I knew that seeing her would be the best medicine for you."

Peter smiled at her. "No. I've already had that."

Caroline blushed and got to her feet. "There's work to be done. Peter, don't tire yourself. Laurel, I leave him in your hands."

Laurel sat beside Peter, and they watched her go.

"She's quite remarkable isn't she?"

"Yes, she is. More than even she realized, I think."

He looked at her. "I love her, Laurel, and this time things are going to work out between us."

Laurel forced a smile. "I think you're right, Peter."

But after a moment he could no longer meet her eyes. "Laurel," he said hoarsely, "can you ever forgive me?"

She said quietly, "Perhaps we'd better not talk about yesterday. It was so long ago. A lifetime ago."

His fingers tightened on hers as she tried to pull them away. "I have to talk about it. The one thing I've been afraid of since it happened was that I would die, or — or you would, before I could tell you . . . how wrong I was. Laurel," he said intently, "I thought I was doing the right thing. But now I see I wanted to get Tait — just because you and Caro and Miss Sophie thought so much of him. As if running him down would build me up. Because he was different, and that difference — scared me somehow. Last night I saw how wrong I was."

His fingers tightened on hers again, making her look at him. He said, "Seth Tait was one of the men who helped pull that wall off me."

Laurel caught her breath, her fingers flying to her lips, but before she could speak he went on, "It wasn't just me. He was helping dozens of others. Chief Henderson said he was the most level-headed volunteer they had last night; men would listen to him, he could get things done —"

"Peter, where is he?" Laurel gasped. "I thought he was dead! Oh, please, if you know —"

Peter shook his head slowly. "He was looking for you, Laurel, making his way out of the city. I don't know what happened to him after I saw him. He said — he told me that if he didn't . . . if I saw you before he did, I was to tell you that . . . that he loved you."

Laurel released an unsteady breath into her fingers. He was alive! At some point last night he had been alive . . . and he loved her. "Peter," she said, getting to her feet, "I've got to find him."

"I understand. I'd help you if I could."

She managed a smile. "I know, Peter. Thank you."

She started moving quickly through the aisles. "Miss? Oh, Miss!"

383

She turned and was startled to see the same police officer she had met outside the station earlier that morning. He had a sheaf of paper in his hand and he made his way carefully toward her. "Aren't you the one that was looking for her husband?"

"Yes." Laurel hurried to meet him half way. "Yes, has there been any word?"

He said, "We're just starting to make up these casualty sheets, listing all the prisoners and trying to find their whereabouts. We're checking out the hospitals and shelters now but we don't expect to have a complete list for a day or two. There were about thirty prisoners; we've accounted for maybe half. You're welcome to look . . ."

Laurel was already reaching for the lists.

Her heart pounded as she scanned the names beneath each column. Missing: Wilson, Carver, Shackleford . . . over a dozen. Brady was not in that column, nor was Tait. How could that be? Frantically she looked at the next list. Injured: Hartford, Wilshire, Kresge, Hammond . . . Confirmed Dead: Hamilton, Harvey . . . Johnson, Willy . . . Brady, Peach . . .

Brady, Peach . . .

The officer was saying, "We let all the prisoners go, it's important that the public understands that. We didn't lock them in there during the quake. We opened the cells right up and most of them made it out alive. Of course, we can't be responsible for what happened to

384

them once they were outside . . ."

Laurel let the papers flutter to the ground.

Brady, Peach.

"Miss? Ma'am, is something . . . ? I'm sorry, ma'am . . . Is there anything I can do?"

Laurel started walking, slowly, blindly, away. Someone touched her arm. Someone else tried to stop her but she pulled away. She walked out of the tent and into the sunlight. She walked across the Battery, into the streets of the shattered city. And she kept on walking.

CHAPTER
Eighteen

EARTH HEAVES, the headline read, CHARLES-
TON STAGGERS. The byline was "Peter Barton."

And in a smaller sidebar on page two the
headline was, "Notorious Outlaw Dies in Quake."
Also by Peter Barton.

> *Peach Brady, infamous outlaw of western
> regions, was apprehended by police here
> Thursday and taken to the Charleston jail to
> await extradition to his native Wyoming,
> where there was an outstanding warrant for
> his arrest on train, bank and horse thievery
> charges. At approximately nine-fifteen, when
> the first tremor struck, the jail cells were
> opened and many prisoners, including Brady,
> escaped. His freedom was short-lived, how-
> ever, as Brady was later confirmed to have
> been killed beneath a collapsing wall on
> Meeting Street. He was buried in a mass
> grave near the site. Over thirty prisoners were*

lodged in the Charleston jail at the time of the quake. Three died inside the building, trapped in the rubble. Brady's death brings the total to four.

Laurel sat on the piazza at twilight, the open paper on her lap, rocking back and forth. The light was too grainy to read by, but it didn't matter. The words were burned into her brain.

A week had passed since the quake, and only now had the presses begun to run again. For much of the world, Peter's story would be the first knowledge they had of the tragedy and drama Charleston had lived through for the past seven days.

Only now were things beginning to take on some semblance of normalcy. Two days ago Sophie had been able to get some boys out to clear away the rubble, prop up the supports, and make their house minimally livable again. Rain had damaged the parlor and the windows were covered with oil paper, but they were home.

But it didn't feel like home to Laurel. Not *her* home.

Caroline and Sophie didn't need her anymore; perhaps they never had. Over the past week they had shown what they were capable of when need demanded, and they were more than capable of taking care of themselves. Caroline still worked long hours at the hospital. Sophie had organized shelters and clothing drives and relief committees, and it was she who had bullied the workmen into getting the roof fixed so that they could move back in. Laurel hadn't done much of anything, except sit, and rock, and remember.

She kept thinking about Chinatree, and the way it had looked that last night, before the quake had torn the earth apart. The way Seth had cleared everything away, so that she could for the first time almost see it as it was meant to be . . . And she remembered how he had talked once, about rebuilding, making it into a horse farm. She had wanted to laugh then. But now she thought, We could have done that. We could have started over, we could have rebuilt . . . we could have made a future. But she hadn't been willing to let go of the past, and she had been too afraid to believe in the future . . . until it was too late.

"Laurel, honey." Sophie stood at the door behind her. "Come on in now and have a bite to eat. You've been sitting here for hours."

With a great effort, Laurel stirred herself to respond. "No thanks, Aunt Sophie. I'm not hungry."

"Honey, you've got to eat something." Sophie came out onto the piazza, her face anxious. "You can't just sit here wasting away. Mr. Tait wouldn't want that."

Laurel almost smiled. "No," she agreed. "He wouldn't."

She knew her aunt was right. It was foolish to sit here wishing for what might have been, remembering what never really was. She just hadn't the strength to do anything else. Not now. Not for a long time.

The sound of carriage wheels made them both look up. The streets had been cleared for vehicular traffic only recently, and the sound of harnesses and wheels was still welcome enough to attract attention.

"Who in the world?" Sophie said as the closed carriage drew to a stop in front of the gate. "And right here at suppertime, too. Isn't that the way it always is? But who do we know, Laurel, who drives a carriage like that?"

Laurel frowned and sat up a little straighter. There was something about that carriage, big and fancy and closed. Who did they know who had a carriage like that? There was only one person in town with a carriage like that . . .

She got to her feet slowly and felt astonishment prickle for the first time in a week when the door opened and Peter got out. His arm was still in a sling, but otherwise he was almost completely recovered. He came up the walk toward them.

Sophie murmured, "Oh dear, I'd better put another plate on. I hope there's enough . . ." She turned back into the house.

"Peter," Laurel said, staring beyond him at the carriage. "Isn't that Miss Elsie's carriage? What are you doing in that woman's carriage?"

He clasped her hand and bent to kiss her cheek. "She let us borrow it. Laurel —"

"Us? Who else is with you? Why in the world

would you want to borrow a madam's carriage?"

She could see the door opposite her open, and people getting out, but she could not make out who they were.

Peter said, "Laurel, I've brought someone to see you."

Laurel noticed for the first time the intense glow of his face, and she turned away tiredly. "Oh Peter, no. I don't want to meet anyone now. You should know better than to bring someone over without warning me. I can't see anyone now."

She turned to go inside. "If they're staying for supper you'd better tell Aunt Sophie. Give them my regrets. Tell them I have a headache."

Peter caught her arm gently. "I don't think you want me to do that." His voice sounded so odd, his expression was so strange that she did not resist when he turned her slowly around.

Chief Henderson came around the side of the carriage, carefully guiding a man on crutches around the uneven stones in the walk. The man's face was bearded, his blond hair tousled, his clothes mended, faded and ill-fitting. He lifted his face and his eyes met hers.

Laurel's heart stopped in her chest. The cry that leapt to her throat choked there and somehow she was down the steps, her skirts flying behind her, her arms outstretched.

One of the crutches clattered to the ground and he caught her to him in a fierce embrace. He was thinner, but his grip was just as strong. Illness had left him with a pallor, and a white bandage scarred his forehead, but he was alive!

"Seth!" she gasped.

She pressed her hands on either side of his bearded face, plunged her fingers into his hair and drank from his lips between sobs of joy. She didn't care who was watching, where they were or who saw them. She clutched him to her; he whispered her name and he kissed her, over and over again he kissed her.

At last Laurel stepped away, her face wet with tears and her vision still blurry, to look at him. "Your leg," was all she could think of to say.

"It's okay. The doc splinted it and it's going to be fine."

She touched the bandage on his forehead, the bristly soft beard on his cheeks, his smiling lips. "Seth," she whispered. "Seth."

The chief interrupted quietly, "Miss Laurel, he's still a mite weak, but he's going to be fine."

Laurel looked at the other man, and so much was whirling through her head that she couldn't speak any of it. Then Chief Henderson smiled and bent to pick up the fallen crutch, and she managed to focus.

"You — I thought he was dead!" Laurel cried. "It's in the paper, and his name was on your casualty list!"

"Peach Brady's name was on that list," replied Henderson evenly. "I put it there myself. As far as I'm concerned — and I'll tell any law officer who asks — Peach Brady died in the quake of

'86. But Seth Tait, now . . ."

He handed Seth the crutch and Seth reluctantly released his tight hold on Laurel's hand to accept it. "Now there's a real hero. This town could use more men like him." And his expression fell as he added, "I wish we could keep him here. But that Pinkerton man, Cassidy, something tells me he's not apt to be as understanding as I am."

Laurel turned stunned, disbelieving eyes from the police chief to Seth, and the expression on Seth's face startled her. It was worried, uncertain, sad. His voice was husky as he said, "I never wanted to do this to you, Laurel. I never wanted to have to ask you this. But if I stay here that Pinkerton man will be on both of us like a hawk on a pair of rabbits. I've got to leave Charleston and I can't even say where I'm bound. I need to know — I have to ask — will you come with me?"

Laurel's eyes flooded with tears. "To the ends of the earth," she whispered. She wrapped her arms around him and pressed him close for an endless moment, and then stepped away. The ardor and relief of Seth's face, the simple unembellished adoration, made her breath stop, and joy brimmed in her chest.

She looked quickly to the chief, and at Peter standing beside him. Then she told Seth quietly, "But you don't have to go, if you don't want to. Neither of us do. Cassidy — he's dead. The earthquake . . . there was nothing I could do to help him. He's dead."

Seth's expression was sharp with curiosity, Peter's was stunned. But the chief merely nodded. "We lost so many good people. I reckon I ought to write his superior, if I can find out who it was." And he looked at Laurel studiously. "Maybe, if it's not too hard on you, Miss Laurel, and when you've recovered a bit, you might want to give me a few more details."

Peter murmured, "Me, too."

Laurel swallowed, and nodded. She just couldn't go into that horrifying story today. This was a time to celebrate with Seth here beside her, alive and strong.

She turned to him then, and said severely, "None of you ever explained what you're doing in that — woman's — carriage."

"Now Laurel, don't you get on your high horse. Miss Elsie has been kind enough to take care of him," Peter explained hastily. "Her place was hardly damaged at all, you know, and she's been letting us use some of the rooms for the injured . . ."

Seth grinned at her, that wonderful, easy, familiar grin. "I know you asked me not to go there," he said. "But I thought maybe you'd overlook it just this once."

"Oh, Seth." Laurel embraced him, but more gently this time, mindful of his leg. "I don't understand. I don't understand at all."

Henderson said, "I'll be going on now. Miss Laurel." He tipped his hat to her, and nodded to Seth. "Tait. I wish you a good life."

Seth looked at him soberly, "Thank you."

And Laurel echoed in a whisper, "Thank you."

Peter said, "Miss Caroline should be leaving the hospital pretty soon. I think I'll just go see if I can't walk her home."

Laurel and Seth were left alone.

"Laurel," Seth said huskily, "there's so much . . ."

"Oh Seth," Laurel said at the same time, "you took such a chance! You shouldn't have stayed here, you —"

"I couldn't leave —"

"I thought I'd lost you."

"I never got to tell you . . ."

"I love you!" Laurel gasped. "Oh, Seth, I do love you!"

"That's what I wanted to tell you," Seth said softly. "I couldn't leave you without telling you that."

The moment between them was too intense for an embrace, too alive for words. It blazed and crackled with soul-searing power and after a time it was too potent to be maintained.

Laurel pressed her forehead lightly against his shoulder. "Oh, Seth," she whispered. "There's so much to tell you. Cassidy, the gold . . ."

"What gold?" he interrupted quietly, and she looked up at him, understanding.

She said softly, "Do you know what this means?"

"A second chance," he agreed soberly. "A new life — for both of us, if you'll have me."

She looked up at him, her eyes glowing. "Welcome home," she whispered. And she smiled. "Even though this isn't really your home — or mine. Oh, Seth, I want us to rebuild Chinatree, just as you said. Not rebuild it as it was — but make it ours. Our home."

"Home," Seth said, "is wherever you are."

Their eyes met and held for another long moment. Then Laurel slipped her arm around his waist, taking his crutch in her hand. They moved toward the house, together.